A LOVE LIKE

Lilly

A LOVE LIKE

Lilly

KAY LYNN MANGUM

**DESERET
BOOK**

Salt Lake City, Utah

Visit us at deseretbook.com

Visit KayLynnMangumNovels.com for more on Kay Lynn's current and planned novels.

Library of Congress Cataloging-in-Publication Data

Mangum, Kay Lynn.
  A love like Lilly / Kay Lynn Mangum.
      p.   cm.
  Summary: Fifteen-year-old Jamie spends the summer after her grandmother's death with her grandfather and learns about her grandparents' courtship and her grandfather's work in the Civilian Conservation Corps when he was a young man during the Depression.
  ISBN-10 1-59038-580-2 (pbk.)
  ISBN-13 978-1-59038-580-7 (pbk.)
  [1. Grandfathers—Fiction.   2. Death—Fiction.   3. Grief—Fiction.   4. Coming of age—Fiction.   5. Civilian Conservation Corps (U.S.)—Fiction.
  6. Depressions—1929—Fiction.   7. Utah—History—20th century—Fiction.]
  I. Title.
  PZ7.M31266535Lov 2006
  [Fic]—dc22   2006009845

Printed in the United States of America
Publishers Printing, Salt Lake City, UT

10   9   8   7   6   5   4   3   2   1

For my grandfather
Harold A. Mangum

PREFACE

I grew up along with my brothers and sister and cousins hearing my grandfather's stories of his time serving in the Civilian Conservation Corps during the Great Depression of the 1930s, mostly during family camping trips around campfires out on the Utah desert. As others have stated, although President Franklin Delano Roosevelt's program, nicknamed the CCC, did much to save America's natural resources by building roads, planting trees, and improving national parks, the most important "natural resource" saved was the young men growing up during the Depression, especially those like my grandfather who had little education and couldn't find work.

My grandfather never tired of telling experiences he had with the friends he made while he was in the CCC, and we never tired of hearing them. When he passed away, I was saddened to think I'd never hear his stories again.

My grandfather had kept a journal on cassette tapes—fifty-eight ninety-minute and sixty-minute tapes, to be exact—by the time he died. I've spent hours transcribing them, and as wonderful as it's been to hear my grandfather's voice again, one of the happiest finds was hearing him tell many of his CCC stories. Just as exciting was finding an album filled with old black-and-white photos of the CCC camps in Utah he was a part of, as well as pictures of himself and the young men he worked with and became close friends with. From the first time I looked through my grandpa's photo album and listened to his stories on tape, I knew I had to include his experiences in a book someday.

The stories in this volume are based on some of the experiences my grandfather had in the CCC during the 1930s. I've remained as faithful as possible to my grandfather's voice and his way of telling his stories, changing only the names for the privacy of others and working with my father to fill in necessary details my grandfather did not include.

The process of writing this book has made me realize that one of the best "natural resources" we could all benefit from—and also the resource most of us take for granted until it's gone—is our grandparents: those we're born having, and those we adopt throughout our lives.

ACKNOWLEDGMENTS

A big thank-you to everyone at Deseret Book, especially Chris Schoebinger and my editor, Suzanne Brady. Thank you for believing in my story and for helping me to make it even better. A huge thanks to my good friend Cheryl Lynn Navas for reading and editing my manuscript. Being such a talented writer yourself, you know how much your opinion and helpful feedback means to me.

Thanks also to my sister, Jill Cazier, and brothers Darrell and Gary Mangum for your careful reading of my book and your comments and suggestions. A big thanks to all my nieces and nephews, too. Your feedback was greatly appreciated.

Gigantic thanks to Ranger Keith H. Stanworth in Cedar City for taking me and my parents up on Cedar Mountain to show us where the old CCC Camp foundations are and for giving us such perfect directions for finding the CCC camp remains in the Uinta Mountains. Your help was invaluable. Another huge thanks to Bill Reardon at Moon Lake Resort for information on the CCCs at Moon Lake and for pointing out the Brown Duck Trail.

Big thanks to Laura Drexl, Lila Huntsman, and Merlin Huntsman for answering my questions regarding the CCC in Veyo and Enterprise, the town of Enterprise, and my grandparents during the 1930s. Your willingness to help meant everything to me.

A huge thank-you to my mother, Janet M. Mangum, for all your support and encouragement in the writing of this book. Likewise a huge thank-you to my father, H. Ben Mangum, for being Grandpa's voice in filling in the details Grandpa left out of his stories on tape and for taking me all over Utah this past year to find all of Grandpa's old CCC camp-sites. We had an amazing time together that I'll never forget, as we truly experienced miracles to help us locate everything I needed to find. We both know Grandpa was there helping us.

And last but certainly not least, an overwhelming "thank you!" to all who read my first novel, *The Secret Journal of Brett Colton,* and took the time to write comments on Deseret Book's website, or to send me a note, or to tell others about my book. Your support and excitement made my first novel a huge success. I hope you'll enjoy this novel, too, as well my novels yet to come.

ONE

The last thing in the entire world I'd wanted to do that day was attend a funeral. And I definitely hadn't wanted to go straight from the church to the cemetery for the dedication of the grave. I shivered, crossing my arms and clutching the funeral program. A cold wind always blew at this cemetery. Every time I'd had to come here, either to visit a grave or bury another relative or family friend, that was the one thing I could always count on. This day was no exception.

Seated on the end of the row of hard white folding chairs on the right side of the casket, I smoothed my wind-tangled hair behind my ears for the millionth time, only to have the wind toss strands back into my eyes again while I irritably rubbed my upper arms. Besides the fact that funerals weren't exactly happy, fun occasions, going to one meant wearing a dress, something I was never comfortable in. Especially with the wind blowing and me in flat sandals with no nylons or socks. I owned three skirts that I alternated wearing to church on Sunday, but Mom had insisted on buying me a true dress a dark, straight-skirted cotton dress—especially for the funeral. I'd drawn the line at a pair of black high heels, though. I didn't care that I was fifteen and that according to my nineteen-year-old sister, Sarah, I should be wearing heels whenever I wore a dress or skirt, the way she did. In my opinion, wearing a dress all day long was bad enough. At least one part of me deserved to be comfortable, since the rest of me definitely wouldn't be. At the moment, I was wishing I was in shorts or jeans and sneakers, shooting hoops at home

1

in the driveway, or riding my bike. Or high in the mountains camping. Anything but sitting quietly in a dress. At a funeral. My grandmother's funeral.

I still couldn't wrap my head around the fact that she was gone. Although my grandma was almost seventy years old, she was in great shape because she took care of herself. Better than most people half her age. But even the healthiest people in the world can develop brain tumors. At least, that's what her doctor had told us when she was first diagnosed.

" . . . on behalf of the Addison family, especially Brother Harold Addison, thank you for your attendance at the services for Sister Lilly Grant Addison. The grave will be dedicated by Harold and Lilly's son, Ben Addison."

I watched my father wipe his eyes and nose with a handkerchief and then quickly stuff it back into his suit pants pocket before rising from his chair farther down the row from me to stand by the bishop from Grandpa's ward. The bishop briefly patted Dad on the back before moving to his seat while Dad bowed his head and folded his arms.

I should have listened to my dad's prayer, but as I folded my arms and bowed my own head, the wind whipped my program out of my nearly frozen fingers. While everyone else was listening to Dad pray with folded arms and closed eyes, I was off my chair, grabbing for my program. I was so rattled by the time I made it back to my seat that I couldn't focus on the words Dad was saying. Instead, I caught my seventeen-year-old cousin, Blake, and his fifteen-year-old brother, Maxwell, grinning, seated together on the folding chairs on the other side of the casket directly across from me. I glared at them both before sticking my tongue out. I only had a moment of satisfaction over seeing Aunt Gracie, Dad's sister, sternly poke them both into good behavior before my seventeen-year-old brother, Trent, seated on my left, jabbed me hard in the side with his elbow. I jumped and glared at him, but he didn't even open his eyes. He only leaned forward until his elbows rested on his knees. Sarah, seated on the other side of Trent, stared at me meaningfully before slowly and purposefully closing her eyelids at me. I rolled my eyes before looking down at the root of the moment's evil in my hands. I stared at the words "In Loving Memory" before I soundlessly opened the funeral program and scanned the words inside:

Funeral Services for

Lilly Grant Addison
April 10, 1985
11:00 A.M.

Born
December 12, 1915

Daughter of
Emery and Ida Barbara Grant

Married
Harold Alfred Addison
June 25, 1937

Died
March 31, 1985

" . . . , amen."

I jumped at the sound of Trent's deep voice near my ear, but I didn't look at him or anyone else around me. When I did look up, I could see Blake and Maxwell standing now, the wind whipping their longish hair nearly into a frenzy, but neither seemed to care. They looked so much alike, both being tall, blond, and blue-eyed, that they could almost pass for twins. Aunt Gracie motioned to both of them to get their attention, and as her blonde head moved close to theirs, I was struck by how much my cousins looked like their mother. They even had her smile. I could see Sarah approaching my aunt now—Sarah, as blonde and blue-eyed and small and petite as Aunt Gracie. The wind gusted again violently, throwing wild brown and red strands of hair into my eyes. Sarah, of course, would never allow her hair to be blown all over her face. She'd artistically combed her hair into a neat French twist and managed to walk in the grass in her high heels without getting a heel stuck in the ground. I watched Aunt Gracie gather Sarah into a hug before both began babbling away as if they'd been best friends their whole lives. I didn't know how Sarah could do that—talk to adults, especially older adults— as comfortably as she did her own friends. I'd never been able to do that. Ever. I could only mumble and stutter and act like an idiot around adults. I was a pro at that.

"Move out of the way!" I stumbled back as Trent nearly pushed me into the chairs, trying to get around me and a horde of people making their way over to my parents.

"Don't let me get in your way there, Trent!" I muttered angrily as I watched him hurry over to talk with Blake and Maxwell. To see skinny, short Trent with his dark hair and eyes standing next to Blake and Maxwell, it was hard to believe they were cousins. It was even harder to believe that Sarah, Trent, and I were brother and sisters, with Sarah so blonde and petite and Trent being on the short side with dark hair and eyes. And me—I had a strange combination of reddish brown hair and bluish green eyes and skin that wasn't fair and perfect like Sarah's or a great-looking tan color like Trent's. And I was tall. I wasn't overpoweringly tall, though, and in fact, I liked my height when I was playing basketball. And when I was running track at school. Even so, I would've been happy to hand some of my height over to Trent. I hated being the tallest, especially since I was the youngest.

"Jamie, darling, go over with your sister and say hello." Mom had moved briefly from Dad's side to harass me into being sociable, even though from the tired way she was looking at me and the defiant way I was looking back at her, it was clear who was going to win. Mom was one of two people who called me by my real name, Jamie, instead of my nickname, James. The only other person who'd refused to call me James had been my grandma.

"I hardly know any of these people, Mom!" I griped.

Mom frowned and shook her head at me before reaching up to her hair as another cold gust of wind blew through, causing more than one woman to hold her skirt down. Mine, luckily, was too straight for me to need to worry about that. But my hair blew in my face again, causing me to push strands back behind my ears for the umpteenth time that afternoon.

"Oh, Jamie, why wouldn't you let me put your hair up like your sister's?" Mom complained, trying to smooth my hair herself.

"Because my hair's thick, and putting it on top of my head would give me a headache." I'd wanted to wear a ponytail, but Mom and Sarah had both thought that would look too casual. So I'd let it hang straight down my back instead. Which had been fine during the funeral but didn't seem like such a good hairstyle choice now that I was stuck in the middle of a wind storm.

Mom sighed and nudged me forward. "Look—your great-aunts are by Sarah now. You know all of them—you need to go say hello. I'm sure they want to say hello to you."

I looked over to where Sarah was and saw her surrounded by my grandma's sisters. The best way to describe my three great-aunts and my grandma was in terms of volume. Aunt Vivian, who loved to dye her hair its original brunette color and was four years younger than my grandma, was Loud. My grandma had always been Medium. Aunt Beth, who kept her hair dyed a light blondish brown and was three years younger than my grandma, was Soft. Aunt Rachel, the youngest sister, who was born seven years after my grandma and didn't worry about dying her hair, was Softest. Although Aunt Vivian wasn't the oldest, being the Loudest, she had always been the ring leader of the four sisters, even though all of them could be pretty stubborn and bossy.

A moment later, Aunt Vivian moved away to draw one of the older men into her circle with Sarah. It wasn't until he smiled—the smile that belonged to my grandma, Sarah, Aunt Gracie, Blake, and Maxwell—that

I realized it was my Great-Uncle Marshall, the oldest in my grandma's family. An only boy with four younger sisters. Knowing how much it annoyed Trent to be sandwiched between two sisters without any brothers, I could imagine how horrible it must've been for Uncle Marshall growing up.

Great-Uncle Landon, Aunt Vivian's husband, and Aunt Beth's husband, Great-Uncle Robert, slowly approached the circle of women and Great-Uncle Marshall while my great-aunts were all taking turns hugging Sarah and admiring her navy blue suit. She'd bought it on a dress shopping trip with Grandma for her nineteenth birthday last year. It was something the two of them had done together every year for her birthday since she turned twelve. And for Trent's birthday in October every year since he turned twelve, Grandpa had taken him deer hunting. Just the two of them. As for me, my birthday tradition with my grandparents didn't extend much beyond getting together for cake and ice cream, but I didn't mind. I wasn't into killing deer, and I definitely wasn't into dresses, but I was very into chocolate cake and fudge ripple ice cream. Besides—my birthday was in August, and summer was the time when my family would go camping a lot with my grandparents and an assortment of extended family, usually to strange, out-of-the way areas up in the Uinta Mountains or down in southern Utah that my grandpa was crazy about. He'd point out roads and dams and reservoirs to all of us kids, but I never paid much attention to what he was saying. I was always too busy catching lizards and trying to scare Sarah with them.

"You've been awfully quiet."

I must've stood clutching my program with my arms folded tightly against the cold wind, deep in my own thoughts, for longer than I'd thought. I jumped before turning to face the person who'd crept up on me to bump my elbow with his. Kyle. Kyle Jansen. After my mom, he was the first to venture over and talk to me since the grave had been dedicated.

"Yeah, well, I guess I don't feel like talking much today."

I watched Mom walk back over to Dad's side to talk to more relatives

I hardly knew, and then I turned to stare hard at my grandma's coffin, ignoring the sympathetic eyes of all the friends and relatives who had gathered around for the dedication of the grave. I could hear a small group of hushed voices near me whispering softly about how lovely the funeral had been and how much my grandma would have liked it. She probably would have, too. One of the speakers had been an old family friend from their ward—Clay Anderson—who'd talked about how much my grandparents loved to go dancing, and how from the day they met, they'd never stopped dancing and had worn out many pairs of slippers dancing to old records in the living room of their home. I wondered then how it must be for the person who's passed on—to look in on an event that's all about her, hearing all kinds of things about her and her life, having to watch everyone being all sad and crying, and not being able to say anything or do anything about it.

"Well, funerals aren't for the person who's died. They're for everyone left behind."

I turned to look at Kyle with a raised eyebrow. "You mean, all of this is supposed to make me feel better?"

Kyle shrugged. "It's not such a bad idea—everyone getting together to remember the person and just be there for each other."

"And it provides a wonderful opportunity to cry in front of people you hardly know. That's always fun. Especially since there are hordes and hordes of people here."

"I know—I can't believe how many people your grandparents know. They've got to be the most social people ever. Unlike some people I know," Kyle grinned, giving me a light shove with his shoulder. "How'd you miss out on that gene?"

"I don't know. Just lucky, I guess," I grumbled back. It was true. My grandparents were friends with just about everybody within fifty miles of them. If people weren't visiting at their house, then my grandparents were usually off visiting someone. They'd always been hard people to track down. Both of my grandparents were "people people," but where my grandma had been more of a no-nonsense, stubborn person who liked to boss my grandpa around, especially in front of other people, my grandpa loved to joke and laugh and do what he could to make everyone around him laugh, too. He'd really beam if he could make my grandma laugh.

"How's your grandpa doing, anyway? He's been pretty quiet all day."

"Yeah, well, he hasn't exactly been himself since my grandma got sick. It's hard to be happy and social and talkative all the time when your wife's dying." I hadn't meant to sound curt and bitter, but I knew I did. I couldn't help it. It'd been a hard day. It'd been hard ever since my grandma had been diagnosed with a brain tumor a few short months ago, to be exact. And it was hard to think about my grandpa. I wasn't worried too much about how he was handling her death. It was thinking about how he was going to handle life without her—and whether he'd actually *be* able to handle life without her—that bothered me the most. He loved my grandma so much. I knew him well enough to know that no one would or could take my grandma's place in his heart or in his life. Ever.

Kyle didn't say anything else but only nodded before looking at my folded arms, unattractively covered with goose bumps.

"Do you want to wear my jacket? You look like you're freezing."

I shook my head. "Nah—I'm sure we'll be heading back to the church for lunch in a second. But thanks anyway, Kyle."

Because I was on the tall side for a girl, and Kyle leaned towards being an average height for a guy, I could easily look straight into his eyes to talk to him. It hadn't always been that way. In fact, until we were fourteen, I'd always had to look down to look into his face, but over the past year since we'd both turned fifteen, he'd started a major growth spurt, and I knew if it continued, it wouldn't be long before I'd have to look up to see into his eyes. I glanced at Kyle but quickly looked away when he turned his head back towards me. Kyle would be taller than me some day. That fact for some reason was unsettling.

Kyle and I had been friends—practically best friends—since we were about eight years old. We'd gone to the same schools since kindergarten, but it wasn't until we turned eight that we discovered a bizarre thing we had in common that few people could boast of.

I'd known for forever that my grandma's best friend was June Jansen and that they'd met when my grandparents moved in next door to June and her husband when my dad and Aunt Gracie were little kids. But Jansen wasn't an uncommon name, and I'd never made any connection with Kyle until Mother's Day Sunday when I was eight years old. I'd been at my grandparents' house visiting with my family when there'd been a knock on the door.

"Jamie, honey, will you get that, please?"

I'd run to the door at Grandma's request, and after flinging the door open wide, stared in surprise at the dark-eyed, brown-haired, eight-year-old boy with a light dusting of freckles across his nose. He was holding a clean, empty casserole dish and staring back at me with just as much surprise.

"Kyle? What are you doing here?"

Kyle's surprise had turned into a happy, elf-like grin. "I'm bringing this pan back to your grandma, that's what!"

"How do you know my grandma?"

"She's my grandma's friend!"

Grandma had joined me at the door then and invited Kyle in as if he was one of her grandkids, too. She started to introduce us before we both cut in and said we already knew each other. Grandma, of course, thought it was just amazing and wonderful to find out that I knew her best friend's grandson. She'd even run to the phone to call June and tell her that Kyle and I knew each other from school. Grandma had insisted that Kyle stay for dessert with us, and since Kyle has always been a friendly, constantly smiling, laughing and joking person who, unlike me, had no problem talking to anyone and everyone, he was more than happy to stay.

We'd spent the evening playing all kinds of games with Trent, and even Sarah had joined in for a game of Hearts. She'd refused to play colored Easter eggs outside with us, though, since that required running around Grandma and Grandpa's yard, and unlike me, she was still wearing her Sunday dress, something I always changed out of as fast as I could once the final amen was said at church. So the three of us had run around outside playing colored Easter eggs, kick the can, and a few other old games my parents had played when they were kids—until it started to rain. Trent had run back inside then, but Kyle and I had jumped into the white painted, double-bench wooden swing with a canvas canopy Grandpa had made for Grandma years before. Seated across from each other on the two benches, we'd taken turns pushing against the wood floor boards to make the swing rock back and forth. It'd been hard work, since both of us had had to sit on the edges of the benches, nearly standing up, to reach the floor boards. We finally got the swing to rock gently back and forth after we'd figured out that we had to work together, but we both couldn't push at the same time. I'd pushed from my end, and then Kyle had pushed from his end, see-saw fashion, and we'd both laughed, loving that we'd figured out how to make the swing work.

That day was the first time I'd sat on the swing with anyone but Grandma. She loved to sit on the swing with me all snuggled up beside her while she pushed the floorboards herself to make the swing rock gently and ask me how I was doing and what I'd been doing. She'd ask if I'd like her to make me something to wear. I knew my grandma could sew better than anyone, and I actually did agree to let her make a dress for me for Christmas a couple of times. She'd listen to me babble away for what seemed like hours, feeding me handfuls of candy. My grandma loved to cook and made the best homemade candy ever. Better than stuff in the stores. Sometimes she'd sing funny campfire songs to me, and when I'd laugh and ask her about the song, she'd say, "Oh, it's just one of your grandpa's silly old songs." We spent time on the swing together almost from the day I was born until she was too sick to go outside.

Kyle had stayed on the swing with me until his parents came to get him. I was actually sad to see him go, but I didn't need to be. Kyle's family visited his grandparents a lot—practically every week—so Kyle came running over every time he saw my parents' green Oldsmobile pull up at my grandparents' home. I didn't dare go over to his grandparents' home, because his grandpa was really sick. But after his grandpa died when we were eleven years old, his grandma invited me over to come see Kyle while I was visiting my grandparents, and we'd switched back and forth, going to each other's grandparents' home when we were visiting our own grandparents, ever since. Sometimes we'd shoot hoops at his grandparents' house, or play catch with a football, or run races against each other, or ride the old bicycles in my grandparents' garage. All kinds of things that my sister Sarah would never want to do in a million years, but because I had a good dose of tomboy blood in me, I not only didn't mind doing sporty stuff with Kyle, I usually preferred it. Although chatting with Kyle and his incredibly awesome grandma—Grandma June— while we ate her famous double chocolate chip cookies was stiff competition.

Our at-home lives had changed after that, too. I still remembered the first time we ran into each other at school after that first day at my grandparents' when we were eight years old. We'd been out playing at recess, and Kyle had been throwing a ball around with some friends. When he saw me, he'd stopped playing to run over to where I was climbing around on the monkey bars with my friends to say, "Hey—your grandparents live by my grandparents!" I'd laughed and said no, *his* grandparents lived by *my* grandparents. It'd become a standing joke way of greeting each other ever since.

But not on this day. I'd almost forgotten Kyle had come to the funeral, which was stupid, because he'd sung a solo for the service. Kyle could sing like nobody else could and was more interested in being in every choir and musical deal Central High had going than in taking time for any serious competitive sports. He'd run track with me in junior high, but he didn't have time for that now. Too many choir concerts and things. And he'd become incredible on the piano. In fact, he'd played the piano while he sang at my grandma's funeral, which was great of him to do, since—besides the fact that no one in my family had any musical talent whatsoever—we would've fallen apart bawling all over the place if any of us had tried singing anything.

"So—are *you* holding up okay?"

I tried to smile, but it was hard, because as I made myself look into Kyle's concerned face, what I really wanted to do was to start bawling. No one else had asked how I was doing or wondered if I was having a hard time dealing with everything. But Kyle had had a grandparent die of something horrible. He knew what this was like.

"I don't know. I guess so. It's all just so—weird. I thought my grandma would be around longer than this. I mean, I hadn't thought at all that she would have to die sometime. I thought there'd be more time."

Kyle nodded. "Yeah, I know. That's how I felt, too."

Kyle turned his face away to look at the casket thoughtfully while I watched him out of the corner of one eye. He looked nice in a suit. The wind was ruffling his hair, but it didn't ruin it the way it ruined mine. His hair actually looked good windblown. It was the same dark brown it'd always been, his eyes the same warm, deep brown, and he still even had some freckles across his nose. The only thing that was different was that he wasn't smiling and joking and laughing the way he usually did, and as he turned to wipe his eyes for a moment, it struck me then that he'd loved my grandma, too. I'd always thought of his grandma as a second grandma. Surely that was the way he thought of my grandma as well. And then I was ashamed of myself for not asking him the same question he'd asked me.

"Kyle—what about you? Are you okay?"

Kyle took a deep breath before turning to me with sad eyes and an attempt at a smile. "You're the best, James, you know that? Just like your grandma."

Before I could think of what to say, Kyle's grandma hurried over and with tears in her eyes, swallowed me up in a gigantic hug that if I could've breathed, would probably have made me cry. A second later, she released me to hug Kyle, and then she put an arm around each of us.

"How are my kids doing?"

"Fine," I said, smiling up into Grandma June's kind but sad face.

"We're ready to head back to the church. Do you want to ride back with us, James?"

I shook my head. "I'd like to, but I better go back with my family."

Grandma June smiled and nodded, and after waving good-bye to Kyle, I watched them cross the grass to Grandma June's car.

The wind had turned colder and stiffer, so I hugged myself tighter, rubbing my arms hard, before turning around to find where my family had run off to.

There was only one person left by the casket. My grandfather was seated on one of the white folding chairs, pulled close to the casket, with a red rose in his hand. I knew I should go to him and try to comfort him. I knew Sarah—even Trent—would have, but I couldn't. I tried to turn away instead, but I couldn't do that, either. And so I watched, spellbound, hardly daring to breathe, while he kissed the rose and carefully placed it on top of the casket before slowly letting his hand slide down the casket to grip one of the side handles, his shoulders hunched and shaking with soundless sobs.

TWO

"Turn off your Walkman, Jamie. We're here."

I jumped nearly high enough in my seat to smack my head on the roof of the car when Mom reached over and yanked my earphones off my head. I'd been slouched in the seat, listening to music cranked high enough to drown out Mom's voice all the way to Grandpa's house. School was finally out for the summer, but instead of being able to spend my first official summer day sleeping in, I'd been rudely yanked out of bed by Mom at 8:00 A.M.

"I still don't get why I'm the one who had to come instead of Trent or Sarah," I grumbled.

Mom sighed as she reached to open the car door. "I told you last night, Jamie. Sarah's staying at the dorms up at the university to take a few summer courses, and Trent has a summer job. You chose not to get a job this summer, so you're the obvious choice to come help."

"I'm not sixteen yet!"

"You will be in less than two months."

"But—"

"No 'buts.' Your grandfather is having a hard time. He needs all of our help and support right now. Please try to think of someone else other than yourself, if only for today."

I slammed the car door extra hard after I dragged myself out of the car. It wasn't that I didn't want to help Grandpa. It was just that I knew both Trent and Sarah would be more comfortable helping him pack up

Grandma's things than I could ever be. And then there was Blake—and Maxwell. And Aunt Gracie. They lived closer to Grandpa than we did—practically walking distance away—but for who knew what reason, they'd found a way to make themselves scarce. Grandpa had called yesterday, asking Mom if we could come out and help, and I'd assumed Sarah most likely would go. In fact, I was sure she'd want to go and help, because summer semester hadn't started yet. And Trent didn't have to go to work until late afternoon. Yet both had claimed they couldn't come. Nothing had been said to them, and yet I'd been the one made to feel evil for being human and complaining. Unbelievable.

Mom pressed the doorbell before turning to me sharply. "If you say or do anything to upset your grandfather—"

"I'm not going to!"

I couldn't say anything else, because a second later Grandpa was there, opening the door wide and motioning us inside.

"Hi, Jan. Hello, James!"

Although he'd put a big smile on his face, the relief to have us finally arrive was painfully clear. I'd almost gasped at my mom's last words to me, but now I was gasping for a completely different reason. Grandpa. He looked awful. He'd lost weight since the funeral nearly two months before, and his eyes were red and watery with such dark circles underneath that I wondered if he'd slept at all since Grandma died. Thanks to too many years of eating candy and doughnuts and drinking way too much pop, he had a heart that had survived more than one attack and triple bypass surgery, too. I watched him rub his chest a bit and wondered if his heart was bothering him.

As we followed him into the house, his step wasn't quick and cheerful like usual but slow and heavy. He usually had all kinds of stories and funny jokes and things to say whenever we came over, hardly stopping to take a breath, but not today.

Mom tried to talk all bright and cheerful with Grandpa while we followed him through the kitchen to my grandparents' bedroom—the old

"How are you today?" and "It sure is hot!" type of shallow conversation, while I did my typical not saying anything. Normally, I loved going into my grandparents' bedroom. The room was painted a light lavender with a fancy ivory painted border around the top of the walls. The bed was covered with a lavender spread, and the end tables on either side of the bed matched the gigantic dresser with a huge mirror attached to it. The room was big and beautiful and had a connecting bathroom that was all done in lavender, too. Everything in the bathroom was lavender—even the toilet paper was lavender! And the carpet and bath rugs were a deep purple. The most amazing bedroom and bathroom ever.

I watched Mom follow Grandpa into the bedroom, but I couldn't make my feet move into the room. I stood in the doorway while Grandpa motioned sadly—almost helplessly—from the large opened closet that took up the entire length of one of the walls to the nearly empty boxes on the floor.

"I tried—really I did. I know it's time, but I just can't—I can't do it—"

I stood there watching, horrified, as Grandpa's eyes started to really water while his voice shook. Mom hurried over and tried to awkwardly put her arm around him, which was nearly impossible to do because he was so much taller.

"Don't worry about it, Harold. That's what Jamie and I are here for. We'll take care of it. All of it. Right, Jamie?"

Both turned and looked at me—Mom with an almost desperate, pleading look on her face, and Grandpa—well, his face didn't look much different, only much sadder.

"Right, Mom. I mean—Grandpa." I moved between the dresser and the bed to stand near the two of them and faced the closet, not wanting to look at Grandpa's sad face again. "So—where do you want to start?"

"Doesn't matter. It all has to go. Unless you want anything, James."

I couldn't help jerking my head up in surprise to look at Grandpa. Grandma had been tiny and petite like Aunt Gracie. Like Sarah. Not tall and all gangly arms and legs, like me.

"You know. As something to remember her by."

I nodded and tried to smile and then turned back to the closet and joined Mom in removing dresses, blouses, skirts, and pants from hangers, carefully folding them before placing everything in the large cardboard boxes at our feet.

After watching us for a minute, Grandpa shuffled forward and reached inside the closet toward the back of it. "I'll help." His voice sounded determined, but one glance at his face and I could see how hard it was for him. His hands shook as he stared at the dress he now held tightly in his hands. I frowned as I turned to look at it. The lavender color had nearly faded away into a strange, dark shade of white, and the style and cut—I knew I'd never find a dress like it in any store. Much too old-fashioned. But it was still pretty. Really pretty, actually.

I smiled at Grandpa and reached out to touch the silky material. "Wow—that's pretty. I don't remember ever seeing Grandma in it, though."

Grandpa's mouth was trembling, and I could tell he was going to start crying again. "I do—I definitely do. She even made it herself. I can't believe she kept it—all these years."

I turned to Mom helplessly, mouthing the words *Now what?* Mom, thank goodness, smiled and reached out to take the dress from Grandpa.

"Harold, why don't you go relax in the living room? You've been working too hard lately—you look exhausted. Let Jamie and me finish this up, all right?"

After a moment, Grandpa pulled himself together. He wiped his eyes and nose with a big white handkerchief from his pocket, but he didn't let go of the dress. "I'm sorry, Jan—I wanted to help—" Mom patted his arm and said more soothing words to him. I couldn't watch—I couldn't stand to see my grandpa like that—so I turned back to the closet with a vengeance and grabbed and folded clothes as fast as I could go. I couldn't stay here any longer—I just couldn't. I reached for the next item—a blue jacket, one Grandma used to wear camping—and tried to hurriedly fold it, but it wouldn't fold properly. One of the side pockets bulged strangely and crinkled loudly in protest, so I stuffed my hand inside and closed my fingers around—an envelope.

I frowned as I pulled the envelope out and read the writing on the outside: "For Harold's airplane trip."

Airplane trip? My mind raced until it hit upon one night last summer, sitting around the campfire listening to Grandpa talk about how much he wanted to take an airplane ride someday and go somewhere. Anywhere. Grandma had rolled her eyes and laughed about how he'd been saying that for years. "Such a waste of money—and for what? To do the same thing you do on a bus, only you're up in the air and there's nothing to see."

Grandpa had just laughed back and said it must not be such a crazy idea, because tons of people did it every day.

"And where exactly are you going to get the money to go on this airplane ride?" Grandma had asked.

Grandpa had shrugged and said he'd better start saving. Everyone had laughed, even Grandpa.

I carefully slipped open the envelope and felt my eyeballs nearly pop out of my head. There was easily five hundred dollars in tens, fives, and ones in the envelope—probably more.

I didn't realize I'd yelled "Holy smoke" as loudly as I must have, or that I'd whooped and squealed pretty loudly, too, until Grandpa came running back into the bedroom.

"James! What's going on? What's wrong?"

I smiled and thrust the envelope at Grandpa's confused face. "Looks like someone's going to be taking that airplane trip after all!"

Mom gasped when she saw all of the ten-, five-, and one-dollar bills inside. I was grinning, absolutely certain that this would make Grandpa's day.

Grandpa stared at the money for a moment before his knees buckled, and he slumped on the bed while the money slowly floated from his trembling hands to the floor. "She never told me—she never— why? Why didn't she tell me?"

I stared while Mom again hurried over to sit down beside him. "Oh, Harold, I think this is wonderful—just wonderful—that Lilly did this for you!"

Grandpa only shook his head sadly but firmly. "No, it's not. She— this isn't the only thing. I've been finding money all over the house. She hid money everywhere. I've already found four thousand dollars. Didn't she trust me to take care of her?"

I could tell that tears were going to start flowing again, and I knew I couldn't handle seeing that again. I mumbled something about taking one of the full boxes of clothes outside and grabbed the nearest one, hustling from the bedroom and out the back door by the kitchen before either one could stop me. I dropped the box by the back door and ran to the swing, where I pumped and pumped with both feet, making the swing rock me back and forth, back and forth. I was shocked to realize I was starting to cry, too.

"Hey you—I thought that was you, James!"

I jerked my head up in surprise. Kyle was leaning against one of the swing poles, grinning his elf grin at me, wearing a T-shirt and cut-off jeans, just like me.

I made a quick swipe with one hand over my eyes to get rid of any possible tears. "You scared me! I didn't even hear you come up the drive-way!"

Kyle laughed. "I noticed. Too deep in thought, I guess." He jumped into the swing and sat across from me and pushed the floorboards with his feet. "So, what's up?"

I shrugged and pushed the floorboards, too, helping Kyle make the swing rock. "Mom and I are helping Grandpa pack up my grandma's stuff. You visiting Grandma June?"

Now Kyle was shrugging. "Sort of."

"Sort of?"

"I got a job for the summer moving furniture at Lakewood's Furniture. It's close by, so I thought I'd check in on my grandma.

Somehow, everything turned from being just a quick visit to taking her to get groceries and some other stuff and mowing her lawn and pulling weeds."

I had to laugh at that. Grandma June was good at getting people to do things for her, but knowing Kyle as I did, I was sure he'd probably been the one to ask if he could take her anywhere and do some yard work for her. He was just that kind of a nice, helpful person. Unlike me. He rarely had to be prodded to be helpful.

"So how's your grandpa doing?"

I shrugged my shoulders. "Not good, I guess." Kyle frowned as I told him how the afternoon had gone so far.

"So you just left him there, by himself?"

"He's not alone—my mom's in there, too!" I nearly yelled. I couldn't help it. Kyle was looking at me as if I'd just committed the crime of the century.

"You shouldn't have left him. Look, I'll go in with you and help."

Kyle had just ground the swing to a stop, gripping the poles on either side of him and digging in with his feet against the floorboards, when Mom came out the back door.

"Jamie, I need to grab some things from the store for your grandpa." Mom definitely looked unhappy with me, but when she saw Kyle, her face lit up. "Kyle! How nice to see you!"

Kyle smiled back, and in seconds, Kyle was waving my mom goodbye with one hand as she cheerfully maneuvered the car out of the driveway and shoving me back inside the house with the other, having promised Mom that we'd both help Grandpa and cheer him up.

"Kyle!"

Grandpa was standing in the bedroom doorway when I reentered the house with Kyle right behind me. If I'd thought the relief on his face was painfully clear when Mom and I had first arrived, it was overpowering now. Kyle grinned and happily jogged over to Grandpa and let him ruffle his hair and slap him on the back. It was then that I began to believe that at least for now, there wouldn't be any more crying.

THREE

Wow! Kyle—Grandpa—look how tiny these binoculars are!"

With Kyle's help, the rest of Grandma's clothes had been safely and quickly folded into the boxes, and Kyle moved them outside just as fast. All that remained now were the dresser drawers, but upon opening the drawers, it was easy to see that Mom had removed every bit of clothing from the dresser. The drawers weren't empty, though. There were all kinds of things in each one—things I'd never seen before. The binoculars, for instance. I turned to squint through the tiny lens at Grandpa and Kyle, who were seated on the bed looking through a stack of old books together. Kyle glanced up for only a second to grin at me before looking back down at his lap to continue thumbing through a thick old book.

Grandpa motioned to me with one hand. "Those belonged to your grandma. And they're not binoculars. They're opera glasses."

"Opera glasses?"

Grandpa smiled. "Grandma liked going to plays. I couldn't afford to get front row seats, so those glasses came in handy."

I frowned and put the binoculars back into their tiny leather case and reached forward to put them back into the drawer.

"You can have them if you'd like, James."

"I don't know—I don't go to plays and operas."

"Maybe not now, but maybe someday you will." Grandpa glanced over his shoulder at Kyle, who was obliviously buried in his book, before turning back to wink at me. "Especially if someone asks you to go to the theater sometime."

I could feel my face getting red and hot. "Yeah, *that's* going to happen," I muttered before turning my back on both of them to dig into the drawers again.

One drawer had tons of flowered paper fans glued to thick popsicle sticks. "For hot summer days at church," Grandpa explained. "Your grandma used them for years." Grandma's jewelry box rested on top of the dresser, and at a nod from Grandpa, I carefully opened the lid to examine all the colorful pins, rings, and necklace and earring sets inside.

"Just costume jewelry," Grandpa said with a sad smile as he picked up a strand of pearls. "She loved jewelry so much. I always wanted to buy her the real thing, but there was never enough money. She didn't complain, though. She didn't mind wearing rhinestones instead of diamonds and plastic beads instead of real pearls."

I dug around in the jewelry box some more until I spied a small gold box underneath a snarl of necklace chains. Inside the box on a bed of tissue paper was a ring. A gold ring, with two tiny, perfectly carved gold tulips on their sides with a small diamond between the two flowers. I'd never seen anything like it in my life.

"Grandpa, look at this ring!"

Grandpa's breath caught funny in his throat as I handed the ring to him. "I married your grandma with this ring. I bought her a nice wedding set years later, when I had the money, but she wore this ring for a long time. I haven't seen it in years. Didn't even know she still had it." Grandpa's hands shook as he carefully put the ring back in the box before pulling his handkerchief out of his pocket to blow his nose and wipe his eyes.

Kyle finally set down the book he'd been poring over to join us in front of the dresser. After staring hard into the box for a minute, he reached inside and pulled out a small red card with a tiny stub of a red pencil attached to it with a thin gold ribbon.

"What's this?"

Grandpa laughed and took the tiny book and pencil from Kyle. "It's a dance card."

Kyle raised both eyebrows. "Dance card?"

Grandpa grinned. "Your grandma went to plenty of these fancy kinds of dances while she was at Dixie College for a year in southern Utah back in 1935. I actually got to take her to one myself before we got married. The Deer Hunters' Ball." Grandpa's face softened when he opened the card, and he chuckled softly and shook his head. "I should've known!"

"Known what?" I leaned over Grandpa's shoulder. The little book had a dozen numbered lines in it, and every line said "Harold Addison" in Grandma's perfect, flowing cursive. "Is this the dance card from the dance you went to with Grandma?"

Grandpa nodded. "I didn't know she'd saved it all this time." Grandpa looked up at me, and I was relieved to see his eyes were twinkling instead of filling with tears. "Your grandma broke the rules. This isn't how dance cards are supposed to be filled out. Usually a girl's card would be filled with the names of a dozen different boys." Grandpa chuckled again. "Yep, these little dance cards were better than gold at a dance."

I frowned down at the little red card in Grandpa's hands. "How so?"

"This made sure that not only would you get to dance at a dance but you'd get to dance with the girl you wanted to dance with the most."

Kyle definitely looked intrigued. "Really? How did it work?"

"See how the lines are numbered? Well, before the dance got into full swing, you'd go ask a girl to dance, and if she said yes, she'd put your name in her card by one of the numbers. Sometimes the card would have the actual type of dances printed on it, so you could pick whether you wanted to dance a fox trot together, or a waltz, maybe. And see—the girl would wear the card all night, so there was no way she could say no to a dance when she'd already written your name down in her card herself." Grandpa slipped the loop of elastic hooked to one end of the card around my wrist and then held up my arm to show Kyle. "And it made for a nice souvenir for a girl after the dance was over."

I couldn't help laughing as I waved the dangling card on my wrist in front of Kyle and Grandpa. "Dance cards? More like a little contract forcing a girl to dance with all the slugs who come asking. And the girl had to wear it all night? That has to be the craziest idea ever."

Kyle shrugged. "I don't think it's so crazy. It'd take away a lot of stress if all the guys are asking for dances before the dance even starts. Kind of like yearbook signing day, I guess."

"It was nice to get the asking for dances out of the way in one big whack, so you could just enjoy the dance and actually dance all the dances, instead of standing around half the night," Grandpa agreed. "You were guaranteed a yes if you got the girl to put your name down. And believe it or not, James, I think most girls thought filling out their cards was kind of fun."

I wasn't about to give in to either of them. "I still think dance cards are lame and stupid."

"You would," Kyle stated dryly. "You think dances are lame and stupid, don't you?"

I lifted my chin to glare at him, even though I could tell he was laughing at me. "For the most part."

"Have you ever even been to a dance, James?"

Kyle knew very well that I hadn't. Not to a fancy dress-up one, anyway, and I'd only gone to one stomp last year. No one had asked me to dance, so after a wasted hour of such lameness, I'd left. "Of course I haven't," I snapped, slipping the dance card off my wrist and tossing it back into the jewelry box. "Have you?"

"Of course. I went to the Spring Formal last month before school let out."

For some reason, not only did Kyle's answer surprise me but it bugged me, too. Though who knew why. We were only friends, after all.

I moved away from the dresser while Grandpa asked Kyle about what dances were like now, and Kyle babbled about going to the Spring

24

Formal and what the dance was like and how everyone danced solely with the date he brought, so dance cards weren't necessary.

"So what were dances like when you were in high school?"

Grandpa laughed. "Oh, they were quite a bit different in a lot of ways, I guess. We didn't have many dance card dances. Most of the time, the dances were pretty informal. More like—what is it you call your Levi's-wearing dances, James? Clomps?"

I burst out laughing. "Stomps, Grandpa, stomps!"

Grandpa grinned. "There was a dance hall in town where I grew up called the Silver Moon Dance Hall. Every Saturday night while I was in high school, people'd come from all over the county to the dances at the hall, and boy, did we cut a rug! But that was during the hard times—the Depression, you know. I didn't have money to buy a ticket into the dance."

Kyle lifted an eyebrow at Grandpa. "So how'd you get in?"

"Well, I either had to crawl in a window or promise to work the next day cleaning up the place after the dance. Ol' Johnny Manatee—he owned the Silver Moon. He was pretty good to let us boys who didn't have any money sneak in or work for him the next day and help clean up the hall or the yard outside or something like that."

"Sounds like a pretty decent guy."

Grandpa nodded. "I used to go to the hall dancing every Saturday night. We danced different from how you kids dance now, that's for sure. We had a live band playing the music for us, and the girls would all congregate in one corner of the dance hall. Once I spied the girl I wanted to dance with, I'd go ask her for a dance. And then maybe I'd get acquainted with her and dance two or three times with her. If I didn't like the way she danced, I didn't have to go back and bother her anymore. And when intermission came to give the musicians a break, if I was pal-ing off with a girl, I might make a date with her for the next dance. And if I really liked a girl and she liked me, I might ask her if I could take her home."

Grandpa's eyes sparkled as he turned to look at me. "That's the way I met your grandma, you know. At a dance."

I nodded without really listening. I'd forgotten that Kyle had turned sixteen months ago and had been driving for quite a while. Of course he'd want to go to the last big dance of his sophomore year when he could actually drive a car to it. Of course he would just have to go. I snatched one of the dusty old books Kyle had been looking at and flipped it open. The name *Emery Grant* flowed in fancy, thin cursive letters on one side of the cover. Grandma's father. I picked up more books and found his name handwritten in nearly all of them. And the publishing dates were mostly in the late 1800s. *Amazing.* I sat down on the bed and, being the klutz I am, lost my grip on the book while trying to be careful with it. A second later, it landed with a loud thud on the ground, causing both Grandpa and Kyle to jump.

"Careful, Grace," Kyle laughed.

"Sorry," I mumbled. I bent over to grab the book. In doing so, I could see the red corner of something sticking out from under the bed near the headboard. I knelt by the bed and reached under it to grab that snitch of red and pulled out . . . a photo album.

The book was old and held together by a thick, red string with the word *Photographs* in faded silver lettering on the front cover. I'd never seen it before, but when I opened the cover, I was amazed at all the strange sizes of black-and-white photos covering nearly every thick, black page inside. A lot of the pictures were scenery shots of mountains, trees, lakes, and roads, but a lot of the pictures were of people. Guys, to be exact. Guys who didn't look like they were much older than I am. And quite a few of them were actually pretty cute, even though they were dressed in strange-looking uniforms with boots that laced up to the knees and pants that tucked inside the boots, looking something like horseback riding pants. They were also wearing long-sleeved shirts with funny stand-up collars, although halfway through the photo album they wore what looked like loose-fitting, flare-legged Levi's and long-sleeved, button-down shirts with a big pocket on either side of the row of buttons. Sometimes the guys were in groups in their strange-looking uni-forms, obviously sitting for a group photo; some of the pictures held only a few guys, clowning for the camera. I could've believed the pictures were maybe army photos from an old war, because tents and barracks that looked like something out of an old black-and-white war movie were in the background, except that in most of the pictures, all the guys were working: digging with shovels, hacking down trees with axes, and riding on tractors. And there wasn't a single photo of anyone wearing an army helmet or holding a gun. I studied the pictures harder, looking at the boys in the pictures more closely.

"Hey! This guy looks like you, Grandpa!"

He did, too. Except the boy wasn't bald, like Grandpa was. This guy had a ton of light-colored, curly hair, and he was thin. Grandpa wasn't fat now, but the guy in the picture was a lot thinner. And he was young, somewhere in his late teens, I would guess, like most of the guys in the photos. The boy in the photo I was looking at—Grandpa, I was sure—was sitting on a short wall made of rocks, wearing a funny-looking, pullover shirt with a strange-looking collar and some sort of knee-length leggings on top of his pants that went from the toes of his boots to his knees. A row of tents tucked between trees were lined up behind him, with mountains rising behind the trees.

"I thought I'd lost that—where did you find my old CCC book?" Grandpa's eyes lit up as he hurried over to sit beside me. He eagerly snatched the book from my hands, while Kyle sat down on the other side of Grandpa to look over the book I'd found.

"It was under the bed. Is that you, Grandpa?"

Grandpa laughed. "Yep. With hair! I'll bet you didn't know ol' Grandpa ever had any hair!" He pointed excitedly to the picture below the one I'd pointed out. "See there? Those were two of my buddies back in the Cs at the Uinta River Camp in Utah. Max and Tucker." Grandpa was standing between the two in the photo. Max looked like he was around seventeen or eighteen. He was tall and thin with short hair slicked over to one side. Tucker looked about sixteen. He was shorter than Grandpa and Max, with lots of dark, curly hair that was long on top and wild looking like Grandpa's. Although the guys were complete opposite in looks, both were definitely very cute. "I met them soon after I joined the Cs, at the first camp I was shipped to in the Uintas. That was before I met your grandma."

It was bizarre to realize Grandpa hadn't always been an old man and had hung out with people I'd never heard of, but it was even more bizarre to realize he'd spent a lot of years not even knowing Grandma existed.

"The Cs?" I frowned. "What are the Cs?"

"Hey, wasn't that the program the government set up in the 1930s during the Great Depression?" Kyle asked.

I was surprised when Grandpa nodded. "Yeah, the Civilian Conservation Corps. The CCC. FDR's program." Grandpa grinned before pinching my arm. "Kyle must've paid attention in history class. What were you doing, James? Sleeping?"

I didn't get a chance to do more than let out a retorting "uh!" and glare at Kyle before Kyle shrugged and spoke again. "Your grandpa's told me a few stories about what his life was like back then, when he was a part of the CCC." His eyes lit up when he pointed at one of the pictures. "Wow! Look at the boots on this guy!"

I leaned over Grandpa's arm to look closer at the picture Kyle was all excited about. The boy in the photo had on a pair of those funny-looking boots that laced all the way up to his knees.

"Yeah, they're pretty weird looking, aren't they?"

"They're not weird—they're cool!"

"You like those funny old boots, huh, Kyle?" Grandpa smiled.

"Heck yes. I wish I had a pair!"

I couldn't help laughing. "Why? You'd look stupid in them. You wouldn't be able to wear them anywhere without getting beat up."

Kyle leaned behind Grandpa and flicked me hard on the head with his thumb and index finger, but before I could do anything appropriate back, Grandpa shushed us both and focused us back onto his photo album.

"I learned a lot in the Cs. Saw a lot of Utah, and did a lot of work. Hard work. Got my career in truck driving thanks to the Cs. I wasn't much good with reading and writing, so I don't know what I would've done if I hadn't had the Cs to teach me how to drive truck." Grandpa sighed and shook his head, looking over pictures of himself in the photo album. "I was just a wild kid back then. A real bad boy with no direction in life when I joined up. A lot of us CCC boys were, actually. Just a bunch of kids who got in trouble too much." Grandpa chuckled and slowly turned more pages. "The Cs definitely helped me to find some direction in my life. Helped me find out who I was, and it helped make a man out of me. It did that for a lot of us lost boys during the Depression." Grandpa shook his head, pointing out other people he'd known. "There's ol' Kurt Harris. And Bud Olsen." Grandpa chuckled. "And even that superintendent I drove crazy every day. I sure did meet a lot of people. Some good, some not so good."

I stared at another young face that looked strangely familiar. In the photo, a dark-haired guy with an olive complexion was sitting on a strange-looking tractor with the word *Caterpillar* in big, black letters along the side of it. He was wearing a funny-looking hat and clenching between his teeth a pipe that looked like something Santa Claus would smoke. He couldn't have been older than sixteen. And he was handsome. Really handsome. "Is that Uncle Landon?"

Grandpa laughed and tapped the photo. "Yep, it sure is. I met your great-uncle Landon in the Cs. He was one of the best Cat skinners in the entire state of Utah. It was quite an honor, being picked to drive a Cat." Grandpa smiled and ruffled my hair a bit. "I met your grandma because of the Cs, too."

"You did?" I knew Grandpa and Uncle Landon had been friends since they were young, but I'd never known exactly how they'd met. But

I did know they'd met my grandma and Aunt Vivian at about the same time and even got married within a week of each other.

"Yeah, I did. The Cs may have made a man out of me, but your grandma helped make a better man of me." Grandpa shook his head, looking over a picture of himself in a long-sleeved white shirt and tie and nice suit pants with suspenders. "I didn't go to church much like I should back then. I have your grandma and her family to thank for helping me to get back on track with the Church and living life the way I should."

That was definitely something new to me. "Really? You haven't always been a good church-goer?"

Grandpa smiled and shook his head. "No, I haven't, I'm sorry to say. I hope neither of you makes the same mistake."

Kyle laughed. "When it comes to making mistakes, I'm not the one you need to be worrying about."

I stuck my tongue out at Kyle behind Grandpa's back while Grandpa obliviously continued to turn the pages of his photo album.

"While I was in the Cs, I learned one of the songs all the guys liked to sing. I think I remember it—I'll sing it to you now."

And then I listened, horrified, as my grandpa actually started to sing.

I joined the C-C's.
I must have been crazy,
For I left a nice, sweet home.
I went for a vacation
And I got a 'noculation,
and the needle scraped the bone.
I got a new shovel,
a half-ton shovel,
and also a brand-new pick.
Oh, heaven forgive me,
I must have been crazy
When I joined the C-C-C.

"That's one of the songs we learned to sing in the Cs. Then there was some more about meeting the little girls so sweet and getting in Dutch with their dads. Well, I forgot all of that."

Secretly, I was glad he had. I sneaked a look behind Grandpa's back to see Kyle's reaction. Even though he was smiling, I couldn't help cringing, wondering what Kyle must've been thinking right then.

"So, remind me what the CCC was all about," I asked, trying to get Grandpa back on track before he scared Kyle off completely. And myself, I had to admit.

FOUR

Grandpa smiled and looked up from the photo album. "I joined the Cs back in 1934, when I was an eighteen-year-old kid living in Price, Utah." Grandpa sighed and rubbed his forehead. "Things weren't so good in the '30s. Not like these days. The Depression was on, and it was hard times."

"Because of the stock market crash, right?"

Grandpa beamed at Kyle while I made a gag face at him behind Grandpa's back. "Right again, Kyle. That was in 1929. Everyone called the day of the crash Black Monday. It caused all kinds of problems for everyone, and before we knew what was happening, we were stuck in the middle of a grand-scale economic crisis. The worst there'd ever been in the U.S. Millions were out of a job all over the United States. There wasn't any work anywhere, and no one had any money. And food—we didn't have very much to eat, I remember." Grandpa sighed and shook his head. "I wasn't any good at reading and writing, so after three tries, I finally passed my freshman year of high school. But things were hard at home, and since I couldn't find a job, in the spring of '34, I decided to leave school for good and join the Cs."

"What did you have to do to join up?"

Kyle actually looked interested, but I was sure he was just being nice, trying to keep Grandpa from being sad by talking about his glory days. And Grandpa—he was obviously loving it. He settled back onto the bed with a truly nostalgic smile and cleared his throat importantly.

"Well, I tell you, it was quite an experience. We had to sign up like soldiers do in the military. I wasn't married, and I was under the age of twenty-five, and because I couldn't find a job and my family had been on the relief rolls of the county for a long time, I knew I had a good chance of getting picked. Plus, I was pretty healthy, and I wasn't afraid of working hard outdoors or of having to defend myself in any kind of fight, be it with words or fists." Grandpa smiled. "Part of Roosevelt's plan to turn things around in the U.S. through the Cs while we fixed up the great outdoors was to keep us young guys out of trouble, learning skills and trades to help us find jobs. And to make money to send home to our families so they could eat and pay bills. I made thirty dollars a month and had to sign that I agreed to have twenty-five of it sent home to my mom each month."

I couldn't help gasping. "Thirty bucks? That's it?"

Grandpa laughed. "Thirty bucks was worth a whole lot more back then."

Kyle was still bent over the photo album's pictures. "So what kind of stuff did you do?"

"Oh, we worked outside in the mountains, building roads and dams and campgrounds, and planting and saving trees, too. Lots of conservation projects that helped protect natural resources that had been pretty neglected. I mostly worked in forests and national parks. So you have us CCC boys to thank for a lot of the national parks you kids like to go camping in these days."

Kyle nodded, thumbing through the photo album with Grandpa. "You guys made the national parks? That's pretty cool!"

Grandpa laughed. "Yeah, the parks are nice, but that was just the beginning of the work we did in the Cs." Grandpa smiled and pointed out another picture. "I worked in the river up at the Uinta River Camp my first summer in the Cs, building river breakers to slow up the river so there'd be ponds for the fish to develop and grow in. We'd cut down great big pine trees, and with the horses, we'd drag the trees over and tie them down in the creek and then pile rocks in behind them. And we'd leave just a little opening between the logs so that the water could go through, and that'd slow the creeks up. But the breakers lasted only two or three years, till there was a good flood up there that took them out. But it was a pretty good summer's work, working in the creek where the water was nice and cool, and then swimming in the creek afterwards."

Kyle nodded without looking up from studying the pictures in Grandpa's book. "Interesting!"

I leaned over by Grandpa's side and looked down at the opened pages of the photo album. Both sides of the pages were filled with young, determined, and hopeful faces staring back at me. "What happened after you got into the CCCs?"

Grandpa smiled. "Well, once I found out I'd been picked for the Cs, I had to thumb my way to Fort Douglas in Salt Lake City to report for duty, something you definitely can't do now. But you could then. And then, after a medical examination that wasn't complete without filling up my back end with needles, I was loaded up with a bunch of other young teenage guys like myself into the backs of a few stake-rack trucks——big old flatbed trucks with holes around the edges. Removable stakes had been stuck in the holes and a few rows of wooden side boards put around the edges to keep us from falling out. We were driven up over the mountains in northeastern Utah, through Indian Canyon to Duchesne, on around and up to Roosevelt, and then up through Neola to the Uinta River Camp, high in the mountains on the Uinta River."

I fell back onto the bed and listened to Grandpa happily chatter, a grin on my face. This was definitely a hundred times better than sadness and crying. And Kyle—I'd been so sure he was just being nice, but he was listening closely to every word Grandpa was saying, too.

Grandpa smiled and thumbed through the book to point out a few black-and-white photos. "It was a pretty camp, right up in the biggest pine trees I'd ever seen. Just look at these pictures, and you can see how nice it was. Our camp had a big building—the mess hall, here—where we cooked and ate our meals. The camp also had a recreation hall and a big shower house where we'd take our showers and wash our clothes. And there was a garage where the trucks and other equipment were kept, and a corral for the horses, too. There were even classes taught in camp for the guys who wanted more schooling, but I didn't have much to do with the education program in the Cs."

Grandpa laughed and sighed, shaking his head. "That first day in camp, right after I jumped out of the stake-rack truck with the rest of the boys, I met Dalton, a tall, twenty-year-old guy with black hair and lots of muscles. He was one of the younger CCC officers who were over us newer enrollees. He coolly looked us all over before pointing behind us.

"'See those barracks on your left?'

"We all looked over our left shoulders and nodded.

"'The officers and foremen sleep there,' he said. 'See those tents behind you to the right?'

"We all looked over our right shoulders and stared at the row of tents pitched in rows in the quaking aspen trees.

"Dalton grinned at us and said, 'All you enrollees sleep there.'

"Our sleeping quarters from then on were old white army tents on a board floor with rails around the sides and flaps over the top to keep the heat out. There were six of us enrollees per tent, sleeping on little army cots with thin mattresses. I'd barely dropped my duffel bag onto one of the empty cots when Dalton and a few other CCC guys came in with boxes. Within minutes, we were issued our equipment: shovels, axes, and picks, mostly—and personal items we'd need, like our bedding, towels, razors, and toothbrushes, and our official uniform.

"Dalton stared us all down and said, 'Reveille's at 5:30 A.M. Breakfast is at 6:00 A.M., followed by roll call at 6:30 A.M. Work call is at 7:00 A.M. Everyone works forty hours a week and until noon on Saturday. After that, you're free to do whatever you want until roll call on Monday morning.'

"After Dalton and the boys with the now-empty boxes left, I picked up my uniform and slowly unfolded it. Holy Moses, I couldn't help busting out laughing!

"'Sakes alive—this looks like something left over from the war!'

"'That's because it is.'

"One of the boys at the far end of the tent shrugged when I looked up. 'What do you mean?' I said back.

"He only shrugged again. 'The government doesn't have money for real CCC work uniforms yet.'

"So there was no getting around it. We all had to wear old, mostly used World War I U.S. army infantryman uniforms: olive drab field uniforms, with boots lacing up to the knees, or leggings to go over the outside of the pants and boots, like I had. The pants were so tight at the ankles that everyone called them choker pants.

"I finally walked out of my tent with the five other enrollees I'd be living with into the bright sunlight. I squinted up and down the row of tents to see the other guys step out of their tents, all of us in these wild World War I get-ups. Boy, I couldn't help but laugh again and wonder if we'd all stepped back in time a good twenty years or so."

"But these uniforms are cool!"

Grandpa chuckled at Kyle. "Well, we didn't think so. They were old and not with the styles of the time. I didn't get more than a second to laugh, though, because we all had to take the official CCC Oath of Enrollment and fall in to learn the rules of the Cs and meet the men who'd be over all of us kids now. Most of us enrollees were from around Utah, but some were from other states. Even states back east."

Grandpa shook his head, smiling down at the old photos. "I wasn't sure how the Cs planned to train us, since most of us had no idea what to expect, but most of our crew leaders and foremen underneath the superintendents and officers were LEMs."

I wrinkled my nose. "LEMs? What's that?"

Grandpa grinned at me. "Local Experienced Men. Mostly married men who had skills and experience handling men and equipment. Enrollees could only be unmarried guys sixteen or eighteen through about twenty-five years old, so LEM positions gave unemployed married men a chance for a job in the Cs, too. And being married and more settled than us wild boys, they were able to train us and keep us from goofing off or fighting too much, and they were able to organize projects and keep everything going so we could stay on schedule."

Grandpa smiled and turned another page in his photo album. "Although the first C stood for Civilian, to make sure everyone knew the CCC wasn't under military control, a lot of the procedures and rules and regulations smelt like the army to me, especially since a lot of the older officers in charge were retired military men. But I wasn't about to complain. I had a job now. I'd be making some money to send home to my mom, and at that time in my life, I couldn't think of anything better I could have."

I sat back up then and turned a few pages back in the photo album to the picture of Grandpa and Max and Tucker. "So what were the guys like? Like the guys in this picture here—Max and Tucker. This is from your first year in the CCC, right?"

Grandpa smiled down at the picture and gently rubbed his thumb across it. "Those guys were some of my tent mates. That first week in the Cs, I didn't learn much about them beyond their names. We worked hard all day every day, and at lunchtime, all I wanted to do was eat, and by the time we got back to camp at four in the afternoon, all I wanted to do was sleep. I was sore and tired every night from all the physical labor, whacking down trees with my ax until I thought both arms would break, and then switching to help pick up and pile giant rocks until I was sure both arms were broken. I wondered if I'd been crazy for signing up. But things looked up considerably once that first Saturday arrived."

Kyle raised an eyebrow at Grandpa. "Oh, yeah? How so?"

Grandpa laughed. "Max lived in the same tent with me. He was seventeen when I met him—a tall, lanky, quiet guy with hair he kept slicked over on the side with religious dedication. He followed me back to our tent after lunch that first Saturday, and once I'd stretched out on my cot to take the long nap I'd been looking forward to all week—since quitting time on Saturday was at noon—he walked over and gave the cot a nudge.

"'You're Addison, right?'

"I opened one eye and squinted up at him. 'Yeah. So?'

"So Max says, 'Tucker—he bunks in this tent, too. You know him?'

"I did. He was seventeen like Max and kind of an ornery kid with a pretty bad temper. So I said, 'The short guy with dark curly hair?'

"Max grinned and nodded, 'That's him. He drives truck. He got the okay to take one of the trucks, and a bunch of us are going into Duchesne later on. There's a dance tonight, so we won't be back until late. You can come if you want.'

"Well, as you can imagine, all of a sudden, a long nap didn't seem so necessary anymore. And I was glad I'd shared my water canteen with Max on Thursday when he'd forgotten his. No doubt I was getting good payback for that service. And I was glad I'd given in and let my mom pack my one good suit into my traveling bag the day I left for the Cs. 'For going to church,' she'd said, although both of us had known I wouldn't likely be going to church."

I frowned as I looked at Grandpa. "How come you didn't go to church?"

Grandpa shrugged and gave me a surprisingly apologetic look. "My life was different then, James. *I* was different then. I hadn't set foot inside a Mormon church in years." Grandpa sighed and shook his head. "Anyway, I knew that suit would get me more dances than that crazy WWI uniform ever could. All that uniform would've gotten me from the girls was lots of laughs. So by four o'clock, I was suited up and ready to go, and less than an hour later, I was part of the pileup in the back of one of the CCC trucks with Tucker driving, and soon I was on my way to Duchesne and whatever adventures were waiting there for me."

As I heard the excitement sparkling in Grandpa's voice, I closed my eyes and waited, listening for more and picturing Grandpa in my mind the way he looked in that old photo album: young and strong and ready to start a new chapter in his life.

FIVE

Duchesne turned out to be a town a lot like the one I'd grown up in, small with just one main street of business and not much going on anywhere in town. It only took us an hour to explore the stores on either side of the street, but the storekeepers were friendly and seemed to be okay with us CCC guys crashing their Saturday afternoon. I watched Tucker throw coins down to get a packet of cigarettes at the grocery store, and my blood nearly froze. Not over the cigarettes—I smoked more of those than I should at the time. It was the realization that I didn't have even one penny in either of my fancy suit pockets. We wouldn't get paid until the end of the month, so here I was, without a dime to spend, planning on going to a dance that evening I was sure would cost money to get into.

Max only laughed when I panicked. "No sweat, Addison. None of us ever pays to go to the dances."

"What do you mean, you don't pay? How do you get in, then?"

Max only laughed again. "We just get in the CCC way. You'll see."

I couldn't figure out what Max meant by that, but since he'd been in camp a month longer than I had, I figured he'd gotten in good with some of the guys who'd been in the Cs even longer, a few of which had come along in our truckload. I didn't get a chance to ask just then, because someone called my name. Someone with a high, musical-sounding voice that definitely didn't belong to any of the guys—and actually sounded familiar.

"Harold? Harold Addison? Is that you?"

I couldn't believe it when I saw her. Mary St. Clair. She'd gone through school with me, only she hadn't stayed around to be a freshman for more than a year, like I had. But she was one of those girls who always got noticed wherever she went. Thick, dark hair that came to her shoulders; huge brown eyes and wide, smiling lips that were dark red from lipstick; plus a killer figure. Mary got a lot of attention from guys. She knew guys always looked at her, but unlike some girls, she wasn't afraid to look straight back.

I couldn't help grinning, because now Max and all the guys in the store, whether they were CCC boys or not, were gawking. "Yeah, Mary, it's me. How've you been?"

She was in Duchesne to visit her grandparents and was staying for the dance. She made me promise to save a dance for her, and with another wide smile, she squeezed my arm and said, "So good to see you—see you tonight!" before sashaying out the door.

Within seconds, Max and everyone else was all over me, asking how I knew Mary and how come I didn't introduce my friend around. Tucker was the only one who kept himself apart from all of it. He only frowned at me before walking casually to the doorway of the store to watch Mary walk out of sight.

When it finally started to get dark, we headed over to the area in town set aside for the open-air dance. A lot of people were already there, dancing on the slab of cement to a small string band that was playing on a raised platform at the far end. There was a fence all around the slab, though, and the only opening I could see was right by the ticket booth. An older couple was manning the booth, and neither looked likely to be sympathetic to a CCC guy without any money.

I grabbed Max and asked again, "How the heck are we going to get in there?" but he just laughed and said to trust him, so I followed him and

Tucker back to the CCC truck that was parked close to the dance where everyone else was lining up their cars in the dirt parking lot.

Open-air dances always had plenty of free cookies and punch for refreshments, but as I expected, some of the CCC guys had brought along some "real" refreshments to share. The bottle had already been passed around a few times by the time I got over to the truck, and as nervous as I was, I didn't hesitate to let a few swallows of that fire water burn a path down my throat. Mom would've been disappointed, I knew, but she'd have been more disappointed if she knew that I'd had better, stronger stuff than what I'd just tasted, many times before.

I definitely felt more relaxed by the time we headed in small groups towards the dance. One of the older enrollees led Max, Tucker, and me in a wide circle around the dance to the back by the band to a neat hole in the fence that was carefully covered by bushes and grass. "CCC expertise," he grinned before cautiously slipping through the fence. I followed Max and Tucker through, doing my best not to snag my suit on the fence. Since there were plenty of town people there already, it was easy enough to hide behind the crowd of people both dancing and standing around so that no one was any wiser to us.

Mary was dancing with one of the town boys when I made my way to the dance floor. She waved and smiled a big smile when she saw me. She'd changed into a fancy pink dress, but when her partner turned to see who she was waving at, I got the opposite look from him. Nothing but a big, sour frown. I learned pretty fast that town boys didn't like CCC boys crashing their dances and stealing their girls. Of course the girls loved it. I'd never met a girl who didn't like riling guys up and being fought over. But I didn't pay the guy she was dancing with any mind. I grabbed the nearest girl—a redhead with freckles—yelled "Wanna dance?" and in seconds, we were out there dancing it up by Mary and the sour-faced guy. I'd always liked to dance. It was one of the main things I was good at, mostly because my older sister had taught me all kinds of dances and steps for years. I guess I made a pretty impressive spectacle of myself. No girl turned me down for dances, and Mary was happy to dance with me quite a few times. I saw Tucker dance with her a few times, too, but a lot of the CCC boys were asking her to dance, so I didn't think anything of it. It wasn't until intermission, when the band was begging for a break, that I realized just how much I'd been dancing with Mary.

I'd gone with Mary to the concession stand, but Max pulled me aside and walked me back to the CCC truck. "Watch out for Tucker. He's not exactly happy with you."

"Tucker? What did I do to him?"

Max drank out of the bottle again and shoved it into my hands. "You were dancing with Mary too much."

"What are you talking about?"

Max shrugged and tried to act like it was nothing, but I could tell by the tight set of his mouth that this was going to end up being a big deal. "Tucker's seen her in town before. He's had his eye on her for a while, I guess."

I had to laugh at that. So Tucker liked Mary. One thing I knew about Mary that I was pretty certain Tucker didn't was that Mary's folks were good Mormons. I didn't know what religion Tucker was, but I doubted Mary's parents would give him much of a chance with all the drinking and smoking he did. I doubted Mary would have anything to do with him, either. Mary's folks would put up with me because I'd known Mary practically since we were in diapers. We were good friends, and she was a dang good dancer, so I'd danced with her a lot that night. But as soon as I saw Tucker marching over to the truck with clenched fists, it was pretty clear I'd been dancing too much with Mary to suit him.

The first thing that came flying out of Tucker's mouth for me was, "You stay away from my girl!"

I still had the bottle of bad whisky in my hands, so I casually took a swallow, turned slowly around, looked Tucker straight in the eye, and said, "What do you mean, 'your girl'?"

About that time Tucker swung his fist hard and hit me in the mouth.

The strength in his arm really took me by surprise. I felt a massive, exploding pain in my mouth and tripped over my own stupid feet before crashing to the ground. I could taste blood, but it only took me a second to figure out why. Something small was rolling around in my mouth, and after spitting into my hand, I could only stare in shock at the bloody bit of me in my hand.

"What the—you knocked my tooth out!"

"Serves you right for dancing with Mary so much. Stay away from my girl!"

I jumped up to plow into Tucker, but Max tried to block me. I was sorry to have to shove him extra hard out of the way, but Tucker had basically handed me an engraved invitation to get to know each other better. In no time, Tucker and I did just that. Max was forced to stay on the sidelines with the rest of the CCC guys, who cheered us on and made bets as to which of us was going to end up losing the most teeth.

Tucker and I had both had too much to drink that night, so the fight didn't last long. Seconds later, we were both lifted, grunting and groaning, and thrown into the back of the CCC truck, where we were piled on by the rest of the guys. I learned pretty quick that that was the standard way of dealing with drunk CCC boys at a dance. The sober boys would gather up all the drunks and put them in the back of the truck, and when the sober ones were ready to leave, they'd sit on the passed-out drunks for the ride back to camp. When they got back to camp, the sober guys would either haul the drunk ones out and take them to the barracks or just leave them in the truck and let them freeze until the next morning.

"We're leaving? Already?" My mouth hurt so much it was like trying to talk around marbles, but Max, who was sitting by me, just laughed.

"Believe it or not, the nice people of Duchesne don't like fights at their dances. We were asked to leave. Most politely, too, considering all the noise you two made."

I passed out quick after that, but lucky for me, Max made sure both Tucker and I were hauled into our tent when we got back to camp. I stayed out of Tucker's way the rest of the weekend, and he stayed out of mine. Poor Max was right in the middle because he and Tucker had been friends a long time, and yet he seemed to want to be friends with me, too.

Monday rolled around too early for me, but by then, my mouth wasn't hurting so bad. Luckily, it wasn't one of my front teeth that Tucker had knocked out. It was back far enough that if I didn't smile too big, no one would notice the hole.

I thought knocking out my tooth would be enough to make Tucker happy, but he had nothing but black looks for me all day Monday while we were chopping down trees for more river breakers. It'd been cold that morning, so I'd taken my army coat with me. By lunchtime I didn't need it anymore, so I rolled it up into a pillow to put behind my head and I leaned against a quaking aspen tree for a nap. Max came over and dropped down to lean against the other side of the tree while we ate our sandwiches and dozed.

"What time is it?"

"Dunno," Max answered, already more asleep than awake.

"Who has a watch?"

"Tucker. It's in his pants pocket."

Tucker. It would have to be Tucker. "Anybody else have a watch?"

"Nope," Max said flatly.

I looked around for Tucker and saw him sitting against a tree not far from us. He looked asleep. Deep in sleep. I figured if I was careful and quiet enough, I could sneak out that watch for a quick look at the time without waking him up. So I crawled over to him and tried to reach into his pocket to slip his watch out and see what time it was without waking him up. While I was trying real carefully to get that watch out of his pocket, Tucker's eyes flew open, and boy, we had a good tussle over that until Max stepped in and broke things up.

I crawled back to my tree and grabbed my canteen, and while I was lying with my head against the tree, panting and taking swigs from my canteen, Tucker stood up, grabbed his ax—one of the brand-new, double-bitted axes that were sharp on both ends—and marched over to where I was. He swung that axe so hard and fast at me so that it chopped thick into the tree and stuck there, making the whole tree shake. The axe stopped only about an inch above my head. If he'd come down about an inch more, he would've scalped me for sure. I jumped to my feet and threw my canteen aside, and we had kind of a tussle about that. Everyone thought Tucker was really crazy to do what he did.

"Is this still about me dancing with Mary St. Clair?" I hollered right in Tucker's face. "Because if it is, you're wasting your time. She's Mormon. A good Mormon. Her dad wouldn't let her go out with someone like you. And she wouldn't want to anyway!"

Well, he didn't like hearing that at all, so after Tucker called me a few choice names, one of the LEMs on duty came over and hauled him away. No doubt about it—there was definitely no love lost there. The sad thing was that I actually thought Tucker was a pretty good guy, and I wanted to be friends with both him and Max. Tucker was a hard worker and had a knack for figuring out faster, better ways to get things done. And he was good with the horses. He could get them to pull more logs up the mountain than anyone else could. But he thought he was quite a hotshot, so although I'd hoped to end up being pretty good friends with him, I'd ended up having some pretty good fights with him instead. And poor Max—he was stuck in the middle. He'd say that the problem with me and Tucker was that we were too much alike, both of us ornery and stubborn and hardheaded. And that we liked the same kind of women and dancing with those dishy girls in Duchesne way too much.

SIX

Well, this is news to me, but you're joking, right, Grandpa? You don't drink—or smoke! And fighting—You never really did stuff like that, did you?!" I couldn't keep the shock out of my voice, because I *was* shocked.

Grandpa smiled sheepishly at me. "I'm sorry to have to break it to you, James, but Grandpa was a bad boy when he was young. Like I said, I wasn't active in the Church when I was a teenager, like you and Kyle are. I hope maybe you'll learn from my experiences as to what *not* to do. That goes for both of you!" Grandpa messed up Kyle's hair with one hand and mine with the other until all three of us were actually laughing.

"Hello? Knock knock!"

I hadn't heard the doorbell ring or any knocking at the front door, and as shocked as I was to realize some stranger was barging into Grandpa's house, I was even more shocked to see Grandpa jump up off the bed and race as fast as he could go for the front door.

"Good grief—who could possibly be at the door to make him move like that?"

And Kyle—he was shocking me, too. He only shrugged. "Probably Anna."

"Anna? Who's Anna?"

I didn't have long to wonder, because seconds later, Grandpa was calling us both to come into the living room.

"I want you to meet my very dear, very special friend, Anna. Anna, this is my granddaughter. And here's Kyle. You know him."

I watched, dumbfounded, while Grandpa put his arm around the stranger in front of me.

"Hello, Kyle. And Jamie! I'm so happy to meet you. Your grandpa's told me so much about you."

"It's James. My grandma called me Jamie."

My voice sounded hard and cold. I couldn't help it. Grandpa's eyes were shining too much. He didn't seem to mind at all that this Anna person had waltzed into the house instead of waiting for someone to open the door and let her in. And he still had his arm around her.

Anna nodded. "James, of course." Anna kept smiling, but I didn't smile back. Her voice was so soft I almost had to strain to hear her speak. "I'm sorry—I didn't mean to interrupt anything. I didn't see any car out front. I just wanted to bring this casserole by for you, Harold."

"My mom's picking up some stuff for my grandpa. She'll be back any minute."

I'd hardly noticed that she was carrying a big glass dish, but in a second, Kyle had taken it from her and was hurrying it into the kitchen.

I thought for sure Grandpa would at least scowl at me, if nothing else, but he was so busy smiling and sparkling over this Anna person that he hardly noticed I was even in the room. "You're not interrupting a thing—you couldn't! And since you went to the trouble of making me some dinner, Anna, why don't you sit down and eat with us?"

"Oh, no—you've got family over. I can come back another time."

"Nonsense. Everyone in the kitchen, and let's eat!"

I watched while Grandpa smiled into her face and she smiled back before he put his hand on her back and led her into the kitchen. I couldn't move until Kyle walked back over to me.

"Don't just stand there, James. Come on!"

"'Very dear, very special friend?' What's that supposed to mean?"

Kyle shrugged and looked away. "Just that. She's an old friend."

I couldn't help looking Kyle over suspiciously. "She knows you, and you recognized her voice when she came in!"

"Yeah, so?"

Kyle had the nerve to actually look defensive. I was ready to pummel him with more questions, but Grandpa put a stop to that. For now.

"James—Kyle—are you kids coming, or are we going to have to start without you?"

Kyle gave me a light shove. "Don't act stupid, James. Come on!"

Between bites of chicken casserole, I studied Anna. In both looks and personality, she was the direct opposite of my grandma. Grandma had been fit and petite, while Anna was tall and fit the more stereotypical look of a plump grandma, complete with a bun at the back of her head. My grandma wasn't afraid to make her voice heard, but Anna—Grandpa had to encourage every word out of her, and she talked so softly my ears were starting to hurt from straining. I couldn't believe he could find this Anna person at all appealing or interesting.

"James here found my old CCC photo album today. I've been telling them about the Cs and some of the experiences I had when I joined up."

Kyle smiled and nodded at Anna. He'd hardly looked at me or talked to me the whole time we'd been at the table. "Grandpa Harold has some great CCC stories."

Now Anna was smiling at Kyle, too. "He does, doesn't he? I've enjoyed hearing a few myself."

My mind had been spinning from the second I'd sat down across the table from Kyle. I couldn't stand the way Grandpa was looking at Anna. I'd never seen him look at my grandma in such a lovesick sort of a way. Ever.

There had to be something I could do. Something less obvious and rude than saying, "Go away." And then, it hit me.

"You met Grandma while you were in the CCC, didn't you, Grandpa?"

Grandpa looked surprised but smiled at me and nodded. "Yes, I did, James."

"I'd really love to hear all about how you met Grandma, and how the two of you got together, and about when you got married. All that good stuff."

Kyle was frowning and shaking his head at me, but I ignored him.

But Grandpa only chuckled happily. "Well, I've been telling you how I met your grandma, James. I met her while I was in the Cs. Because of the Cs, actually. I never would've ended up in southern Utah or even in the same room with her if it hadn't been for the Cs. So in order for you to learn how I met your grandma, you have to understand the events that led up to the time we actually met."

"Your grandpa told me he met your grandmother at a dance while he was in the CCC. In Enterprise, wasn't it, Harold? Or was it in Veyo?" Anna was smiling at me now, but I ignored her, too.

And Grandpa was back to smiling at Anna. "Veyo. During a Shoe Dance."

Kyle raised an eyebrow at Grandpa. "A Shoe Dance? What's a Shoe Dance?"

Grandpa grinned. "Oh, it's not really a dance. Just a silly sort of a way to get a girl to dance with you. Happened when I was in the Cs and crashed a dance with a bunch of the C boys while we were in southern Utah." Grandpa turned to Anna then and reached for her hand. "Anna met her husband in a pretty interesting way, too. He was a pilot. Why don't you tell the kids how the two of you met?"

I had no desire to hear how this Anna person had met her husband, and lucky for me, she didn't seem to have any desire to tell me.

"Oh, maybe another time, Harold."

Grandpa just kept smiling at Anna. "Anna and her husband and Lilly and I have been in the same ward together for years. We've all been friends a long time."

"Yes, we've all been friends."

I realized then that I had no desire to hear anything Anna had to say.

At all. "Yeah, well, same with the Jansens, but I don't see Grandma June coming over all the time without knocking and staying for dinner."

I only muttered that under my breath, but Kyle kicked me under the table. I thought for sure Grandpa would get after me for being rude, but he didn't. He just smiled his patient smile at me. "Anna and I understand each other, James. You see, Anna's husband passed away a few years ago. He had a brain tumor, too."

I didn't know what to say to that, and luckily I didn't have to say anything.

"Hello, everyone! Sorry I'm so late."

Mom was back, and after she plunked two armloads of groceries on the table, which Kyle of course had to run over and help her with, I had the satisfaction of watching on her face the surprise bordering on shock that I knew had been on mine when Grandpa introduced her to Anna. I gave Kyle my best "See—it's not just me who's not thrilled" look. He only rolled his eyes at me, while Mom did her best to be polite and pretend she was happy to meet Anna.

"Well, it's getting late. Jamie, are you about ready to go?"

"There's still a lot of stuff that needs to be boxed up. And there's some cleaning around the house to do. I wouldn't mind staying for a few days or so, if Grandpa doesn't mind."

Kyle frowned and shook his head, but I turned my back on him to face Grandpa.

I was surprised to see a huge smile on Grandpa's face. "You know you're welcome to stay as long as you want, James. You can stay all summer!"

I grinned and looked around at everyone. "You know, that's sounding pretty great, since I don't have a summer job or anything. Spending all summer here helping Grandpa and hanging out with him could be really fun. Besides, Grandpa needs some company right now, and I'm more than happy to stay."

For some reason, Mom actually looked worried. "But, Jamie dear, you don't have any clothes or any of your things here."

"Oh, that's no big deal. You can throw some clothes and my toothbrush and hairbrush and stuff into a bag. Kyle's working out at
Lakewood's for the summer. He's going back home tonight, so he can
drop off my stuff tomorrow on his way to work. Right, Kyle?"

I turned and gave Kyle my best triumphant smile, but Kyle only nodded stiffly and said, "Sure. Whatever, James." I kept smiling and said
thanks, but then I had to hurry and look away. It wasn't just because he
had his arms folded across his chest and was still frowning at me.
Something in his eyes and the way he was looking at me made it clear
he doubted my motives for wanting to stay. Completely.

SEVEN

Grandpa had warned me before I went to bed that he went swimming every morning at the city pool with his friend Clay Anderson, the speaker from Grandma's funeral, so I wasn't surprised to wake up the next morning to an empty house. What did surprise me was to find three bags of my things sitting on the living room floor.

"Good on you, Kyle—you didn't forget!"

All of my favorite jeans, shorts, and shirts were inside the bags, as well as my favorite sandals and another pair of sneakers. My Walkman and a bunch of cassettes, as well as my toothbrush and hairbrush and other personal items, were carefully packed in the bags as well. I wrinkled my nose at the denim skirt and nice blouse that were also inside. My scriptures tucked inside the skirt weren't really necessary to get the message across loud and clear that I was supposed to go to church every Sunday with Grandpa.

I'd been whistling around the house after my shower, munching on buttered toast and a few granola bars, enjoying poking around in the books and plunking on the keys of Grandma's old piano and organ, until I went back into the kitchen for a glass of juice. There in the sink was proof that last night hadn't been a mere figment of my imagination. I stared at the dirty casserole dish filled with water, knowing that I should be nice and wash it and take it back to Anna. And knowing that if I did, it would at least keep her from having an excuse to come over tonight, if she dared, now that I was here. But instead, I grabbed the spare key on a nail by the back door and hightailed it over to Grandma June's.

"You wouldn't believe all the cool stuff Kyle and I found at Grandpa's yesterday. The wildest thing was finding money everywhere. Grandpa said he's found thousands of dollars already!"

Grandma June smiled and joined me at her kitchen table with a plate of something that smelled wonderful. "How exciting! I can only imagine. Here, James, have a cookie. I made double chocolate chip cookies. Extra gooey, just like you like them!"

It didn't take me long to finish off two and a glass of milk. "I thought it was pretty weird that my grandma would hide money all over the house."

Grandma June only shrugged. "Well, your grandparents lived through the Depression. If you'd had to watch all the banks fail, you wouldn't trust banks completely, either. You'd be surprised how many people from my generation kept money hidden around their homes, just in case. Better safe than sorry again."

I nodded, slowly munching my next cookie, while Grandma June studied me closely.

"Something else is bothering you, James. I can see it on your face. What's wrong? Is Harold all right?"

I almost laughed at the worried look on Grandma June's face. I knew she was thinking about Grandpa's bad heart and the strain my grandma's death had put on it. I couldn't wait to see her reaction when I told her what was really going on with Grandpa and his heart.

"Grandma June, do you know someone in your ward named Anna?"

"Anna Stanley?"

I shrugged. "I don't know her last name. I just know an Anna from your ward came over last night and had dinner with us."

"Don't you like her?"

I shook my head hard. "I don't like that she came over to have dinner with my grandpa. I mean, you'd never do that—just come over with some food and invite yourself to dinner."

Grandma June actually laughed. "Well, I hate to admit it, James, but I have."

I frowned at Grandma June's laughing face. "What do you mean?"

"Anna's not the only lonely woman in our ward who's taken dinner to your grandpa since your grandma passed away."

My mouth dropped open at that. "You, too?"

Grandma June laughed again. "Not just me. You'd be surprised at how many widows in our ward have had dinner dates with your grandpa. It's a good thing, too. He'd been losing weight since Lilly got sick, so those dinner dates meant your grandpa was getting at least one good meal a day." Grandma June smiled and shook her head. "Your grandpa loves company, so it was only natural that he'd invite anyone in who brought him food for dinner, or even invite a woman out to dinner himself. He's made quite a stir in the ward. Your grandpa's an attractive—"

I put my hands over my ears. "Stop it! I don't want to hear this."

Grandma June yanked my hands down. "Your grandpa's single now, and he's lonely, James. I think it's wonderful that he's trying to do something about it."

"Do something about it?"

"He's spent time with several widows in the ward, and now he's dating Anna."

That made me drop my cookie. "Dating? What do you mean, 'he's dating Anna'?"

Grandma June shrugged. "Your grandpa calls her up, invites her to do something, picks her up, and pays for everything. You know—dating."

I couldn't help feeling horrified. "It's just—I don't know—gross!"

"Gross? Why?"

"Well, for starters, my grandma passed away less than three months ago, and, well, they're old!"

Grandma June laughed out loud. "What has age got to do with

dating? Dating is two single and available people getting to know each other better. There's no age limit to it."

I couldn't help shuddering. "It's just—I mean, I didn't think old people actually—*dated.*"

Grandma June laughed again. "Just because a person's had a lot of birthdays doesn't mean a person's 'old,' James. If mirrors weren't around to prove that I'm not twenty-five anymore, it'd be hard for me to believe, because I still feel pretty young. It's a shock for me now to look in the mirror. I hardly recognize the face staring back at me. It's not the way I picture myself in my mind." Grandma June moved around the table to put her arm around me. "That's why I love you and Kyle so much. Most people only see an old, gray-haired lady who moves slowly, not the person I really am inside. But you and Kyle—you see *me.* Just like your grandma did, and your grandpa still does. The way your grandpa sees everybody, including Anna."

I tried to mull over everything Grandma June had told me once I got back to Grandpa's, but I was still in shock. I sat on the old swing, and even though it was hard to pump it much by myself, I did my best to do just that before heading back in the house.

Grandpa's CCC photo album was still sitting on the dresser where Kyle had left it yesterday when we'd been called out to meet Grandpa's "special, dear friend," so I picked it up to sit cross-legged on Grandpa's bed, thumbing through the small black-and-white pictures.

"You like that old CCC book of mine, don't you, James?"

His voice made me jump. "Grandpa! I didn't hear you come in!"

He smiled and sat down beside me on the bed. "Nope, you didn't."

"Did you have a nice swim?"

"Real nice." Grandpa tried to act all casual. "So, James, what do you think—"

I knew he was going to ask me about Anna. Or even worse, maybe about him *and* Anna. I didn't want to hear or talk about either subject, so I pointed to the page opened on my lap at a photo of a cute guy with short, dark, curly hair.

"Wait—is this another picture of Tucker?"

Grandpa leaned over my shoulder to take a look. "Yep, that's him."

"What happened after the dance in Duchesne—and after you two fought over his watch?"

Grandpa smiled. "Oh, Tucker and I had more adventures together after that, whether we wanted them or not!" His eyes started to twinkle in a way that meant I was going to hear some good stories, and I knew that at least for now, I wouldn't have to hear anything about Anna.

EIGHT

*A*fter the tussle over the watch, I stayed out of Tucker's way as much as possible. Once we'd finished building the river breakers during that first summer I was in the Cs, the LEMs at the camp got us all busy building roads way up on top of the Baldy Mountains. That required more backbreaking work with our axes against the trees, clearing a path to lay down the road with the Caterpillars. Or Cats, as we liked to call them. Big, bulldozer machines that we used to flatten out the ground to make a road. And the drivers—we called them "Cat skinners." That was a good project for me, because I was put on a different crew from Tucker, since he was building part of the road further up on top of the mountains. I could go all day without having to see him, and by the time we were driven back into camp on trucks at the end of the day, we were both too tired to fight with either words or fists.

Max still made sure I got a place in the back of the truck on Saturday nights for the open-air dances in all the neighboring towns, but after that first dance, I made sure not to dance with any girl too many times in a row. If I hadn't had to both live and work with Tucker, I wouldn't have cared, but because of that and for Max's sake, I did my best not to do anything to get Tucker all riled up. And luckily for me, after the incident with Mary St. Clair, I didn't run into a girl at a dance I wanted to dance with a lot. Strangely enough, neither did Tucker.

One day while we were working on the roads, way up on top of the

Baldies, Max and I were rotated to the front of our road-building crew, and we were the first to see it: a great big field of wild strawberries. It was like manna from heaven, all spread out on that mountaintop. The second we could stop for lunch, Max and I took off at a dead run into that field and stuffed our faces on all of those wild berries. Oh, they were as big as lemons. Great big delicious strawberries. Max and I told the LEM over us about the field, and he gave Max and me the go ahead to leave the road crew and spend the rest of the day picking strawberries to take back to the camp for dessert. Somehow Tucker found out—probably thanks to Max running to find him and give him some berries—and so he got the okay to pick strawberries, too. I wasn't thrilled to have him help out, but he brought a few guys from his crew with him, and together, the six of us were able to pick a ton more berries than Max and I ever could've picked on our own.

I'd been picking away, filling up my sack, eating one here and there as I went, when I heard a sort of swish-swish sound in the field not too far up the mountain ahead of me.

"Tucker? That you?"

Tucker had been a little way ahead of me, but I figured he must've gotten down on his hands and knees to crawl around and get a few berries near the ground because I couldn't see him anywhere. I could see Max some distance ahead in a thicker part of the field but still pretty far back from the other guys from Tucker's crew, who were way ahead and farther up the mountain from Tucker and me. And then I heard that swish-swish sound again, sounding more like an animal moving smoothly through the strawberries than a guy clomping around, stopping to pick berries here and there.

"Tucker?"

A second later, Tucker popped up a few yards ahead of me to scowl at me and yell, "What, Addison?" I would've been relieved, except that Tucker wasn't where I'd heard the swish-swish, and the swish-swish hadn't stopped. And then, a second later—out of nowhere, really—there was the most bone-chilling screech I'd ever heard. Max yelled, "Look out!" and right where I'd heard the steady swish-swish sound not far behind Tucker, a big ol' mountain lion sprang up to show us all just how big he was before he leaped towards Tucker and me, jumping fast and mean through those strawberries!

I screeched Tucker's name again, and he whipped his head around just long enough to see that mammoth lion bearing down practically on top of him. Tucker screamed and turned back to run towards me. I was scared—scared right out of my wits—and I yelled as loud as I ever had, making sure the whole world knew how scared I was. Tucker and I kept on screaming and running for our lives down that mountain. Max and the other three guys were behind the lion, and they kept busy chucking strawberries and rocks at the animal as they flew down the mountain right behind it. At least one of them must've been living right, because the lion got clobbered with a few strawberries and even more rocks, so he veered off our trail. I guess he'd been as surprised and scared to see us as we'd been to see him! He took off to the left towards a thick grove of trees, but even though he was off our tail now, neither Tucker nor I stopped running until we got back to where the LEM and the road-building crew were working.

We'd lost most all our strawberries, but Max and the others went back for the sacks and finished filling them while Tucker and I stayed with the LEM, trying to calm down and not think about how we could've been maimed pretty good by that lion, if not killed.

When Max came back with the other three guys and our sacks refilled with strawberries, Tucker and I were still quaking away, so Max put an arm around us both.

"You two going to be okay?"

Tucker nodded, and I said sure, even though I wasn't okay at all.

The LEM sent Max and Tucker and me with the strawberries back to camp so everyone could have strawberries and cream for dessert that night. Once we all dug into those strawberries, both Tucker and I cheered up considerably, and instead of being scared over that mountain lion anymore, we enjoyed all the attention we got telling everyone about our adventure running with the mountain lion through the strawberry patches on Baldy Mountain.

NINE

After the race with the mountain lion, late in the summer of '34, a bunch of us helped fight a forest fire. We'd all had a little training fighting fires that first week in the Cs, but nothing really prepares a guy for the real thing.

The LEMs told us there was a forest fire over by Swift Creek, up on the Yellowstone River, deep in the primitive area. No motor vehicles were allowed up in there. Max, Tucker, and I volunteered right off, so we were hauled with a bunch of other volunteers from our camp and a few neighboring camps clear down to Neola and across to Altona, and up the canyon, deep in where the fire was blazing.

It was a long, slow trip, riding up the mountain on the windy road between the quaking aspen trees. We stood up in the back of the CCC stake-rack trucks, gripping the tops of the stake racks, and followed the trail of smoke in the sky, looking for the actual fire.

I was standing by Max and Tucker, watching the smoke path, when something huge and black came hurtling out of the trees straight at us.

"WWHHHHOOOO! WHHHHHOOOOO!"

"Holy Moses!" I yelled and ducked fast. Problem was, so did everyone else in the back of the truck, both yelling and ducking, with all of us leaning to one side of the truck to get away from whatever monster was headed straight for us.

"Holy Moses!" I couldn't help yelling again, because with all of us piled on one side of the truck, the truck tipped onto its two right wheels, and if it hadn't been for the driver screeching the brakes and twisting the wheel hard in the opposite direction, we all would've been dumped out in a heap with that old CCC truck on top of us.

"Idiots! Stupid idiots! It was only a dumb old owl!"

Tucker had been squished under two big guys and was ready to let everyone have it. No amount of sheepish apologies could make him happy again. But we made it up on top of the mountain without further incident, as near as we could get to the fire by truck. At that point, we had to hike five or six miles up to the actual fire.

The fire was burning hot and strong, right up in the ledge rocks. The local guys that our CCC group was supposed to relieve had been fighting the fire for hours and were just coming down the mountain when we arrived. They were all black faced and tired, ready to head for home and some sleep. Unfortunately for us, they'd eaten everything in the grub boxes. There wasn't anything left for us but coffee.

An officer on charge took all us new guys in hand before we could get into any trouble on our own. "Okay, boys, there's more than enough experienced men already in fighting the fire. It's going to be dark soon, and since most of the fire's already out, we'll put all of you on fire guard."

He put us in groups of three and four. I was with Max and Tucker. We had to go out on patrol, and when we found little spot fires, we'd pound them out with our shovels. We didn't talk much—just stayed together, the three of us, as night came on, keeping our eyes peeled for hot spots. We would run off to stomp and smother the fires wherever we saw a small one, and then we'd regroup together once they were put out. The problem, though, was that I was regrouping less and less and going off on my own more and more. I'd get a spot fire put out, then I'd see another small one a ways off and go put it out, then I'd see another, and so on.

I'd just finished stomping out another small spot fire, when I looked up and saw one smoldering down off the ledge of the mountaintop a little ways. Even though I was green and inexperienced with putting out fires, I figured I could handle something more dangerous, so I climbed down off this bigger ledge on the edge of the mountain I was on, down onto a little smaller ledge to put that spot fire out. I stomped and smacked at the fire with my shovel and got it out, but once the fire was gone, it was pitch black all around me. With the main fire calmed down and quite a ways behind me, I was now stuck in thick darkness like I hadn't been caught in by myself in a long time.

As my heart hammered fast in my chest, I realized I couldn't see which way to go. I couldn't *not* move, though, so I gingerly tried to climb my way back up off that small ledge to get back onto the bigger one and then back onto higher ground again. I thought I'd caught a good toe hold, but those stupid World War I boots didn't have near enough traction on them anymore, and a second later, my foot lost its grip, and I did a combination of sliding and falling down the mountain, a good hundred feet, I was sure.

"Holy Moses!"

When I finally ground to a halt, face flat in the dirt, I lay there and just tried to breathe and get my heart to stop hammering in the thick darkness that was suffocating me. There was no way for me to regroup with Tucker and Max unless I got back up and over those stupid ledges, so once my hands and legs stopped shaking, I felt around and got a hold of the rocky ledge that I'd fallen off of, relieved to find out I hadn't fallen that many feet after all. I threw my shovel up onto the ledge and finally managed to heave myself back up on top of it. Then I threw my shovel up over the bigger ledge and pulled myself up on top of that. I looked around and saw other little spot fires—and then, I could see the figure of a guy smacking a spot fire with a shovel, and I hollered out as loud as I could. He turned, came running over, and helped me the rest of the way back up on the top of the mountain.

"Are you Addison?" His face was so black from smoke that I couldn't tell who he was.

I nodded, gasping for air. "Yeah—Addison."

The guy turned away from me and yelled, "Hey, I found Addison!"

Seconds later, Tucker and Max came running out of the darkness over to me, and Max actually gripped me in a hug for a second.

"Stupid idiot! What did you think you were doing, climbing down over a cliff like that? You could've been killed!"

Tucker was leaning against his shovel a few feet away, staring stonily at us both. "It's what stupid idiots do, Max. He couldn't help himself."

I was still shaking, so I decided to ignore Tucker. We spent all night fighting those little fires and staying on guard in case we were needed deeper into the real fire, but we were too inexperienced for anyone to consider throwing us into the pit of hell. Instead, Max, Tucker, and I stayed with the other boys from our camp, putting out the little spot fires. And this time, I really did stay with the others.

When we got through at about two, three o'clock in the morning, another group came to relieve us, so we went back to where the main bunch was to get some sleep. All we had for warmth were the big old army coats we'd brought with us. We put those around us to sleep, and we all just sat on the ground, leaning our heads against the quaking aspen trees, and tried to get as much sleep that way as we could.

By morning, the main fire was put out, and our CCC camp finally got some food to us. We were dead tired by the time we got back to camp. I decided I'd had my fill of volunteer fire fighting, and I swore I wouldn't volunteer for another one ever again.

TEN

Did you tell James about the mountain lion in the strawberries? That's a great story."

Kyle was standing in the doorway to Grandpa's bedroom. He was actually smiling at me, and for some weird reason, the fact made my heart jump strangely.

"I thought you were at work!"

Kyle kept smiling. "I *am* at work. It's my lunch break."

I'd started to smile back until I saw who had silently followed Kyle into the house.

Grandpa smiled huge and jumped off the bed to hurry to Anna's side. "Anna! I was just about to ask James to come along with us on Saturday to go on the new water slides. You know—the ones we saw down by the city park?"

I frowned. "Water slides?"

"Sure! It'll be fun. Just the thing for a hot summer day, and boy, Saturday's supposed to be extra hot! Kyle, why don't you come with us? Or do you have to work?"

Kyle couldn't stop grinning. "No, I don't have to work this Saturday."

"Water slides? You can't—I mean—"

Kyle lifted an eyebrow at me. "Why can't they?"

Grandpa laughed. "There's no age limit, James. In fact, we should get in cheaper since we're senior citizens! Got to take advantage of that, you know!"

I couldn't believe what I was hearing. "But I don't have a swimming suit and—"

"Yeah, you do. I know your mom packed it. So what time on Saturday are we going, maybe around eleven or so?"

"I'm not going!"

That shut everyone up fast, and Anna, who hadn't spoken a word, just looked uncomfortable, as I felt she well should. I ran past her and didn't stop running until I'd made it to the swing. A second later, though, Kyle opened the back door, so I jumped out of the swing, ran into the garage, and slammed the door shut.

I'd been pacing around for a minute when Kyle quietly and carefully opened the garage door. I stared at him for a second before I went back to pacing. Kyle watched me for a minute, and then he stuck his hands in his pockets and wandered around the circumference of the garage, poking into one box and then another.

"Hey, I didn't know your grandpa had one of these!"

I turned around to see Kyle sitting on a fancy, nearly brand-new riding lawn mower, happily checking out all the controls. I folded my arms and slowly walked over to him until I was standing in front of the mower.

"You knew she's been coming over to see my grandpa, didn't you?"

Kyle looked up at me evenly. "Yeah—so?"

"For how long?"

Kyle shrugged but didn't look away. "I don't know. A couple of weeks, I guess."

"A couple of weeks? And you didn't say anything?"

"Hey, you'd know for yourself if you'd cared enough to come out and check on your grandpa before now. It's not my job to keep you informed. Besides, it's none of my business what your grandpa does."

I wanted to scream. I couldn't believe Kyle didn't think what my grandpa was doing was a big deal, when it *was* a big deal. A very big deal. In fact, all Kyle did in response to my saying that thanks to him, Grandpa was alone with this Anna person in Grandpa's house, was to jump off the mower and head for a bicycle in back of it. A minute later, he'd muscled it out from under some old lawn chairs.

"Look at this, James—a Schwinn bicycle built for two!"

"Who cares?"

Kyle ignored me. "It's in great shape. It just needs air in the tires." He ran around the garage looking for a tire pump, which he of course found, and quickly pumped up both tires. "Come on!"

"Come on where?"

"Outside. Don't you want to try it out?"

"Not really. I'm going back inside."

"I've got to get back to work soon. Come on!"

If anyone else had been coaxing me to try out the bicycle built for two, I would've said no. But this was Kyle, and for some reason, I couldn't turn him down.

"I don't even know how to work this thing."

"Just get on."

So I did just that, and from the get go, we had problems. The thing jerked around like it was alive and tried to buck us off, but after the second failed attempt, Kyle at least had figured something out.

"You've got to stop trying to control the bike from behind. So don't start pumping the pedals until I'm ready, too, James. And we have to start on the same foot."

"Which foot?"

"The right foot. Ready? One—two—three!"

This time, it worked. I even laughed out loud, I was so surprised. It was like figuring out how to make Grandma's swing work with Kyle all over again. We breezed around the neighborhood a few times while I watched the wind ruffle Kyle's thick dark hair and giggled as he did the proper hand signals to warn me and everyone else when he was going to make a left turn or a right turn. I didn't know how much fun I'd been having until Kyle turned the bicycle back into Grandpa's driveway, and I realized I was disappointed the ride was over.

Kyle jumped off and held the bike steady so I could get off before he pushed it back into the garage.

"That was fun!"

"Yeah, it was." Kyle leaned it back in its place against the far wall of the garage before facing me with a smile. "And the water slides on Saturday will be fun, too."

"I said I'm not going!"

Kyle shrugged. "Okay. Then I guess your grandpa and Anna will just have to go have fun by themselves."

There was no way I was going to let that happen. I couldn't let that happen.

Kyle laughed and gave me a light shove. "If you go, I'll go with you. Just come with us, James! You know you want to."

I didn't want to, but I wanted even less to have Grandpa and Anna spend an entire day alone together.

ELEVEN

I can't believe I'm going to a water slide with my grandpa and his 'date.'"

I stared at myself in the bathroom mirror before I pulled a T-shirt over my old red one-piece swimsuit. I always wore a pair of blue, boy's swim trunks on top of my suit, and I did so today. It definitely didn't make me look very girlish, but it kept me covered, and that's what I needed when I was being flung down a water slide into a shallow pool.

I'd heard Kyle's knock and knew he was sitting in the living room chatting with Grandpa and Anna. I'd just about finished wrapping an elastic around the bottom of my one long braid when the sound of more knocking and what sounded like a half dozen strange voices froze me in place, both hands clutching my braid.

I could hear little voices yelling, "Grandma, Grandma!" and my own grandpa laughing and calling out hello to what sounded like at least three different kids. I couldn't stand it anymore, so after slipping my sandals onto my feet, I stuffed a towel into my overnight bag and cautiously stepped into the kitchen and then into the living room.

"There she is. James, say hello!"

Grandpa looked so excited to introduce me to Bobby, Tommy, and Michelle, three of Anna's grandkids, that it made my heart hurt.

"And this is Anna's daughter, Marilynn, and her husband, Paul. They're all coming with us to the water slide."

Bobby and Tommy were somewhere around seven and nine, but

petite, tiny, blonde Michelle—she looked developed enoug
een, even though she claimed to be only thirteen. And she'd
attached herself to Kyle, who didn't seem to mind that a thi
old girl insisted on hanging around him and talking his ear off.

"Well, it's getting late. Let's get a move on!"

Anna's family piled in their car, while Kyle and I drove with Grandpa
and Anna. And Michelle, who insisted on coming with us. Grandpa was
in high heaven. He couldn't stop singing silly little songs he called "dit-
ties" and making comments the whole way to the water park.

"Just look at all the traffic! Don't these people have homes?"

We drove along with Grandpa laughing and telling jokes until we
passed a cemetery.

"Hey, Michelle, did you know the people living on the left side of the
road can't be buried in that cemetery on the right side of the road?"

"They can't? That's stupid. Why not?"

"Because they're not dead yet!"

Anna laughed and laughed. So did Michelle and Kyle, but I could
only roll my eyes. That was one of Grandpa's oldest car jokes ever.

Kyle, Michelle, and Anna continued to laugh at all of Grandpa's
jokes, but I kept my face turned to the window and ignored everyone.
Even when Kyle bumped his shoulder against mine and whispered,
"Don't be a pain!" I still refused to move my nose from against the glass.

Kyle and I got our water mats and were the first to stand in the water
slide line. Kyle tried to joke with me, but it wasn't working today.

"Did you know all of Anna's family was coming, too?"

Kyle nodded. "Yep. Anna told me on Saturday."

"Gee, thanks for letting me know. Why didn't you tell me?"

"Because I knew you wouldn't come if I told you."

From where we were standing, I could see Grandpa, Anna, Michelle,
and the two boys leaving the dressing room. For an old man, Grandpa
didn't look too bad in a swimsuit, but Anna—I was shocked to see her
in one. And Michelle—her suit was easily a size too small for her. I was

surprised Kyle didn't seem to notice, but he was too busy trying not to hyperventilate around all the girls who had bikinis on. I looked away from Kyle and watched while Grandpa chased the two boys around. All three were laughing hard, along with Anna and Michelle.

"Why do I need to be here? Grandpa doesn't need me here. I mean, just look at him. Those kids aren't even his grandkids, yet he's acting more excited to be with them than he ever acted around any of his real grandkids."

Kyle sighed loudly and shoved me. "I don't know why you can't just be happy for him. I wish my grandma had someone in her life. She gets so lonely it's hard to watch."

I chose to ignore Kyle's remark. "Just look at Anna. I can't believe she'd actually get into a swimsuit and go on a water slide. You couldn't have gotten my grandma to do something like this in a million years."

Kyle lifted his eyebrow. "Maybe that's part of why your grandpa likes Anna."

I scowled at Kyle, but all he did was turn and yell for everyone to come get in line with us. Michelle kept squealing about being scared to go down the slide. I was ready to tell her to just go sit on the grass if she couldn't handle a water slide, but Kyle cut me off instead.

"You can go down the slide with me if you want, Michelle."

I couldn't believe it. When we got to the top, Michelle snuggled in front of Kyle on his water mat with his chin above her head before they raced down the slide, Michelle screaming all the way.

"That looks fun. Come on, Anna—come sit in front of me!"

Grandpa and Anna doubled up on a mat going down, and the two boys did as well. That left me riding my mat by myself, which I was happy to do almost the whole afternoon, while Michelle conned Kyle into riding with her on her mat again and again. And again.

For the hundredth time, I got on my mat, muttering, "Why am I here?" before shoving myself down another slide to land with an unceremonious plop in the shallow pool at the bottom of the slide that always separated me from my mat, no matter what I did to hang onto it.

Towards the end of the afternoon, I had the absolute joy of watching Michelle come racing down the slide to be thrown mercilessly into the pool. She stood up, spluttering, trying to get her hair out of her eyes, as if she had all the time in the world to just stand there in front of the slide. I could see her two brothers racing together down another slide that also landed in the same shallow pool and realized she was forgetting the rule of getting out of the way the first second possible to avoid getting slammed by other sliders. I knew I should've warned her, but instead, I happily leaned against the side of the shallow pool while Tommy and Bobby slammed head on into Michelle, sending her flying and screaming out of their way and being dunked in the process as well.

I couldn't stop laughing. "Now that was worth coming for!"

Michelle had no desire to go down the slides any more after that and ran to join her parents on a grassy area near the pool. I grabbed my mat and ran for the slides, grinning the whole way.

"Hey, James. Wait up!"

I stopped and turned to see Kyle lightly jogging up to me with his mat under his arm. We'd hardly said a word to each other the whole afternoon. He looked good in his suit, and his hair looked great wet. Even though he wasn't on any of the athletic teams at school, I could tell he'd been lifting weights. I knew I only looked drippy and soggy, and I was sure I didn't look great in my old red swimsuit, so I looked away and started walking fast towards the slides.

"What do you want?" I threw that over my shoulder and hurried up the slide stairs.

Once we got to the top, Kyle grabbed my braid and gave it a light tug. "Hey, want to go down the slide with me?"

My heart did its strange jump it'd been doing around Kyle too much lately, but I just shrugged and said, "Sure."

Kyle put the mat down and got all settled on it. "Well, come on, James. Sit in front of me."

It felt awkward and strange, but I did just that. I waited for him to give us a shove down the slide, but he didn't, so I turned my head to look at him.

"Ready, Kyle?" I could feel myself blushing all over when I saw that he was looking at my legs. "What are you staring at?"

Kyle just kept looking at my legs. "You've got long legs."

"What?" I flipped my head around to look at him again, not sure I'd heard him right. But Kyle actually looked irritated now.

"Nothing." Before I could say anything back, Kyle grabbed my braid and flipped it over my shoulder. "Try not to hit me in the face with this."

I didn't have a chance to say anything back, because Kyle gave us a hard, fast shove, and a second later we were flying down the slide. We leaned from side to side at the exact same time at the appropriate moments for the turns and made ourselves go through the loops and tubes faster and faster. When we finally made it to the bottom of the slide, we were going fast enough that we flew through the air before slamming into the water. But it was fun. Really fun. I was laughing hard, and shockingly enough, so was Kyle.

"Wanna do that again, James?"

I did, so we shared a mat for a half dozen more times until Michelle decided she'd recovered from being slammed by her brothers, but of course, she couldn't handle going down the slide alone, so Kyle shared his mat with her for the last bit of the afternoon.

I didn't realize how much Michelle and her insistence on flirting with Kyle irritated me until we arrived back at Grandpa's house and Kyle pulled me aside by the swing.

"What's your problem, James?"

I stared at Kyle without smiling. "Problem? I don't have a problem."

Kyle sighed and ran a hand through his hair. "Look, Anna's family is only going to be in town for a few days. I was just trying to be nice. Would it have killed you to be nice?"

"Is that what you call what you were doing?"

"That's all I was doing. Good grief, James. She's only thirteen."

"I'm glad you remembered." I shoved past Kyle and hurried into the house. Grandpa was sprawled on the couch, and luckily for me, Anna's family left pretty soon after that. I thought Anna would go with them, but she didn't.

Grandpa smiled once I'd seated myself on the floor to lean against the couch. "Did you have fun, James?"

"Sure, I guess."

"Sure, you guess?" Grandpa laughed. "Well, I'm bushed. Do you want to watch some TV?"

Anna was settling into a chair in the living room that Grandma had always liked to sit in, and for some reason that bothered me. A lot.

"No, let's not watch TV. You told me you met Grandma in the Cs. I want to hear all about when you met her. At a Shoe Dance. In Veyo. Isn't that where you met her?" Kyle was leaning back in the recliner across from me, giving me his "not now" look, but I turned myself on the floor in front of Grandpa so that I didn't have to see Kyle or Anna at all.

"Hey, weren't you telling James about the forest fire you fought up in the Uintas the other day?"

Grandpa nodded at Kyle. "Yep. That happened while I was still up at the Uinta River Camp. I told her all about it. And about finding that mountain lion in the strawberries!"

"Tell us the canteen story. Didn't that happen right after the forest fires?"

Grandpa chuckled. "Yeah, that happened not too long after that fire."

I turned around and glared at Kyle, but he only grinned his elf grin back. "It's a funny story, James. You'll love it!"

Grandpa laughed again. "It *is* a pretty good story, James. Would you like to hear it?"

I scowled at Kyle's grin before turning to look at Grandpa with a resigned shrug. "Sure—why not?"

TWELVE

After the fires were brought under control, we got busy building a road from the Uinta River around the mountain that crosses over to Moon Lake. To build that road, we used our picks and shovels and axes to clear the ground of trees and debris to make a space at least six feet wide so a Cat could walk through it and flatten the land out into a road. It took a long time, but we finally made a road that wound up and around the hill from the Uinta River over to Moon Lake. We'd work there all day—pick and shovel, picking away—and then, when evening came, we'd just leave our shovels there and only take our pick heads back into camp, because by the end of the day, they were always dull and had to be sharpened for the next day's work.

At lunchtime, a truck would come up with our lunches. Our lunch sacks usually had a cheese sandwich, or maybe a peanut butter sandwich or apple butter sandwich. Sometimes we'd build fires and toast the cheese sandwiches over the fire. That made them really good. We didn't go much for the peanut butter, but the apple butter was pretty good.

The worst part, though, was the Canteen Problem. It was a pain to carry a canteen on your hip, because it got in the way of picking and shoveling a little, but it was better than going without water. The Canteen Problem came up because half the guys decided it was easier not to carry their canteens and instead bum water from the guys who did carry their canteens. It went on everywhere, in every CCC camp, and no one seemed to have figured out a way to make it stop. Tucker, Max, and I were three of the guys who'd bring water, and so we got accosted on a daily basis by guys begging water off us. I got really tired of it after a week of giving half my water away, so one day during lunch, I wandered off a short ways and found an interesting little pond area surrounded by trees. I leaned down really close to look into the water and couldn't help grinning at what I saw. My canteen was nearly empty, so I reached down to stick it into the pond. A second later, I felt a hard slap on my back.

"What the—"

Tucker was standing over me, scowling at me like he always did.

"What was that for? You nearly knocked me in!"

"The water's full of pollywogs, idiot."

I grinned and stuck my canteen back into the water. "I know."

Tucker watched me fill my canteen a minute more before he grinned, too, and ran off to get Max. After Max looked at the water, he laughed, and we all got busy filling up our canteens. It didn't take long before a bunch of the guys asked for a drink of water, and with a shrug, we handed over the canteens.

Tucker, Max, and I tried to act all casual and uncaring, but we were all watching out of the corners of our eyes, waiting to see what would happen when the first three got a mouthful of pollywogs. The second the guys tasted the pollywogs, they threw the canteens to the ground, spitting and gagging and swearing, while Max, Tucker, and I nearly split our sides laughing. We knew there'd be a fight, and there was, but it was worth it. And the result was that every day after that, everyone had canteens full of clean, cold water riding on their hips. No one trusted anyone for a drink after that, so we cured the whole camp of the Canteen Problem with our pollywog water.

THIRTEEN

randpa Harold, you need to write all this stuff down. Your stories about the CCC are the best."

"And then you need to write all about how you met Grandma and when you got married. I can't wait to hear all of those stories." I looked pointedly at Anna, but she only smiled.

Grandpa laughed. "I can barely write my name, and you want me to write my life history?"

"But, Grandpa, it's important. You know everyone's supposed to keep a journal—"

"You don't have to write your history down on paper, Harold. Why don't you use a tape recorder instead?"

I stared at Anna's smiling face and couldn't help but wonder if she was throwing down the gauntlet at me. Maybe she didn't want to fight, but she was challenging me in some kind of way, that much I was sure of.

I smiled thinly back. "What do you think, Grandpa? If I bought some tapes, would you let me tape your CCC stories? And how you met Grandma because of the CCC and when you got married?" If Anna didn't feel threatened or intimidated by me or Grandma's history with Grandpa, I was sure it wouldn't last for long, once I got him going telling every memory he had about my grandma when they were young. I knew no woman could ever compare in Grandpa's eyes to my grandma. Ever.

Why would she want to keep hanging around with Grandpa when it would be obvious he was in love forever with my grandma?

"Well, now, James—I'd never thought about keeping a journal that way before, but recording my life on tapes—I think that sounds like a pretty interesting idea!" Grandpa's eyes were shining excitedly, and as for me, I was feeling pretty excited myself to see Grandpa so happy about doing something huge like this.

"I made an apple pie for dessert. Is everybody ready to have some?"

Anna had stood up and was smiling at everyone. Of course, Kyle and Grandpa were up for dessert. And even I was curious to find out what Anna's pie was like, though I knew it couldn't possibly be as good as Grandma's pies.

"James, would you mind coming into the kitchen and helping me with the pie? I've got vanilla ice cream to go with it."

I looked at Anna's smiling face steadily, but my heart was thumping. "Sure." Anna needed help serving pie? I doubted it. But I figured if Anna wanted to have a private talking-to with me to put me in my place, I was up for it. In fact, the more I thought about it as I walked slowly into the kitchen, the more the whole idea started to appeal to me. Here was my golden opportunity to get rid of Anna for good.

"I'll cut the pie if you wouldn't mind scooping out the ice cream onto each piece. Will you do that for me?"

I shrugged without looking at her. "I guess."

Anna was already getting the pie out. "The ice cream scoop is in the drawer—"

"I know where the ice cream scoop is!" I snatched the scoop out of the drawer. "I've gotten it out hundreds of times for years."

But Anna kept smiling. Almost kindly. Almost as if she felt sorry for me. "I'm sorry. I guess I should've realized that. The ice cream's in the freezer. I won't tell you where that is."

I knew she was trying to get along with me, but I didn't want to get along with her. Ever. She wasn't my grandma, and she never would be. I hated seeing her puttering around the kitchen, touching Grandma's kitchen things. But at least it put me into the best frame of mind for when she was ready to get after me for being unkind to her all the time. I could tell she was getting ready to say something to me. Any second now—

"So, James—"

"Yeah?" Even I was taken aback a little. I definitely sounded like I had my fists up, all ready to swing my first punch.

"That Kyle Jansen sure is a sweet boy. Is he your boyfriend?"

She couldn't have knocked me over more completely. "Boy—boyfriend? Kyle?"

Anna laughed and continued to cut into the pie. "Well, he does come over a lot now that you're here. And it's obvious he thinks a lot of you. I just haven't been able to help wondering for some time now if the two of you are—you know—an item."

I burst out laughing. "An 'item'? That sounds like something my grandma—" I shut my mouth tight. I wasn't about to see Anna as anything like my grandma. Ever. I frowned and turned away from Anna's painfully hopeful face and dug viciously into the ice cream with the scoop. "No, we're not an 'item,' or 'boyfriend-girlfriend,' or anything retarded like that."

"Why not? Don't you like Kyle?"

I dug even harder into the ice cream. I wasn't going to talk about whether or not I liked Kyle. Not with her. Not with anyone!

"Kyle's just my friend. He's been my friend forever."

Anna smiled again. "That's the way the best relationships start."

I grabbed two plates of pie and ice cream and hurried out of the kitchen, nearly tripping all over my feet. After I handed Grandpa his pie, I almost dumped Kyle's dessert in his lap.

"Careful, James!" Kyle laughed and grabbed the plate from me. "Are you okay?"

I was blushing, and I hated that Kyle could see it. "I'm fine. Just fine." I ran back into the kitchen, but Anna was standing in the doorway, smiling as she handed me a plate of dessert. "I've already put the ice cream and pie away. Let's go back into the living room."

I couldn't look at Kyle the rest of the evening. When he tried to coax some conversation out of me, I hardly answered, and when I did, my voice was as muffled and quiet as Anna's. Poor Kyle—I glanced at him once and saw the baffled look on his face as he stared back.

"Hey, James—want to go outside on the swing for a while?"

My heart leaped funny inside me, but when I looked at Kyle, he casually nodded in Grandpa and Anna's direction. I frowned while Kyle pointedly looked over at Grandpa and Anna again before looking back at me. I turned my head to look at the two of them on the couch and saw that they were whispering together and holding hands.

I frowned and shook my head firmly. "Too many mosquitoes are out now."

Kyle rolled his eyes again before standing up to say his good-byes to all and left.

As annoyed as I was that Anna and Grandpa were getting far too attached to each other, by the time I went to bed, my brain was too busy mulling over Anna's comments about Kyle to worry about the two of them. I couldn't begin to fall asleep and lay awake in bed half the night.

FOURTEEN

I was still thinking about Anna's comments the next day as I scrubbed the dirty dishes in the kitchen sink while Grandpa was off taking his morning swim at the city pool with Clay. Kyle and I had been friends forever. Nothing more. I couldn't imagine that Kyle would ever see me as anything but a friend, but then—I stopped in mid thought, holding a plate up for inspection, and stared at my reflection instead. He *had* looked at me funny when we'd been on the water slide together, and he *did* come around a lot. A second later, the wet, soapy dish slipped from my shaking fingers and nearly crashed in a million pieces on the floor. I grabbed frantically for it and saved it from certain death before giving myself a firm mental shake.

"Stupid, stupid—stop thinking stupid things about Kyle!"

Grandpa had left some money on the kitchen counter with a note saying, "For cassette tapes." I'd grinned and grinned over it the second I'd noticed it. *Thrilled* was too tame a word to describe how happy I was that Grandpa was still willing to record his life history on tape. That he was up for it meant his stories would be told in great detail, and he'd likely spend some time thinking about what he wanted to say before I stuck his cassette recorder in front of his face and pressed Record. This was a solid yes. I wasn't going to let myself focus on things in my life that were anything less. I was determined about that.

I scribbled a quick note to Grandpa in case he got back home before I did and then scooped up the money on the counter into one of my cut-off jeans pockets. I grabbed the spare key off the hook and opened the back door.

"Hey—I mean, Knock knock!"

Kyle. He even had his fist up, ready to knock.

"Sorry—I mean—I'm just on my way out—"

Kyle leaned against the inside of the door. "Oh, yeah? Where to?"

"Just that corner store to get some stuff."

Kyle smiled and shrugged. "Okay if I come with you?"

"Shouldn't you be at work?"

"I'm taking an early lunch. It's been a slow day at Lakewood's. I guess not many people ordered new furniture last week. Want to take that bicycle built for two?"

I shrugged and gave Kyle a light shove so I could shut and lock the door. "Sure, I guess."

"So what do you need to pick up at the store?"

I kept my head down, focusing on locking the door. "Nothing. Just some cassette tapes."

"For your grandpa?"

I turned to look at Kyle and caught him frowning at me. "Hey, he left the money and a note for me. I didn't make him! Besides, recording your life history is important!"

Kyle rolled his eyes. "Whatever. I know you don't want my advice, James, but I'm giving you some anyway. Leave the thing with your grandpa and Anna alone."

I shook my head and moved around Kyle to walk quickly to the garage. "I can't do that."

It only took Kyle a second to catch up and block me from walking into the garage. "Why not?"

I frowned and stared straight into Kyle's eyes. "Look. You claim you wish your grandma was seeing someone, but that's because you don't know what it's like. You have no idea how this is for me. It's humiliating, thinking of my grandpa running all over town, chasing all the old widows—"

"Really? Or are you just jealous because he's dating and you're not?"

My mouth fell open at that. "Jealous? I'm not even sixteen yet!"

"You will be in a few weeks. We'll see if you're as busy as your grandpa after that!"

I couldn't stand to hear Kyle laughing. "Oh, shut up!"

I ignored Kyle's annoying remarks after that and stuck my tongue out at his back while we pedaled the bicycle together in silence. I couldn't believe how many people were inside the store. Only one cash register was in operation, and there were easily ten people in line waiting. I sighed and fidgeted in the back of the line, tapping my package of cassette tapes against my leg, trying my best not to scream. I looked around for Kyle, who'd been wandering up and down the few short aisles, picking up one thing and looking it over before putting it back and then doing the same again with something else.

The little bell above the door rang out, and like everyone else in line, I turned idly to see who had come in, even though I knew it would be a stranger. Only this time, it wasn't.

The girl with long, dark black hair and what I knew Kyle would refer to as a killer figure and a fancy face breezed into the store like she owned the place. Even though I wasn't friends with her and had never even exchanged a hi in passing, I knew who this girl was. In fact, everyone at Central High knew who this girl was. Samantha. Samantha Colton. She'd been on the drill team all three of her years at Central High and been voted homecoming queen and senior prom queen last year. She was going with Mike, the captain of the varsity football team, who was also the student body president. Obviously, I hated her. The only thing redeemable about her was that she had two very hot younger brothers, Alex and Brett Colton.

Even though I knew she wouldn't have known me from Adam, I turned my back to her and hoped she hadn't seen me.

"Kyle—is that you, Kyle?"

"Hey, Sam. What's going on?"

I had to be hallucinating. I had to be. After all, Kyle wasn't that unusual a name.

I slowly turned around, but to my utter horror, Kyle was laughing and smiling and flirting with the biggest flirt Central High had ever known. I couldn't believe Sam even knew Kyle's name, but worse than that was being forced to realize Kyle knew Sam—

"So, I hope you're still playing the piano, Kyle. You are, aren't you?"

"I am."

"That is so great—I'd love to hear you play sometime!"

"Come on over anytime you want."

I couldn't believe what I was hearing. And seeing. Kyle was saying stupid things, his tongue tripping all over the place, while his eyes—his eyes were sparkling all funny. *A crush? On Sam Colton? Of all the girls at Central High*—I felt sick. Absolutely sick.

A second later, I watched, dumbstruck, while the two of them walked out of the store together. Since I was tall, even though there were people standing around in front of me, I had no trouble seeing over everyone's heads, and so I was easily able to view the horrible scene going on outside through the store's front windows.

Sam was looking over the bicycle built for two—Grandpa's bicycle—and touching the handle bars and seats and laughing up into Kyle's smiling face. I watched her tug at Kyle's arm, pleading with him over something, and the next thing I knew, the two of them had jumped onto the seats and were pedaling in a circle in the parking lot in front of the store. Without any jerks or stops or repeated starts, either, like when Kyle and I had tried the bike out the first time. They glided all over the place as if they'd ridden the bike together for years.

"Miss—miss? Can I help you?"

The old man behind the cash register motioned me forward. Somehow I made my legs move, and through a red haze, I was able to drop the tapes and money onto the counter and get the purchasing moment over with. By the time I shoved through the store door, making the bell ring, Kyle and Sam had finished riding the bike and were standing together talking at the far end of the store by the phone booths. Kyle still straddled the bike, holding it upright.

I couldn't make myself move any farther, but once Kyle saw me, he smiled and gave me a "come over here" head jerk as if everything was fine and he hadn't done anything wrong.

I glared at Kyle and moved stonily forward while his smile faded, and he looked nothing but baffled back.

As soon as Sam saw me, she touched Kyle's arm and said "Talk to you later" before swinging her hips unnecessarily as she walked towards me, cool and confident as a sleek, black cat. She grinned wide without opening her mouth once we were eyeball to eyeball and gave me a nice condescending nod before brushing past me to reenter the store.

"I'm sure I was just hallucinating, but for a second there, I thought I saw you giving Sam Colton a ride on my bike. But I had to be wrong. I mean, you don't even know her. You wouldn't have done something like that without asking if it was okay, since it's my bike and everything, right?"

Kyle raised an eyebrow. "It's not your bike. It's your grandpa's. He wouldn't have cared. In fact, he would've done the same thing. Besides, it wasn't my idea. She asked for a ride."

"And you couldn't have just said no?"

"Unlike some people who'll remain nameless, it's not in me to be rude."

I decided to ignore that remark. "How in the world do you know Sam Colton?"

Kyle shrugged. "I was in a mixed grade biology class last semester. She was in there, too, and sat in front of me. She couldn't stand cutting into anything whenever we had to dissect something, so she'd ask me to help her out."

"I'll bet she did."

"What's that supposed to mean?"

Kyle still looked baffled, and truth be told, I was just as baffled. I shouldn't have cared that he'd given Sam Colton a ride on Grandpa's bike, but being forced to watch the two zip around the parking lot together and seeing how Kyle had looked at Sam—I didn't know—I'd felt strange. More than just angry. Hurt. Sure, I felt hurt. Maybe even a little jealous. Almost—betrayed. And yet, Kyle and I were just friends. Just friends.

"Nothing. I hope you realize she was just being nice."

Kyle frowned at me suspiciously. "What are you saying?"

"Oh, come on, Kyle. Everyone knows she has to flirt with everything and anything remotely male."

Kyle laughed. "Jealous, are you?"

I almost snorted. "Jealous? Over Sam Colton? Hardly."

"Then how come you're acting all weird?"

"I'm not acting weird. You're the one acting all weird. You should've seen how stupid you looked, drooling all over her. I can't believe you'd act so stupid around someone like Sam Colton. You know she'd never go for you in a million years."

Kyle's face hardened funny for a second. "Maybe, maybe not. I just know that no guy can help being attracted to a really pretty girl."

I almost felt slapped. I didn't want to think about what Kyle was implying. I knew I wasn't pretty. I'd always known that. I was too tall and skinny, and my hair had too much red in it, and I had no idea how to use makeup to hide everything about my face that I hated.

"Obviously, I don't know anything about that. Let's just go home now, okay?"

I couldn't believe I was fighting with Kyle. With Kyle—one of my best friends ever. I jumped off the bike the second we bumped up into the driveway at Grandpa's and ran into the house, leaving Kyle to put the bike away.

"Whoa there, James. Where's the fire?"

Grandpa was sitting on the couch reading a newspaper, but he lowered it to peer over the top of it at me.

"There's no fire. I'm fine. Just fine." I sat down beside Grandpa, who put his arm around me and squeezed my shoulders.

"You sure, James?"

"I'm sure. And look—I bought your tapes." I opened my sack and handed Grandpa the package of tapes, but when I looked up at his face, I was shocked to see tears in his eyes. "Grandpa—I'm sorry—I'm pushing you too hard, aren't I? I mean, you don't have to record anything if you don't want to—if it's too hard for you—"

Grandpa shook his head as he quickly wiped at his eyes with his handkerchief. "No, no, James. It's not that. I'm just happy, that's all."

"Happy?"

"Happy that you want to hear about ol' Grandpa's life. And that you want to keep my history on something that will last, so it won't be forgotten too soon."

I couldn't help giving Grandpa a quick hug. "Someone like you could never be forgotten, Grandpa, you know that! Besides, this is going to be fun, right?"

"That's right. It *is* going to be fun! Our special project together, James!"

Our special project. Something I'd always remember sharing with Grandpa.

"I know you want to hear how I met your grandma most of all, and we're getting there, James—I promise!"

I smiled up at him. "I know we are. Just don't forget to go back and record all the stories you've already told me—and why you got into the CCC in the first place. You don't want to leave anything out!"

Grandpa laughed. "Go grab the cassette recorder. I won't forget!"

FIFTEEN

Once the road we were building up the mountain reached Moon Lake, we built a new camp near the lake that we called the Moon Lake Camp, up on the Yellowstone River. We moved into Moon Lake Camp in the fall of '34 for the winter. Since it was a winter camp, we built wooden barracks down by the river to sleep in so we could be inside out of the snow. There was a good-sized ditch we had to jump across to get to one part of the camp, and there was a small bridge across another stream to get to the other end of camp.

We had four big barracks for us enrollees to sleep in, a recreation hall, and a shower house. The barracks had wooden bunk beds instead of the army cots and a big old pot-bellied stove at one end to keep the barracks heated. The shower house was across the creek, along the road by the river. There was a big, long area inside the shower house where the basins were, with both hot and cold running water, and a little section portioned off in the shower house where we'd go in and scrub our clothes out by hand. And then there were some steps on the hill that led up to the mess hall, the officers' barracks, headquarters, the doctor's office, and recreation hall. We used to play pool and have dances in the recreation hall.

That first winter, we really had a lot of snow, so in no time, we were snowed in. As a result, we spent a lot of time out on the CCC trucks and the Cats pushing snow to open the road to Duchesne. We hadn't been able to get out on the weekends much, and I for one was going completely stir crazy. One Saturday, after we'd finally opened the road from camp all the way to Duchesne, Tucker was able to secure a CCC truck with a canvas top over the back to keep the snow off us for the drive down to Duchesne for the Saturday night dance.

Mary was at the dance, but this time, I only asked her to dance a few times. The strange thing was that Tucker didn't ask her to dance at all. He disappeared after a while, so Max and I went looking for him and found him huddled in the back of the CCC truck nipping on some whisky with a half dozen of the guys we'd come with. He gave me his customary scowl while he offered the bottle to Max. But I got my fair share, and before long, the whole group of us had passed out in the back of the truck, not waking up until early Sunday morning.

It was cold that morning, and the roads were snowy, icy, and slippery, going up and down through the mountains to get from Duchesne back to the Moon Lake Camp. I was sitting in the back of the truck with a dozen of the guys, while Dalton, the official leader of our group, and Tucker, the official truck driver, and one other guy—Enrollee Collett—rode up front.

Tucker was driving around 35 miles an hour, which wouldn't have been so bad, except that the roads were snowy and icy and the road through the mountains had some sharp turns that needed to be taken slow and careful. And it didn't help that he'd had too much to drink and that Dalton and Collett had each had too much to drink, too.

After leaving Duchesne, Tucker couldn't get the truck to climb a small hill at the big dugway about one and a half miles north of Mountain Home. Tucker ground the gears like crazy, but he couldn't get that truck to move up the hill. Max and I were sitting in the back, and I had my head cranked around, watching Tucker fight with the gears, when Max elbowed me in the back.

"Tucker's never going to get this truck up the hill with all twelve of us in back. We've got to lighten the load." So Max and I and a couple of other guys jumped out the back and trudged up the hill on foot. I saw Tucker glare at us, leaning out the window.

"What der ya think you two are goin'?"

I cringed at the slurred words, but Max just stared stonily ahead while he yelled over his shoulder, "At the rate you're going, we'll make it up the hill faster by walking."

I turned to see Tucker scowl blackly at us before grinding the gears even harder, making the wheels squeal and spin circles hard and fast in the snow. But the truck still stuck and couldn't get up the hill. It only fishtailed a little before grinding to a sad halt again.

Max and I kept crunching our way through the snow up the hill with the rest of the guys who had jumped out of the truck with us, but we were stopped by a CCC truck at the top of the grade, heading straight for us and honking like crazy. The truck stopped, the passenger door flew open, and a man in uniform stepped out and stomped through the snow over to us. Lieutenant Stewart, one of the officers from our camp.

"What in the world is going on here?"

"We're stuck," Max stated calmly.

We both pointed down at our truck stuck at the bottom of the hill and waited while Lieutenant Stewart watched the truck's pitiful tries for a few seconds with an ugly frown on his face. A minute later, he mumbled under his breath before marching back to jump into his truck and order the driver to drive down to where our truck was stuck at the bottom of the hill.

Max and I walked back down the hill a little—enough to see that Lieutenant Stewart still wasn't smiling when he again jumped out of his truck to approach Tucker sitting at the wheel. He smiled even less when it was clear he could smell liquor on Tucker's breath.

"What's the problem, Tucker?"

Dalton was pretty easy to understand, but both Tucker and Collett were slurring their words.

"Get out of the truck and put chains on these tires!"

I couldn't help wincing, seeing how unsteady Tucker and Collett were on their feet, trying to get those chains on. Once the chains were on, Lieutenant Stewart turned to Dalton.

"You—Dalton. Get behind the wheel and drive."

Dalton quickly did just that. Tucker clearly didn't like that at all, but he followed Collett back to the passenger side, slamming the door hard once he was inside the truck.

It was almost laughable how easily Dalton was able to get the truck up the grade. The chains probably had a lot to do with it, but Tucker was drunk enough that he couldn't have gotten up that hill if it'd been the middle of summer. Lieutenant Stewart watched until Dalton got the truck safely to the top, passing Max and me and the others who'd jumped out of the truck, and he kept watching until the truck had cleared the grade. At that point, Lieutenant Stewart stepped back up inside his truck and continued on his way to Duchesne.

Once Lieutenant Stewart was safely out of sight, the CCC truck ground to a halt. Tucker jumped out of the passenger seat, and while Max and I hurried to catch up to the truck, we could hear him yelling at Dalton.

"It's my job to drive truck—I'm the regular truck driver, not you!"

Dalton didn't want to give in, because Stewart had ordered him to drive the rest of the way, but Tucker wouldn't let up. So Dalton, to our surprise, finally gave in and jumped out of the truck, stomping around the front end of it to jump in on the passenger side and slam the door as hard as Tucker had a few minutes before.

No one said anything, but we all knew we were in trouble with Tucker back at the wheel. Tucker knew Max and I and the rest of the guys on foot were close behind the truck, but the second he was behind the wheel, he got the truck moving again. It was clear he wasn't about to wait for us. But we were able to catch up with it easy and climb aboard, because the truck was still going pretty slowly due to the slight uphill grade.

Max and I got a hold of the endgate, and I was about to heave myself over the gate into the back of the truck with the other guys, but Max grabbed a handful of my coat.

"Addison, wait!"

"What?"

Max shook his head. "Tucker's drunk. Don't get in. Just hang on!"

Max was right. In any other circumstance, riding on the endgate was against CCC rules, but this time, riding on the endgate of the truck was the best place to be. We could get off quick in case anything happened, with Tucker being drunk and all.

Tucker went back to driving too fast—way too fast with all the ice and snow on the road. He took all the turns at high speed, making the old truck heave and sway back and forth. We were clipping along, easily going around 30, 35 mph.

About two miles from camp in the late afternoon, we reached one of the sharpest turns we had to maneuver on the mountain passes. It was bad enough that the road was slick, but even worse, we were now on a downhill grade and picking up momentum as we headed for the turn. Traveling at that rate of speed with a drunk driver behind the wheel, there was no way that truck was going to make the turn. When we got to that bad turn, instead of using the gears to get around it, Tucker slammed on the brakes. Since the road was covered with snow and ice, Tucker couldn't slow the truck enough to make the turn. I heard Max yell, "I knew this would happen!" and when I felt the truck tipping instead of making the turn, I jumped off and rolled out of the way, slamming my back into a giant rock.

Max wasn't so lucky. He should've jumped before everything happened, like I did. Instead, he was thrown off as the rear end of the truck skidded off the road, and he went tumbling and crashing into some snow-covered rocks. A second later, the truck was completely off the road and rolling over an embankment. It turned a complete loop in the air before finally landing on its wheels on the right side of the road.

The worst I got out of the mess was a bruised back and bruises on my right arm. But Max wasn't moving much from where he was, quite a few yards away, so I knew he was hurt pretty bad. Everyone was banged up, but Max got the worst of it. I ran over to him as soon as I saw the truck had landed on its wheels.

"You okay, Max?"

Max could hardly talk. "I don't think so—I hurt everywhere—"

"Don't move. We're only a couple miles from camp—we'll get help!"

I took off my coat and threw it over Max, who was starting to shake pretty bad. I wanted to clobber Tucker and clobber him good. He and the two other clowns in the front only had a few cuts and bruises on their heads. It was easy to tell who was sober and who wasn't: the sober guys were hurt, and the drunk ones had nothing more than a few scratches and bruises.

Those of us who were sober and not hurt too badly, like myself, ran to camp to get help. I saw Tucker fall out of the truck and slowly crawl over to Max before I started running as fast as my legs could go with the rest of the guys who could still run. Nobody was traveling the highways in those days way out in the mountains where we were, so we had to run the full two miles to camp in the snow to get the camp doctor. We had an ambulance in camp, which rushed back out those two miles minutes after we arrived.

I wanted to ride in the ambulance back to the scene to see how Max and Tucker were doing, but no one would let me go. After our injuries were looked over, we were ordered back to our barracks to rest while the ambulance picked up the rest of the injured guys.

Max got to ride in the ambulance, though. He suffered the worst injuries of any of the boys. His left arm was broken, and he had what the doctor called a "severe laceration of the forehead." And "contusions of right cheek and eye." Plus a "moderately severe bruise of about the 10th and 11th left ribs mid-auxiliary line."

The biggest shocker was seeing the truck come into camp. One look, and it was clear that it had suffered the worst damage of all. The cab, front fenders, front axle, front bumper, and the left side of the cowl were battered. The window in the passenger door was broken, and the driver's door was bent in pretty bad. Three oak bows were broken, too, and the canvas cover of the truck was torn almost in half. Still, the engine itself ran okay, and the truck was able to return to camp under its own power.

Of course, an investigating board of officers was appointed to make a thorough investigation of all the facts "leading to and connected with the accident on or about Jan. 6, 1935," so they could make their report about whether our injuries occurred in the performance of official duty and whether the accident was the "result of the injured's own misconduct."

Rumors flew that Tucker wouldn't be allowed to drive the trucks any more and that the camp officers would be looking for a new man to be a camp truck driver. I actually felt sorry for whoever would be unlucky enough to take over for Tucker as an official truck driver, because Tucker would make life miserable for that poor soul for taking his driving job away.

The crazy thing, though, was that Max wasn't mad at Tucker at all. Not for the accident, and not for nearly getting himself and everyone else killed. I got pretty exasperated with him one day when he was going on and on about being worried about Tucker when he should've been worrying about himself—sleeping and taking it easy with all of his injuries and everything.

"I don't understand why you care what happens to Tucker. I can't believe you're even talking to him!" I myself had been avoiding Tucker ever since the accident. Max only shrugged.

"Tucker and I—we've been friends since we were kids. We've been through some pretty tough times. Besides, I'm all he's got."

I didn't get a chance to ask Max what he meant by that, because one of the LEMs shooed me out of the barracks so Max could take some pain pills and get some sleep.

SIXTEEN

I didn't venture out the next day, but instead, moped around Grandpa's house and stared at myself in the mirror a lot. Something had to be done. The following day, I went along with Grandpa grocery shopping and casually strolled down the supermarket's cosmetics aisle. Mom had put some money in one of my suitcases, and with a wad of dollars in my shorts pocket, I was ready to try something I'd never done before: buy makeup.

As I stood staring at the massive amounts of lip stuff, gunk for the eyes, and powders and gooey-looking liquids for the face, for the first time in my life, I was really wishing my sister, Sarah, was here. She'd know exactly what to get so I'd look nice instead of like a clown. I sighed and dived in and grabbed a tube of black mascara, a reddish shade of lip gloss, and a little palette of purple and pink eye shadows and hoped for the best.

I practiced with the makeup a little that evening, but the word *clown* kept coming to my mind as I did my best to apply all of the stuff to my face. Even so, I finally figured out how to put the eye shadow on my eyes in a way that I liked, along with two good coats of mascara. Before I went to bed, I took some old rags, cut them into strips, and rolled pieces of my hair in the strips like I'd seen Sarah do. I did my best to sleep with all of the rag knots all over my head. I looked ridiculous, but if Sarah's hair always turned out great, I was sure I had no reason to fear.

The next morning I put on the most girlie shorts outfit I had, a pink top-and-shorts set Sarah had bought me for my birthday last year that I'd never worn yet, and I did my best to apply the purple and pinks to my eyelids. With the black mascara and fancy red lip gloss in place, I thought I looked okay—until I took all the rags out of my hair.

"Poodle—I'm a red-haired poodle!!"

I never would've believed that hair as straight as mine could turn into Orphan Annie hair just from sleeping with pieces of rags twisted into it. Granted, I'd used tons of strips of rags, and I'd twisted tiny sections of my hair around each piece pretty tightly, but still, I couldn't believe how out of control my hair looked.

I didn't want to dunk my head in the sink after all my hard work tying it up in rags for a good solid hour the night before, so I did my best to drag a brush through my hair. The brushing, unfortunately, only made my hair look frizzy, and it stood out like a circus tent even worse.

It was Saturday, and Grandpa was off for his morning swim with Clay, so after grabbing an elastic band to pull back my hair into a pony-tail and slipping on a pair of white sneakers, I casually strolled over to Grandma June's house.

I could hear the thwang-thwang of a basketball bouncing on cement the moment I stepped outside and knew Kyle had to be shooting hoops in Grandma June's driveway. I hadn't spoken to Kyle since our tiff a few days ago, and my heart—it didn't just leap funny like it'd been doing lately, but it started to thump fast and hard. Nervous to see Kyle again? Who, me? Impossible. It was just Kyle, after all.

Kyle was so busy bouncing the ball and getting ready to try for a jump shot that it was easy enough to sneak up behind him and snatch the ball away from him. While Kyle just stood there staring stupidly at me, I laughed and tossed the ball myself, grinning when it swished through the hoop.

"What happened to you?"

I ran for the ball, since Kyle still hadn't moved, and casually bounced it up and down, up and down, before tossing it through the hoop again. "What do you mean?"

This time, Kyle finally came alive and lunged for the ball, grabbing it before I could get it again. And then, he just gripped the ball in both hands and stared at me. "You look—I don't know. Why did you do it?"

"Do what?"

I didn't like the look on Kyle's face as he stared at me. He actually looked horrified. "All—this. Your hair—the stuff on your face—"

I scowled at Kyle and self-consciously shoved my messy curls behind my ears. "Because I felt like it, okay?"

Kyle shook his head, obviously still baffled. "Okay, fine!" He stared at my hair, my face, and my outfit again for a second before shaking his head some more and bouncing the basketball. "So, do you want to play a game of one-on-one?"

I shrugged and turned so I didn't have to look at him. I was wishing like crazy that I'd dunked my head under the sink after all and scrubbed the makeup off my face, too. "I don't know."

Kyle gave the basketball a toss. That it missed the basket by a foot and bashed into the backboard instead was incredibly satisfying to see. "We haven't played hardly any basketball this summer. You need to get practiced up for girls' basketball next year."

"I don't know if I'm going to try out for the team after all."

Kyle stopped chasing after the ball to give me his annoying, horrified stare again. "What? Why not?"

I shrugged again and twisted a curl around my finger. "I'm thinking of seeing if I can try out for the drill team or the dance team or something instead."

Kyle actually looked angry now. "Why in the world would you do that? You're an awesome basketball player. The team needs you!"

"Maybe I want a change. You ever think of that?"

Kyle shook his head again before jogging off to rescue the basketball from where it'd landed inside a bush. "Does that mean you're not going to play one-on-one with me?"

"Maybe."

"That's okay. I would've beaten you anyway."

A second later, a high-pitched shriek came flying out of my mouth, and in a second, I'd stolen the ball from Kyle. "First one to eleven wins!" And with that, the game was on.

We played pretty rough, fouling each other like crazy, but I didn't care, because I wanted to win. I had to win. If Kyle wasn't going to appreciate my efforts to look—well, different—then I was determined to kick his rear end in basketball. Unfortunately, Kyle was playing to win just as hard as I was. Every time I scored a basket, Kyle quickly followed up with one of his own, and if he missed a shot, I missed my next shot, too. Things were getting pretty heated once we both had ten points each, until I slapped the ball hard up into the air from behind Kyle. We both dived for it, and somehow, my feet got all tangled up in his, and the two of us went flying, landing in an awkward heap on the cement. Worse still, I could hear laughing. And lots of it.

"Well, well, well. We were hoping to play you guys in a game of two-on-two basketball, but it looks like you're pretty busy playing tickle and slap. Though considering how big James here is, I'm guessing there's more slapping than tickling going on."

Blake. My cousin Blake. I shoved Kyle away and jumped up as fast as my scraped right knee would let me. Both Blake and his brother, Maxwell, were leaning their backs against the fence inside Grandma June's yard. Since Aunt Gracie lived only a few blocks from Grandpa, it shouldn't have surprised me to see them finally come around.

I scowled at Blake and carefully brushed the dirt from my cut knee. "Don't be gross!"

Maxwell laughed and turned to Blake. "Are you kidding? I'll bet it's more like punching, not slapping. James could probably knock Kyle out easy."

Kyle frowned at both of my cousins while he stood up and then turned his back to them to rescue the basketball from the bushes again before bouncing it slowly. "Hey, Blake—Maxwell. What's going on?"

Blake grinned and shrugged before moving forward. "Nothing much. We just—"

"Holy cow, Blake! Check out James's hair!" Maxwell burst out laughing, and a second later, once Blake took a good look at me, he grinned and reached out to tug a lock of my hair.

"Got your finger stuck in a light socket there, James? I mean, Cleopatra, queen of the Nile?"

"Stop it!" My makeup job couldn't have looked that bad!

I could hear Kyle sighing loudly. "Leave her alone, guys."

I'd had enough, though. I snatched the elastic band out of my pocket and ruthlessly yanked my hair into a tight ball at the back of my head before saying something ugly to all three of them. Blake and Maxwell only burst out laughing again, but Kyle looked shocked. I scowled at all three guys before turning and running into Grandma June's house as fast as I could.

Before I made it into the house, though, I could hear Maxwell teasing Kyle about me again. I wanted to climb under a rock somewhere, but Kyle's answer to Maxwell's teasing, "so is James your girlfriend?" made me stop cold with my hand on the screen door handle.

"It's not like that. She's just a friend. Practically a sister."

And Blake—he burst out laughing. "Practically a sister? More like a brother!"

"Something like that, I guess."

I was trembling. Kyle had laughed. He'd actually laughed!

I wrenched the door open and stumbled into Grandma June's house, slamming the door behind me as hard as I could.

SEVENTEEN

ames, honey, just forget about those boys. And don't you worry. I'll have a talk with Kyle."

I'd been sitting at the kitchen table with Grandma June, eating double chocolate chip cookies and wiping the makeup off my face with tissues, but I quickly grabbed her wrist before she could stand up.

"No, please don't do that, Grandma June!"

"For heaven's sake, why not? I thought he had better manners."

"It'll only make things worse. Please, just forget it. Forget I told you anything," I said miserably.

Grandma June eyed me carefully before tossing the used tissues into the garbage. "All right, all right. I'll leave well enough alone." Grandma June picked up a cookie, and we munched together in silence while she continued to study me. "So, James, how's your grandpa doing?"

I scowled down at the table. "Why don't you ask Anna?"

"Don't you like Anna?"

"Not really." But I knew it didn't matter that I didn't like Anna, because Grandpa did, and that was all he seemed to care about. I hated the fact that from the very start, I couldn't deny that the two had a natural friendship that had grown over years and years of living in the same ward and becoming friends. Or the fact that the two were attached to each other, in a whole different kind of a way than my grandpa was with Grandma June. Or even with my grandma.

"Every day they're getting closer. More than I ever dreamed they would. I just hate it."

"Why, James?"

I shrugged. "I don't know. I miss my grandma, and it just—it just hurts, seeing him so happy with Anna."

Grandma June smiled and patted my arm. "Well, isn't it better to see your grandpa happy with Anna and doing wonderfully, rather than sad and crying all by himself, rattling around in that house all alone? You know your grandma wouldn't want that. She wouldn't want him to be sad. Isn't it nice not to have to worry about him? Don't you want him to be happy again?"

"Of course I want my grandpa to be happy. I'd do anything to make sure he's happy. You don't understand—it's not that. It's—"

Grandma June continued to look at me steadily. "What is it, James?"

I shook my head in frustration. "You don't know how hard it is to watch my grandpa with her. He's—he's happier with Anna than he ever was with my grandma."

Grandma June looked shocked and jumped out of her chair to run over to give me a quick hug. "Oh, honey. That's not true at all. Not at all!"

"You haven't seen them together—you don't know!" My throat caught funny, and I was shocked to think I might start crying. Grandma June didn't say anything about it, though. She just kept hugging me and patting the back of my head.

"James, honey, you have to remember that your grandpa's situation with Anna is brand new. Everyone acts silly and mooney at first over someone new."

I shrugged without looking up. "I guess."

Grandma June gave my shoulders a final squeeze and then moved to sit back down in her chair at the table. "You only knew your grand-parents as an older couple. You never had the chance to see them when they were courting." Grandma June winked and pushed the plate of cookies towards me. "I'm sure if you were able to see your grandparents when they first met and were in their romantic phase, you'd see how crazy your grandpa was about your grandma. Why, I knew them when your dad and your Aunt Gracie were just tiny kids, and even then, I could tell they had something pretty special between them."

Grandma June had given me something to munch on mentally for a while, but as soon as I could hear Kyle, Blake, and Maxwell coming in through the back door, I gave Grandma June a quick thank-you hug and hurried out the front door.

Grandpa was home resting on the couch with his eyes closed and his feet up on an ottoman, while Anna sat right by him holding his hand.

I frowned before moving into the living room to sit down in one of the recliners. "You don't look so good, Grandpa. You okay?"

Grandpa opened one eye to squint at me and laughed. "Don't you start in on me, too, James!"

I kept on frowning, but before I could say anything, Anna jumped in with, "You see, Harold? James agrees with me. You've got to stop pushing yourself so hard and give that poor heart of yours a rest now and then!"

That made my heart do a hard, funny jump I didn't like at all. "Grandpa, you didn't have a—a heart attack, did you?"

"No, no, James. Nothing like that. My chest felt a little funny after my swim, and I felt tired, too, so Anna came over to check on me, and now she's babying me real good. Nothing for either of you two to worry about, all right?"

"Are you sure, Grandpa? Is there anything I can do?"

Grandpa smiled and stretched. "Well, how about you go round up my recorder, and I'll tell you some more experiences I had in the Cs. Have I told you how I met Uncle Landon?"

"No, you haven't."

"Well, you have to hear about that before you can hear about how I met your grandma, so go get that recorder, and I'll tell you all about how your great-uncle Landon and I met."

EIGHTEEN

Once the spring of '35 was underway, we moved back to the summer camp on the Uinta River, and we were back to living in tents again. The government finally had some money for real uniforms for us by then, so we were issued Levi's work pants, good work boots, and blue, long-sleeved, button-down, work shirts. A lot of the guys kept wearing the World War I uniforms, though. Even some of the superintendents and LEMs kept wearing their choker pants and knee-high boots.

We built a fire road that spring and summer clear across the mountain, up Swift Creek, up through the Indian reservation, and over to the Uinta River. I was on a cutting crew, working from where the campgrounds are now, clear to Swift Creek, cutting down quaking aspen trees that were in the way of the road we were building. The Caterpillar bulldozers would come along after us and push out the stumps. Then we'd put our backs into it, piling the quaking aspen logs off on one side of the road.

We also went over onto the Moon Lake side of the Uinta Mountains during the summer and killed trees by Moon Lake. The trees near the lake would get full of bugs and turn brown, so we'd cut them out with our axes and burn up the ones too filled with bugs to save.

And then during the fall of '35, we got a bunch of new guys in camp. A lot of them came from the camp in Vernal, Utah. We got acquainted with most of them, but during the winter, I got to know one guy in particular from the Vernal Camp pretty well.

That winter of '35—'36 after we'd moved back to the Moon Lake Camp, back into the barracks on the Yellowstone River, I went to work in the garage greasing the CCC trucks. I was officially known as a grease man. Probably about a dozen of us worked in the garage greasing trucks. Our camp was big, and we had lots of trucks and Caterpillars and all sorts of heavy equipment that needed proper greasing practically every day so that none of them would bind up out on the job sites. My job was to help grease the trucks that pulled into the garage at the end of the working day. I'd lie down underneath the truck with my grease gun that was hooked up with a hose to an air compressor and a big old barrel of grease and carefully shoot grease into all the vital parts on a CCC truck that needed. It took a good amount of time to grease a truck properly. It wasn't about squirting grease every which way underneath the truck. Each wear point of the truck had to receive a precise amount of grease. It definitely took a certain amount of finesse and control. I actually felt pretty honored to get the chance to work as a grease man on the trucks.

And Max—he was trained as a grease man, too, and got busy greasing the Cats at night that were pushing snow out on the roads during the day. The road from Swift Creek up over the mountain wasn't quite finished by winter, so we had the Cats working up on top of the mountain pushing snow and finishing up the fire road all winter long. During that winter, we were both off schedule from most of the enrollees. I'd help grease the trucks in the shop at night once they'd all pulled in for the day, Max would help grease the Cats, and then we'd have the next day off to sleep in until late afternoon.

The grease trucks were loaded with two big drums of grease in the back, along with the grease guns and air compressors, ready to be driven up the mountain if greasing was needed out on the road on the job site, which happened more often than not, usually late in the afternoon. Sometimes it was because of the weather. The trucks and Cats would seize up from working in the cold too long and hard. But a lot of the time, it was because the other grease men weren't doing a good enough job. Sometimes both Max and I would end up on one of the grease trucks together, heading down the road to grease down a Cat stuck somewhere up on the mountain.

One day around about noon, I'd been happily asleep for a few hours after a back-breaking session with the old grease gun only to have someone shake my shoulder, hollering, "Addison! Addison!" in my ear. When I opened one eye and saw it was Max shoving at me, I yanked the pillow out from under my head and smacked him with it before rolling over onto my stomach and covering my head with it.

"Go away—I'm sleeping!"

"You've got to see what I snagged, Addison—you've got to try these. Come on!"

Max wouldn't give up, so I muttered about a hot place I wished Max would rot in before I stumbled into my pants and boots and grabbed my coat and gloves to see what Max was all fired up about.

Once I stepped outside the barracks, I could see Max standing in the snow, proudly waving two long, skinny boards at me.

"What the heck are those?"

Max laughed. "Skis, dummy! What else?"

Skis. I'd forgotten all about the camp putting in requests for those. For recreation, the camp had gotten a hold of a bunch of snow skis for us, and somehow Max had sneaked off a pair for us to try that day.

"How the heck do you put the dumb things on?" I griped after looking them over.

"Like this—"

The skis back then only had one strap that would go over the toe of our work boots. I watched Max slip a booted foot into each ski and tromp around the snow in them, telling me all he said I needed to know in order to ski, before letting me try them on and stomp around in the snow myself. I tripped and fell face flat into the snow, which Max thought was incredibly funny.

"Just pretend your foot's as long as the ski. Pretend you have really big feet that you need to maneuver, and then it'll get easier."

Max carried the skis over to the grease truck. We tied a rope on the back of the truck and took turns pulling each other up a hill near the barracks to get used to the feel of the skis under our boots, one of us holding the rope, wearing the skis, while the other drove slowly up the hill to the top. Max already knew how to ski, so he shimmied down the mountain like a professional. I figured it couldn't be that hard, but once it was my turn, I found out it was harder than it looked. In about two seconds, I was flying way too fast down the hill, and when I tried to jerk myself upright, one foot went flying up, and a half second later, I'd flipped and landed hard on my rear end. Unfortunately, I'd gained too much momentum to stay where I landed. Instead, the skis flew off my feet, and I rolled and slid the rest of the way down the mountain. Luckily, Max found the skis. Once he caught up to me and helped me into the truck, I got up the courage to ask him if I'd looked really stupid.

"Well, let's just say you can be glad I was the only one who saw you." And then he laughed and laughed. When we made it back up the hill, he had to show me exactly how I looked trying to ski. Based on his performance, I must've looked liked a liquored-up lunatic with his pants on fire. That was enough to keep me from wanting to ski anymore that afternoon.

We had to travel farther up the next hillside to meet up with the Cats and trucks that needed to be greased on the job site late that afternoon, so we drove over to the top of the hillside to the job site and left the skis sticking out of the back of the grease truck after we'd pulled up near a Cat that needed greasing. The guy who drove the Cat was leaning near a tree, waiting for us, calmly smoking on a little pipe. He had really black hair and wasn't a very big guy at all. He couldn't have been more than sixteen years old. I didn't recognize him and figured he must've been one of the new guys from the Vernal Camp. Max and I got busy greasing the

Cat, and by the time we finally got done, the driver of the Cat—the guy with the pipe—was nowhere to be found. But that wasn't all.

"Hey, Addison, what did you do with the skis?"

Max was standing in back of the grease truck, right by the spot where the skis should've been sticking out. Only problem was, they weren't there anymore. But there were plenty of tracks in the snow, making it clear someone had come along and swiped our skis.

We asked around, but none of the guys on the jobsite even knew we had a pair of skis with us. It was getting late, and we needed to get the grease truck back down to the shop for the night greasing, and since we still hadn't found the skis yet, the next thing we did was to get cranky, blaming each other for the missing skis.

"You should've shoved 'em further behind the grease drums, Addison. Then no one would've seen 'em and swiped 'em!"

"The skis were your dumb idea in the first place, so don't go blaming me for anything!"

I was pretty mad at Max for trying to point the finger at me for anything to do with the skis, so I stomped off away from the truck. Two seconds later, I stopped and just stared at the tracks going down the hill in the snow. Two identical tracks in the snow that were definitely not made by boots but were clearly made by two skinny boards. Skis, to be exact. When I looked up from the ski tracks, my mouth dropped open at what I saw trudging up the hill through the snow. The guy with the pipe—still smoking it—was climbing up the hill with the skis thrown over one shoulder. I stood there with my arms folded, but once he got close enough to make eye contact with me and my scowl, he didn't look at all scared. He knew he'd just come along and grabbed the skis and went over the hill, trying to ski, without asking for my or Max's permission, and yet he didn't look at all nervous to face me. In fact, he acted like he had every right to take the skis and give them a try.

As soon as he was within a couple of feet from me, I yelled, "Thanks a lot for asking!" before I lunged and grabbed the skis off his shoulder. Problem was, somehow in the process I decked him in the head with the skis, knocking the pipe out of his mouth while he stumbled forward and nearly joined his pipe in the snow. The guy may have been shorter than me, but he was every bit as tough as anyone in camp. Before he could straighten up, he charged me in the gut and knocked the wind out of me, sending the skis flying back down the hill. So we wasted a good five minutes trading insults and punches before Max jumped in to break it up. We were both gasping for breath, leaning heavily against the same tree, while Max hightailed it down the hill, chasing after the skis.

"Where'd you learn that jaw uppercut? I thought for sure I'd lost another tooth." I complained about that and my bleeding lip while I leaned down to pick up the guy's pipe where I could see it just barely sticking up out of the snow. My jaw was going to be stiff for a few days, but I couldn't help being impressed with his ability as a fighter. His jabs were fast and accurate, and he could hit hard.

The guy laughed as I shoved the pipe into his hand. "I was about to ask you where you learned your kidney punch. It was pretty impressive."

I laughed and told him my name and asked him his. He stuck out his hand and said, "Landon. Landon Hayward. From Vernal."

That's the way I got acquainted with Landon. Sure, he took the skis without asking, and we had a few words, and even got into a fight that left me with a split lip and a sore jaw, but somehow I knew that from then on out, not only would we become friends but we'd be friends the rest of our lives.

NINETEEN

I stayed out of Kyle's way for the next few days, which was easy, because he didn't venture over anyway. I had to assume he was as mortified as I was over my self-makeover attempt, and I at least wasn't ready to face him yet.

Aunt Gracie had called earlier that day asking if Grandpa could come help her with a broken kitchen cabinet door, but knowing Grandpa, he was likely still busy chatting with her and Blake and Maxwell and had forgotten how long he'd been there.

I was idly flipping through stations using the remote control Grandpa had bought to go with his brand-new TV when the back door was carefully and quietly opened.

"Knock, knock, Harold!"

I gripped the remote tight. "He's not home, Anna!"

I didn't mean to yell as loudly as I did, but the sound and tone of my voice brought her soft footsteps moving forward into the kitchen to an abrupt stop before slowly starting up again a second later. I didn't look up from the television when she entered the room but slouched deeper into the recliner.

Anna settled herself carefully into the recliner near mine, also facing the TV. "Mind if I wait for him and watch TV with you?"

I shrugged and kept staring at the screen. "Suit yourself."

Anna shifted around in her chair. I wondered if she was as uncomfortable as I was. We'd never had to be alone together for longer than a minute at a time, so knowing that this "minute" could stretch into an hour or hours definitely was not my idea of fun.

"What are you watching?"

"I have no idea. Nothing, I guess. I was just checking through all the stations with this remote control thingy here." At the moment, the show on the screen in front of us looked suspiciously like the beginning of an old musical. Everyone was dressed in peasant-looking costumes, and from the characters' names I could catch here and there, I was pretty sure the story took place in Russia. Early 1900s time period, too, would've been my guess.

"Oh, it's *Fiddler on the Roof!* That's one of my favorite movies!"

Realization hit me hard. "My grandma liked the songs from it."

"Your grandma had excellent taste. This movie has some wonderful songs in it. Have you seen it before?"

"No."

"Well, then you're in for a real treat. Unless you wanted to watch something else?"

"No, nothing's on. If you want to watch this, then fine." I handed Anna the remote and reached for a magazine and thumbed through it. I didn't want to do anything with Anna. Not even watch a stupid old musical with her, even if my grandma had liked the songs in it.

Anna sat holding the remote for a minute before she turned in her recliner and smiled all bright and cheerful at me. "Well, I think we should have some treats while we watch the movie. How does that sound?"

I shrugged. "Whatever. I don't care."

Anna actually laughed. Softly, of course, since her voice was so quiet I was practically straining to hear her speak. "Well, I do! You need popcorn if you're going to watch a movie. I love lots of butter on mine. Do you like popcorn?"

I shrugged again. "It's okay."

"Well, on the first commercial, let's get busy and make some!"

I tried not to watch the television, but Anna kept throwing in comments every few minutes, like "Oh, I love this song!" "Oh, that Topol is such a wonderful actor. No one else could play Tevye like he did!" "Oh, tradition—tradition—We're all slaves to it, aren't we?," so I finally screamed "Uncle!" in my head, tossed the magazine to the floor by my side, folded my arms, and scowled at the television.

True to her threat, the second the first commercial came on, Anna stood up out of the recliner. "Time for some popcorn, James!"

I didn't move, so after a second, Anna went into the kitchen without me and started banging cupboard doors.

"James, I can't find the popcorn popper. Do you know if your grandpa has one?"

I rolled my eyes and dragged myself off the recliner. "I'm pretty sure he has one. Didn't you make popcorn just last week?"

Anna pretended not to hear me, so after I snatched it out of the bottom cupboard near the sink where it was sitting in plain sight, she pointed to an outlet. "Just plug it in there, dear, and I'll get the popcorn."

Before I could escape, Anna handed me the popcorn bag and a measuring cup. "Would you mind filling it up and turning on the popper? I'll get started melting the butter."

I muttered under my breath, but Anna pretended again not to hear anything.

"We haven't seen Kyle around in a while. Is everything okay with you two?"

I gripped the measuring cup and turned to face her. "Just because he hasn't come over in four days doesn't mean there's anything wrong. And anyway, there is no 'you two.'"

Anna smiled and moved to get two cans of soda out of the fridge. "If you say so. I wouldn't worry, though. I'm sure we'll be seeing plenty of him in no time."

"I can see him any time I want. He's only next door," I griped. "Besides, it's been nice to have a break from him. He can be pretty annoying sometimes."

Anna laughed. "Yes, men can be like that sometimes. But they are usually nice to have around. I've sure missed having one in my home. It's been three years now."

I wasn't sure what to say to that. "You've been alone for three years?"

Anna smiled. "Yes and no. I've lived by myself for three years, but I wouldn't say I've been alone. Good people in the ward have reached out to me. Your grandma was especially good to me after my husband died."

"She was?"

"Oh, yes. She always called to see if I wanted to go with her and June to every Relief Society activity the ward had going on." Anna sighed and looked at me wistfully. "Your grandma was such a wonderful friend. I miss her so much."

I didn't say anything for a second while I stared at the popcorn popping out of the popper and into the bowl. "Me, too."

I could hear the swell of the music starting on the television again, and since neither of us was saying anything anymore, I grabbed the bowl of popcorn. "Well, it sounds like the movie's back on."

"Oh, hurry back into the living room. I don't want you to miss any of it!"

We munched the popcorn and drank our sodas, and Anna continued to make her quiet comments while we watched the movie. I even found myself laughing out loud over parts with her. I couldn't believe I could actually like an old Hollywood musical, but I did like it. And it was fun watching it with someone who liked old musicals.

I was actually impressed with the dancing celebrating Motel and Tzeitel's wedding, although I couldn't help giggling a little when four of the men held hands and danced around with wine bottles on their heads. Anna insisted it was considered an impressive part of the movie, but still—it was guys holding hands with bottles on their heads, and I just couldn't get past that.

"I've always wanted a man who can balance a bottle on his head and dance at the same time."

Hearing Anna say that so calmly and matter-of-factly made me giggle even harder. "Who doesn't?!"

And then Anna started to giggle, too. "I've been trying to get your grandpa to learn, but he's just not catching on."

The idea of my grandpa dancing around with anything on his head made me burst out laughing. Anna laughed, too, and for some reason, having a good hard laugh with her felt nice. The happy, hopeful look on her face after we both calmed down enough to watch the rest of the movie and finish downing the entire big bowl of popcorn was impossible to miss. I knew if Grandpa came in and saw us, he'd be happier than a kid on Christmas Day.

No doubt about it, the musical was a pretty good one. The "Matchmaker" song was pretty catchy, and "Sunrise, Sunset" was definitely a pretty song. The type of song I knew I'd probably like even more each time I heard it.

"This is nice. The musical, I mean."

Anna smiled at me and reached over to pat my hand. "Yes, it is, isn't it?"

And then I did something really weird and unexpected. I actually smiled back at Anna. I couldn't help it. Whether I liked it or not, I knew I was grudgingly starting to like her and had been for some time. She wasn't at all like my grandma, but what got to me more was that I was beginning to see things in her that were pretty great. Qualities that even my grandma never had. Qualities that would make anyone want to be with Anna a lot.

I couldn't deny that she'd definitely brought a lot of life back to my grandpa, and I had to appreciate that, even though at the same time, it made me incredibly sad watching Grandpa be happy with someone who wasn't my grandma.

TWENTY

Grandma June brought by a plate of double chocolate chip cookies for me the next day, and when Anna, Grandpa, and I finished them off two days later, still without any sign of Kyle, I waited until Grandpa and Anna left to go to the funeral of someone in their ward that afternoon before venturing over with the washed plate.

Grandma June never expected me to knock, and because her door was always unlocked, I stepped inside and shut the door before I realized Grandma June was probably at the funeral, too.

"Great. Just great," I grumbled. I set the plate on the kitchen counter and reached for a pen and paper to leave Grandma June a note, but I froze when I heard something coming from the piano. Something so beautiful I could hardly breathe as I slowly walked into the living room.

Kyle was seated at the piano, his head bent over the keys, but a second later, his fingers stopped and he frowned, looking down at his hands.

I leaned against the wall nearby. "Don't stop now. That song's amazing!"

Kyle jumped, but when he saw me, he scowled and grabbed the sheet of music in front of him, stood up to lift the piano bench lid, and shoved the paper and a few pencils inside it.

"I didn't hear you knock."

I shrugged. "That's because I didn't. I never do. You know that."

Kyle glanced at me but looked away just as fast. "You should've knocked."

"I didn't think you'd be here. How come you're not at work?"

Kyle sat back down on the bench. "I have the day off. You should've knocked."

I stuck my hands in my back pockets before slowly moving forward. "Sorry. Grandma June told me it was okay to just come in."

"Well, she's not here right now, and I don't know where she is."

"She's probably over at the funeral. My grandpa and Anna are there right now."

Kyle looked up at me in surprise. "Someone in their ward died? Again? There was a funeral over there just last week!"

I rolled my eyes and sat down on the piano bench beside Kyle and plunked on a few keys. "What do you expect in a ward full of old people?"

"How come you didn't go, too?"

I shook my head firmly. "I'm done with funerals for now."

I could almost taste how tense Kyle was. I'd definitely interrupted him, and he was definitely annoyed. I wasn't going to give up and leave, though. Not yet.

"So, what were you just playing? It sounded nice."

Kyle frowned and wouldn't look at me. "Nothing."

I gave him a good bump in the shoulder with my shoulder. "Well, play 'nothing' again. I want to hear some more."

"Nah, not right now."

I could feel a good glare coming on, especially for Kyle. "Why not? If I remember right, you told Sam Colton you'd play for her anytime, but you won't play for me. How come?"

Kyle shrugged and stood up again to walk a few feet away and fidget with the switch on a lamp nearby. "Because I just don't feel like playing anymore right now, okay?"

"Okay—fine!" I gripped the piano keys cover and in frustration banged it down harder than I meant to, hiding the keys. I twirled myself around on the bench and leaned my elbows against it. "So, I haven't seen you for a while. What have you been doing?"

Kyle shrugged again, but his eyes wouldn't stay on my face. "Just some stuff."

"What kind of stuff?"

"Just—stuff."

I sighed nice and loud. "Well, I was going to get out the bicycle built for two. Do you want to go for a ride?"

"Not right now. Maybe later or tomorrow or something."

Enough. I'd definitely had enough. "Tomorrow or something? Fine. I'll just go. Tell Grandma June I said hi."

I heard Kyle say, "James, hold on," but I'd slammed out the door by then and run as fast as my long legs would take me back over to Grandpa's house.

I'd barely rounded the curve to Grandpa's when the sight of two unfamiliar cars parked in the driveway made me stop hard and fast. I stared blankly at the red one before I realized it was Aunt Gracie's Buick. I wondered for a second why she would've driven over when she only lived a few blocks away, and then I was staring hard at the white car, trying desperately to place where I'd seen it before.

"Only one way to find out!" And with that, I hurried in through the kitchen door.

"Who just came in? Is that Harold?"

Aunt Gracie stuck her blonde head into the kitchen doorway. "No— oh, it's James. Hello, James!"

Great-Aunt Vivian's car. Of course. I'd seen it at Grandma's funeral without really seeing it.

Aunt Gracie gave me a quick hug. "Hello, sweetie. Come say hi to everyone."

Aunt Gracie hustled me into the living room where my grandma's three sisters were keeping themselves busy. Great-Aunt Vivian was digging through boxes Kyle and I had packed away my first day at Grandpa's.

Great-Aunt Beth was looking over the knickknacks lined up on the old pump organ, and Great-Aunt Rachel was pulling out books on the bookshelves.

I frowned, suspicion creeping up my spine like an old snake. "What's going on?"

Great-Aunt Rachel tried to look cheerful. A guilty, caught-out sort of cheerful. "We're just trying to help your grandpa out. You know—doing some spring cleaning."

"But it's summertime. And I've already been cleaning this place."

Great-Aunt Beth walked over to stand by Great-Aunt Rachel. "We just thought you could use some help giving this place a really good, thorough cleaning job."

"That's funny. I don't see any mops or brooms or dust cloths in motion."

Great-Aunt Vivian didn't stop going through the box in front of her. "Well, we'll be getting to that later. We're just going through some old things your grandpa was going to throw away."

"He's not throwing any of that stuff away. He's just putting it away. There's a difference!" I watched Great-Aunt Beth gather up a few books and put them in a smaller box by her purse. "What are you doing?"

"Nothing, dear. Just—"

I hurried over to look into the box and lifted out the book on top. It was an old book, and with one quick flip of the cover, I could see my great-grandfather's signature inside.

"Why are you moving Grandma's books into this box?"

Great-Aunt Rachel put her hand on my arm. "Honey, these books belonged to our father. Now with Lilly gone, they can't mean anything to your grandpa. They mean something to me, though, since they belonged to my father—"

"They mean something to me, too, since they belonged to my great-grandfather!"

Great-Aunt Rachel smiled and tried again. "I don't think Lilly would mind me taking these books."

"Yes, she would. They were given to her to keep in her family!"

I snatched all three of the old books out of the box and hustled them into Grandpa's bedroom. When I came back into the living room, all three of my great-aunts were studying the old pump organ that had been in my grandparents' living room for forever, talking with their heads close together.

"What are you talking about?"

All three turned around and smiled at me before Aunt Gracie hurried over and put her arm around my shoulders. "We were thinking that the organ ought to be returned to the old family home in Enterprise. You know, the home your grandma was raised in. Aunt Rachel owns the home now, and since it used to be there anyway, she and Aunt Vivian and Aunt Beth thought it ought to be returned."

I couldn't believe what I was hearing. In a flash, I'd moved out from under Aunt Gracie's arm so I could face her. "Returned? How do you return something when it was given to Grandma by her own parents? She wanted the organ, and they let her have it. You can't just take it back because she's gone now!"

Aunt Gracie sighed and reached for me. "James, honey, you need to calm down—"

I moved backwards a few steps and turned to face my great-aunts, who were staring at me as if I was insane. "You can't take anything—you can't!" I whirled back around to face Aunt Gracie again. "Aunt Gracie, I can't believe you let them think this was okay. I wish my dad was here. He wouldn't let this happen—I know he wouldn't!"

Great-Aunt Vivian stared at me before shaking her head and putting her hands on her hips. "Strong willed and stubborn—you sound just like—"

I froze and stared at Great-Aunt Vivian. "Just like who?"

But it was Great-Aunt Rachel who softly answered me. "Just like Lilly, of course."

I could hardly breathe. No one said a word after that, but a second later, we all heard the kitchen door creak open.

"Knock knock—James, are you here?"

There was only one person I knew who had such a quiet, soft voice. "Anna—"

Aunt Gracie was the first to hurry into the kitchen, followed by me and my three great-aunts. "Who in the world could that be?"

I tried to catch up with Aunt Gracie first. "Hey—"

"Oh, good." Anna was inside now, smiling and looking painfully hopeful while Aunt Gracie approached her with a big, beaming smile of her own. "You're the one from the ward who's been checking in on my father a lot lately, aren't you?"

"Why, yes, I've been seeing Harold—"

Aunt Gracie nodded without listening. "We really appreciate your help. In fact, if you have time to help us do some cleaning right now, that would be better than wonderful. James here is letting her grandpa live in an absolute pig sty. Sister—I'm sorry, I know I should know your name, but I can't think of it right now—"

"Anna. Anna Stanley—"

"The broom's just in the closet there behind you."

I was so shocked I couldn't get my mouth to work. Which didn't matter, because my great-aunts stepped right in.

Great-Aunt Beth moved in first. "Yes, this kitchen could use a good sweeping."

Anna's hopeful look was gone, and instead, her smile just looked sad. "All right. I can do that. I'm happy to help." She spoke so quietly I wasn't sure anyone heard her but me. I was cringing so badly from a mixture of shock, anger, and pure embarrassment that I was sure if too many more seconds went by, I'd explode.

"Oh, and by the way—there's a feather duster in that closet, too. Could you get that out and dust off all these knickknacks? I can't believe how many Lilly collected over the years—"

Thanks to Great-Aunt Vivian, enough seconds had now gone by. I was ready to explode. "Wait—just hold on—Anna, you don't have to do anything!"

Great-Aunt Vivian turned to stare at me as if I'd grown horns. "Really, James! What's the matter with you today?"

I couldn't help it. I actually gasped. "Anna isn't a ward lady or a cleaning lady. She's Grandpa's friend! Actually, she's more than Grandpa's friend!"

Great-Aunt Vivian frowned at me. "Just what exactly are you saying, James?"

"Anna and Grandpa are—"

I didn't have to say what they were, because Anna quietly spoke up. "We've been seeing each other."

No one spoke for a good whole five seconds at least. Great-Aunt Vivian was the first to finally break the awful, tense silence. "Oh. I see."

No one else spoke for another few uncomfortable seconds until the kitchen door banged open and shut loudly, and Grandpa's cheery humming filled the room.

Grandpa beamed at everyone, happily oblivious to all of the drama he'd just missed. "Well, hello, everyone! Looks like we've got a full house here!" Grandpa hustled around the circle, giving everyone a huge hug. "Gracie—and Vivian—and Beth and Rachel, too? If I'd known everyone was coming for a visit, I would've hurried taking Brother Brown home. He's in a wheelchair now, you know."

"They're not here for a visit, Grandpa," I said flatly.

Grandpa turned to look at me in surprise. "Oh?"

"They're housecleaning. In every sense of the word."

Grandpa just smiled. "Oh, yeah? Well, while everyone's here—Gracie, I've got something I've been meaning to give you for some time now that I thought you'd like to have." No one moved while Grandpa gave Anna's hand a quick squeeze, which made Great-Aunt Vivian choke and Great-Aunt Beth's and Great-Aunt Rachel's eyes bulge, before he hurried out of the kitchen and into his bedroom.

Grandpa returned a few uncomfortable seconds later and presented Aunt Gracie with a tiny baby blue jewel box.

"I know your mother would want you to have these."

I watched while Gracie frowned before slowly taking the box from Grandpa's hand. She opened it just as slowly and stared at whatever was inside.

"It's your mother's wedding ring set."

"It's not the original ring you gave her."

Grandpa smiled. "No. I've still got that. She wore this set most of her married life though, up until the day she died. I promised I'd get her something nice when I could afford to, and I'm glad I did. I just couldn't bury her in it. She loved those rings too much. I thought you'd like to have it, being our only daughter and all."

Aunt Gracie just kept staring at the rings dumbfoundedly. "I—I'm not sure what I'm supposed to do with them. I don't have a daughter to pass them on to—"

But Great-Aunt Vivian couldn't wait any longer. "I want to know what in the world is going on here!"

Grandpa frowned at her. "Going on? What do you mean?"

Great-Aunt Vivian stretched a hand out towards Anna. "Harold, James has been telling us you've been seeing Anna Stanley here. Is that true?"

Grandpa smiled and nodded before walking over to stand by Anna's side, putting his arm around her. "Yes, we've been seeing each other. I've been meaning to plan a time all of us could get together for dinner so I could introduce Anna properly to all of you. She's the most wonderful person—"

"So is Lilly!" Great-Aunt Beth had had enough, too.

And Great-Aunt Rachel looked shocked. "Do you mean to say you've been dating her?"

"I've been taking her out, yes."

Great-Aunt Vivian gasped. "Dating? At your age? If that isn't the most ridiculous thing I've ever heard of!"

Now I'd had enough, too. "It's not ridiculous—*you're* all being ridiculous!"

Aunt Gracie reached over and shook my arm. "Hush, James!"

Poor Grandpa tried again desperately. "She understands what I'm going through, losing Lilly—"

But Great-Aunt Vivian wasn't finished. "You're not the only one who lost Lilly! She's our sister!"

"I know that—I know you miss her, too—"

"How can you possibly miss her? You're seeing this woman now!"

And I wasn't finished, either. "This woman has a name, and she's standing right here. Stop talking about her as if she isn't even in the room! And anyway, you don't even know her."

Before Aunt Gracie could grab me again, Anna stopped everything with her soft, quiet voice. "Harold, I think it's best that I go home now. James, it was good to see you again."

I hurried over to Anna's side. "I'll walk you to your car, Anna."

Anna only patted my hand and tried smiling again. "That's not necessary, James. You stay with your family."

I followed Anna outside anyway, and after she drove away, I slowly climbed into the old swing and just sat there for a full five minutes until I could come to grips with what had just happened. I pushed against the floor boards and made the swing rock gently and was shocked to realize I was trying not to cry. I was mad—so mad—and yet, I wanted to cry. I took a few good, deep breaths before jumping out of the swing and walking resolutely back into the house.

When I opened the kitchen door again, I could hear Great-Aunt Vivian going at it, giving Grandpa a shocking once-over in the living room. I stood frozen in the kitchen, not knowing exactly what to do except guiltily listen.

" . . . I'm sorry—I thought you'd be thrilled with Anna—she's made me so happy—"

"How long have you been seeing her?"

"I ran into her a month or so after Lilly died—"

"And you haven't been separated since?"

"No, I guess not—"

"I can't believe this, Harold—I really can't!"

"What's wrong with me wanting to be with someone who under-stands and cares?"

"It's wrong because you're rushing it—you're not showing any respect for Lilly, rushing into marriage." I could hear Great-Aunt Vivian's angry voice rising higher and louder. "And another thing. I saw that mon-strosity in your garage—that big old tractor, riding lawnmower thing. You had absolutely no business buying that. Or this silly television set with this channel changing thing. We gave you three thousand dollars from the family to help you pay off Lilly's medical bills, and what do you do? Run out and buy a bunch of frills you don't need!"

"Vivian, listen to me, please!"

But Great-Aunt Vivian clearly wasn't in the mood to listen to anyone. "I can't stop you from seeing your lady friend, but I can tell you this, Harold. If you want to come and visit me and Landon, or Beth and Robert, or Rachel, or any of us, or even go to the Grant Family Reunion this August, you're still welcome to come, just as long as you don't bring her with you."

Things couldn't get much worse, but this time, I chose to keep my mouth shut and quietly tiptoed back outside and stayed on the swing, slowing swinging back and forth, until Gracie and my great-aunts had pulled out of the driveway in their cars.

When I walked back into the house, Grandpa was sitting on the couch, staring dully into space, looking as close to shell shocked as I'd ever seen him.

"Grandpa, are you okay?"

Grandpa tried to smile. "I'm not sure, James. I haven't been chewed out like that in a long time." He touched my hair and looked at me with sad eyes. "I heard your great-aunts say the way you stood up for Anna reminded them of Lilly, 'Loyal to her friends, right or wrong.'"

He shook his head slowly, still staring at nothing I could see. "Anna and I—we haven't been talking marriage—not at all! I'm just going with her. No one's even mentioned marriage yet." He shook his head again. "And the money—I used every cent of that three thousand dollars on Lilly's medical bills. Lilly saved the money I used for the lawnmower. She wanted me to buy it, knowing how bad my heart has been. I used what was left for the TV . . ."

"It's okay, Grandpa. You don't have to explain anything to me."

"Oh, James, I haven't seen much of my own family in so long. Lilly's family is really all I've got now." Grandpa's voice was shaking, so I reached over and held his hand.

"I think you should just forget about them. What do they know about anything going on with you anyway, right?"

Grandpa leaned over and kissed the top of my head before moving his arm around my shoulders to give me a squeeze. We sat like that without talking until I heard Grandpa's stomach rumble. "You need some food. Can I fix you anything to eat?"

"No, thanks, James. I'm not hungry."

If anyone needed to get their mind off of the present, Grandpa did. "Okay. Well, if I go grab the tape recorder, do you feel like working on your history project with me? How about telling me the next stories about your CCC days? That'll cheer us both up!"

Grandpa sighed and shook his head slowly. "Well, I have to warn you, James. The next thing I remember happening in the Cs was pretty sad. I don't know if you want to hear a sad story right now. Maybe we should wait until tomorrow night."

I shook my head and squeezed Grandpa's hand. "Today hasn't been exactly happy, Grandpa. I'm in a good state of mind for a serious story. Even a seriously sad story. If you think you are, that is."

Grandpa fished for his handkerchief and wiped his eyes before he smiled and ruffled my hair with his free hand. "I think I am. Go grab the recorder."

TWENTY-ONE

At the end of the summer of '36, right before I was transferred out of Moon Lake Camp, a forest fire started in the mountains again like the summer before, up high in the primitive area of the Uintas. No one knew how it started. Some fires were started by lightning, but usually they started from campfires and careless campers and smokers throwing lit cigarettes along the trails or roadways. All of us enrollees were confined to camp on fire alert in case we were needed to fight the fire. Everyone was pretty tense from the strain of just thinking about getting sent out on the fire line and into the middle of the flames.

Tucker and Max were assigned to the same fire squad as me. So was Landon. Since Tucker had been fired as a CCC truck driver, no one had wanted to try for his position except for one big guy named Madison. Tucker didn't try to bully him out of being a truck driver, like he'd done to the rest of us, so Madison got the job. The day the alarm was given for our camp to head out to help fight the fire, all four of us climbed into the back of Madison's truck with a dozen other enrollees, our fire-fighting gear, and some food supplies.

Madison drove us in as close to the fire as he possibly could. I knew we had to be pretty close to the flames, because the air was getting thicker with smoke, making it harder to see, and the farther we drove up the mountain, the hotter it got. The heat from the fire made the air ripple, and all of us started to sweat there in the back of the truck. Finally, the road disappeared into practically nothing—nothing that was driveable, anyway—so Madison screeched the truck to a halt. At that point, we all had to jump out of the truck and walk the rest of the way, carrying all our gear and food on our backs.

"Holy smokes, Addison! Look at that!"

Max hadn't moved but was just standing and staring. I jumped out of the truck and landed near him, squinting through the haze to see what Max was staring at so open mouthed. A second later, my own mouth hung open at what I could see. It was more than just a forest fire. The mountain looked like *it* was on fire. It was the most horrible and at the same time most spectacular thing I'd ever seen.

A few other CCC trucks piled in behind us, and soon a good few dozen enrollees were grouped around, trying to get our bearings in the smoke and heat. Madison jumped out of the truck cab and ran over to where all of us were standing, clutching our blankets and shovels.

"There's a stream further ahead. Take your blankets and soak them so you can beat the flames better!"

I couldn't stop staring at the mountain fire ahead. At that moment, I finally knew what a forest fire running out of control really was. This blaze was going to take the combined efforts of all the CCC camps in the area and probably all the available local men in the area to combat. Our group could only fight it by hand, and I knew that blankets and shovels weren't going to be enough to tame the fire all around us.

"Come on, idiots!"

Tucker had jumped out of the truck first and was already halfway down the path towards the stream, fading into the haze. Landon jumped out of the truck, squinted at the flames, and then gave me a huge grin before he jogged down the path after Tucker and the rest of the crew.

We found the stream and drowned our blankets in the water, squinting into the inferno in front of us, before fanning out around the stream, beating at the flames with our blankets and shovels for all we were worth. The further we got into the burning mess, the more I had to stop to cough and choke and gag from the heat and the smoke. The more I pounded at the flames, coughing and choking, the more I knew we weren't going to be able to beat this fire out with shovels like we'd done to the spot fires last summer.

I could make out forms in the haze—the enrollees from our truck—beating the flames around me as hard and fast as they could. I squinted through the smoke and flames, but I couldn't make out Tucker or Max anywhere, or even Madison, for that matter. Every lungful of air I took in had me coughing. I'd soaked my bandana in the stream, too, and tied it around my nose and mouth, but it didn't help enough.

Like the rest of the enrollees, I'd beat the flames for a while and then run back to the stream to dunk my blanket before running back to beat the flames some more. I'd been beating the flames with my soaked blanket in all that heat shimmering from the fire, getting hit by the hot cinders that kept landing on me and burning little holes in my pants and jacket for what seemed like hours, when I saw Landon running towards me through the haze.

"Addison, we gotta get outta here now!"

I'd been so busy smacking flames directly around me with my blanket that I hadn't realized the inevitable. Without any warning, the wind blew up and changed direction, causing the blaze to "crown," which meant the fire was blown by the wind from the top of one tree to another, hundreds of feet at a time with each gust of wind. Our crew was too deep in an area that was burning too fast and thick for blankets and shovels to be of any use, and now we were surrounded by the fire. The crowning had happened so fast that we were trapped pretty good. We had no choice but to give up and try to get out of the area and back to our truck. The fire was jumping fast in the tops of the pine trees, and fanned by the wind and the fire's own updrafts, the roaring blazes were running fast along the mountain.

The winds were getting worse, and between the winds and the flames, I could hear the screeching of trees toppling over. The smoke was so thick and blinding it had blocked out the sun, making it seem more like night than day.

I followed Landon, screaming, "Where's Max and Tucker?" but Landon just kept running, yelling over his shoulder, "We gotta get outta here, or we're all going to be burned alive!"

We made it back to the stream and everyone threw in their coats and blankets and soaked them in water before putting them over their heads to make a mad dash for the trucks. By the time I got to Madison's truck, Tucker was already there, so I hurried over to yell above the wind into the back of the truck at him.

"Where's Max?"

"Isn't he with you?"

Madison wasn't anywhere in sight, either, so Tucker jumped back out of the truck, and he and Landon and I went back into the flames, screaming for Max.

I'd heard a few trees falling, but the screech and whine of a tree falling nearby followed by a scream that was definitely human made my blood freeze. Landon stopped to look over his shoulder at me with the same horrified look I knew was on my face, but Tucker took off like a rabbit straight to the sound. We followed him through the hazy smoke and finally found Max, trapped good by a burning tree, with Madison kneeling on the ground, trying to lift the tree trunk off him. The tree was gigantic. It took all four of us to lift the tree enough to drag Max from underneath it. And Max—he was burned. Burned worse than I'd ever seen someone burned. But even so, he tried to grin before whispering, "Hey, what took you guys so long?" When Madison tried to carefully throw him over his shoulder, he moaned before passing out cold.

Before we made it back to the truck, I could tell Madison had been burned bad, too. His hands, mostly.

"Tucker, Landon, get in the back of the truck!"

Landon ran around to the back of the truck and jumped in, but Tucker had other ideas and shook his head frantically at Madison.

"I'm staying up front with Max!"

"There won't be enough room to lay Max down on the front seat if you get in the front, too!"

Tucker cursed a blue streak at Madison and jumped into the cab of the truck anyway. Madison cursed back but finally gave up, and between the two of us, we carefully laid Max in the cab with his head on Tucker's lap. We wrapped him in wet blankets, but I knew there wasn't anything we were going to be able to do for Max.

And then I was in for another surprise.

"Addison, you're going to have to drive."

Madison wouldn't give me a chance to say no. His hands were too badly burned to drive, and he couldn't make them stop shaking. So I had no choice but to jump in the cab after Madison and get the truck in gear as fast as I could before the fire ate us all. I drove as fast as I dared through the trees down the road with the fire jumping over the top of us. The fire was spreading so fast on both sides of the road that I had no choice but to drive through the fire with all the guys in the back with nothing but a canvas cover over the truck and hope for the best. At one point, sparks from the burning trees caught a part of the canvas top on fire, but Landon and the guys in the back attacked it with their blankets and got it out fast. I couldn't stop. I had to keep on driving until we were out of the inferno. I couldn't let myself look over at Madison with his shaking hands that looked almost black, or at Max, not even moving, or Tucker, who was whispering to Max and running his hands through Max's hair and trying to keep from crying.

I thought we'd never get down the mountain through the flames and back to the outside of the fire, but we finally did. I drove that truck at lightning speed back to camp, but it didn't matter. Max had already died long before we made it to camp. The camp doctor figured it was actually the falling tree that killed him and not the burns from the fire. Even if he'd survived the blow from the tree, he would've been in bad shape for the rest of his life.

I went numb all over when we got the news that Max hadn't made it. I'd never had anyone close to me die before. I had no idea how to handle it. Landon stuck by my side pretty close after that, worried, I guess, that I might do something stupid. Stupider than just getting really drunk, that is, which is exactly what both of us did, first chance we got, but it was Tucker who needed looking after much more than I did. Tucker took off and disappeared for a few days. No one knew where he went, but everyone was too busy fighting the fire until it got put out to do anything about it. There was too much fire to fight for those first couple of days to have time to think about the fact that I wouldn't see Max again.

Once the fire was out, the LEM over our crew pulled me aside and said that Madison had told him all about my fancy driving down the mountain the first day we'd fought the fire and how cool a head I'd kept the whole way down through the fire. He'd said that I seemed to have a knack for driving those huge CCC trucks, and since his hands were still in bad shape, Madison had recommended that I take over his position as a CCC truck driver—Tucker's old position.

I knew me taking over Tucker's position wasn't going to be a good idea at any time, but Madison wouldn't stop pushing, so with his help studying with me, I was able to pass the exam and road test pretty easily. Landon had a knack for driving, too, and had been training to drive the Cats, so when Madison wasn't up to it, Landon and I studied for the test together. I passed my test first. After that, we got the news that most of us would be transferring down to Duck Creek Camp near Cedar City, and my main job there would be to be a truck driver, transporting men and equipment to and from the job sites every day.

It'd been nearly two weeks since the first day of the fire, and due to Madison being laid up, I'd taken over as one of the truck drivers while plans were being made to move down to Duck Creek. I'd driven my load of enrollees back to camp late that afternoon and had just stepped into my tent when I about jumped out of my skin at what I saw.

Tucker. Lying flat on my bunk, legs crossed, one arm under his head, the other holding a cigarette that he was casually smoking, flicking ashes all over my stuff.

I tried to say, "Hey, Tucker, where've you been?" but Tucker ignored me to smoke his cigarette. Didn't hardly even look at me. As soon as he'd finished the cigarette and flicked it aside, he slowly sat up and stared at me. Hard and mean.

"You driving my truck now?"

I barely had a second to say yep before he charged me, knocking me flat to the ground. Landon was part of the group who came running, trying to break up the fight, but what he and everyone else didn't realize was that it actually felt good to fight. Neither of us had had a chance to get out the pain of having Max die, and fighting was probably the best thing for both of us.

One of the LEMs came barreling in and helped pull us apart before dragging Tucker away. Tucker had deserted the camp for too long, and since he hadn't had any kind of an official leave pass, he was officially kicked out of the Cs. I wanted to talk to Tucker, but I didn't get a chance. The LEM thought we'd just start fighting again if we were left alone together. Tucker wasn't even allowed back in the tent to get his stuff. Someone else came in to pack his stuff up for him, but I sent him back out and packed up Tucker's stuff myself. I shoved a couple of dollars I had into his duffel bag, along with a picture someone had taken of him and Max and me together one day in camp, and then all I could do was hope that everything would get better. For both Tucker and me.

TWENTY-TWO

*J*ames, I'm going to take my riding mower over to Beth and Robert's to cut their grass. Wanna come along?"

We hadn't talked to any of my great-aunts since the big explosion a week ago, but I'd been thinking about Grandpa and his CCC buddies too much to notice. Grandpa had cried after he'd told me about Max's death, and I'd cried with him, but ever since the morning after the explosion, Grandpa had been trying to act like everything was fine and that he was fine, too.

I knew Grandpa had been driving out to Great-Aunt Beth's once a week to mow the lawn all spring and summer. I wasn't sure if he'd still try to go over there now, but considering that Grandpa was working so hard at pretending nothing was out of the ordinary, I figured it made sense that he'd want to keep up his normal routine and make sure everyone knew he didn't have any hard feelings.

"Is Anna going to come along?"

"No, she said she's got some things she needs to get done this afternoon."

I had to assume possibly dealing with more family drama wasn't one of the things she wanted to "get done" that day, so I couldn't blame her for not wanting to tag along.

Grandpa was unusually silent during the half-hour drive over to Great-Aunt Beth's, and when he finally did speak, the sound of his voice filling the silence made me jump.

"James, what would you say if I said Anna and I had been thinking about maybe getting married?"

Married? I couldn't answer for what seemed like forever. "You want to get married?"

Grandpa looked briefly at me before nodding. "I went and had a talk with the bishop after church on Sunday. Told him I was sure he knew that Anna and I've been seeing a lot of each other lately and that we were concerned about whether people were talking or what might happen. And do you know what he said?"

"I have no idea."

Grandpa smiled. "He said, 'I'm going to tell you right frank, Harold. I don't give a darn what people think. I know you two kids are great people, so don't worry about everyone else. You two just enjoy yourselves.' That made me feel good about everything. I told Anna, and the more we talked, it just made sense that we should do everything up right and get married so we can keep on being together for as long as the Lord allows us to be here."

This was my chance, and I knew it. Grandpa was glancing over at me so hopefully while we drove along, waiting for my response, that I knew whatever I had to say could possibly make or break what he wanted to do.

I was all ready to say that I thought it was too soon for him to be thinking of getting married again. Grandma had only been gone about four months. It was too soon to get married. It was! I loved Grandma, and I missed her. I missed her so much.

I turned in the seat to face Grandpa—and bit my lip when I looked at him. Grandpa had been lonely, and now he was happy. And he *had* known Anna forever anyway in his ward. Surely that made it more okay.

I swallowed hard. "I—I think—I think you should do whatever will make you happy, Grandpa. Whatever you and Anna decide to do, I'll support you. I just want you to be happy, Grandpa. That's all."

Grandpa's eyes teared up as he reached over and squeezed my hand. "I've prayed about it, James, and I feel so good about it—so good."

I reached over with my other hand and squeezed his hand back.

"It'll all be okay, Grandpa. It will." It wouldn't be easy or fun, of course. I knew my family well enough to know that. But in the end, it would all work out. It had to.

When we arrived at Great-Aunt Beth's, I jumped out of the truck to help Grandpa get the mower out, and together we muscled it out of the little red utility trailer Grandpa had hooked to the back of the truck. A few minutes later we were through the back gate and into Great-Aunt Beth's backyard.

"Hi, Aunt Beth!"

Great-Aunt Beth was busy hanging up wet laundry on her old clothesline. She smiled big at me in surprise, but when she saw Grandpa, her smile faded.

Grandpa smiled and waved. "Hello, Beth!"

Great-Aunt Beth didn't say hello back. Instead, she snatched up the laundry basket by her feet, stuck her nose up in the air, and hightailed it back to the house, slamming the door behind her.

Grandpa stared at the back door in bewilderment. "What was that all about?"

I shook my head sadly. "I can only guess."

A second later, Great-Uncle Robert hurried out the back door and over to Grandpa with a smile that looked too tight and forced.

"Hello, James. Do you mind if I talk to your grandpa alone for a minute?"

"Sure. I'll just go inside, if that's okay."

I went inside, but Great-Aunt Beth wasn't in the kitchen or the living room, so I watched Grandpa and Great-Uncle Robert through the kitchen window. I had a feeling the conversation wasn't going to be pretty, since I was asked to leave, and I was right. Within thirty seconds, Grandpa was angrily pushing the mower back towards the gate we'd just brought it through. I jumped up and ran back out the kitchen door and into the backyard in a flash.

"What's going on?"

"Just help me get this back onto the trailer here, James. We're going home."

Grandpa looked so angry and upset that I waited until we were safely on the road again before I dared to speak.

"So, what happened?"

Grandpa stared straight ahead, gripping the steering wheel hard with both hands. "Beth's decided she doesn't want me to come around with the lawn mower anymore. Doesn't need me to cut the lawn with my riding mower. I wanted to talk to her, but she wouldn't even talk to me or speak to me. You saw that."

"What did Uncle Robert say?"

"Oh, you know him. He's kind of got a ring in his nose. He didn't have much to say for himself. So I figure I just better stay away and let things go as they are."

I didn't know what to say. What could I say? This was how Trent and Sarah and I acted when we were mad at each other, but we were just kids. Grandpa and my great-aunts and uncles—they were old. It was strange, seeing people so much older than me act like me.

"Just because people change on the outside as they get older doesn't mean everything's going to grow up on the inside, too. That kind of change takes a lot of hard work done on purpose. It doesn't just happen, like gray hair and wrinkles."

I was mad—so mad. I couldn't believe it, but I dared say a few mean things about all my great-aunts and uncles, but Grandpa stopped me fast.

"They're your family, James. They deserve more respect from you than that. Besides, they loved your grandma very much, and they miss her. They're still grieving, too."

Grandpa patted my hand and sounded okay, but one look at his face told me he wasn't.

It was at that second I realized I was smack in the middle of experiencing an "ah ha" in my life—a major realization that my great-aunts and uncles, people I'd respected and looked up to my whole life, weren't as close to perfect as I'd always thought they had to be by now. The fact that they still were making mistakes, big mistakes, actually floored me.

"No one ever reaches an age where you're guaranteed to know it all and never make a mistake again, or be jealous, or mean, or spiteful, etc. and etc. Believe me, I know. No one ever stops learning, and when you're learning, you're bound to stumble and do some tripping—even down and out falling flat on your face along the way."

I knew I'd have to mull this over for a while. It'd been too strange to see my great-aunts and uncles in a whole different light. One that wasn't exactly flattering, but I had to content myself with the fact that at least it was real.

I sighed and looked out the window for a minute before turning in my seat again to look at Grandpa. "Well, the good news is that now we've got the whole afternoon to ourselves, we can stop for hamburgers and ice cream!"

Grandpa laughed out loud, and the sound made me feel better, as if everything really was going to be okay.

"All right. We'll find some place with soft ice cream. You know I love soft ice cream!"

I couldn't help smiling, but I soon became silent as Grandpa continued to drive. Then I said, "I've been thinking about the CCC story you told me last week. About Max and Tucker. What happened after Tucker was kicked out of the CCC?"

I knew asking Grandpa to tell me more of his stories would get him in a good mood again, and thankfully, I was right.

TWENTY-THREE

I didn't have much time to mourn for either Tucker or Max, because we were all kept busy working hard, getting ready to move to Duck Creek Camp in Cedar City. On our last Saturday night in the Uintas, I got permission to take a load of enrollees down to Duchesne for one last dance. It was during a slow dance with a real cute girl named Alice that I had my first big shock of the night. One second I was laughing at something Alice said, and the next, I turned my head and saw Tucker. Leaning casually against a tree, watching me. I wanted to talk to him, so after the song ended, I went looking for him, but he'd disappeared.

About halfway through the dance, I went back to the truck with Landon and a few other guys for a smoke and a quick drink. Landon came along and smoked on his pipe for a while before heading back to the dance. I stayed behind to make sure the whisky bottles were properly tucked away.

The second I turned away from the truck, I got my second big shock of the night. There was Tucker, leaning against a truck a few yards away, smoking a cigarette, still just watching me. I stared back and waited until he finally ground the cigarette under his heel before slowly walking towards me with his hands deep in his pockets.

"Hey, Addison."

"Hey, Tucker."

We leaned against the CCC truck and talked about nothing for a minute. I wanted to say something about Max—I knew I should—but Tucker beat me to it.

"Max and I—we grew up in the same small town. Did you know that, Addison?"

I nodded slowly. "Max said something about that once."

"Yeah, well, my home situation wasn't so good. Max's was, but mine wasn't. He saved my life, you know. More than once."

"Oh, yeah?"

Tucker nodded and stared off with a funny, sad smile on his face. "Yeah. My old man used to beat on me, so Max would let me stay at his house when it was bad at my place. One time, it got really bad, and Max found me with one of my dad's guns, playing Russian roulette."

My eyes bulged out of my head a little. "Yeah? What did Max do?"

Tucker shrugged. "Took the gun away from me, of course, and told me I was being an idiot. Then he told me to sign up for the Cs with him, so I did. Max said it would help us and make our lives better, because we'd be making a difference for generations to come."

I nodded again. "That's true. I think that's what we're doing."

Tucker only snorted. "Some difference. Max got killed, and I got kicked out."

I held my tongue just for a second. "Max was still right, though. We're doing something that's making a difference now and *is* going to make a difference in the future."

Tucker didn't say anything to that, and when he finally spoke again, the words that came out of his mouth surprised me more than anything else had that night.

"So, you really think a girl like Mary St. Clair wouldn't give a guy like me a chance?"

I couldn't help it—I burst out laughing. "Ah, Tucker, all I can tell you is that it's been my experience that good Mormon girls don't give guys like us a chance."

Tucker frowned. "How can you be so sure about that?"

I shrugged. "I grew up in a town full of Mormons, and I didn't go to church enough to suit them. I could hardly get a nice Mormon girl to even look at me. Believe me, I know."

I didn't see Tucker again after that. Those of us transferring to Duck Creek Camp on Cedar Mountain in southern Utah were kept busy getting everything ready to move out, and the following Saturday morning, we were on the road headed for Duck Creek Camp.

TWENTY-FOUR

After huge double burger hamburgers, fries, and large chocolate soft ice cream cones, Grandpa and I spent the rest of the afternoon doing some grocery shopping, and just for fun, some engagement ring window shopping until Grandpa settled on a ring that I'd spotted first.

"Holy Moses, James, it's almost six-thirty! I needed to take my heart pills a half hour ago!"

Time had run away from us, so we sped home to Grandpa's pills as fast as we could. Even so, we sang crazy campfire songs at the top of our lungs the whole way home.

"Hey, James, isn't that your dad's car?"

I frowned, staring hard at my dad's old green Oldsmobile. "Yeah, that's our car. Did you invite everyone over?"

Grandpa looked at me in surprise. "You mean you didn't?"

"No, of course not!"

But our car wasn't the only one there. Aunt Gracie's red Buick was there, and so was Anna's car. When Grandpa and I walked through the kitchen door, we were both pretty surprised at the room full of people gathered in the living room.

"Jamie—you're back!" Mom came at me first with a huge hug. "How are you, sweetie? Are you all right?"

"All right? Of course I'm all right. Why wouldn't I be all right?"

Dad stood up from where he was seated between Trent and Sarah and smiled at me before going over to Grandpa.

"Hi, Dad, how are you doing?"

"I'll be doing just fine once I take my pills. Give me a second to do that, will you?" Grandpa went back into the kitchen while Trent and Sarah looked at me as if I were a criminal on trial.

"What?" I demanded, walking over to both of them.

"Having a fun summer, James?" Sarah's voice was cool. Too cool.

Trent only snorted, but I ignored him. It was usually the wisest thing to do when it came to dealing with Trent.

Aunt Gracie was sitting stiffly in a hard chair between Blake and Maxwell, who were slouching on the floor. And Anna looked about as uncomfortable as she possibly could.

"Knock knock—hey, James—"

Kyle. I couldn't believe he'd found his way back over to Grandpa's again. It figured he'd show up when the entire world was in Grandpa's house, but he just grinned his elf grin in surprise at everyone.

"Hey—full house! How's everyone, anyway?" Kyle could easily work a room, and within seconds, he'd said his hellos to everyone and seated himself near Sarah, who was more than happy to suck up all of Kyle's attention to herself and blah-blah-blah to him about her boring summer classes up at the university. Even worse, Kyle, being overly nice like he always was, said something to Sarah about how nice she looked.

"Oh, thanks. I haven't worn this dress for a while. I got it shopping with my grandma a few years ago for my birthday. I can hardly believe it still fits . . ."

I felt a strange numbness go down my spine, and a weird, sad lurch in my chest as I stared at Sarah in her dress. Her birthday dress that she'd shopped for with Grandma on her actual birthday, like she'd done every year since she was twelve. This dress was a loose cotton summer jumper in pink, Sarah's favorite color. But not Grandma's favorite color. Grandma loved lavender.

I turned sideways a little so I didn't have to see the dress anymore and tried not to think about my own birthday coming up fast. There wouldn't be any Grandma shopping trips for birthday dresses for me. Ever. I turned a little more so I didn't have to see Kyle smiling and laughing and talking with Sarah in her pink birthday dress and telling her how pretty she looked. I'd never cared about getting dresses for a birthday before. There was no reason to let myself get worked up over a stupid dress. I didn't want, or need, a new one anyway. My Sunday skirts were holding up fine . . .

Grandpa was smiling when he came back into the living room. "I'd almost believe this was a surprise party, except it's not my birthday yet."

Dad was still standing, waiting for Grandpa to come back. "Gracie called us and asked us to come over, Dad."

And now Aunt Gracie was standing up, too. "Yes, Dad, I just thought we ought to discuss—you know—the situation that's going on here."

Grandpa frowned at both my dad and Aunt Gracie. "There's a situation?"

Aunt Gracie sighed. "You know there is, Dad—"

"I guess I have you to thank, then, for getting Ben and his family out here so quick?"

Dad shrugged and tried to act casual, even though I knew he was concerned. Majorly concerned. "She said it was an emergency."

"Well, it is! This whole thing with Anna is—is—"

Grandpa stared at Aunt Gracie. "Is what, Gracie?"

"It's—it's unacceptable. Yes, that's what it is!"

Grandpa folded his arms and nodded at Aunt Gracie. "I agree, Gracie. It is. It really is."

Aunt Gracie's mouth fell open, as did everyone else's. "You do? I mean, it is?"

"Yes. I don't want to date Anna anymore."

"You don't?" I couldn't believe what I was hearing. That couldn't be true—I knew it wasn't.

Grandpa smiled at me and winked. "That's right, James. I don't. I want to marry her. And lucky for me, she told me she wants to marry me, too." Grandpa walked over to Anna, who smiled in relief and reached out to take his hand.

Aunt Gracie looked like she was going to faint. "When did this happen?"

"Two days ago." Grandpa was beaming, oblivious to the fact that everyone else looked as if he'd just announced he was going to have a lobotomy just for fun. "All of you are the first to know—"

Aunt Gracie fell back into her chair and rubbed her temples with both hands. "I—can't believe this—I just can't!"

No one else did or said anything but just stared at Grandpa. Even Kyle looked a little stunned. As for me, I was shocked, too. Not so much at Grandpa and Anna's announcement, but at the way everyone had reacted. Grandpa deserved so much more than that. And, I realized, so did Anna, who hadn't said a word yet.

I'd been slouched against the wall near Kyle, Trent, and Sarah, but I straightened myself angrily and walked purposely over to Grandpa and Anna. "Well, I'm glad I get to be the first to congratulate you. So— congratulations, and everything. I'm happy for you!" I turned and gave Grandpa a big hug and then shocked Anna by smiling at her and actually giving her a little hug, too.

Anna's voice shook when she quietly whispered in my ear. "Thank you, James. That means so much to me. You don't know—"

Kyle finally sprang to his feet to come over and hug them both, too. "Yeah, congratulations! So when's the big day?"

Grandpa was still beaming and still pretty oblivious to the dead, shocked silence from everyone else in the room. "We want to get married as soon as possible, so we thought we'd like to get married before the reunion at the end of August. We thought we'd shoot for August 14th. We'd like to get married in the temple, though of course, it'd just be for time—"

Aunt Gracie let out a high-pitched, short shriek that made everyone jump, but a second later, she'd brought herself under control, snatched up her purse, and yanked it open.

"Sarah, darling, here. This is for you."

I watched dumbfounded as Aunt Gracie thrust the baby blue jewel box I knew contained Grandma's wedding set into her hands.

"Since these rings obviously mean nothing to your grandpa anymore, and since you had a special closeness with your grandma, I thought you'd like to have them."

Grandpa's voice choked. "Gracie, honey—"

Aunt Gracie's eyes were flashing pure fire. "And thank you so much for planning your wedding day on my birthday! I guess I'm next in line to be forgotten by you!"

Grandpa looked as if someone had stabbed him in the heart. "Oh, Gracie, honey—I wasn't thinking, like I always do—I didn't mean to—"

Aunt Gracie was trying hard not to cry. "I don't want you to get married on my birthday. There. I've said it. And I mean it!"

Anna actually looked scared. "I'm so sorry. I didn't know that was your birthday. Of course we won't get married on that day. We never would have planned it on that day if—"

"If my own father had had the decency to remember his only daughter's birthday!"

I could see tears welling up in Grandpa's eyes. "Gracie, please—I'm so sorry—I—"

Anna spoke firmly but kindly. "We'll postpone it. Let's wait until after the family reunion to talk about setting a new date. Maybe in the fall. How does that sound?"

I couldn't help it—it was their day, not anyone else's. "You should get married whenever your want to! Don't worry about anyone else."

Mom was standing nearby and reached out to grab my arm and yank me closer to her side. "Hush, Jamie. It isn't your place to be saying anything about this!"

"It doesn't matter what you say, Mom, or anyone else. They're going to get married, so everyone might as well just get used to it! Good grief—it's not the end of the world here."

Mom gave my arm another hard yank and gave me her worst warning look ever. "That is enough, Jamie! Not another word out of you! I mean it!"

"Fine!" I pulled away from Mom, ran outside, and sat down hard in the old swing, pushing viciously against the floor boards as hard as I could to make it move back and forth. I was so busy staring at my feet, trying hard not to cry, that I didn't know anyone else was around until someone reached out and jerked the swing to a hard stop.

Trent glared at me, holding tight to the supporting bars of the swing. "So, what's it like?"

I stared at his glaring face, not sure I'd heard him right. "What?"

Trent only glared harder at me. "How does it feel being a traitor?"

My mouth dropped open fast. "What are you talking about?"

"You know, you getting all cozy with Anna!"

"Are you kidding? That's nothing compared to how cozy James has been getting with Kyle."

Both Trent and I turned to see Blake leaning casually against the house, his hands deep in his pockets, grinning like a Cheshire cat.

Maxwell was only a foot away, laughing. "Yeah, better check her out for chapped lips."

Now both of my cousins were laughing, and I was the one glaring. "You're sick!"

Trent didn't laugh, though. He turned back to me in disgust, shaking his head. "I should've been the one to stay with Grandpa this summer. If it'd been me, none of this would've happened."

"If you mean helping Grandpa to stop being sad all the time, then you're right—none of that would've happened if you'd been here instead!"

Trent ignored my words and leaned his angry face in towards mine. "The thing that amazes me the most, James, is that out of all of us, I would've thought you'd fight this disaster the most. I thought you loved Grandma. Obviously I was wrong."

I gasped. Twice. "I can't believe you just said that to me!"

"Hey, James—everything okay?"

Kyle came banging out of the back door then, looking at me worriedly. Of course everything wasn't okay. That much was obvious.

I only glanced at Kyle for a moment while he walked over to stand by me. "Yeah, I'm fine."

Kyle kept looking at me before turning to face Trent and my cousins. "Your mom's looking for you, Trent. And Gracie asked where you guys went."

Trent shrugged. "Fine. I don't have anything else to say to her anyway." And with that, Trent turned his back and stomped back into the house, followed by Blake, who grinned, looking first at Kyle and then at me. Maxwell winked at both of us and made disgusting kissing noises before disappearing into the house, laughing.

I looked back down at my feet and waited for Kyle to go back inside, too, but he didn't.

"Mind if I sit down?"

I shrugged and didn't look up. "Do what you want."

Kyle slipped into the seat across from me and pushed at the floor boards with his feet. I numbly did the same, and soon we had the swing gently rocking back and forth. Kyle didn't say a word while we alternately pushed against the floor boards until I looked up into his face and finally made myself speak.

"You know, just because I'm supporting my grandpa in this marriage deal doesn't mean I don't love my grandma. You know that, don't you?"

Kyle smiled and shook his head. "Of course I do, James. I've watched my grandma be lonely for a long time. Like I told you before, I wish my grandma would find someone, too."

"Do you think she ever will?"

Kyle shrugged. "I doubt it. She's gotten too used to being by herself.

She keeps telling me she doesn't want a man around to mess everything up. And that she likes having the television to herself."

I smiled into Kyle's grinning face. "My grandpa still loves my grandma. I know he still does. He has to, right?"

Kyle nodded. "Truth is, the fact that your grandpa wants to get married again is proof of how much he really loved your grandma."

"Oh, yeah? How do you figure that?"

"Well, the fact that he wants to get married again soon means he was really happy married. And that for him, being married is better than being single. If he hadn't been happy with your grandma, he wouldn't be looking to get married again."

I frowned. "How do you know?"

Kyle laughed and shrugged. "Well, I don't, really. My grandma told me all that. But it makes sense to me. So don't let Trent or anyone else get to you."

I nodded and looked back down at my feet until Kyle spoke again quietly.

"James, it's okay to like Anna. It won't change how much you love your grandma. And just because your grandpa likes Anna doesn't mean he doesn't love your grandma anymore. He's always going to love her. I'm sure of that."

"You are? How can you be so sure of that?"

"Just from the way your grandparents always were together. Whenever I'd come over, they'd sit and hold hands the whole time we were talking. And they'd smile at each other a lot and laugh at each other's jokes."

I shook my head in surprise. "No, they didn't. I never saw them do that."

Kyle shrugged. "Maybe not when you and everyone in your family was over. I'm talking about when I came over by myself."

That truly surprised me. "You'd come over to my grandparents by yourself, when I—I mean, my family—wasn't around?"

Kyle laughed again. "Sure. Lots of times."

"Like when?"

"Whenever we came to check on my grandma after my grandpa died. Usually at least once a week, so I'd always go over and see your grandparents, too."

It was strange to think of Kyle spending time alone with both my grandparents all these years without my knowing about it. "I had no idea."

Kyle shrugged again. "It's nice to see your grandpa happy again. I hated seeing him so sad. I miss your grandma, too, but I know that letting myself like Anna doesn't decrease how much I cared about your grandma." I looked up and was surprised to see Kyle watching me. "That's the great thing about love, James. Loving someone new doesn't take away any of the love you feel for anyone else. In fact, when you love someone new, I think putting the process into practice again helps you to love everyone else in your life even more."

I nodded and didn't look away until Kyle smiled.

"Now, how about that ride on the bicycle built for two. You up for it?"

I smiled. "I think I'm up for just about anything, Kyle."

TWENTY-FIVE

I stayed outside on the swing with Kyle until everyone left. Mom and Dad gave me a hug good-bye once I'd convinced them I wanted to stay all summer with Grandpa, but Sarah only frowned and shook her head at me, while Trent left me with a nice black scowl. Aunt Gracie, Blake, and Maxwell didn't say one word to me when they finally left, but Anna insisted on giving both Kyle and me hugs before she drove away, waving good-bye.

Kyle jogged back over to Grandma June's soon after Anna disappeared down the street. "You know it's all going to work out, James. So don't worry so much about it, okay?"

I could only nod back before walking the bicycle back into the garage.

There was no sign of Grandpa in either the kitchen or the living room when I quietly entered the house again. I stepped into the doorway of Grandpa's bedroom but stopped when I saw Grandpa lying on the bed, flat on his back with his eyes closed.

"Are you okay?"

Grandpa opened one eye at me and smiled. "Oh, my chest hurts a little, but I'm fine. Probably that darn soft ice cream!"

"Do you want me to get you another pill?"

Grandpa shook his head. "No—no, I'm fine."

"Well, I'll let you get some sleep."

Grandpa opened both eyes and struggled up into a half-sitting position. "Stay and keep me company for a while, James?"

I nodded and walked around the bed to sit on the other side of it but stopped fast when I saw my grandma's face smiling from a gold metal frame on the bedside table in front of me. The frame held an old 5 x 7 black-and-white photo of my grandma leaning against a gigantic oak tree. She could've only been about twenty years old at the time. I picked the picture up carefully and looked it over closely, dumbfounded.

"I can't believe I missed seeing this before!"

Grandpa turned his head to see what I was holding. "Seeing what?"

I turned the frame around so he could see. "This picture of Grandma. It's beautiful!"

Grandpa smiled. "Oh, that's because it hasn't been there very long."

"It hasn't?"

Grandpa nodded. "The original's a lot smaller. I took that picture of your grandma when I was in the Cs when I met her in Enterprise. It's always been my favorite picture of her."

I looked down at the beautiful picture again. "When did you get it blown up and framed?"

"I didn't. Anna took it out of my CCC photo album, had a negative made of it, enlarged it, and framed it for me."

I couldn't believe Anna would do something so selfless and sweet. A second later, though, I was shaking my head at that thought. Knowing Anna, of course I could believe she'd do something that nice.

I stared at the picture, and soon, not only was I seeing Grandma with her wavy, platinum-blonde hair, big blue eyes, and delicate features but I could see Gracie, and even more, I could see Sarah. In fact, anyone who'd never seen my grandma would think it was a picture of Sarah dressed up in 1930s clothing.

"I can't believe how much Sarah looks like Grandma."

Grandpa lifted an eyebrow. "Do you really think so?"

"Of course. Just look at this picture!"

Grandpa leaned over to examine the picture more closely before nodding uncertainly. "Yes, I guess she does have her build. And her face."

I couldn't help laughing. "You don't sound convinced, Grandpa."

Grandpa only smiled as he steadily looked in my eyes. "Well, I guess it's because you remind me of her more."

My mouth fell open while I stared back at him. "Me? Why? I don't look anything like her! How could I possibly remind you of Grandma?"

Grandpa kept smiling and shook his head. "It's not just looks that remind you of a person. Your spirit is like hers."

"My spirit?"

Grandpa chuckled. "You're strong and stubborn like her. You don't let anyone walk all over you or the people you care about. She never let anyone, either. You have a way of standing straight and tall, letting the sun shine on both the good and the bad about you without apologizing or making any excuses. That always makes me think of her."

I considered everything Grandpa had said for a minute before quietly speaking again. "Anna's not like that."

Grandpa nodded in agreement. "No, she isn't."

"She always wants to make sure everyone's happy. She's not happy unless everyone else is, too. She's quiet and sweet—"

"Yes, James, I know. She and your grandma are almost complete opposites. I love that about them both."

I kept silent for a few seconds before carefully replacing the picture on the bedside table and moving to sit on the bed by Grandpa. "Grandpa, I've been wondering—how did you get together with Anna?"

Grandpa smiled, and when I looked at him, I could see tears forming in his eyes. "You know something? You're the first person to even ask."

My heart lurched, seeing those tears in his eyes. "You don't have to tell me if you don't want to. I mean, I understand if it's none of my business."

"No, I want to tell you. I'm happy that you want to know." Grandpa reached into his pocket for his handkerchief and wiped his eyes and nose before stuffing it back into his pocket.

"After losing Lilly, I knew I had to start a new life, and it was hard. And lonely. I was doing all right taking care of myself, living up to the requirements that she'd set. Your grandma told me when she was sick that after she was gone, if I didn't keep the house clean and neat, she was going to dig out of her grave if she had to dig through China and come back and haunt me."

I couldn't help laughing. "She did?"

Grandpa chuckled, too. "Oh, yes. She was very particular about that. So I've strived to do that and take care of the yard, too. It wasn't so bad around here in the morning, especially once I got busy doing something, or went visiting. Landon and Vivian, and Beth and Robert, and Rachel— they all had me over for dinner a lot. They were awful nice to invite me over, and have me help with projects at their places, too, and just spend time talking, but without Lilly there, too, it just wasn't the same. But even so, evenings were the hardest part, having to be alone here in the house. Nobody realized it or understood how hard it was for me. But I was doing the best I could and kept my spirits up by going to church as I should. Your grandma would've wanted me to do that because she knew that would help me not to feel so alone, and she was right."

Grandpa's voice shook, so I slipped my hand into his and felt him squeeze it before he took a deep breath and continued.

"Well, conference came in April. I didn't pay too much attention to the talks, since your grandma had just passed away, but after I spent my time moping around, my priesthood class assigned us to bring one of the talks from conference. I thumbed through the *Ensign* conference issue and then looked through the conference issue from the year before, and I felt inspired to choose Elder Marvin J. Ashton's address. He gave a real special talk, all about how much the single sisters need our love, encouragement, and respect. As I read Elder Ashton's words, it was as if he were talking to me, asking me not to forget the widows. There were a lot of them around, and they needed some companionship, too. I figured I could offer to help them clean their yard, or invite them out for dinner, or just spend time with them. So I got to thinking about that after I gave my presentation on Elder Ashton's talk in priesthood, and it hit me that I needed to take that counsel. It was almost like I could feel your grandma shoving at me to pick up the phone, so I decided to do it."

"I don't remember that talk."

"Well, you should read it. It was a good one. At least, I thought so."

I smiled, trying to picture myself enjoying a talk meant for widowers. "I'm sure it was. Is, I mean."

Grandpa sighed and squeezed my hand again. "At first, I thought of your grandma's dear friend, Victoria Allen. They were really close in the Relief Society together, and she'd been a widow for a number of years. And then, of course, I thought of your Grandma June. I took them each out to dinner, and everything went really well. It wasn't as hard as I thought it would be. Both women were quite excited to be asked out on a date, and it was pretty fun for me, too. It'd been so long since I'd gone dating that it brought back all kinds of memories of dating your grandma and how happy and exciting those times were. It felt so good to feel happy and excited about something again. You just don't know, James."

I could feel tears in my own eyes at the wistful sound of Grandpa's voice. It wasn't fair—it wasn't right—that he should've spent time so unhappy. Not my grandpa.

"So time went on, and I was enjoying spending time with other widows in the ward, too, but I didn't have anyone specific in mind that I wanted to see more of. Then one evening while I'd been working in the yard, I thought, 'Well, I'll walk over to Gracie's and see how everyone at her house is doing.' And as I was walking down the block, I had to wait for a car to pull into a driveway, and as I waited, the woman in the driver's seat smiled and waved. It took a second for it to register in my brain that it was Anna Stanley. I stood there and watched while she pulled into the driveway and climbed out of the car before I remembered that she was a widow in the ward, too. I hadn't thought of Anna before as being one of the widows in the ward, even though she'd spent two and a half years by herself by then."

"How come you forgot she was a widow, too?"

Grandpa shrugged. "She's a good ten years younger than me, so I don't think of her as a widow. I guess that's also the reason I didn't think of asking her out. And, well, she wasn't coming out to church regular and hadn't in a long time. I think I'd almost forgotten she was even in the ward. It was kind of funny, because your grandma and I had been friends with her and her husband. He worked for the airlines, you know. A pilot."

"Yeah, you told me."

Grandpa smiled. "Oh, they were the sweetest, friendliest people you could ever meet. Always greeting people. I remember when her husband became sick. He had a tumor on his brain, like your grandma did. It paralyzed him on one side, so he had a hard time getting around. She'd bring him to church in a wheelchair, and during the week, sometimes I'd see her with him where I go swimming with Clay in the morning. I'd help get him in and out of the pool, and then she'd exercise his legs and arms, hoping that that would help. But now that I've gone through this with Lilly, I know that with tumors like he had and like Lilly had, getting better at all—it was just out of the question. But she was so strong, bringing him to church every Sunday."

I squeezed Grandpa's hand again. "So what happened next?"

"Well, after he passed away, Anna kept coming to church for a while, and then we'd notice that one Sunday Anna wouldn't be there. Then she'd show up again, and then it would be two or three Sundays that we wouldn't see her. And then more Sundays before we'd see her again. But we all assumed that since she had married kids, she was maybe spending time with them. And so we just left things alone, not thinking that she needed more companionship in the ward, as we should have done."

Grandpa sighed and shook his head. "So there I was, standing in Anna's driveway, with all of this racing through my mind. It was just getting dark, and when she got out of the car, I could see on her face that she knew exactly what I was going through. She smiled and said, 'Hi, Harold,' and I said, 'Hi, Anna,' and then she hurried right over to me and gave me a big hug and some sympathy. And while I was hugging her back, it hit me right then, why not ask Anna for a dinner date? So I asked her, and she said, 'Oh, I'd like that. I'd like it very much.' I was pretty excited. I couldn't wait for our date the next weekend."

I shook my head slowly. "It still blows my mind that you were asking women out on dates, Grandpa."

Grandpa laughed and squeezed my hand again. "What is it people say? You're only as old as you feel? I guess that describes me pretty good!" Grandpa cleared his throat and continued. "We had dinner at a restaurant and talked and talked. Oh, it felt so nice! The two of us had the same thing in common to talk about: our sympathy for each other and understanding what each other was going through—knowing what loneliness was and what it was like losing someone you love so much. But we also had some fun, enjoyed our dinner, and tried to forget about the past a little bit. So when we left the restaurant, I said to her, 'Anna, I'd like to go for a ride up in the hills above town and see the city lights.' Why rush home? We had plenty to talk about. So we rode up where we could get a great view of the city, got out, and sat on the back end of the car, just talking and looking at the lights below. And while we were talking and looking at the lights, I don't know what came over me, or how it happened, but one second I was thinking how pretty she was, and the next, I reached over, took her by the hand, pulled her over to me, and we kissed. Just one nice little kiss. It was a thrill to me, and I hope it was a thrill to her."

I wasn't sure what to think about Grandpa telling me he'd kissed someone other than my grandma, but at the same time, I couldn't stop listening to everything he wanted to tell me.

"We had a beautiful evening. Once I took her home and parked in her driveway, we sat together for quite a long time just talking some more. I knew she liked to travel, because she'd flown all over the world with her husband while he worked for the airlines. And listening to her stories, I could see that we had a lot in common. All our thoughts fit together. I kissed her again that night before I left. While I drove home, I was whistling and singing—I was in high heaven, so excited that I'd found someone I wanted to get to know better. Someone who might end up being a special companion for me. I couldn't wait for the next day so I could talk to her again."

"And so did you? Call her again the next day?"

Grandpa grinned. "Yes, I did. We got together again the next evening and walked up town. We walked for a long time, held hands, and shared a nice evening together. And so the next evening, we saw each other again. And we just kept seeing each other every evening after that. We really enjoyed getting to know one another, just talking. It was so nice being with her. And it wasn't just that I was feeling good because I wasn't feeling lonely anymore. I could see that she'd been lonely and discouraged, too. What really felt wonderful was knowing that I might be able to help her, just like she was helping me. It felt so good to be needed again. I could see that she needed someone to be with just as much as I did."

I nodded quietly but didn't say anything, waiting for Grandpa to tell me more.

"So before I knew it, four weeks had gone by, and we'd spent every day together, going walking, visiting places and people, going out to eat, swimming—all kinds of things to pass the time together. I think we fell in love easily because we needed each other. But the thing that was best of all was seeing Anna coming to church again every Sunday. I'd go over to her place every Sunday morning and walk to church with her. Boy, your grandma would've been surprised, seeing me be the one to get someone to go back to church again!" Grandpa laughed before squeezing my hand again. "So, that's how it happened, and that about brings us up to date. Does that answer your question okay, James?"

I turned my head to look at him and slowly smiled. "It does." We were both quiet for another minute before I spoke again. "Grandpa?"

"Yes, James?"

"I'm sorry you were lonely. I'm sorry—" I had to stop, because my voice was shaking funny.

"It's okay, James. Everything's okay." Grandpa squeezed my hand again, and then he placed his other hand on top of mine and patted it softly. "Hey, if you want to break out the ol' tape recorder, we can work on our history project. I'll tell you about our move to the new CCC camp at Duck Creek in Cedar City before we both hit the sack. How does that sound?"

I brushed away the tears that were starting to fall and smiled. "It sounds good, Grandpa. Really good."

TWENTY-SIX

I t was quite a deal, moving down to Duck Creek in the spring of '36. We loaded the big CCC trucks with all our gear and things and piled all the mattresses in camp in the back of one of the open stake-rack trucks. A bunch of the guys rode in the back of the trucks, while I drove the one and only dump truck, loaded with the oil and grease for all the other trucks. Landon and Madison rode in the cab of the truck with me, and we brought up the rear of our convoy along with the ambulance. That was one big string of us CCC boys, like a covered wagon caravan from the ol' pioneer days, but with CCC trucks instead.

We made short stops along the way, but when noon rolled around, we stopped for a good hour at a big, wide spot in the road where we could park and eat the sandwiches the cooks had made up for us. By the time we got down by Richfield, it was getting dark. We'd left early Saturday morning, and as we started down Marysvale Canyon, Landon and Madison and I were belting out some old drinking songs when Landon happened to look out the passenger window, squinting hard into the dark.

"Hey, Addison, look over there!"

I could see some lights strung up, and after a few seconds of squinting into the dark to get a look at what Landon was seeing, sure enough, I could see there was a dance hall off to the side of the road.

Landon grinned at me, waiting, while I grinned back, wondering if we ought to. Then Madison finally yelled, "Well, what are we waiting for?" We all hooted and howled, and while Landon scrambled in his pockets for a comb, I gave the wheel a hard turn off the road and made my own road over to the open-air dance hall. We had our dirty old CCC Levi's and button-down shirts on, but we didn't care. A few turns on the dance floor with a dishy girl or two was just the thing we needed. No one would ever know, seeing as how we brought up the rear of the convoy and had to stop a lot along the way, anyway, to fill up trucks with oil and gas. They'd expect us to be late.

I wheeled the dump truck by the cars parked in the dirt near the dance and squealed it to a halt that sent dust flying. I snatched the comb out of Madison's hands to try and do something with the snarl of curls under my hat. Didn't do me much good, but I didn't care.

"Ready?" Landon had already jumped out of the truck and was ready to run for the dance floor. Madison and I jumped out either side and gave the doors a hard slam, ready to sneak into the dance with Landon, but a second later, we were all caught in the glare of headlights. A CCC vehicle, I was sure of it. We all just stood there, staring like big dumb deer. All three of us swore under our breath, wondering who'd caught us.

The vehicle slowly ground to a halt near our truck, and as I squinted at it, trying to figure out who was driving, Landon muttered, "The ambulance!"

I had to take a deep breath and just hope for the best. I wasn't well acquainted with the ambulance guys, but since they worked with the doctors, I was sure they'd lord it over us and get us in Dutch. I watched while a guy jumped out of each side of the ambulance. It took them forever to walk over to us, but once they did, I could see that neither of them was smiling. My heart was pounding really hard and fast. I couldn't get in trouble over this—it wasn't worth it.

One of the guys finally opened his mouth. "So, are we going to go dance or what?"

Landon, Madison, and I just let our mouths hang open while the two ambulance guys burst out laughing. I was sure we were done for, and Landon kept saying as much to the ambulance guys, who thought the fact that we were scared of them was the funniest thing they'd ever heard of. A second later we were slapping each other on the back, laughing in relief before all five of us carefully sneaked through some shrubs to get into the dance the CCC way.

We must've danced for about five songs with some of the cute Marysvale girls before Landon yanked at my sleeve.

"We better get going—they're gonna be looking for us."

We had to make Duck Creek that night by getting over to Panguitch and then up the mountain to Duck Creek, so we hurried out of the dance and drove like lightning to catch back up with the rest of the convoy, but once we got going down through the canyon, it started to rain.

"Hold up, Addison—what's that in the road?"

I ground the dump truck to a halt and squinted in the rain to see what Landon was looking at.

I couldn't believe what I was seeing. "Looks like a mattress!"

"It *is* a mattress!"

"What the—I know we tied those down good. I know we did!"

We found mattress after mattress lying in the road, so we had to stop and run out in the rain and pick up each mattress as we came to it. We loaded the mattresses inside the ambulance so they wouldn't get even more soaked, until we had the ambulance full of mattresses. We finally caught up to the convoy in Panguitch and found out that a bunch of the guys had been riding in back of the truck loaded with thin bunk mattresses. Once it started to rain, they'd crawl under a mattress so they wouldn't get wet, and then the mattress would blow off. So they'd crawl under another mattress, and then it would blow off, too. We weren't about to deal with stopping and picking up mattresses again, so we and the ambulance guys loaded the mattresses back onto the stake-rack truck and tied them down good so they wouldn't blow off again.

It took us all night to climb up the mountain from Panguitch to Duck Creek Camp, our new CCC home. Like in the Uintas, we were up in the quaking aspen and the pine trees, high in the mountains. It was definitely a pretty camp up there on Cedar Mountain. Since it wasn't wintertime, we lived in tents. There was a big mess hall by the side of the road, and the tents were set up a ways behind the mess hall. The garage where we kept the trucks and all kinds of supplies was across the road that ran by the camp. We even had horses and two mules at the Duck Creek Camp to help pull out the timber while we were building roads. Once we had the camp all set up, we lined both sides of the paths and trails to each of the buildings and to our tents with rocks a little larger than softballs, like we did at the Moon Lake Camp and the Uinta River Camp.

We had quite a time there at Duck Creek Camp up on Cedar Mountain. We hauled logs up around Navajo Lake, cut out the bug trees, and built all the campgrounds at Duck Creek. We made little wooden coolers at each campsite for campers to keep food in that needed to stay cool, and we fixed up some nice fireplaces for each campsite, too. And we built the Little Duck Creek Dam, way down below the CCC camp, with a pond area where people could go fishing.

While I was at the Duck Creek Camp, my job was to run the supply truck. I'd run into Cedar City and get the parts we needed for the shop in the garage to repair the trucks. And I'd pick up the cement and any wire and tools we needed for our projects, along with freight or mail that came in for the Forest Service, too. I'd make a trip every day into Cedar City, and the guys would take turns going with me to help bring back the supplies.

About a month after we'd moved into Duck Creek Camp, we started tapping the spring at Navajo Lake—the Blue Spring near the lake—so we could put in water for the campgrounds. There was a big, blue spring above Navajo Lake with real deep, cold water. That spring was about thirty feet around. We had to drive over to Marysvale to get the pipe we needed for the campground's water system, so I started making regular trips with a few other guys in the stake-rack trucks that we usually used to haul the guys to their work projects, and we used the trucks to haul loads of pipes that we needed from Marysvale over to our camp.

Once we got all the pipes we needed for running water into the campgrounds, I went back to running the supply truck into Cedar to pick up supplies. While I was up at the Duck Creek Camp, the camp was given a great big Walter dump truck. It was a huge, four-wheel-drive truck, and since I was one of the guys who'd been driving truck the longest, I was one of the first to be trusted to learn how to drive it. The seat was right up on top of the front wheels, and the motor stuck out in front. Six people could easily sit across the seat, it was so huge.

The first time I drove the Walter into Cedar City, Landon went with me and drove one of the stake-rack trucks I'd been driving. I'd trained Landon during the summer on how to drive the stake-rack trucks, so he went with me to get a big load of supplies that required two trucks, because we were going to move camp that fall from Duck Creek down to Veyo.

Landon hadn't been able to stop eyeing that new Walter truck all morning. "Hey, Addison, which one of these trucks do you think goes the fastest?"

"Don't know, but probably this big ol' Walter."

"Ah, I don't think so. This stake-rack truck is smaller and lighter. It's got to run faster."

"I doubt it. The Walter's new, and it's got a great big engine in it. It's got a lot more power than that stake-rack truck."

Landon scratched his chin, looking back and forth between the two trucks before grinning at me. "Wanna find out which one's the fastest?"

Landon was determined, so since we had plenty of time to get to Cedar City, we raced those trucks down from camp off of Cedar Mountain. The road was all gravel and not very wide. We were side by side for a lot of the ride. Sometimes Landon pulled out in front, and sometimes I got in front, but I finally got the lead and kept it, driving on the wrong side of the road.

"Woo hoo! Told you this Walter was faster!"

We turned off onto the road to Navajo Lake. Back up by Navajo Lake, we squealed around a tight curve in the road, with me still on the wrong side of the road and Landon close behind me, and as we raced around the bend, a car came towards us around the corner out of nowhere. Everyone slammed on their brakes, making the tires scream and dust fly like mad. I had to turn out off the road to let the car get around the Walter and Landon's truck and crashed into the rocks along the side of the road.

I screeched the Walter to a halt and just sat there with my heart pounding in my chest and throat. I took a few deep breaths once I realized I was fine, Landon was fine, and the other car was fine and not even around anymore. I wiped my sweaty palms on my pants and reached down to start the Walter, but when I tried to start up the motor, I could hear something banging real loud underneath.

I hurried and turned off the motor. "What in the world is that?"

Landon could hear the noise, too, so he jumped out of his truck and jogged over to the Walter to see what the trouble was while I tried starting the Walter again. But turning off the engine and starting it again didn't change anything. The loud banging was still going on underneath the truck.

"Sounds like you probably bent the oil pan barreling over the rocks here by the side of the road."

I knew from the sound of it that Landon was probably right. We used Landon's truck to pull the Walter clear of the rocks and then climbed underneath it, and sure enough, lying on our backs and looking at the engine under that big Walter, we could see I'd bent the oil pan, and the ol' crank shaft right above the oil pan was banging into it instead of going around in circles like it needed to in order to get the engine going.

"Holy Moses! What's the Supe going to say? This Walter's brand-new!"

Landon laughed and crawled out from under the truck to grab the tool box.

"Just be glad nothing else got hurt in the process, and help me get this oil pan off."

We muscled the oil pan off, and I found a baseball-sized rock that we used to pound out the dent. We did our best to mold the pan back into its normal shape so it wouldn't get in the way of the crankshaft when it went around, but it didn't look very good.

"Well, we've fixed it as best we can. Let's get the oil pan back on and see if it'll start up for you now."

The Walter did start up and move forward, and I nearly cried from relief when I could tell that it still drove the same. We drove on into Cedar City, and the second we got there, we took the Walter right into ol' Al DeBrisky, the mechanic in town. He was somewhere in his forties, but he was in good shape and looked like he still liked to have a good time whenever he could.

"There seems to be something wrong with the oil pan."

Ol' Al climbed underneath the Walter after making a big fuss over how huge the truck was, and when he crawled back out from under it, he grinned at both of us.

"So who won?"

I could hardly get my voice to work. "Uh, I don't know what you mean, sir."

"Bent oil pan, lots of dirt on the tires, and dust all over the sides of the Walter. And on that stake-rack truck, too. I'd say the two of you had some kind of fun getting into Cedar today!"

Both Landon and I just stood there looking dumb and scared. But ol' Al just threw back his head and laughed. He proved himself to be a pretty good guy. He took the oil pan off and fixed it without saying anything more, and then we were able to get our supplies and haul them back to Duck Creek Camp. The Supe never found out, and neither did anyone else. But things like that always seemed to happen when wild guys like Landon and me got together doing things we shouldn't.

TWENTY-SEVEN

The next morning was Saturday, and since I'd been up late with Grandpa the night before, I slept and slept and slept. I would've slept longer, but I heard the back door slam hard, followed by a crash and a dull thud.

"James? James, are you here? James!"

Anna's voice. Loud and frantic and almost hysterical. I sprang out of bed faster than I thought was possible and raced into the kitchen to see Anna trying to help Grandpa into a chair at the dining room table. Grandpa looked terrible, all white faced and wincing in pain, leaning on Anna.

I hurried over to Grandpa's side to help Anna ease him into a chair while he tried to take some deep breaths. "What—what happened?"

"It's his heart. He brought his tractor over to mow my lawn, but before he was through—"

Grandpa's voice was hoarse and winded. "Just having a little pain in my chest, James. Anna's making something out of nothing, I'm sure."

"Don't pay any attention to him, James. I think we need to get an ambulance over here!"

"Maybe—maybe I should call my dad first. Is that okay?"

Grandpa shook his head and coughed a funny, dry-sounding cough. "Oh, that's not necessary."

Anna turned to me and spoke more firmly than I'd ever heard her speak. "Yes, it is. Please call your dad, James. That's an excellent idea."

So I did. My hand was shaking while I tried to dial the numbers on Grandpa's rotary phone, but somehow I finally got the number dialed. Thankfully, Dad was at home.

"I'll be there in twenty minutes. Just keep him calm and quiet."

It seemed like forever before Dad finally arrived, but after taking one look at Grandpa, Dad was ready to load him in his car and drive over to the hospital as quickly as possible.

But Grandpa wasn't finished being difficult yet. "I have an appointment tomorrow with my doctor as it is."

"Tell me about the pain, Dad. What does it feel like?"

Grandpa frowned and closed his eyes for a moment. "Well, it didn't—and it still doesn't—feel like a heart attack, but it's a pretty awful pain I've got in my chest. It hurts—hurts bad."

Dad shook his head fast and helped Grandpa stand up. "To heck with it. I'm taking you up to the hospital now, because for all we know, you're having a heart attack right now."

The three of us carefully loaded Grandpa into Dad's car before piling in behind him while Dad drove faster than he should have to the hospital. Dad swung up to the emergency room double doors, and within a matter of what I'm sure was only minutes, although it seemed more like hours at the time, Grandpa was in a room with his heart doctor. Dad, Anna, and I waited outside for at least an eternity before the doctor finally came out of the room.

"You can see him now, but only for a few minutes. I've given him something to relax him, and he's going to need some sleep."

I gave the doctor's sleeve a quick tug. "When can he come home?"

"I'd like to keep him here for a week so I can monitor his heart . . ."

I didn't wait to hear anymore but pushed through the circle of adults to get inside to see Grandpa.

When I stepped into his room, it shook me to see how still he was lying in the hospital bed, all hooked up to quietly beeping monitors. He was still almost as white as his hospital gown.

"Grandpa?"

Grandpa slowly opened his eyes and turned his head to the doorway to smile sleepily at me. "James . . . come here, sweetie."

I walked slowly over to him. "Are you okay?"

Grandpa reached for my hand and patted it. "Oh, I will be. My heart's just acting up a little. Nothing to worry about, all right?"

I nodded. "All right, Grandpa."

Anna stayed with me at Grandpa's house that week. We got up early every day and drove straight over to the hospital to spend as much time as possible with Grandpa. Mom, Dad, Sarah, and Trent came a few times to see him, too. So did Aunt Gracie, Blake, and Maxwell. But it was Anna who took care of him better than any of the nurses or doctors. She brought him magazines and books and was quick to make sure he had enough ice water in his room at all times. She fluffed his pillows behind his back and also beeped for a nurse at the slightest sign of trouble. She even brought his tape recorder in case he felt up to telling more stories.

I'd been sitting on Grandpa's bed the second day he was in the hospital, helping him with a crossword puzzle while Anna went to grab us some sandwiches, when Grandpa sighed and pushed the book away.

"Where's that tape recorder, James?"

"Right here, Grandpa." I reached for the recorder that had been tucked away under the table by his bed. "Are you sure you're up for this?"

Grandpa sighed again and nodded. "I need to forget about this place for a while. This is the best way I know." He grinned and his eyes sparkled at me knowingly. "How would you like to hear about the time when I first met your grandma?"

I couldn't help grinning. "I'd like that. Very much."

TWENTY-EIGHT

We broke camp at Duck Creek and moved down to the CCC camp in Veyo in early October of '36. Besides fixing up the campgrounds in Duck Creek and putting in water lines for the campgrounds, we'd spent the summer building the road from Duck Creek out to Strawberry Point. I didn't see a lot of Landon during the day, because he was running the Cat up on the mountain at Duck Creek. In fact, Landon drove the first Cat out to Strawberry Point and helped build the road over to the point where it's possible to look right down into Zion's Canyon.

The day we left Duck Creek for Veyo, I was driving the Walter dump truck with a big, flat trailer attached to the back of it to haul the Cats on. The trailer wasn't real steady and only had a four-wheel swivel dolly in the front of it. Landon and I loaded a Cat up in the back of the Walter truck, and then we loaded a big old road grader on the flat trailer behind.

No one rode in the cab of the truck with Landon and me. We came down slowly off Cedar Mountain, and soon we were headed for the bend in the road that was closely followed by a narrow bridge with wooden guard rails on either side of it.

Landon was puffing away on his pipe and turned to raise an eyebrow at me, nodding at the bridge up ahead right beyond the curve. "You think we can clear that?"

I shrugged. "Only one way to find out!"

The Walter cleared the bridge okay. That wasn't a problem. It was that trailer with the grader on it that caused all the trouble. Even though I crossed over slow and careful, it was impossible to keep both the truck and the trailer in a straight line going over that bridge. I could hear the trailer banging from side to side against those guard rails as we drove over the bridge. I guess I should've known we wouldn't be able to make it over the bridge straight with that bend in the road right before the bridge. We'd climbed clear over the side of the mountain, taking it easy the whole way, but by the time we got across that bridge coming out of the bend, I was sure I'd knocked the guard rails off both sides of it.

Landon leaned out the window, craning his head as far as he could to see what kind of damage I was causing.

"Well? Did we make it okay?"

Landon pulled himself back into the cab and grinned. "Nope. Guard rails on both sides are history."

I couldn't help swearing. "No one could get straight over that bridge with the bend in the road and driving this big old Walter with that stupid trailer on the back!"

Landon just laughed and puffed on his pipe some more.

We finally finished the long, careful drive down off Cedar Mountain and turned out west to Cedar City before turning off on the Pinto Road to cut over to Veyo. Landon wanted to stop in Cedar City, though, since some of the boys coming down off Cedar Mountain in other CCC trucks would probably still be there loading up some supplies. Landon and a couple of the guys who'd been there waiting for us wanted to grab something to drink, but I didn't, because I had to drive the Walter. After knocking off one set of guard rails, I figured I better stay sober for the rest of the ride, so I waited in the truck for Landon to come back. Some of the CCC trucks lined up near my truck were overheated and boiling over. They'd gotten way too hot coming down off the mountain. I sat and watched some of the guys climb under the hoods of as many trucks as they could to dump water on the radiators until the water supply everyone else had brought down Cedar Mountain on their trucks had run out.

By the time Landon made it back to the truck, he was pretty lit up with whatever he'd been drinking. He and Kurt Harris, a big, eighteen-year-old funny guy from Pleasant Grove, came stumbling up to the cab of the truck by me, each of them with an arm around the other.

"Hey, Addison!"

"Hey yourself, Kurt."

"My truck won't run!"

"What do you mean, your truck won't run?"

Kurt grinned up at me, trying to hold himself and Landon up. "I need some water for the radiator."

"We don't have any more water."

Kurt laughed. "My truck—she don't register at all on the temp gauge, but she dang sure gets hot!"

Both Landon and Kurt burst out laughing, but I didn't, because I knew that meant I'd be responsible for both of them now.

I normally carried water on my truck, but I hadn't this time around. Since Kurt's truck had overheated and was all boiled over and wasn't about to start for love or money, the three of us had no choice but to hook his truck onto the back of the trailer on my truck. I knew the Walter could handle the extra baggage, but it'd been slow going already with my truck carrying a heavy load and having to haul a loaded trailer besides, and now with Kurt's truck in tow, I had to grit my teeth to make myself not think about how much slower we'd be going now. It was even more painful to have Landon and Kurt in the cab of the truck with me, half drunk and singing all kinds of songs I was sure they were making up, laughing their heads off every other line, as we got back on the road and went on over to Pine Valley.

"Pine Valley? What're we doin' there?" Landon had been waving his pipe around under my nose while he'd been singing, so I grabbed it out of his hand and chucked it onto the dashboard of the truck.

"We're supposed to unload the Cat and the grader there."

"Oh, yeah?"

"Yeah. We're going to build a dam and a reservoir there, so we need to unload the Cat and the grader and then get the trailer back over to Veyo. Not that either of you is going to be any use to me getting this equipment unloaded," I grumbled.

Landon raised his eyebrows and exchanged looks with Kurt, who burst out laughing. I could only grind my teeth and mutter under my breath about what I'd like to do to both of them for getting liquored up.

We finally got over to Pine Valley, and before I could finish grinding the Walter to a stop, Landon and Kurt shoved open the passenger door and jumped out. Somehow the two of them got Kurt's truck unhooked and out of the way before I could get out of the Walter, and a second later, they had the trailer unhooked from the back of the Walter. I hurried behind the trailer to help pull the grader off, and before the three of us were finished doing that, Landon leaped into the back of the Walter truck and into his seat on the Cat and jumped it out the back of the Walter. It was a miracle none of us broke or wrecked anything.

We got the empty trailer hooked back onto the Walter in nothing flat, and minutes later, we were back in the cab and heading out of Pine Valley down through Central and over to Veyo. We just went a-flying down through the hills, making it over to the camp in record time. With all of the equipment off the truck and the trailer, and only having an empty trailer behind me, I could finally reach a decent speed. Landon and Kurt went back to their singing, and I realized that most likely if Landon hadn't had anything to drink, he wouldn't have gotten anything unloaded. He would've been too careful and taken his time, especially unloading the Cat he drove, and we would've been in Pine Valley half the night. But since both he and Kurt were feeling pretty good, he unloaded all the equipment like Superman.

By the time we got to Veyo it was late anyway, and I was tired. Luckily, the CCC camp was set up right next to the town, only a mile or so from the main street, which was a nice change after being way up on Cedar Mountain, far from Cedar City. Landon and Kurt had finally passed out in the truck, but once I unloaded the truck, I poked and prodded them awake enough that I was able to half drag them into the barracks and dump them each onto a cot before flopping on a cot of my own.

Morning came all too early, and the next thing I knew, I was being poked in the ribs by a guy I hadn't ever seen before.

"You Addison?"

I was only half awake, so I didn't get a good look at the guy except to see he was on the tall side like me with light brown hair and a huge grin.

"Who wants to know?"

"Well, the superintendent outside the barracks, for starters."

The guy said his r's funny, and almost didn't say them at all, so I knew he was one of the new East Coast guys. I didn't think about that too much, though, because all I could really concentrate on was the sick feeling in my stomach that having a superintendent outside waiting on me wasn't good.

I got myself into a sitting position and grabbed my pants. "The Supe wants to talk to me? What about?"

The guy just grinned even bigger. "Not just you. You and Landon and Kurt over there," he said, poking at Kurt with his foot. Then he laughed and strolled out of the barracks.

I roused Landon and Kurt out of bed and got us in line outside in time for reveille, ready to report for work. The Supe—a big guy with a mean look on his face—marched right over to the three of us lined up together with the new East Coast guy standing next to me. After glaring at the three of us with his hands clenched behind his back for a good thirty seconds while everyone in camp stood stock still in line, he opened his mouth big and wide and loudly jumped all over us in front of the whole camp. All kinds of stuff about what irresponsible, brainless, useless, sorry excuses we were. Disgraces to the camp and to the CCC in general.

"I expected a lot better from all three of you!"

I don't know how I dared to do it, but I guess I started to get angry myself, since I couldn't have been more confused at the Scotch blessing we were getting in front of everyone. I sneaked a look at Landon and Kurt and saw the same open-mouthed daze and confusion I was feeling, so when the Supe finally stopped to take a breath, I took my chance.

"Excuse me, sir, but what exactly did we do wrong?"

The Supe just stared bug-eyed at all three of us before he got right in my face and yelled, "You knocked all the guard rails off of every single bridge from Pine Valley to Veyo!"

I was stunned. So was Kurt and Landon. I could hear the East Coast guy snort, trying to hold in laughter. The Supe yelled some more, and I soon figured out what had happened. There were lots of little bridges with wooden guard rails on either side that we had to cross to get over to Veyo, and since it was dark and the truck was light and the trailer was empty and I'd wanted to get back to camp as soon as possible, I'd driven fast. Too fast, obviously. It wasn't the Walter that took out all the guard rails. It'd been that danged empty trailer bouncing from side to side as we barreled over the bumpy old washboard roads on the bridges. I couldn't believe I hadn't noticed, but since the roads were pretty straight, I figured I'd cleared them just fine. But I was wrong. I really *had* knocked the guard rails off every bridge coming back to camp! So all I could do was stand there and get a belly full of heck for that from the Supe.

The East Coast guy thought the whole thing was pretty funny. I thought for sure we'd all get put on guard rail repair detail, but they needed Landon on the Cat and me in the Walter to help out building the dam and reservoir in Pine Valley. We were sent over with a crew to Pine Valley where I ran the Walter, four-wheel-drive hauling the dirt for building the dam.

Once the Supe finished chewing us out up one side and down the other, the three of us jumped into the Walter, followed by the East Coast guy.

"Bud. Bud Olsen," he said when I asked his name.

"You're not from around here," Landon said while he packed his pipe for a smoke.

Bud grinned. "Nope, I'm not. But I like it here. It's not bad. Not bad at all."

The site for the dam and reservoir was pretty. Lots of Ponderosa pine trees everywhere, and a nice stream running down the mountain. The town of Pine Valley itself was pretty, all snug up against the mountains and trees, so it figured that farther up into the mountains, we'd find the perfect spot for building a reservoir and some nice campgrounds.

A bunch of the guys dug a pit down on the side of the mountain, and those of us driving trucks would back up near the pit. Landon on the Cat would push dirt into our dump trucks, and we'd haul out loads of dirt and spread it all out on the dam. A guy on another Cat would use the roller on his Cat and go back and forth, spreading out the dirt and packing it down so we could get that dam built.

The following Friday, the four of us had spent all day working on the dam up in Pine Valley, as usual. Landon was running the Cat, and while he was pushing a load of dirt into the back of my dump truck late in the afternoon, we both heard the sound at the same time—like he'd smacked hard into a boulder. I jumped out of the Walter, and Landon, clenching his pipe between his teeth, jumped down off the Cat, landing beside me to look over what I'd already seen.

"You knocked the radiator into the fan."

Landon shook his head and swore. "Looks like both the fan *and* the radiator are ruined."

The last thing we needed was to have the ol' Supe screaming at us again, so once he'd hustled over to see what the matter was, before he could say anything, I hurried and told him I remembered that there was a fleet tractor all tore down and waiting for parts in the garage shop in Cedar City.

"I know Al, the mechanic in Cedar City. Since that tractor in his shop is waiting for parts anyway, I bet he wouldn't mind putting its radiator and fan on the Cat and order a new radiator and fan for the tractor in his shop."

"You sure he'd do that?"

I nodded fast. "I'd bet anything he would, sir."

The Supe looked me over carefully and then reached into his pocket and tossed me a set of keys.

"Take my pickup."

I couldn't believe it. The Supe had one of the new Dodge pickups. I was shocked he dared to trust me with it after the guard rail disaster, but I'd learned my lesson from that experience and had been a much more careful driver ever since.

"Go into town and get that radiator and fan and bring it back here. We'll get it put on the Cat in the morning."

Before he could change his mind, I said okay and jumped into his fancy pickup truck. Before I could start the truck up, though, Kurt was banging on the window of the cab. A bunch of the guys, including Landon and Bud, were standing by him. I rolled down the window, and Kurt stuck his head in and leaned both arms across the inside of the door.

"You're going to town, huh?"

I frowned at them all. "Well, yeah."

Kurt grinned and shoved a wad of bills in my hand. "We passed around a hat. Get us a few bottles of whisky while you're in Cedar City."

I stuffed the bills in my pocket, and since the afternoon was almost over and dark clouds were settling in, I rolled the window up tight and tore up the road for Cedar City. It rained hard all down Pinto Canyon, and I about went off the road at one point. The wheels slipped all over the slick, wet roads, nearly sending me off into the bank at the side of the road. I thought I was done for then, but I got back on the road and made it on into Cedar City and over to Al DeBrisky's garage in one piece. He took the radiator and fan out of the fleet tractor and even gave me a few other parts he thought we might need. It was raining pretty good and hard by then, and I wasn't too excited about driving back to Veyo on all of those slick, muddy roads just yet.

"So, Addison. It's officially the weekend now. Got big plans for tonight?"

"Nah, not really. The guys—well, they asked me to pick up some hooch, so I guess that'll be the entertainment for tonight." I showed Al the wad of cash the guys had given me and grinned.

Al grinned back. "If you let me have one of those drinks, I'll pick you up some good stuff from the liquor store. Unless you really just want a lot of cheap beer?"

I wasn't about to make him ask me twice, so Al went out and bought some good whisky for me and the guys. The rain was slowing up by then, but even so, after I got the truck gassed up, I decided to go around by St. George so I could use the oiled road to get back to Veyo. It was just starting to get dark, about six or seven o'clock, when I finally got to St. George. The bag of whisky on the seat beside me started to call my name, and before much time had passed, I pulled a bottle out of the bag and started nipping on it a little bit. Not the smartest thing to be doing, but I was alone on the road, and the rain had stopped, so I figured I'd be okay.

TWENTY-NINE

Drinking and driving? Not the smartest thing to be doing, Grandpa Harold."

Kyle. My back stiffened funny at his familiar voice behind me while my heart skipped. I quickly turned around to see him lounging just inside the door, leaned up against the wall, grinning his elf grin and holding a paper sack in his hand.

Grandpa was beaming all over the place. "Well, Kyle, come on over here!"

Kyle smiled and walked over to us before tossing the sack into my lap. "From Anna. There's your sandwich."

I peeked inside the bag. Turkey with cheese on wheat bread. "Where is she?"

"She's outside talking to one of the nurses." Kyle slid easily into one of the chairs by Grandpa's bed. "So how are you, Grandpa Harold?"

"Oh, I'm doing all right. James and Anna are taking good care of me."

I chewed a bite of sandwich. "The doctor's helping out a little, too."

Kyle grinned. "And the nurses, I guess?"

I grinned back. "Yeah, they come in once in a while, I guess."

Kyle laughed before turning back to Grandpa. "Any more pain in your chest, Grandpa Harold?"

"Nah, not too bad. I think my doctor must be saving for a sports car.

That's the only reason I can think of as to why he's keeping me here longer."

Kyle laughed again. "As long as being here for a while will help get you back on your feet, that's all that matters."

"I really am feeling better. I can't do too much yet, though. I think it was a diaphragmatic problem that I had, or something like that, more than a heart attack, because after the doctor checked my heart, he said he couldn't see much wrong with it."

"Well, that's good news. Definitely good news. Right, James?"

I smiled and swallowed another bite of my sandwich while I wiped the back of my hand across my mouth. "The best news ever!"

Kyle laughed and reached inside the sack to hand me a napkin. "Well, you were right in the middle of your story when I barged in. So did you make it back to Veyo in one piece or what?"

Grandpa laughed. "Well, hand me back that tape recorder and I'll tell you!"

THIRTY

Once I made it to Veyo, I could see a string of cars and trucks headed in the same direction off the main road onto a side road that led down a shallow gully to Veyo's open-air dance hall. I parked the Supe's truck at the CCC camp, and as I staggered into the barracks, I realized the stuff Al had bought was a lot more potent than I'd thought. The room swayed, but when I got inside, the guys grabbed the bag out of my hands and cheered when they looked inside. They cheered even more once they'd broken open a few of the bottles and had a taste.

Landon laughed but grabbed me before I fell in a heap. "You better pull yourself together, Addison, or you'll never make it to the dance."

"Dance?" I mumbled.

"Yeah—we're all going, so get ready."

The stuff had gotten to me so bad there was no way I could shave myself or shower—I was that lit up—so Landon grabbed one of my arms, and Bud the other, and together they took me over and shaved my face and helped me shower. Bud would take a swig out of my bottle of whisky, then Landon would, and soon I was taking my turn drinking, too.

By the time all of us CCC boys got in our trucks and drove down into the gully to the open-air dance hall, all surrounded by trees and mountains, I was feeling pretty happy. A little too happy. The dance was in full swing when we got there, with a real nice, live band with a piano, drums, and guitar. And lots of people were dancing. I had a great time, dancing with a lot of girls and sneaking out to the truck now and again for some of that A-1 whisky good ol' Al picked up for us. I really got plastered that night.

I'd just come back from taking a swig at the truck when I heard someone yell, "Shoe Dance! Boy's choice! Come on! All you girls throw a shoe into the center of the floor!"

I was sure I'd heard something wrong, but a second later, all of the women were running to the middle of the cement floor to toss in one of their shoes. Once the girls had all run back to the edges of the floor, giggling and laughing, a few of the older guys got into the middle of the floor and mixed up all the shoes together in one big pile.

I walked over to where Landon and Bud were standing and tugged on Landon's arm. "What the heck is going on?"

Landon shrugged my arm off. "Don't bug me—I'm keeping my eye on a shoe!"

Bud laughed. "Haven't you seen a Shoe Dance before?"

I shook my head. "Never."

Before Bud could explain, the guy who'd yelled for the girls to throw in a shoe yelled, "Okay, boys. Come get a shoe, go find the owner, and you'll have your next dance partner!"

Before I knew it, I was part of a big, pushing mob of guys racing for the shoes. I reached into the pile, too, and almost got hit in the eye with a shoe that went sailing by my head. It was a big, ugly, brown loafer, so I shoved it back into the pile. And then, right by my hand, I saw a small, dainty black shoe with a high heel. The shoe was shiny but not new. Looked like it had been polished over and over, but it had been kept in good shape. Reminded me a little of what I'd expect Cinderella's shoe to look like except it wasn't made of glass, so I grabbed it before anyone else could and made my way around the edges of the dance floor with the other guys, looking at the girls' feet, trying to find a shoe like it, asking, "Is this your shoe?"

About halfway around the floor, I finally saw a foot wearing a shoe just like the one I was holding, and when I looked up and said, "I'll bet this is your shoe!" I couldn't stop staring at the girl sitting in front of me.

I was buzzing from the whisky. I knew I was, but at the same time, I felt my heart jump, like it did when I was asked on the spot to do something that was going to be nerve wracking. The girl was pretty. Really pretty. To me, anyway, although by the way other CCC guys and old Kurt in particular looked at her that night, I knew they thought she was pretty, too. She had wavy, bombshell-blonde hair that just hit her shoulders. And she had a slow smile and big, light blue eyes that sparkled in a way that made me want to not only ask her to dance but get to know this girl. Somehow, I knew I had to get to know this girl.

The girl nodded, still wearing that smile. "Yes, that's my shoe."

She held out one tiny, bare foot at me, and as I slipped the shoe onto her foot, I definitely felt like I'd stepped into that Cinderella story. A second later, the girl stood up and straightened her skirt. Even with her high heels on, she wasn't very big. Hardly reached my shoulder.

"Would you like to dance?"

The girl smiled again and nodded. I was about to lead her back onto the cement floor of the dance hall when Bud and Landon hurried up to me.

"Addison—hey, Addison! Wait up!"

Bud had a tall, pretty girl with red curls grinning next to him, and standing with Landon was a short, dishy brunette with dark eyes who was looking at me as if she thought I stank.

"Marshall—the school teacher here—he's from Enterprise. That's not too far from here," Bud said. "He and his friends brought a few pickup loads of girls from Enterprise for the dance."

"Oh, yeah?" I said, trying to shake the buzz out of my head. I couldn't be sure anymore if the buzz was from the booze or from the pretty girl I was about to dance with.

"Oh, yeah," Landon grinned. "They're easy to pick out. They're the pretty ones here." That at least brought a smile to the brunette's face. "Addison, this here is Vivian. From Enterprise. I met her earlier tonight, and lucky me, I found her shoe for the Shoe Dance!"

Bud burst out laughing. "Landon was bent on finding that shoe. He would've punched out any guy who tried to touch it before he could grab it!"

Bud introduced me to Faye, the redhead, who happened to be friends with Vivian.

Landon was grinning at the girl by me. "And who is this?"

"Well, this is—" And then it hit me I had no idea what the girl's name was, but before I had to ask, she stepped up and whispered into my ear.

"Lilly. I'm Lilly."

Lilly. I liked her name. I liked it a lot. "And I'm Addison."

Lilly smiled that slow smile of hers back at me. "Addison."

I turned back to Bud and Landon and said, "This is Lilly," before turning to Lilly again. "And this is Bud and Landon, my CCC pals, and this is Faye and Vivian." I thought I'd got the girls' names right. In fact, I was sure I had, but I knew I must've messed up somehow, because all three girls burst out laughing. But even Bud and Landon looked confused, so we all waited until they could stop laughing and talk normal again. Faye was the first to get herself under control.

"I would hope that Lilly and Vivian already know each other. They're sisters!"

That made us guys laugh, but what I really wanted to do was dance with Lilly, so I asked her again.

Lilly nodded, so we headed back onto the dance floor, all six of us, and danced a couple times out there on the cement floor. Lilly was wearing this light purple, shiny dress that fanned out a little whenever I twirled her around.

"It's not purple. It's lavender. I made it myself." Lilly informed me of that when I tried to tell her I liked her dress.

I didn't know anything about ladies' fashions, but looking around the dance floor, I could tell she was easily wearing the prettiest dress of all. As great as twirling her around in that dress was, it was a lot more fun to waltz with her. Made conversation a lot easier, so I was happy to hear the band slowing down and even happier when she agreed to dance with me again.

"So, Mr. Addison—I heard you have a church in your CCC camp. Is that true?"

"A church? Well, sort of. I mean, there's meetings on Sunday in the mess hall for those who want to go."

"Do you?" Lilly looked me straight and serious in the eyes when she said that.

"Do I what?"

Lilly sighed. "Go to church, of course."

"Well, you know, I've been meaning to. I'm guessing you never miss, huh?"

Lilly smiled her slow smile. "Not often."

I coughed nervously. "And I'd bet you're probably Mormon?"

"Does that really surprise you?"

I grinned. "I guess it shouldn't, since we're in Utah."

"And what about you?"

I grinned. "Actually, I'm Mormon, too."

"Really!"

"I'm from Utah, too. I didn't think any other religion was allowed in this state."

I was surprised when she laughed, but she did. I would've danced the rest of the night with her, but all of that liquor I'd been drinking was catching up with me, and my stomach started to roll. Too much liquor, too much dancing, and too much of a jumpy stomach dancing with a cute girl I was feeling happily nervous around because I wanted to get to know her so much added up to me feeling sick. Really sick. Luckily, the song was dying out anyway, so I wouldn't have to run off the floor and embarrass Lilly. And me.

"Let's sit this one out, okay?"

Lilly nodded, and we went over to the edge of the floor to sit on some old metal folding chairs. My head was really spinning. Almost as fast as my stomach.

"Are you okay?"

I didn't get a chance to answer, because Bud's redhead had slid into the chair by me, giggling at Bud, who sat down next to her, while Lilly's sister and Landon sat down on the other side of Lilly. I was wishing everyone wouldn't have bunched up so close to Lilly and me, since I was feeling all sweaty and hot, because a second later, my stomach did a dance of its own. I turned away from Lilly and faced Bud's redhead, and the next thing I knew, I put everything that had been in it right in her lap. She screamed, Lilly and her sister screamed and jumped up and away from me—and Bud and Landon hollered "whoa!" and jumped away, too. As for me, I stood up and stumbled right straight off the dance floor and headed for the outdoor privies.

I'd seen a little wooden building hiding in the trees near the dance floor when I'd first arrived and had made a mental note of it, so I hardly had to look as I staggered off in its general direction. I never even stopped to look to see whether it was the men's or the women's privy. All I knew was that I needed to calm my stomach down before facing anyone again and give myself a second to stop being sick.

The privy had six holes in it with no stall dividers between the holes, and since it was nearly pitch black in there, I felt my way over to the side and sat on the one farthest away from the door. My hands were shaking, but since my stomach wasn't rolling anymore, I lit a cigarette. I didn't care to think about the fact that I was supposed to have quit the weed. I needed one too badly just then.

I could hear noise outside—girls giggling, mostly. The privy door opened, and the giggling got louder. I about died when two girls came in and sat down on the holes near the privy door and started talking. I thought if I stayed real quiet they wouldn't notice me, and I'd sneak out after they left, but no such luck.

"Hey—do you smell something burning?"

I froze when I heard that, because it sounded suspiciously familiar. Too familiar. Vivian familiar—

"Smells like—a cigarette!"

The second voice made my mouth drop open enough that I nearly lost my cigarette. It couldn't be Lilly—it just couldn't—

"It *is* a cigarette!"

Stupid me—I'd kept smoking, and in that pitch black dark, they could see the glow of my cigarette. Both girls let out a yell and jumped off the seats, screaming, "There's a man in here!" Boy, they left in a hurry. I felt kind of funny, too, because I'd gotten myself into the wrong cranny. But even worse was knowing who I'd just scared off. I stayed to finish my cigarette and figured no big deal—no one would know anything about it. Least of all, Lilly and Vivian wouldn't have known it was me. But as soon as I got some fresh air into my lungs and walked back onto the dance floor, I could see Kurt standing by Lilly, and Landon and Vivian, and all the rest of the CCC guys. Except for Bud and the poor girl he'd met at the dance who was now wearing my whisky. They were nowhere to be seen. The second the CCC guys turned and saw me, they all started to laugh and clap.

"What, can't you read?"

"You got in the wrong cranny, huh?"

All of the guys—especially Kurt—had a great time making fun of me in front of the girls. Lilly, in particular. I learned a lesson that night never to step into a privy again without looking for a sign on the door first. Lilly looked pretty horrified and wouldn't meet my eyes, but Vivian had no trouble looking me straight in the eye. She definitely had her "you *really* stink" look on her face for me again. I must not have looked happy at all, because Landon stepped forward and threw his arm around my shoulders.

"Don't be mad. The girls couldn't help telling on you!"

I was even more embarrassed now, thinking of both Lilly and her sister in that privy with me, but at the same time, it was pretty funny, so I went ahead and laughed along with everyone else and made a few jokes of my own. And after a minute of that, I walked right straight off the dance floor and passed out cold on the grass. That whisky was definitely too good for me.

When I finally came to, I was in for a surprise. The dance was over, and when I pried my eyes open, I found myself in the back of the CCC truck I'd come in—with Lilly sitting on my lap! I jumped and about knocked her to the floor of the truck.

"What the—what are you—" I could hardly get my mouth to work right, it tasted so nasty and full of cotton. I would've given my last dollar for a drink of water, since besides the fact that my mouth tasted awful, I was thirstier than I could stand.

Lilly looked down at me before turning her face away, sticking her nose in the air really high to say all matter-of-factly, "I needed somewhere to sit where it would be comfortable and warm. It's cold outside, you know. And I didn't want to get my dress dirty. It's new." And then she carefully smoothed out her skirt as if it was perfectly normal for her to be sitting on the lap of a guy passed out from drink in the back of a truck. "Besides—that large friend of yours is incredibly persistent. I needed a break from his undying attention."

"You're hiding from Kurt?" I said stupidly.

A second later, Landon poked his head into the back of the truck. "You okay, Addison?" He took one look at Lilly on my lap and grinned. "Yeah, I guess you're fine. Hey, the girls need a ride home. Vivian's going to sit up front with me, okay?"

There were other CCC guys passed out in the back of the truck, too. A few of Lilly's friends giggled when they saw her on my lap, and thinking that looked like a good idea, they sat on the other guys passed out in the truck. Lilly and I didn't say anything to each other the whole drive from Veyo to Enterprise. I was still too much of a mess from the whisky, and she didn't seem too pleased with me. She hardly even looked at me the whole way. The second we pulled up in front of her home, she jumped off my lap, hopped out of the back of the truck, and left me without even a wave good-bye. I didn't know what to make of that as I watched her run into the house, but I was still too sick to care. I could see Landon talking by the cab of the truck with Vivian, but I fell back into a stupor and didn't wake up again until morning.

THIRTY-ONE

For most of the day on Saturday, I felt like I'd been hit by a truck. Somehow I got through work, mostly by reminding myself that we only had to work until noon. I dodged Bud the whole time, because I was sure he had it in for me for ruining his chances with the redhead.

Once we got back to the barracks at noon, there was no hiding from Bud. He came right up to me and lunged for me. I jumped back a little and got my fists up, and ol' Bud—he looked all surprised and burst out laughing.

"Addison, what's the deal with you? Here I am, trying to thank you, and here you are, ready to punch me."

"Thank me? For what?"

Bud couldn't stop grinning. "If it wasn't for you, Faye wouldn't even remember my name, but as it is, I'm takin' her out tonight!"

"A date?" I couldn't believe it, but it was true. The redhead—Faye—hadn't been all that interested in Bud at first, but he'd helped her clean her dress up, gave her his coat to wear, walked her back to her place to get changed, and then the two of them had spent the rest of the evening talking on her front porch. She was pretty impressed at how he'd stepped right up and taken care of her after that ugly moment of mine I'd shared with her at the dance.

"The best part of it is since she's not too crazy about you, I don't have to worry about you stealin' her away from me!"

Landon went to Enterprise that night with Bud to see Vivian, since he'd finagled an evening with her. He tried to get me to come along, but I was sure Lilly never wanted to see me again. Even so, when I found out on Monday that the next CCC project was to build a new ranger station in Enterprise, complete with a home for the ranger, a barn, and a shop, while another crew would keep working on the reservoir in Pine Valley, I made sure I was first in line to be part of the new project.

All that week, I hauled supplies for the ranger station. It was hard not to think about Lilly, because nearly every afternoon that week when I drove my truck over to the ranger station site, she always just happened to be taking a walk around the area, usually with her sister or Bud's girl, although sometimes she was with a couple of other girls with light brown hair who looked a little like her, so I figured they could be sisters of hers, too. She'd casually loiter near the site, and sometimes I could swear she was looking straight at me, but she'd never say hello.

I gave up trying not to think about her, so when Friday came, the second I'd pulled up to the site with my load of lumber, I jumped out of my truck and walked right up to her and asked her if she was planning on going to the dance in town that night. She said she was, so right in front of Vivian, who still looked at me as if I smelt funny, and the two other girls who had to be sisters, too, I got brave and asked her if I could escort her to the dance. She smiled and said, "Of course." I couldn't believe I was having such good luck. I whistled and sang and didn't feel a bump in the road all the way back to Veyo and the CCC camp.

Since I was one of the drivers, I was able to swipe a pickup truck, so while Landon and Bud had a truckload of CCC boys in one of the big Walter trucks, I had a nice little pickup truck to myself.

Enterprise had a nice, open-air cement dance floor with a low fence around it built right by the high school. It looked more like a tennis court than a dance hall, but it didn't have a net, so I figured tennis wasn't played there very often. It looked like the whole town was at the dance, including all the kids and older people. And the dance band was impressive. The band was up on a platform on one end of the dance floor, and there was a piano, drums, banjo, trumpet, and trombone—even a violin and saxophone! And the players were really good.

I was nervous—way too nervous—to be with Lilly again, so I'd stuck a bottle of some cheap whisky behind the driver's seat. I didn't have any of it on the way to pick up Lilly, but once I'd jumped out of the pickup, old Kurt Harris showed up with Landon and Bud and the rest of the guys in the big CCC truck. Kurt made a beeline for Lilly, and once I finally got a chance to ask her to dance, he couldn't stop cutting in. She introduced me to the two girls with light brown hair who, as I'd guessed, were sisters of hers, and she told me to ask them to dance, too, so I did. I couldn't tell if Lilly really minded my asking them or not. She definitely didn't seem to mind that I had to compete for her attention all night, since other CCC boys and local boys, too, couldn't stop hanging around her. All I could do about it was stomp out to my truck for that bottle behind the seat whenever someone else asked her to dance and she said yes. And sometimes I reached for a cigarette. By the time the dance was over, I had a nice, decent buzz going on. I actually felt happy, and that made me loud. A little too loud, because Lilly didn't seem to be enjoying my company anymore. I knew I'd had too much to drink, so once the dance was over, I asked Landon if he wanted to drive the pickup home with me, but he'd had too much to drink himself and had fallen out of favor with Vivian. Bud still had Faye thinking he was something special, though, so he agreed to drive the pickup with me while Landon and the rest of the guys passed out in the back of the Walter.

When we pulled up in front of Lilly's home, I got out of the truck to hold the door open, but Lilly jumped out in a flash and shoved around me and walked with fast, angry steps up the path to the front door. I had to jog to catch up to her and only did that when she reached the front door. She had her hand out, ready to grab the doorknob, but I jumped ahead of her and stood in her way. I was all ready to try joking her out of her bad mood, and if that didn't work, I was planning on going straight to apologizing for drinking and smoking and whatever else I'd done. But I didn't get a chance to do either, because Lilly stepped back and stuck her hand out as if we were concluding a business deal. I stared at her hand for a second before slowly taking a hold of it. She gripped my hand hard and gave it a firm shake before sticking her nose up in the air like she'd done before.

"Thank you for yet another interesting evening, Mr. Addison. However, unless you give up your smoking and drinking, please don't come calling for me again."

With that, she pulled her hand away and shoved past me to open the front door and close it nice and firm behind her.

I stood there dumbfounded until Bud hollered at me to hurry up. I waited until we'd dropped Faye off to tell Bud what happened. On the one hand, I had to admit I was pretty surprised a good Mormon girl like her would go anywhere with me, but at the same time, it was annoying to have some little chit tell me I had to give up a few things or never see her again.

"All I know is that for a girl like her to give a guy like you a chance, she must see something in you. You'd be a fool to throw that away."

Maybe Bud was right, but it still rubbed me wrong, having her tell me she wouldn't go with a guy who drank and smoked. Especially since I'd already quit the smoking. Basically. While we were up on Cedar Mountain at the CCC camp, I'd been smoking a lot. Thought I was big and tough and smart, although I didn't smoke a pipe like Landon or roll cigarettes like he did, either. When Landon wasn't smoking his pipe, he was a Bull Durham smoker. I had to smoke Tailor Mades—ready-made cigarettes. But I knew smoking wasn't helping me breathe real well up in the mountains, trying to get a lot of physical work done, so I'd quit the weed. Basically. Oh, I'd had a few since I'd met Lilly, but the girl made me so nervous it was almost her fault that I'd picked up the habit again. Almost.

When we got back to the barracks in camp, Kurt was hollering it up, yelling all these crazy rhymes, giving Landon a bad time about something. He was drunk—that much was clear. And he was loving getting under Landon's skin. I couldn't figure out why Landon had such a black scowl on his face until one of the other guys filled me in.

"He got rejected by a high school cheerleader!"

"Vivian's a cheerleader?" I had to throw a pillow at Landon's face for that. "What are doing, chasing a high school girl?"

Landon glared at me and threw the pillow right back at me. "You forget I'm not an old man like you. Me and Bud are seventeen—it's perfectly normal for us to like girls our own age! And Faye's a cheerleader, too, so why isn't everyone bugging *him* about liking a cheerleader?"

I was a little taken aback, because Landon hadn't ever yelled at me like that before and because I'd forgotten he and Bud were practically babies. Both Lilly and I were twenty-one, and yet we were still pretty young ourselves.

I didn't get a chance to say something back, because Kurt plopped himself down on Landon's bunk right by him. "Aw, don't get all sore, Landon. Just because Miss High and Mighty thinks she's too good for you doesn't mean the rest of us think that, too! Besides—who wants a prissy little Mormon girl when there's plenty of real women around?"

Boy, Kurt couldn't keep the liquor flowing fast enough that night, and poor Landon was right there with him, drowning his sorrows over Vivian. I didn't know where it would all lead until the next night— Saturday night—when Landon and Kurt disappeared without a word to anyone. Landon woke me up well past midnight by accident, stumbling around and falling all over me in the dark trying to find his bunk. I was ready to lean all over him for that, but the poor guy was so depressed I decided to listen to him babble instead. Both he and Kurt had gone back to Enterprise that night to try and teach Vivian a lesson. And Lilly, too, since she'd have none of Kurt. They'd driven into town in one of the pickups and then parked at the church house around the corner from Lilly and Vivian's house while they drank some cheap whisky Kurt had bought. Well, eventually Kurt got drunk, and soon Landon was, too, so to play a prank on the girls, Kurt got Landon up on his shoulders, and the two romped down the street in the dark. Once they got to Lilly and Vivian's house, Landon would reach over and hook onto a picket of their white picket fence and pull it right out of the ground.

"You guys did what??"

Landon only groaned and said he couldn't believe what they'd done and wished he was dead. I was wishing the same thing, too.

"Why in heck would you do something that stupid just because a girl changed her mind about you?"

Landon shook his head at me. "It wasn't just that. Vivian told me last night that her school-teaching brother, Marshall, told her and her sisters they shouldn't be associating with us wild CCC guys. That his sisters can all do better. So you know if that's what their brother thinks, then her parents probably think the same thing."

"And you think trying to get back at her brother is going to make any of them change their minds?"

Landon groaned again and held his head in his hand. "I don't know. It seemed like a great idea at the time."

"Whose idea was it, anyway?"

Landon shrugged miserably. "Don't remember. Kurt's, I guess."

Of course it was. I ran my hand through my hair. "Yeah, I thought so."

The only thing I could think of to try and fix everything, even though it was now officially Sunday, was to hightail it for Enterprise and get working on fixing that fence as soon as possible. Poor Landon—he got next to no sleep at all. We pulled into Enterprise an hour later and got to work running up and down the street, gathering up all of those pickets and trying to hammer them back into place without waking anyone up, but of course that was impossible to do. Lilly's brother—he must've been staying over for the weekend, because he came outside after the first knock of the hammer and stood there on the front porch with his arms folded, scowling at us, before he finally ventured over to take a look at our fix-it job.

"I hope you don't expect to get paid, since we already know you two were the ones who damaged our fence anyway."

Landon froze, and I could tell he was pretty sore thinking Marshall thought we were fixing the fence for money.

"Don't try to deny it. Vivian, Rachel, and Beth saw you both from the upstairs window. You woke up half the neighborhood, drunken fools that you are!"

Marshall railed on us some more, telling us what bums we were. I could see Lilly and Vivian and the two other sisters watching us from the main window of the house. Landon was an inch away from punching Marshall in the mouth, but I kept myself between the two of them. So instead, Landon tried to tell Marshall I had nothing to do with the fence, but I shut him up.

"We're sorry about your fence. It won't happen again."

Marshall only said "Huh!" and finally stomped back into the house. I kept my back to the house, working fast with my hammer and nails while Landon moved farther down the fence. I'd just finished with my half of the fence and yanked my handkerchief out of my pocket to mop my face when I saw something that made me just stand and stare. I hadn't heard the front door open, but there was Vivian standing on her side of the fence, leaning over it to hand Landon a big ol' glass of lemonade with a smile. He was saying something to make her laugh, and for some reason, the whole thing made me feel sad and jealous and mad all at the same time, even though I was glad Landon was patching things up with Vivian. I didn't see Lilly anywhere in sight, so since I was finished anyway, I stomped back to the truck and yelled for Landon to hustle it up, because we needed to get back to camp.

THIRTY-TWO

As soon as the seven days were up, I couldn't wait to bring Grandpa home. Anna and I drove in together to pick him up, but when we made it up the four floors to his room, we could hear voices coming through the slightly opened door. Dad's voice. And Grandpa's.

Anna gave my arm a small tug before I could barge into the room. "Let's give them a few more minutes, okay, James?" I looked at Anna for a moment before silently nodding. "I'm going to get a soda from the snack bar. Would you like one, too?"

"Nah, I'll just wait here in the hall."

As soon as Anna had disappeared around the corner, I carefully pushed the door open a little, just enough so I could see them both, and shamefully listened in on Grandpa and Dad's conversation.

" . . . oh, James has been here a lot. Don't know what I would do without her, Ben."

"If she's getting in the way, I'll take her home. You just let me know, Dad."

"She's not in the way at all. She's been a great help and comfort to Anna. I appreciate you letting her stay with me all summer."

"As long as she's not causing any trouble—"

"Oh, no. Not at all." Grandpa chuckled. "She caught Anna snuggling with me in the hospital bed the other day. I thought by the look on her face that she was going to get all upset, but she just laughed and got Anna's camera out of her purse and took some pictures of us together, wires and tubes coming out of me and all. I think she got quite a kick out of us."

Dad's voice sounded funny, like he didn't believe Grandpa. "Well, that's good."

"She even told the nurses that we're planning on getting married. The nurses wanted us to get married right here in the hospital, but Anna and I have already made a couple of arrangements with the temple to get married after the family reunion in August."

"You're still planning on trying to go to the reunion? It's only a couple of weeks away—are you sure you're up to it, Dad?"

"Oh, I'll be fine by then. Just fine. I'm feeling better already, and the doctor said that as soon as I got feeling better, we could go ahead and get married. You know that airplane money Lilly left for me?"

Dad's voice still sounded funny. "Well, yes—"

"I'm using it to surprise Anna with a honeymoon in Hawaii!"

"Dad—"

"Don't worry, Ben. We won't be going right away. The doctor told me I couldn't go and do all the things I want to do yet. I have to stick around so he can watch me for a while."

"You're still planning on getting married—in the temple?"

"Of course. A temple marriage, but just for time. That's what the bishop recommended."

Dad was silent for so long I almost decided to walk in.

"Has any of Mom's family been in to see you?"

That made me stop and listen harder. Grandpa didn't answer for a moment, and when he did, he sounded sad. So sad.

"Landon's the only one of the in-laws that's come to see me. But I don't mind."

Dad didn't say anything for a few seconds. "He called me on the phone the other day, after he'd been to see you."

"Oh, yeah? What'd he have to say?"

I could see Dad shrug, looking about as uncomfortable as I'd ever seen him look. "He was all upset and said he thought you're making a mistake, getting married. He thinks it's all happening too soon. He said you need to listen to Aunt Vivian."

Grandpa snorted. "Yeah, he said the same thing to me when I told him I'm going to marry Anna in a few weeks."

"Well, he wouldn't stop going on about it, so I—I sort of came—unglued."

"Unglued? What did you say to him?"

Dad sighed and ran a hand through his hair. "I told him—I told him, 'Dad's never had a ring in his nose. He can think for himself. If he wants to get married, I'm for him.'"

Grandpa's eyes nearly bulged out of their sockets, as I'm sure mine were nearly doing as well. "You said that—you really said that?"

Dad nodded and ran his hand through his hair again. "Yes, and I'm sorry—I shouldn't have gotten so upset."

Grandpa shook his head fast while he stared at Dad hopefully. "No, not that. The 'I'm for him' part. Do you mean it, Ben?"

Dad stepped back a little as if he'd been slapped. "Of course I do. You're my father!"

Grandpa's voice caught funny like he was trying not to cry, and while my own vision blurred a little, I watched my dad reach for Grandpa at the exact moment that Grandpa reached for him before I quietly closed the door.

THIRTY-THREE

Grandpa loved buffet-style restaurants, so I wasn't too surprised when Kyle drove into the parking lot of one near Grandpa's house. The four of us—Grandpa, Anna, Kyle, and me—were celebrating Grandpa's return home from the hospital after he'd been able to rest at home for a couple of days and was ready to tackle getting out and about again.

"More food for less money, James. And this one's got an especially good lineup of food. You'll see!"

I loved Grandpa dearly, but I would never be able to get excited over food buffets. But I could get excited over seeing him up and around again. Easily.

Grandpa poked me in the shoulder until I turned around in the front seat, where I was seated by Kyle, to look at his grinning face. "This is going to be fun. Kind of like a double date. Right, James?"

I was so horrified I couldn't look at Kyle. "It's not a date. I'm not even sixteen yet!"

"But you will be soon, James. Only a few more days to go before the big day!"

"Whatever!" Thankfully, Kyle had wheeled the car into a parking space and had just turned off the engine. I jumped out of the car, ready to run into the restaurant, but Kyle jumped out of his side of the car and grabbed me by the arm when I tried to circle around.

"Wait up, James. Don't you want to make sure your grandpa gets out of the car okay?"

I quickly shoved Kyle's hand away. "Of course I do!"

Kyle frowned at me before we both hurried over to Grandpa's passenger door. "Need some help, Grandpa Harold?"

"No, no, I'm fine. Anna's right here, so if I start to fall, I'll fall on her instead of the pavement."

Anna laughed as she held Grandpa's arm. "Oh, Harold, you're not going to fall!"

Dinner wasn't so bad, except that I hardly talked, because I couldn't get that stupid double date comment of Grandpa's out of my head. And maybe I was crazy, but Kyle seemed quieter than usual. I had to believe Grandpa's double date crack bugged him, too. I was sure the idea of going on any kind of a date with me, James, his tomboy friend who was practically a sister to him—practically a brother—was the most repulsive idea to him ever.

I kept my head down, shoveling in food without looking at anyone while Grandpa and Anna talked and laughed. Mostly about arrangements for their upcoming wedding. Kyle got involved in their conversation a little and even laughed at a couple of Grandpa's jokes, but I couldn't focus on anything.

"Come on, James. What do you think?"

I jumped and was shocked to see Kyle looking across the table at me, obviously waiting for me to say something. "Think about what?"

Kyle sighed. "Your grandpa just asked if we want to go play miniature golf. Do you?"

I could feel my face starting to flush. "Um, I guess. I mean, if you want to. Since you're driving and everything. Unless you need to get back home soon?"

I sounded stupid and I knew it. Like I was nervous to be around Kyle. He frowned and raised an eyebrow.

"I just said I wanted to go. Didn't you hear me?"

I shook my head and stirred my fork around in the food on my plate. "Sorry."

Grandpa grinned at us both before wiping his mouth and standing up. "Well, if you two are done, then I'll take care of the bill."

Kyle jumped up so fast he nearly knocked his chair over. "I've got money, too. You don't need to pay the whole bill."

Money! I didn't have a dime with me. "I—I'm sorry. I don't have any money."

"Don't worry, James. This is a double date, right? I've got you covered." Kyle grinned his elf grin and winked at me while he followed Grandpa over to the cashier. I could feel my face burning a nice, hot red. Anna smiled and winked at me, too.

I rolled my eyes and stabbed at the food on my plate with my fork again. "He's just being nice. That's all!"

Anna kept on smiling. "Sure. That's all."

Miniature golf was the perfect thing to follow up the weirdness at dinner. I needed something to whack to get my strange, jumbled-up insides to calm back down again. It didn't help that Kyle insisted on paying for his game and mine as well, grinning and loudly saying again, "We're on a double date, right?"

"Whatever!" I rolled my eyes, hoping Kyle wouldn't notice that my hands were shaking a little when I reached for the pink golf ball and putter he handed to me.

Grandpa was already halfway to the first hole. "Come on, kids—we're up next!"

I didn't do too badly, but my aim wasn't entirely on. I hit the ball too hard at first, causing it to ricochet and fly over the fence surrounding the golf park. Grandpa and Anna laughed, but Kyle leaped over the low chain link fence before I could move and handed me the golf ball. From his elf grin, I knew I'd gone beet red again.

"Try again, James. With a little less muscle this time."

I tried my best to ignore everyone after that and just focus on putting, but I didn't do too well. In fact, I lost to everyone. Even to Anna, who wasn't good at miniature golf at all.

Grandpa insisted on some soft ice cream at the snack bar after the golfing was over, so we all sat around a little table under a big red-and-white striped umbrella with our cones.

"My treat!" Grandpa insisted. He wouldn't let Kyle slide even a nickel forward to help pay.

Grandpa watched me thoughtfully while I fixed a napkin around the bottom of my cone. "So, let's see, it's about, what, four days exactly before you turn sixteen. Right, James?"

I shrugged without looking up. "I guess."

Grandpa burst out laughing. "You guess? I thought you'd be more excited about turning sixteen than that!"

I shrugged again. "It's not that big of a deal."

"Of course it's a big deal. My youngest grandchild is turning sixteen years old. Now that makes me feel old!"

Anna laughed and put her arm around Grandpa. "Oh, you're not old, Harold!"

Kyle bumped me in the shoulder, almost making me drop my ice cream. "Tell me the truth, James. Is it going to be a Sweet Sixteen birthday for you or not?"

I gave Kyle a good, hard jab in the ribs for that one and nearly made him drop his ice cream cone right in his lap. "None of your business!" He opened his mouth, ready to say something back, but I quickly cut him off with a good, black glare. "I'm going to give you the silent treatment if you bug me about this anymore, so just stop, okay?"

Everyone had a nice laugh over that, but thankfully everyone, including Kyle, left the subject alone while we finished off the last of our ice cream.

On the drive back home, I kept my eyes straight ahead, staring out the front window. Kyle tried to tease me into a better mood, but I only grunted and rolled my eyes in response and wouldn't look at him.

We were almost home when Kyle had to stop for a red light. Before Kyle could say anything, I turned around in my seat.

"Hey, Grandpa—"

That was all I could say, because at that exact moment, Grandpa was leaning in towards Anna to give her a kiss. My voice turned into a shocked, high squeak as I whipped my head back around face forward again. Kyle glanced in the rearview mirror, and by his grin, I knew he'd seen exactly what I had.

I finally managed to gasp, "Grandpa! What are you doing back there?" Kyle just laughed and whistled. A loud wolf whistle, which made both Grandpa and Anna laugh.

"I'll bet Kyle wouldn't ever dare do something like that!"

Now that made me burst out laughing, because it was nice to have someone else get teased about something embarrassing tonight besides me.

"I'll bet you're right, Grandpa—"

"Oh, yeah?"

I turned to look at Kyle, and in the next second, his face was way too close to mine. I jerked my head back and turned my face in a flash, but not before I felt Kyle's lips awkwardly brush against my cheek, missing the mark he'd shockingly tried to aim for. And would've made, if I hadn't moved a split second faster than he had. For the hundredth time that night, I could feel my face burning while Grandpa hooted it up, clapping, and Anna squealed in obvious delight.

"Hey, you're not supposed to do that!"

I glared into Kyle's laughing face. "Well, you weren't supposed to do that!"

"Just trying to give you an early birthday present, James. Since you're turning Sweet Sixteen, you know!"

"You can keep your presents to yourself! And the light's green, so how about you go back to driving, too?"

Kyle laughed and laughed and didn't seem to notice I was the only person in the car not laughing. I stayed scrunched by the passenger door with my arms folded, trembling all over, and didn't look at Kyle the rest of the drive home. The second Kyle turned into Grandpa's driveway, I exploded out of the car and ran into the house as fast as my long legs could carry me. I didn't stop until I'd run into Aunt Gracie's old room, my bedroom for the summer, and slammed the door shut tight. I dived head first onto the bed and buried my face in the pillow—and stayed that way until I could hear Grandpa tapping at the door.

"James—James—aren't you going to tell Kyle good night?"

I didn't even lift my head out of the pillows. "No way!"

Grandpa laughed softly. "It's okay, he's not coming in. He has to get home, so it's safe to come out."

Another set of footsteps approached my shut door, and a second later, I could hear Anna's voice. "You shouldn't have teased her so much, Harold. And you shouldn't have goaded Kyle into trying to kiss her."

"I was just having a little fun—that's all!"

"Well, obviously James didn't think it was fun."

Grandpa tapped at the door again. "James, honey, I'm sorry." This time, I chose not to respond. Grandpa waited a few seconds before trying again. "Hey, we were just getting into some good stories about Enterprise and your grandma the other day. Would you like to work on our history project and hear some more tonight? I've got the tape recorder out here ready and waiting!"

I lifted my head and frowned before slowly climbing off the bed to open the bedroom door. "Only if you promise not to mention what happened tonight. Not to me or anyone else!"

Grandpa smiled and held out his hand for me to shake. "I promise, honey. It's a deal!"

THIRTY-FOUR

I stayed away from Enterprise that week and helped out back in Pine Valley on the dam and the reservoir again. But come the weekend, Landon insisted I go with him to the dance in Enterprise.

"It's the last open-air dance in Enterprise this fall before the Deer Hunter's Ball, and you'll need a date for that. So you've got to go to the dance on Saturday!" I tried to ignore Landon, but he kept getting in my face. "Lilly's going to be there. Vivian told me she would."

I frowned and folded my arms. "What about this Deer Hunter's Ball?"

"Vivian told me all about it while we were fixing their fence, so I'm taking her to that Wednesday night. You ought to ask Lilly—I'll bet she'd go with you."

I wasn't as optimistic as Landon, but since it was the last open-air dance before the dances would be moved inside the church house and the high school due to cold weather, I decided I ought to show up.

Landon, Bud, and I had decided not to get into dances the CCC way anymore and instead had our money ready to buy an official dance entry ticket. The guy sitting in the ticket booth taking money and handing out tickets was definitely a sorry sight. He looked like a cowboy who'd been out riding on the range too long. He hadn't shaved, and he had on old dirty Levi's and cowboy boots and a shirt that had seen better days years ago.

We were polite to the old guy but couldn't help laughing at him, since he looked like he'd been dragged behind a few steers. He didn't smile at us at all but looked us over carefully from head to toe before taking our money without a word and handing us back our tickets.

Bud saw Faye with Vivian and Lilly right off and made a beeline for them.

"C'mon, Addison!"

I guess my feet had frozen solid, because Landon couldn't get me to move. It wasn't until Lilly looked right at me and gave me one of her slow smiles that I finally relaxed a little and followed Landon over to where she was standing.

I'd made the conscious decision not to drink a swallow of whisky tonight, so that meant I was going to have to rely on my own personality and above average sense of humor to have a good time. I looked over my shoulder for a second and saw the old guy in the ticket booth looking steadily in our direction with his arms folded, his eyes not wavering from the three of us.

I turned back around and forced out a laugh, jerking my head in his direction. "Who's that old-time rancher there, Billy Whiskers?"

Landon and Bud burst out laughing, but I watched the smile on Lilly's face fade, while Vivian had her "you stink" look on her face again.

Lilly folded her arms and stared hard at me. "That old rancher happens to be my father."

Boy, Landon and Bud really exploded over that. They had a nice good laugh while I was thinking how much I wished I was about a thousand miles away with a nice big bottle of whisky. So in one blow, I'd met Lilly's dad for the first time and most likely the last.

I mumbled an "excuse me" and I think an "I'm really sorry" and hightailed it out of there to the other end of the cement floor. I hid from Lilly for the next half hour or so, dancing with other girls while I told myself whatever had almost begun was officially over now.

So there I was, dancing it up as if I'd been drinking all night, when somehow—I wasn't sure how it happened, but I was monkeying around on the dance floor, horsing around like us guys were always doing—the seam in my trousers, right in the crotch, split in one loud rip. The girl I was dancing with—her eyes got all big while she covered her mouth with her hand, and then, trying not to laugh, she grabbed my hand and hustled me off the dance floor to hide in the ticket booth. Lilly's dad was still in there, so I really didn't want to be in there with him, but there was nowhere else to go. He took one look at my situation and calmly stepped out of the little ticket booth to walk slowly onto the dance floor. I saw him talking to Lilly, and not five minutes later, sitting in the ticket booth with my head in my hands, I felt a tap on my shoulder.

I couldn't believe it when I looked up and saw Lilly looking down at me.

"Take off your pants."

I was shocked. "What? What did you just say?"

"Your pants. Take them off!"

Before I could bellow again, Lilly held up a needle in one hand and a spool of thread in the other.

"Would you mind turning around?"

Lilly smiled that slow smile of hers before turning around.

"Where'd you get the thread and needle?"

"My dad sent me home to get it. He said you were in some sort of trouble."

Lilly grabbed a folding chair nearby and sat down right by the ticket booth while I sat inside it in my underwear, feeling about as awkward as a guy possibly could, while she silently stitched up the crotch of my pants.

"You owe me an apology, you know." Lilly didn't even look up when she said that. Just said it matter-of-factly and kept stitching away.

"Apology? What did I do to you?"

"You left without giving me a chance to thank you for fixing the fence, even though you weren't the one who broke it in the first place."

I guess I must've looked pretty surprised to hear her say that, because she smiled at me.

"Now, tell me you're sorry and that you want to make it up to me."

"And how am I going to make it up to you?"

"You can start by taking me to the Deer Hunter's Ball."

"Deer Hunter's Ball?"

"Yes. This Wednesday night. Landon's taking Vivian, and Bud's taking Faye. And I thought we could go, too. If you want to, I mean."

"I do."

Lilly smiled again. "That's good."

After she finished sewing up my pants, we danced the rest of the night together. Kurt tried to cut in at first, but Lilly gave him a polite no every time he tried, so he finally gave up and passed out from whisky with a bunch of the other guys in the back of the CCC truck before the dance was over.

I'd written to Mom and told her about my pants mishap at the dance and that there was a certain girl I was planning on escorting to the Deer Hunter's Ball, but before she could've gotten my letter, she'd mailed me off a new suit that arrived on Tuesday. She'd gone into Salt Lake a week before and bought me a new suit with some of the CCC money I'd been earning. I thought I looked pretty spiffy in it. I thought Lilly would like me in it, too, but when I put the suit on Wednesday night, Landon and Bud laughed at me. Neither of them was dressed up a bit, and even looked a little like twins in big red sweatshirts, old Levi's, and hunting caps they'd gotten from somewhere, so I laughed right back at them.

"You two are going to be sorry showing up like that for a fancy dance!"

They both just laughed some more while I rounded up some flowers for Lilly. We'd been stuck with one of the big Walter trucks, but since it was big enough for all six of us to fit across the front seat, I knew missing out on getting a pickup truck wouldn't be so bad.

We stopped at Lilly and Vivian's house first. I was driving and hopped right out and headed for the front door with my flowers before

Landon could catch up with me. But Landon—he was happy to loiter down the path, chuckling as if he knew some secret I didn't.

Lilly opened the door, and after taking one look at her, my mouth dropped open about the same second Lilly's did, too.

"You can't go dressed like that!"

We both said the same words at the same time, but I was shocked that Lilly had, since I figured I had more of a right to say anything than she did. She looked just like Bud and Landon, dressed in beat-up Levi's, old hiking boots, and a big red sweatshirt that was easily a few sizes too big for her. And on top of that, she had a big red handkerchief on her head tied in the back behind her ears.

Lilly tried to get me to change, saying she was sure they had something I could wear, but I knew I was taller than her brother, and bigger than him, too, so I just thrust the flowers at her and said I wasn't about to change my brand-new suit for a pair of grubby short pants, and if she wanted to go to the dance with me, then she might as well come on.

Vivian came running out of the house next, dressed just like Lilly. She burst out laughing when she saw me and then ran over to Landon while they both laughed their heads off. It didn't help that Faye was dressed the same, and while everyone kept laughing, I jumped into the CCC truck, slammed the door hard, and squealed the tires over to the high school where the dance was being held.

It was worse there than I thought it would be. Not only was everyone dressed in old pants or Levi's and deer hunter red shirts and hats, but the gymnasium was covered in red, too. Red streamers and balloons. Even the dance cards handed out at the door were red with little red pencils attached. Deer hunting red was all over the place, and boy, did I stick out like a huge, sore thumb in my new navy blue suit. And Lilly's dad—he had his eyes glued on Landon and me from the second we walked through the door. He never even smiled once. The only thing that made me feel any better at all was the fact that Lilly was given a hard time for not giving me the needed details on the Deer Hunter's Ball.

"We tried to tell him, Lilly, but he wouldn't listen," Landon laughed.

"Suits are for dances. Everyone knows that," I grumbled. "And what about these dance cards? No one's dressed up, so what do we need these for?"

Lilly put her hands on her hips and raised an eyebrow in surprise at me for saying that. "Well, this *is* a ball, you know!"

Everyone went back to ribbing me and saying dumb things about my suit until Faye finally spoke up. "I wish someone would put on a nice suit for me and bring me flowers."

Boy, that made Bud nearly choke on his laugh, which gave me a chance to laugh.

"Yeah, I guess that would be nice." I nearly fell over to hear Vivian say that. It was great, though, because both comments worked like a charm to shut Bud and Landon up for the rest of the evening, with all of their laughing and their jokes about me in my suit. And Lilly—she was finally looking at me differently and didn't seem to be embarrassed by my suit anymore.

"Come on, let's dance!" Lilly tried to drag me onto the dance floor, but I held my ground and wouldn't move. "What's wrong, Harold?"

I grinned into her confused face. "I'm not sure my name's on your dance card."

Lilly smiled that slow smile of hers. "Your name's next on the list!"

I kept grinning at her. "Really? Let's see!"

I tried to swipe the dance card off Lilly's wrist, but she surprised me by whipping her hand away from me even faster before carefully tucking the little card into her Levi's back pocket. "No need for you to worry about that, Mr. Addison!"

Once I had her in my arms and smiling up at me, I couldn't have cared less about dance cards or who was wearing what for the rest of the night.

The gymnasium got hotter than Hades, so after a while, we grabbed some punch and took a stroll around the high school. Lilly had her arm linked with mine, and I was feeling pretty good about that. So good that I didn't hear what she said at first.

"I said, did you happen to go to church in the camp on Sunday?"

"Believe it or not, I actually did poke my nose in there for a while." And I had, too. It wasn't the most comfortable meeting I'd ever gone to. Besides the fact that it was hot inside the mess hall on Sunday, the topic was the Word of Wisdom and the evils of drinking and smoking. And coffee drinking. I was doing my best to give up all three, but I was still a long way off from being completely done with all of them for good.

"And what did you learn?"

"I learned that it's going to take a lot of hard work for me to ever be a good Mormon."

Lilly laughed at that. "Do you think it'd be worth it to try?"

"It would be if it means someone I like will agree to keep putting up with me if I give it a try."

Lilly was quiet for so long I was sure I'd said the wrong thing. "You can't do something as big and important as becoming a good Mormon just to make someone else happy."

"But it would make you happy if I became a good Mormon, wouldn't it?"

"Only if it was what you wanted for yourself."

I found out later once we'd dropped the girls off and made it back to the camp in Veyo that Vivian had been working on Landon pretty hard, trying to convince him to change his ways. I'd stopped buying my Tailor Mades, so that made it a little easier for me to quit smoking. Poor Landon—he had a hard time giving up his pipe, but he was definitely trying.

But at least now Landon and I both knew where Lilly and Vivian stood and had pretty much from the day we'd met them. We both respected them for that. They were good Mormon girls who wanted good Mormon guys, and yet they were letting us wild CCC boys hang around them. That part sort of mystified me, since it'd never happened to me before, and it was something I thought about every day, whether I was driving into Cedar City for supplies for the ranger station in Enterprise or driving the dump truck in Pine Valley helping out at the reservoir and dam project. But as long as the girls were going to keep letting us see them, then Bud and Landon and I were going to continue to get acquainted with them.

We started to go over to Enterprise quite a bit after that to chase the girls and visit and date them and have a little fun, and not just on the weekends. Every time I brought a load of lumber from Cedar City over to Enterprise, I'd stay in town for a while and chase Lilly around until I thought the Supe would come looking for me if I didn't get back to camp.

THIRTY-FIVE

The week after the Deer Hunter's Ball, Bud and Landon and I wanted to go over and see the girls in Enterprise. We'd told them at the dance on Friday night that we'd try to come over during the week, so after work on Wednesday night, we swiped a big Walter truck out of camp, and with me driving, we headed over to Enterprise. We were afraid some of the superintendents might see us, so whenever a car came by, we'd drive off the road into the cedar trees and turn off the lights and hide until the car was gone.

By the time we got to Lilly's house in Enterprise, all three of us were pretty jittery from being on Superintendent Watch, and when I jumped out of the truck, Landon followed me out on the driver's side. Somehow, he slammed the door on my thumb. Holy Moses, did he smash my thumb! I screamed like a girl, it hurt so much.

"Addison—good grief, Addison—what happened?!"

I would've decked him if I could've made a fist, so instead I shoved my thumb in his face.

"Look what you did, you—"

Landon's eyes got as big as my thumb when he and Bud got a look at it in the headlights of the Walter truck. Within minutes, it had swelled up as big as my foot, and hurt! Boy, did it hurt! But I wasn't about to turn around and go back to camp, so Landon and I walked up to Lilly's house while Bud took off to get Faye so we could all visit with the gals. I had to suck my thumb most of the night because it hurt so bad. It turned blue, and I about lost my nail and everything. It was a mess. The only thing that made it worthwhile was Lilly's reaction to it.

"Oh, Harold, what happened?!" She held my hand carefully and inspected my poor, almost purple thumb and raked Landon over the coals for not being more careful. I enjoyed every second of that.

As soon as Bud and Faye arrived, we loaded the women up in the Walter. All six of us could easily sit across the seat beside each other. Lilly actually sat on the left side of me, between me and the driver's door, next to the steering wheel. The Walter was so big there was plenty of room for her to sit there.

We went riding around town, and then we went out north across the wash and up and around and onto the back of Winsor Hill, a little hill just north of town. We climbed the hill around the back and made it up to the top in the Walter and had a great time, making the girls scream and squeal going over the bumps and dips in the road. That big ol' four-wheel-drive truck was a hundred percent traction. It could just go any-where, and it had two big, really bright headlights on each side of the windshield. We got up on top of Winsor Hill, and those two headlights shone out there quite a ways. We found out later that a lot of people in town saw the lights that night and couldn't imagine what the devil that was up on the hill.

Bud and Faye wanted to get out and walk around, and soon Landon and Vivian had the same idea.

"We can get out and walk around, too, if you want to, Lilly."

"Let's just sit and talk. Is that okay?"

I nodded and smiled at her. "Sure."

I showed her a bunch of the controls on the truck, and she did the right amount of oohing and ahing to make me feel pretty big and impor-tant.

"So, Harold, can I ask you a question?"

I shrugged, but inside I was a little worried about where this was going to lead. "Sure."

"It's kind of personal. Is that okay?"

"I guess I won't know for sure until you ask."

"You could ask me a personal question first, if you want to."

I was sure she thought I'd say no, but I figured I couldn't let this golden opportunity slip by. "Okay, I will. Your dad doesn't like me and Landon much, does he?"

Lilly looked away and shifted uncomfortably around on the seat. "Why do you say that?"

"We get plenty of black looks from him at the dances, and you've never once invited me over to meet him, or have dinner with your family, or do anything inside your home. I have to believe that's because your dad doesn't approve of us."

"My dad wants to see me and my sisters marry good LDS men in the temple. Does that surprise you?"

I shook my head. "No, I guess not. What does surprise me is that you're hanging around with someone your dad doesn't like instead of with a good LDS boy from your town."

Lilly looked me straight in the eyes. "If I was interested in any of the boys in my town, I wouldn't be with you right now."

I stared at her back before nodding. "Good to know."

"Now do I get to ask you my question?"

"Go ahead."

Lilly nodded and then dived in pretty fast. "You told me you were born into a Mormon family."

"That's right."

"Well, then, when did you stop going to church, and why?"

I guess I shouldn't have been surprised. In fact, I should've been more surprised that she hadn't asked me all of this before. "My parents got divorced when I was little. I guess I didn't like going somewhere where I was different from all the other kids, so by the time I was, oh, about thirteen, I stopped going to church."

"Your mother didn't make you go?"

"She tried, but she had a hard time, I guess partly because I was big for my age."

"Didn't your friends go to church?"

"Most of my friends didn't. I guess we thought it was more fun to see what kind of trouble we could get into. By the time I was fifteen, I'd gotten myself into enough trouble that I didn't feel right sitting in a church as if I was perfect when I knew I wasn't."

Lilly sighed loudly. "Church isn't for people who are 'perfect,' because none of us are."

I couldn't help smiling at her. "You are."

Lilly just laughed. "No, I'm not."

"Well, you're as close to perfect as anyone I've ever known."

Lilly shook her head. "That's sweet of you to say, but it's not true. I have a long way to go before I'll be perfect, just like everyone else. That's why I go to church. It helps me learn how to become better."

"Well, if you think you have a long way to go, then I'm doing even worse than I thought!"

Lilly grabbed my arm and gave it a shake. "No, you're not—you're not!"

I laughed and then looked at her face. "You're the prettiest girl I've ever known."

Lilly laughed again and let go of my arm. "Now you're just flirting with me."

"I can't help it. Who wouldn't want to flirt with you, the prettiest girl in town?"

"Stop it!" Lilly laughed again and gave my hand a slap. Unfortunately, my sore thumb got included in the slap.

"Ow!"

"Your thumb—I'm so sorry!" Before I knew what was happening, Lilly put my hand to her lips and carefully kissed my thumb. She stared at me, and I stared back at her for what seemed like hours before I could get my mouth to work again.

"What would you say if I said I really wanted to kiss you?"

Lilly gave me another one of her slow smiles. "I'd have to confess that I really want to kiss you, too."

I wasn't about to give her a chance to change her mind, so I put my arm around her and leaned in and kissed her. Best of all, she kissed me back. When I looked down at her little face in the moonlight, her eyes still closed, I couldn't believe it when she leaned in towards me again. My heart was racing as I leaned in again, too.

"Hey, what's going on in here?"

A stick of lit dynamite thrown between us couldn't have made Lilly and me jump apart faster. Landon laughed as he and Vivian climbed back in the truck, with Bud and Faye close behind.

Landon elbowed me hard in the side. "Oh, doing some lip reading, huh?" Before I could yell at him, he grinned and whispered, "Me, too!"

We sat there in the truck, all six of us, and monkeyed around for a while, joking and laughing for I didn't know how long, but we all knew it was getting really late, so I turned the truck back on and drove back down the hill and into town. We had to leave for Veyo before it got too late, because I had to get the truck back to camp before the ol' Supe could raise heck with me. He still hadn't forgiven me for knocking those guard rails off, so I had to be careful to try and stay on his good side. But we gave the women—the girlfriends, actually, since they all officially were now—a really nice ride in the big ol' Walter truck that night. And we got the Walter back to camp early the next morning before the go-to-work time. None of the superintendents ever did find out about it, so that made our good time with the girls that night even better.

THIRTY-SIX

I'd lied the night before when I'd told Grandpa turning sixteen wasn't a big deal to me. And I'd lied when I pretended not to remember my birthday was coming up. No one turning sixteen forgets their birthday is coming up. Ever. I'd been thinking about my birthday for some time now. More so since the night the whole family had come over to freak out about Grandpa dating Anna, only to find out Grandpa was planning on marrying her as well.

My birthday usually called for a family camping trip, complete with a birthday cake and candles somewhere in the mountains. I knew there was no way that was going to happen, with Grandpa's bad heart acting up and his doctor's strict orders to take it easy. And with Kyle acting so stupid lately, the idea of going somewhere fun with him wasn't sounding good, especially if he was going to dive at me as a kissing joke again. And as for shopping for a birthday dress with Grandma like Sarah always did—that obviously wasn't going to happen. And that was too bad, because I'd been thinking maybe getting a pretty dress—a real dress, not just a casual, plain skirt—wouldn't be such a bad idea after all. But I figured the idea of having someone help me shop for a dress who had fashion sense like my grandma was just a dream, and the fact actually made me feel sad. On all sorts of levels that were confusing and strange.

When I woke up early on my actual sixteenth birthday, I had absolutely no idea how I was going to spend my day. For the first time in my life, I had no big plans for my birthday, and the idea depressed me considerably. So I did the only thing I could do. I pulled the covers over my head to block out the sun filtering in through the window and went back to sleep. Or tried to, anyway. A mere five minutes later, I could hear Grandpa tapping at my door.

"James—James, are you up yet?"

"No, I'm still asleep!"

"No, you're not—I'm comin' in!" Grandpa threw open the door, marched over to the bed, and tossed the covers off of me with a big grin. "Happy birthday, James!"

"You remembered!"

Grandpa grinned down at me and threw a pillow at my head. "You didn't think I'd forget, now did you?"

I laughed and threw the pillow back. "I guess not."

"Well, now that you're sixteen years old, how about saving your first date for me?"

That was the last thing I was expecting Grandpa to say.

"A date?" To say the least, I was dumbfounded. I would've thought for sure Grandpa was only teasing me if I hadn't seen a strange mixture of hope and pleading in his eyes.

"Yeah, a date. How 'bout it?"

"I guess. I mean, Sure. Why not?" I felt a little idiotic, but seeing Grandpa's face light up made me glad I'd accepted.

"Well, get yourself up and at 'em—I've got breakfast about ready!" Grandpa turned to leave as I hurried and sat up in bed.

"Hey, wait. Where are we going for this date? Do I need to get all dressed up?"

"No. Shorts or jeans will be fine. I'll take you to lunch first, and the rest is a surprise!"

It wasn't until after Grandpa left, whistling back down the hall to the kitchen, that I was able to ponder the whole thing. Grandpa and I, going on a "date." I couldn't deny I was curious to see what the day would bring.

Grandpa hugged me when I walked into the kitchen a minute later, still in my PJs. "How about some chocolate chip pancakes? How does that sound, James?"

I laughed as I slipped into a chair at the kitchen table. "You know that's my favorite!"

Grandpa grinned as he tossed a few with a spatula onto the plate in front of me. "Well, good, because that's what kind of flapjacks I've got for you here!"

I couldn't help laughing again. Grandpa was way too excited about our "date."

"I wish every guy was this excited to go out with me!"

Grandpa smiled and patted me on the shoulder. "Don't you worry, honey. The ones who realize how beautiful you are will be thrilled to have the chance to go out with you."

I almost snorted. "Beautiful? That's pushing it, Grandpa."

Grandpa looked surprised as his face turned all serious. "But you are, James. You are!"

After Grandpa and I had finished eating way too many pancakes, Grandpa slapped my hands when I tried to clear the table.

"Not on your birthday, James! I'll get those. I have a few stores I need to visit after I clean up here, and then I'll be back. Will you be ready to go about eleven thirty?"

I nodded. "Sounds good. I'll be ready!"

I was showered and dressed in the pink shorts outfit I hadn't worn since the basketball incident with Kyle, minus the fancy hair and makeup, by eleven-thirty on the dot when Grandpa returned, honking the car horn.

"I shouldn't have done that, James. That's not the way a boy should pick up a girl on a date. Remember that for the future, all right?"

"Sure, Grandpa." I couldn't see any guy honking or knocking or yelling or doing anything for me any time soon, but Grandpa looked so happy I just nodded and smiled.

Grandpa wheeled the car into the parking lot of a restaurant a few short blocks away. "How about this place for lunch? Do you like this restaurant?"

"I do, Grandpa." And I really did. It was a nice casual soup, salad, and sandwich type of place that had fast service and good food. Grandpa tried, but he couldn't contain all of his crazy excitement and acted somewhat like a teenager himself. The second our waitress arrived at our table, Grandpa couldn't hold back any longer.

"Today's my granddaughter's sixteenth birthday, so I'm taking her out on her first date!"

I knew I was blushing, but the waitress only beamed at me. "Oh, that's sweet. Well, dessert is on the house. And to make it extra special, I promise not to let anyone here sing at you. How does that sound?"

I beamed right back at her. "Perfect!"

Besides the waitress, Grandpa had to tell the guy who cleared our table, another waitress who came to check on our table and refill our water glasses, and the cashier when we left, that he was taking out his granddaughter for her first date on her sixteenth birthday today. Embarrassing as it was, it was pretty sweet and cute, too, so I let it go without grumbling like I could have.

Once I'd climbed back into Grandpa's car and snapped my seatbelt into place all snug around my waist, I turned to Grandpa and smiled. "Thanks for lunch, Grandpa. And for breakfast this morning!"

Grandpa smiled and nodded but didn't start the car. Finally he turned to me with one of his hopeful smiles. My own smile faded when I saw a little sadness on his face, too.

"You know, honey, since your sister Sarah turned twelve, your grandma always took her shopping for a new dress on her birthday."

I nodded and looked down at my hands. "Yeah, I remember."

"I'm sorry the two of you weren't able to do that before she passed on."

"So am I."

Grandpa sighed. "Well, I know I'm not your grandma, but I'd really like to do the same for you, like your grandma would've wanted to on your sixteenth birthday today. So how would you like to go shopping for a brand-new, special birthday dress? With me?"

I could hardly believe it. My throat was closing funny, and I could feel myself wanting to laugh and cry at the same time.

"Yes, Grandpa, I'd like that very much."

For the next three hours, Grandpa drove me all over the city, looking in every store for that special dress. Anybody else would've been furious with me for taking so long, but not Grandpa. He had the time of his life, watching me try on dress after dress after dress. I only wished I could find *the* dress for me. My sixteenth birthday dress. When I found the right one, I'd know it. If a dress didn't jump out at me the first time I saw it, then I knew it wasn't the one, although I did try on several Grandpa picked out, and even more that the sales girls at the stores pushed on me. But none of them were it. They just weren't. I apologized to Grandpa like crazy for dragging him around all over creation, but he insisted that he was enjoying every minute of it.

"Why don't we try that big new mall down at the bottom of Fifth Street? How does that sound?"

Grandpa was still smiling, but he was looking tired. "Are you sure, Grandpa? We've been at this three hours as it is—"

"I'm sure. We're not going home until we find that dress you're looking for!"

The mall was huge, so while I hopped from store to store looking at dresses, Grandpa sat outside on the long benches lining the halls and walkways resting, which worried me. He'd lost weight since Grandma died. He'd always been in good shape and was pretty lean anyway, but he looked thin to me. Thinner than he'd ever been in his life, and as I watched him slowly sit down on a bench and take a few deep breaths as I turned to smile and wave at him before running into yet another dress shop, I was angry at myself for keeping him from his home where he needed to rest. It would've been useless, though, to try and make him go home now. Even though he wasn't in the best of health, I knew he wouldn't take me home until I found my dress.

By four-thirty, I was feeling pretty depressed and frustrated, especially since the only dress shop left in the mall was an expensive one.

Grandpa gave me a shove when I hesitated in front of the shop's doorway. "Come on, James. Let's look around inside anyway."

My spirits soared when I saw all the beautiful, elegant, and fancy dresses in every color imaginable—and then some. "Wow, would you look at these dresses? I've never seen such nice, fancy stuff as this!"

Grandpa's eyes were sparkling every bit as much as mine. "Well, don't just stand there. Go try some on!"

So I did. I tried on quite a few, and although Grandpa thought I looked pretty in each one, he'd say what I was thinking as he'd look at me.

"It's real pretty. And you look pretty in it. But it's not the one, is it?"

I'd slowly made my way to the back of the shop, looking at all of the beautiful tea-length dresses, when one dress caught my eye.

"Oh—that one. That's it—that's the one!"

It was a lavender dress that felt like silk with a three-inch thick, silky lavender sash that belted tight around the waist with a vertical row of tiny lavender pearl buttons in the back. The skirt fell a good four inches below the knee with a net-like slip underneath it that made it stand out a bit. It had inch-wide shoulder straps, but the whole dress was covered with a short-sleeved, matching lavender-colored lace with sparkly, tiny beads that went over the silky material like a second dress. It was so pretty that I knew it was the dress for me. I snatched it off the rack and raced past Grandpa and into the fitting room.

Once I'd carefully slipped it on, I stared at myself in the mirror. And stared some more. It wasn't so bad, trying on these pretty dresses. And this one—I took a deep breath as I turned around halfway to see the back of the dress. It was absolutely amazing. I turned again to face the mirror and watched myself slowly smile. Wearing dresses wasn't so bad. Not bad at all.

I finally emerged from the fitting rooms and floated over to where Grandpa was seated in one of the overstuffed wingback chairs by the three-way, floor-length mirrors. His face lit up when he saw me in the dress. My dress. He couldn't stop saying, "Oh, honey—that's the one. That's the one!"

I laughed and twirled around. "It's pretty, isn't it? I've never seen such a pretty dress!"

"You want this one, then?"

I smiled and nodded, but my smile faded as I stared at myself in all of the mirrors. "I love this dress. I really do, but where would I ever wear something like this?"

Grandpa moved to stand behind me and squeeze my shoulders. "You're sixteen now. You'll find lots of reasons to wear a fancy dress like this. A girl always needs a pretty dress to go dancing in!"

I shook my head slowly, looking at our reflection together in the mirror. "Girls don't wear this kind of a dress unless they're asked to a fancy school dance."

"Don't worry. You'll be asked!" Grandpa squeezed my shoulders again. "And in the meantime, you'll need something nice in case someone was to ask you to go to the theater. So you can use those opera glasses of your grandma's!"

I turned to face him and lifted an eyebrow. "'Someone,' Grandpa?"

Grandpa shrugged and grinned. "You never know. You're sixteen now, after all! You're not a little girl anymore."

I looked at myself in the mirror again and sighed. "Well, I won't have any place to wear a dress this nice any time soon."

Grandpa was quiet for a moment before he looked into my eyes in the mirror's reflection. "How about to mine and Anna's wedding? It'd be just perfect."

My heart leaped inside my chest. "It would, wouldn't it?" And just as if I'd stepped into Cinderella's shoes and heard the first loud, annoying stroke of midnight, I remembered something. Something important.

The price tag for the dress was dangling under my right arm, and with a sick feeling in the pit of my stomach, I slowly turned it over in my left hand to see how much this dress—a designer dress—cost.

One hundred dollars. Another loud bong before midnight. I stared at the price tag again. *One hundred dollars!!* And it was on sale, too. Another ear-deafening bong in my head.

"What's the matter, honey?"

"No," I said, shaking my head firmly. "This dress isn't the one after all."

Grandpa's mouth dropped open. "What are you talking about? You look so beautiful in it—"

I couldn't stop shaking my head. "I'm sorry. This dress is way too expensive. Way too. And it's too fancy for someone like me anyway. Lacy, fancy dresses like this aren't meant for tomboys like me—"

Grandpa looked so hurt I almost started crying. "Oh, James!"

"I need to look for something more appropriate. Something I could really use. It was crazy of me to try this dress on—any of these dresses— in the first place."

"That's not true—"

I glanced down quickly at my watch. "And—wow—it's late. Give me two minutes to change, and then maybe we can find a dress some other time."

I ran back into the dressing room and shut the door tight before sagging heavily against it. I couldn't let Grandpa spend so much of his money on an expensive dress like this. No way.

I allowed myself one final, wistful look in the mirror before slowly taking the dress off and handing it to the fitting room attendant. I sighed and fought the urge to cry in frustration. It was such a beautiful dress. I'd never tried on such pretty dresses before in my life. I couldn't help feeling horribly, sadly disappointed. I yanked my shorts and shirt back on and slipped my feet into my sandals before taking a deep breath and opening the dressing room door.

When I finally made my way out of the dressing room area, Grandpa was waiting for me by the mirrors and overstuffed chairs with a dress bag over his arm.

"Happy birthday, honey!"

My feet stopped moving, and all I could do was stare disbelievingly at the dress bag that he was holding out to me with a huge smile on his face. I couldn't believe it. I couldn't. He couldn't have bought that beautiful dress for me.

"Oh, Grandpa, you really shouldn't have done this," I said softly.

Grandpa nodded his head firmly. "Yes, I should have. You're a beautiful young lady inside and out, and at the very least, you deserve a beautiful dress!"

"But it's expensive—way too expensive!"

Grandpa waved that aside with one hand and gently tugged a lock of my hair, smiling into my eyes.

"No, it's not. Besides—I've been wanting to do something really special to thank you for a long time now."

I could feel my brow creasing in confusion. "Thank me for what, Grandpa?"

Grandpa smiled and smoothed my hair. "For being my hero."

I looked straight into his eyes in surprise. "Your hero?"

Grandpa nodded. "You've been my hero all summer."

I shook my head. "I'm not a hero."

Grandpa only nodded determinedly again. "Yes, you are. Heroes save lives, don't they?"

I nodded, still confused.

"Well, that's what you've done. So thank you, James. For saving mine."

Tears filled Grandpa's eyes, and I could feel tears forming in my own as well. Grandpa smoothed my hair again with a trembling hand and smiled. "Did you know, James—you're so much like my Lilly. Just like her, you've become one of the best friends I've ever had."

I knew I was crying when I buried my face in his chest and hugged him tight while he hugged me back.

"I should have done this a long time ago. I'm just glad we did before it's too late." Grandpa's voice was hoarse with his own tears, and I wasn't quite sure I'd heard him right, but at that moment, I was too happy to think about or worry about anything.

When we reached Grandpa's house shortly before six o'clock, Anna had a rainbow of helium balloons floating until they touched the ceiling all over the kitchen and bright-colored streamers taped along the walls with a big "Happy Birthday!" sign. In the middle of the kitchen table was a huge chocolate cake with "Happy Birthday, Jamie" in white icing with lavender roses.

I couldn't help giving them each a big hug, but I hugged Grandpa longer and tighter than I usually did.

"Thank you so much for today—it was wonderful. I'll never forget it." I pulled back to look into Grandpa's happy, shining eyes. "Grandpa, I love you."

Grandpa's eyes teared up fast as he hugged me tight again and whispered, "I love you, too, honey."

THIRTY-SEVEN

After I'd tried on the dress for Anna, who insisted on taking a few pictures of me in it and a few with Grandpa as well, I changed back into my shorts outfit. Grandpa threw some burgers and bacon on his outdoor grill and cooked the three of us some wonderfully greasy bacon burgers.

"These can't be good for your heart, Grandpa!"

"Oh, just this once won't hurt anything. It's a special day. You're sixteen now!"

It really had been a perfect day. We sat outside in the swing and rocked back and forth, me on one side and Grandpa and Anna on the other, and munched our burgers and potato chips and drank pop and joked and laughed and just had the best birthday I'd ever had.

"Do you miss being up in the mountains on your birthday, James?"

I smiled at Anna and shrugged. "I thought I would, but it's been too great of a birthday to be sad about that."

Grandpa grinned and lightly kicked my right shin. "Well, the summer's not over yet. We can still go up into the mountains before you have to go back to school."

I grinned and lightly kicked him back. "Speaking of going up into the mountains, what happened after you and Uncle Landon had your hot date up on Winsor Hill with Grandma and Aunt Vivian?"

Grandpa smiled. "Oh, there were big changes in Enterprise shortly after that."

"Really? How come?"

"Because the winter set in."

"That made a difference?"

Grandpa nodded. "A big difference. If you'll go grab the tape recorder, we can work on our history project for a while, and I'll tell you all about it."

THIRTY-EIGHT

We spent the rest of the fall of '36, after the new ranger station got underway, working on some more road-building projects during the week, going over to the dances in Enterprise on Friday nights, and having a lot of fun with the girls every chance we got in between. Vivian and Lilly never invited us into their house, though, so we knew their dad still didn't approve of us wild CCC boys dating his daughters. But the girls liked us, and that's all we let ourselves care about. We'd swipe CCC pickups, or someone in Enterprise would send a special truck over for us for the dances or something, but we usually managed to get the CCC pickups over to Enterprise for the dances and monkeying around with our girls.

Winter came in late November, and it snowed hard in southern Utah. Boy, I'm telling you, that was a heavy winter. There were three or four feet of snow on the level, and at that time, Landon and Bud and I were working on building the Gold Strike road from Enterprise over to the Enterprise dam and reservoir, with Landon on the Cat, me in the Walter truck, and Bud on a road grader. When the snow came, the Supe had everyone stop working on the road-building crews and start pushing snow with the Cat and trucks instead. We pushed snow on the road from Veyo over to Enterprise until we finally got that road opened. The officers in camp set up a temporary, smaller CCC camp known as a spike camp in Enterprise a couple of weeks before the snow came. They wanted to move some of the guys from the Veyo Camp into it. Spike camps only lasted until a specific project was done, which could be anywhere from a few weeks to a few months. As soon as I heard about the Enterprise Spike Camp, I talked the Supe into adding my name to the spike camp list so I could be right *in* Enterprise.

Bud and Landon and I all got picked to be in the spike camp, but ol' Kurt Harris had to stay at the Veyo Camp. A few days before we were supposed to head out to Enterprise and help push all the snow off the roads both to and around town, just when there was a ton of work that needed to be done packing up stuff for the spike camp, Landon couldn't get himself up and moving out of bed. I tried to drag him out of his bunk, but he refused to budge.

"Lazy, good-for-nothing—you're just doing this so Bud and I'll do all the work!"

Landon only moaned, "I'm sick! Can't you tell I'm sick?"

I just grumbled about his lazy self some more.

"I've got a sore throat! No—more than that—I think I've got the mumps. My ears ache—oh man, they ache bad!"

I ignored Landon, but Bud had a better idea for getting Landon well fast. He walked over and grabbed Landon around the throat, and none too gently.

"Open your mouth."

Landon did just that, and Bud nodded seriously again.

"All angry and red down there. A sore throat for sure. And your ears ache?"

"Yeah, something fierce!"

"Well, then, I'd say you've got the mumps. What do you think, Addison?"

I took a look at Landon and nodded all serious like, too. "Yep, looks like mumps. Your face should be swelling up nice any day now. Since you're all sick with the mumps, you shouldn't get out of bed at all, so you know what that means, don't you?"

Landon looked more suspicious than worried. "What?"

"You can't go over to Enterprise with us and be in that spike camp. We're leaving in two days, and they're only taking healthy guys who can push snow off the roads."

Bud nodded and grinned at Landon, too. "I heard we're going to dig out cattle ranchers and sheepherders, too. A bunch of them got stuck on the mountains when the snow came. They can't get their animals back into town with the snow being so deep as it is."

I shook my head sadly. "Too bad. It's going to be great being so close to the girls. Vivian's going to be disappointed."

That's all it took to get Landon to spring out of bed as if it were filled with hot coals. He pulled on his pants and boots and said he was going to Enterprise, too, even if it killed him.

"Pickles—that's what I need!"

Both Bud and I laughed and said, "Pickles?"

Landon acted like both of us were stupid. "To test for mumps!"

I laughed some more. "How does that work?"

"If it hurts to chew, I've got mumps. But the pickle juice should kill off the swelling."

Landon hobbled out the door for the mess hall, and by noon, he'd eaten all the pickles in camp to test to see if he had mumps. And once all the pickles were gone and his sore throat hadn't died down at all, he smoked and smoked his little ol' pipe until he turned so green I was sure he was going to make himself even sicker.

"If the nicotine doesn't kill off the mumps, nothing will. The Supe says if I can get rid of whatever's wrong with me, then I'll be able to go to the spike camp, too."

The day we were set to move out, Landon finally got rid of the sore throat, so he was able to go with Bud and me and a bunch of other guys to the Enterprise Spike Camp and run one of the Cats to help push all the snow. All his hard smoking and pickle eating didn't pay off, though. The snow wouldn't let up, so none of us was able to see any of the girls much. I was spending all day with Landon, Bud, and the other guys at the spike camp trying to keep all of the roads around Enterprise plowed and open. That alone was a full-time, back-breaking, freezing job.

While Landon and Bud were driving the Cats, I was running one of the big Walter trucks. The guys in the garage at the Veyo Camp built a big winged blade they attached to the front of the truck. My first official day in the spike camp, I'd taken my Walter truck from Veyo into St. George with the superintendent, who I knew would never like me. We spent most of the day clearing the road from Veyo into St. George.

There was about a foot of snow in St. George that year. It was the first time anyone had seen snow in St. George in a long time. Once the Supe and I headed back to Veyo in the Walter truck to finish opening the road, as soon as we got down into the desert, the truck kept getting stuck. The guys in the garage hadn't made it so the blade could be lifted, so I was dragging snow back under the wheels. The truck was moving slower and slower through all that thick, heavy snow and kept getting stuck on top of all the snow trapped under the wheels. The Supe kept yelling, "Punch the gas! Just punch the gas!" It didn't take too long before I was good and ready to punch something, but it wasn't the gas.

After a few more minutes of trying to shove through the snow at a slow crawl with all that snow stuck underneath, it was impossible to keep going. The ol' Supe was about ready to blow a gasket and nearly shoved me out the door.

"Move over, Addison. Lemme take the wheel. I'll show ya how it's done!"

I had no choice but to get out and stomp through the snow over to the passenger door and scrape the snow off my boots and climb inside while the Supe slid over into the driver's seat.

"Now watch, Addison, and maybe you'll learn how to drive a truck in the snow."

I sat calmly in the truck, not saying a word, while the Supe went back and forth from reverse to all of the gears, revving hard on the gas as he tried to get the truck moving in some direction. Any direction. In no time, the truck made a horrible, loud breaking noise, and both of us knew he'd torn the transmission out. The Walter was no good for anything then. I listened in satisfaction while the Supe waved an impressive string of obscenities, and I tried not to let him see me grinning. We had to flag down some of the CCC guys who were plowing roads in a Cat nearby to pull the Walter into town and park it until spring.

The superintendent took over the Cat from our rescuers and demanded I stay with him, so the two of us made our way across the desert in the Cat, pushing the snow close to Enterprise. When night came, we quit and left the Cat in the desert by the road near Enterprise and caught a ride in a CCC pickup over to the spike camp.

"It'll be fine, Addison. Don't worry about it!"

I wasn't so sure about that, but the Supe didn't want to hear anything from me on the ride back to camp, so I kept my mouth shut.

The Supe and I went out the next morning to get the Cat, but neither of us could get it started. I tried first, but the Supe again shoved me out of the way, certain he could do it, but he couldn't, either. The Cat had been out there in the wind and the snow all night, and it was really cold. We tried and tried, but the engine wouldn't crank over.

"Go run back to camp and get some guys to help us get this thing moving again!"

I ran back and grabbed Landon and Bud and some supplies, and we all got busy and dug the snow out around the Cat, wide enough so we could put a tent over it. The Supe claimed I brought him nothing but bad luck and told me to stay as far away from him as I could from now on. I could've told him that was fine with me and that he was the one always chasing me down, not the other way around, but I didn't. Even so, the Supe got in and helped Bud and Landon and me with the Cat. We built a fire inside under the tent and took turns keeping the fire going, and boiled the water and heated the oil that needed to go in the Cat. The oil had gotten so thick it couldn't move, but after a while, the oil was at last like liquid again, and we were able to dump it back into the Cat. Finally we got it started so we could get back to pushing snow.

THIRTY-NINE

T he snow was so deep in Enterprise that winter it actually covered the fences around the houses in town. The second day in camp, because Bud and Landon and I were the three main guys who'd been trained to drive the two Cats and had the okay to drive them, we used them to clean the road from the barracks up to Andy Winsor's store and Lilly's home, and back down and over by the post office, in front of the church house, and down the street and over by Faye's house. Anywhere that the girls needed to get to in town, Landon and Bud and I made sure they had a plowed road from their homes to wherever they needed to go. And in return, Lilly and Vivian talked two of their next-door neighbors into letting us use their potato cellars at night to store the two Cats in so they'd start in the morning instead of freezing up.

When Lilly found out Bud and Landon and I were being sent with a handful of other CCC guys to clear the road from Enterprise to Modena, she talked another neighbor into giving us an old sheep wagon so we could attach it to the back of the Cat and sleep in it at night out on the desert on our way to Modena. The wagon looked a lot like an old pioneer covered wagon, only it had a door in the back of it and at the front of it near the tongue that we attached to the Cat. It had a rounded canvas top, a stove inside for heat and cooking, and a bed. We got the wagon hooked onto the Cat, and once it was all hooked on and ready to go, the three of us said good-bye to the girls and started out for Modena.

Besides clearing the road to Modena, the three of us had instructions to go up into the hills near Modena to dig out the sheep and cattle herds that were snowed in, as well as a mining camp, too. We headed out on the Modena road and out around the hills north of Enterprise around Winsor's Hill. Once we got out on the desert, the wind really blew hard and cold. That first night, while we opened the Modena road with the Cat, we had a good fire going in the stove in the sheep wagon, but it was about thirty, forty degrees below zero outside. We had to have the headlights on in the snow the whole way so we could see. Landon would sit on the Cat and drive in the cold for five or ten minutes, and then I'd run out on the tongue from inside the sheep wagon to take Landon's place while he ran back across the tongue to go inside and get warm, and then five or ten minutes later, Bud would come running across the tongue and climb up the back of the Cat and take my place at the wheel for as long as he could stand. We took turns at the driver's seat that way until we got to Modena. We about froze, but we finally made it across the desert that night.

FORTY

"hat did you do once you made it to Modena?"

Grandpa stretched and cleared his throat. "Well, the first thing we had to do—"

"Hi, all! Happy birthday, James!"

I hadn't heard any car pull up in front, and when I turned to see who'd yelled my name, it was easy to see why. Aunt Gracie had come on foot and was hurrying around the corner, with Maxwell and Blake dragging their feet a short distance behind her. Before I could get out of the swing, Aunt Gracie leaned in to smack a kiss on my cheek and drop a small package in my lap.

"Blake and Maxwell helped me pick it out. I hope you like it!"

"Oh, thanks, Aunt Gracie." Blake and Maxwell had "helped"? I set the gift aside to open later in case anything jumped out of it.

Aunt Gracie leaned against the swing with her back to Grandpa and Anna and faced me with a grin. "Tell me you haven't cut the cake yet, James!"

"No, we're still waiting for Mom and Dad and everyone else."

"Good. I would've felt really bad if we missed singing to you!"

"Hello, Gracie." Anna's voice was so quiet I almost didn't hear her, but Aunt Gracie turned her head to look in her direction.

"Oh, hello, Anna." Aunt Gracie whipped her head back around so fast I wanted to give her a good kick in the shin, but Grandpa had stood up and was trying to get out of the swing.

"Well, give your dad a hug, Gracie!" he said. "And where are those boys of yours? Get over here, you two! Come wish your cousin a happy birthday!"

Blake and Maxwell smirked and muttered something that might have been "happy birthday," but I wasn't sure. Luckily, I didn't have to strain to try and make small talk with them for long, because a few minutes later, I could hear a car horn honking down the road.

"That must be Mom and Dad!"

And thankfully, it was. With Sarah and Trent and gifts galore. Trent gave me a new basketball, and Mom and Dad brought a new pair of basketball shoes and a couple of new shirts, but Sarah had bought me a pair of off-white, fancy semi-high-heeled shoes.

I stared in wonder at the shoes, one in each hand. "How did you know?"

Sarah laughed. "Oh, Grandpa mentioned he might take you dress shopping, so I took a chance. I figured this color would be safe, and see— this place dyes shoes to match dresses, so you can change the color if you want."

I looked over the card from the shoe shop that Sarah had tossed into my lap. "Oh, well, I think I'll leave them alone so I can wear them with other dresses, too."

Trent burst out laughing. "What other dresses? You mean your Levi's skirts?"

I gave him a black glare. "Shut up, Trent!"

Mom stood up and flicked Trent in the back of the head with her fingertips before turning to me. "Jamie, I'll let that slide because it's your birthday." Mom looked back and forth at the two of us. "How about everyone play nice and get along for once, okay?"

I was still looking at the shoes when Kyle knocked and Anna let him in.

"Happy birthday, James!" Kyle had his elf grin on as he slid onto an empty kitchen chair by the recliner I was in.

"Oh, hey, I wasn't expecting you!"

Kyle's grin faded. "You weren't?"

I could feel my face turning hot. "Well, I wasn't sure—I mean—never mind. I'm glad you came over."

Kyle grinned again and poked at the box in my hands. "What's this?"

"Oh, some new shoes Sarah bought for me." I quickly removed the lid and tilted the box so Kyle could see inside.

Kyle whistled and shook his head. "Think you'll be able to walk in these?"

I laughed. "I'm going to try."

"Hey, let's get this cake going. Come on into the kitchen, James, so we can sing to you. I'm putting the candles on now!" Grandpa was already halfway to the kitchen with Anna close behind.

And so with all of the lights off and nothing but my candles glowing to light up everyone's faces in the room, I grinned and laughed uncomfortably while everyone, including Kyle, sang to me. My heart jumped when I thought I saw Kyle wink at me right before I blew out the candles. But he laughed and clapped along with everyone else once I got all sixteen candles out with one breath, so I was sure I must've been seeing things.

I'd been so busy chatting with my parents, Aunt Gracie, and Sarah, and painfully noticing how Anna was being left out of the conversations floating around the room that it wasn't until I was almost finished eating my cake and ice cream that I noticed Kyle, Trent, Maxwell, and Blake were missing. I waited until I'd finished my last bite of cake before taking a turn around the room to collect everyone's empty plates and forks so I could dump them in the kitchen garbage.

The kitchen was empty. And no one was in any of the bedrooms or bathroom, either. Frowning, I wiped my hands on a kitchen towel before pushing open the back door into the yard, where I could just make out Blake's tall form and blonde head in the moonlight.

"I'll bet he won't do it."

And Maxwell, standing next to Blake, said, "Yeah, well, I'm betting he will—"

I stepped into the doorway and let the screen door rest against my hip. "You're betting who will or won't do what?"

All four guys standing around together turned at the same time to look at me. Blake and Maxwell had evil grins on their faces, and Trent was trying hard to look innocent.

"Hey, there's the birthday girl now!" Trent grinned and punched Kyle in the arm before turning back to me. "Come on over, James."

I frowned and folded my arms. "What's going on?"

Trent only laughed. "Come over here, sis, and find out!"

Blake leaned over and tugged on my arm, dragging me off the back porch. "Kyle's got a little something for your birthday!"

Kyle hadn't given me a gift yet. Not that I was expecting anything, but from the strange look on his face, I couldn't deny I was curious.

"What is it, Kyle?"

Kyle tried to smile, but it looked tight and strange. "Nothing, James. They're just—"

"We're just playing a game. You like games, right? Like one-on-one with Kyle? Basketball, I mean, of course. One-on-one basketball." Blake kept his face serious, but Maxwell was smirking and laughing beside him.

Kyle jumped in to try again. "They're just being stupid, James. Ignore them—"

Blake turned to give Kyle a shove. "Being stupid? We're not the ones being stupid!"

Maxwell got in my face then. "Are you going to play or not, James?"

I looked from one grinning face to the next, and then to Kyle, who just looked incredibly uncomfortable. "I guess—"

"Well, come on—let's play!"

I frowned and moved to stand by Kyle. "What are you playing?"

Blake grinned. "Just a little game of Truth or Dare. I just dared Kyle to kiss you, James. Right, Kyle?"

"What?!" The word burst out of me before I could stop it.

Kyle shook his head and folded his arms. "I don't remember saying I was even playing your stupid game—"

Trent laughed loudly. "Oh, come on—it's not like you guys haven't had plenty of practice all summer long!"

Maxwell burst out laughing at the look on Kyle's face. "What's wrong, Kyle? Scared?"

And now Kyle just looked angry. "It's not like that—we're friends—"

"Oh, so you don't want to kiss my sister?"

"Wait—that's not what I meant—" Poor Kyle looked like he'd gotten his foot stuck in a bear trap.

Trent pointed at Kyle and laughed. "So you *do* want to kiss James—I knew it!"

I tried desperately to fight my way into the argument. "Leave Kyle alone—He's not going to—I told him not to!"

Based on the dumbfounded looks on everyone's faces, and even worse, a strange mixture of hurt and embarrassment on Kyle's, I was wishing I'd kept my gigantic mouth shut. The words had burst out of me in sheer stressed out panic. I couldn't even look at Kyle. Everyone was silent for a second before Blake, Maxwell, and Trent burst out laughing.

Blake was the first to try and speak around his laughs. "What? That's hilarious! See, I told you James wore the pants! Kyle wouldn't dare kiss her even if he wanted to!"

Maxwell could hardly breathe, laughing and trying to talk at the same time. "Yeah—he knows James would beat him up if he did!"

"Kyle doesn't even want to kiss me, so just stop it—"

"Yeah—he's way too much of a wimp to try, right, James?" Now Trent was gasping from laughing, too.

All three guys were laughing so hard that I was ready to scream at all of them, but the next instant, Kyle had forced a laugh and said, "Oh, yeah?" and roughly grabbed me by both upper arms. I gasped and tried to wrench myself away, but Kyle pulled me to him. The next thing I knew, he'd pressed his mouth hard on mine.

It only lasted for a second, but I couldn't move. Kyle let go of me fast, and while I stared in shock at him, I was surprised to see that he looked pretty startled himself.

I didn't realize how quiet it had suddenly become until my brother and two cousins erupted back into their annoyingly loud laughing again. I couldn't stop staring at Kyle, who was trying to act like none of this was that big of a deal but failing miserably in the attempt.

"Wow—I didn't think you had it in you, Kyle!"

"You need to pay up now, Blake!"

"Yeah, I guess I do. Here's your twenty bucks, man. You earned it!"

A second later, Blake had tossed a twenty-dollar bill at Kyle's feet, and then all three boys ran off, laughing their stupid heads off.

I looked down at the crumpled twenty-dollar bill on the grass that Kyle hadn't made a move to pick up yet and realized I was trembling.

"James—"

"You—you guys made a bet?" I said dully, my voice quivering in a way I didn't like. I couldn't lift my eyes from that horrible piece of paper on the grass.

"It wasn't me, James. It wasn't my idea!"

"Twenty bucks. I hope it was worth it." Now my voice was quivering harder.

"James—"

I wasn't about to let Kyle see me cry. No way. It was bad enough that whenever I thought about my first kiss, I'd have this horrible memory to deal with. I couldn't let crying in front of the guy who'd given me my first kiss—especially since it was Kyle, my friend since forever—be part of this horrific memory.

So I did the only thing I could do. I stretched my legs and ran back into the house as fast as I could, letting the back door slam hard behind me.

I was quiet the rest of the evening, even after Aunt Gracie finally took my two mean, smirking cousins home. Mom and Dad gave me a hug and kiss good-bye and made an effort to smile and say good-bye to Anna, too. I avoided Trent and gave Sarah a smile and a wave as she followed my parents out the door.

Grandpa followed after them with a "be back in a minute, girls" thrown over his shoulder. I sat down in one of the recliners near Anna, but even after the house had been quiet for a solid minute, Anna didn't move from her chair. She just sat there without moving and stared out the front window.

Anna finally sighed. "You know," she began quietly, "I really love your grandfather. So much. Just like I love my husband, and your grandfather loves your grandma."

Anna sighed again and rubbed her eyes before turning to look at me. "I know I'm not your grandmother, and I'm not trying to replace her. Not in your family, and not in your grandfather's heart. I wouldn't ever try to do that, because I know I never could. And I wouldn't want to. You know that, don't you?"

I looked at her and nodded slowly.

Anna smiled at me and nodded back. "I appreciate you trying to accept me, James. You have no idea what it means to your grandpa. And to me."

"I know you're having a hard time, but, well—I like you." It surprised me a little to be saying it out loud, but it was true. I really *did* like her. She'd tried harder than anyone I'd ever known to make everyone happy.

Anna reached out and put her hand on top of mine for a moment and patted it awkwardly. "I like you, too, James. I like you a lot. You remind me more and more of your grandma—"

The kitchen door slammed again and a moment later, Grandpa entered the living room with a big, cheery smile on his face. "Well, did you have a happy birthday, James?"

I turned to give Grandpa a big smile. "I did, Grandpa. Thanks to you. I still can't believe you bought me that beautiful dress! I can't wait to wear it to your wedding."

Grandpa walked over to me and kissed the top of my head. "It's so nice to have someone else be happy about our special day coming up. Looking forward to it, too, and all that."

"Well, thank you for making this day special for me."

"Well, thank you back for making this whole summer special for us."

"It means so much—" Anna's voice caught in her throat. I watched her wipe her eyes for a moment before she smiled and continued. "We appreciate that you're willing to accept our marriage and be happy for us. You just don't know how much, James."

It hit me then that all summer long, I'd never seen anyone come to visit. Not people in the ward and definitely not any of my relatives—the older ones that my grandparents had always been close to through the years. Like my grandma's sisters. Kyle and I had been Grandpa and Anna's only friends and social life all summer long, and although the realization made me glad we'd spent time with them, at the same time, the thought made me sad.

"Well, Harold, if I remember right, you were in the middle of a great story just as everyone arrived for James's birthday party!"

I smiled at Anna's brave smile as she handed him the recorder before turning back to Grandpa. "That's right, Grandpa. We were getting somewhere good with our history project, before we were so rudely interrupted!"

Grandpa laughed. "Rudely interrupted—that's right!"

"So what *did* you do once you made it to Modena?"

FORTY-ONE

We didn't end up staying in Modena but left early the next morning and headed towards the mountains to get busy digging the mining camp out of the snow. We went up to the state line, about eighteen miles north of Modena on the Nevada border, back up into the mountains, and met up with some other CCC guys on Cats and in trucks who were helping to dig people out, too. Besides the mining camp, we were supposed to dig out some cattle ranchers along the way who were stuck in the snow up in the mountains, too.

When we finally made it over to the cattle ranch, the ranchers waved their hats and cheered when they saw our Cat making its climb up the hill. All the guys at the ranch clapped us on the back and hustled us into the ranch house for some food. I was surprised when we sat down to a big mountain-man type of meal with steak and eggs and all the trimmings.

"Doesn't look like being snowed in has hurt you guys too much!"

One of the cowboys grinned at me, scratching his head. "Oh, no— we've got plenty of food. It's the cattle that're suffering."

Bud slid in beside me at the table. "You run out of hay?"

"Peat, actually. That's what we'd been feeding them 'til we ran out."

Landon didn't look up, he was so busy stuffing food into his mouth. "So what are you feeding them now?"

"Cornflakes. It's all we've got to keep 'em going."

I couldn't believe they could keep cattle alive on cornflakes, but I gave the ranchers a gold star for coming up with the idea. Since they had plenty of food for people, we bedded down at night in the bunkhouse and got a couple of good meals at that ranch house while we finished opening the road down the mountain and into town for them. After that, the ranchers were able to take their trucks and go into town to where the railroad had brought in hay, and then they were able to get hay to the cattle and take care of them properly. It felt good, knowing us CCC boys were able to help them out. They called us heroes, but what really felt great was knowing we'd been able to help them save their cattle.

The Supe had given us directions to get to the mining town, which included following a road from the ranch to where an old state road guy was stationed. He was supposed to instruct us where to go to get to the mining camp and over to some sheepherders as well. We found him all right—a grizzled-looking little guy with a big gray beard and squinty eyes.

"See that canyon up a ways to the left? That's where you're headed. You'll see a stream that's ice now. Stay to the left of it."

That didn't sound right to me at all. "I thought the mining camp was over to the right—"

"Oh, you did, did you? And who told you that?"

"I've been around here before. There's no mining camp up to the left in that canyon."

The state road guy let a few obscenities fly. "I'm sending you to dig out a miner. That's all that matters—"

"But the Supe told us to dig out a mining camp—"

"Just do as you're told, boy! I'm not taking any back talk from any of you—get going!"

The ol' state road guy jumped in his truck and followed us on the path the Cat was breaking up the mountain to make sure we did as we were told, so there wasn't anything we could do but dig out the road in the opposite direction from the mining camp. I figured maybe there were some miners stuck in an actual mine, but once we got the road dug out to the mine head, there was just one guy there at the mouth of the mine. The mine was a small one, and he was the only one who laid claim to it. He was friends with the state road guy and had worked it with him to get a clear path down the mountain so he could haul his ore in. Bud, Landon, and I ground our teeth watching the two old guys toss loads of ore into the state road guy's truck. All three of us swore our way back down the mountain in the Cat, but when we got back to where we should've turned off for the mining camp, we were in for a real treat. The Supe had just arrived with some more CCC boys in trucks and Cats.

The Supe glared at me. "Somehow, I knew you three would be involved in this!"

The Supe looked ready to kill, and I just knew we'd get thrown out of the Cs for sure. But luckily for us, the Supe had already found out what had happened from the cattle ranchers we'd dug out. The Supe jumped off the Cat he was on, ran as best he could in the snow, and yanked that ol' state road guy out of his truck. He got him down in the snow on the road and, boy, he and that state road guy went around and around before the Supe wrestled him good and hard down in the snow. That ol' state road guy found out the hard way that he'd better not send CCC guys to do selfish work like that again.

"Too much daylight's been wasted as it is. Gas up the Cat and get going to the mining camp."

The Supe jumped back onto his Cat as if nothing big had happened, so we hurried and gassed up and did the same. We went on up to the mining camp and dug the people out of the snow up on the mountain so they could get into town.

After we'd finished digging out the mining camp, Landon and Bud and I and a bunch of other CCC guys were sent to dig out a lot of sheep herds that were stuck out on the desert, too. By the time we finally got to where the herds were with the Cats, we were in for a horrible sight.

"Holy Moses—would you look at that!"

None of us could speak after that, because what we were seeing was terrible. Most of the sheep were frozen. Some of the sheep that weren't frozen would struggle through the snow over to us and get in the way of the Cat. Once they'd get in the track where we needed to open up the snow, there was no way to get them back out. We didn't have any choice but to run right over them with the Cat. Otherwise, we'd have to start over and make a new road.

I saw frozen sheep piled up like stacks of hay out there on the desert. The wool was worn away from their legs and bellies where they'd tried to break through the crust of the snow. The sheepherders had tried to keep them alive by cutting branches off of the piñon pines so the sheep could chew on the branches.

It was a horrible, sad sight, but even though a lot of sheep were lost, whole herds would've been lost along with the sheepherders if us CCC boys hadn't rescued them off that mountain. The sheepherders were so grateful they were in tears, and Bud and Landon and I—we did some crying, too. We finally got enough roads made to get the sheepherders and their sheep back into Modena where hay had been hauled in for the sheep to eat.

It took us a few weeks to get all the mining camps, cattle ranchers, and sheepherders dug out of the snow on that mountain and paths plowed for them to get into Modena. It was hard work up there in the mountains and in the cold, but it was good work. It was up there digging out those people trapped on the mountains that I realized I felt better about myself than I had in a long time. Mostly, I think, because I wasn't thinking about myself at all.

milk. Hey, Grandpa—where's the milk?"

I'd tried to sleep in the next day, but after sleepily dreaming about my beautiful new lavender dress and my wonderful day with Grandpa, the second I remembered my moment with Kyle the night before when he'd kissed me, I was wide awake and couldn't sleep anymore.

I had the refrigerator door open with a bowl of cold cereal waiting nearby, but no carton of milk was inside.

"Sorry, honey. I finished it off this morning. Anna's coming over soon to talk wedding plans. Would you mind walking over to that corner drugstore and picking up a carton?"

I couldn't help laughing. Go buy more milk myself? My birthday was definitely officially over now. "Sure, Grandpa. No problem."

I tried not to think about Kyle or that stupid, lame excuse for a kiss while I yanked on my favorite cut-off jeans and a red jersey T-shirt. I pulled my hair back with a banana clip and slipped my feet into my white sneakers without socks before jogging over to the drugstore, moving extra fast past Grandma June's once I spied Kyle's car in the driveway.

I was still jogging when I rounded the corner to the drugstore, but I jammed my feet to a screeching halt when I saw two fine-looking boys walking out of the drugstore toward a car parked a few yards away. Two fine Central High guys, to be exact. The hot blue-eyed blond was Kelly Baxter, a center on the junior varsity football team. He'd been in my seminary class last term. And the way-too-handsome, blue-eyed, black-haired guy couldn't be anyone but Brett Colton, the varsity team's star quarterback, even though he'd only been a sophomore last year. I remembered how shocked I'd been to find out that someone as healthy and in shape as Brett Colton had leukemia. But it was great now to see how good Brett looked. Really good, in fact. He was still on the lean side, but he'd bulked up some since he'd gone into remission.

Kelly was holding a can of pop, but Brett was actually carrying a baby in his arms. A pretty little girl dressed in a pink sundress who was giggling at Brett while he goggled at her, saying, "Hey, Kitty. How's my girl?" He looked so cute rubbing noses with her that I couldn't help laughing myself. I must've laughed louder than I thought, because a second later, instead of opening the car door, Kelly turned to look in my direction.

I was standing there in the parking lot, staring like some freak, so I forced myself to look away and walk a wide circle around them towards the open door of the drugstore. I carefully glanced over my shoulder as I walked by and nearly tripped when I saw Kelly Baxter was leaning against the car, staring right at me and grinning.

"Hey, I know you. You're Jamie, right? Jamie Addison?"

My eyes were too wide open while I nodded. "Yeah, that's me."

Brett turned with the baby all snuggled tight in his arms, and when he saw me, he grinned his gigantic, wide grin at me. At me!

"Hey—you go to Central, too, don't you?"

"Yeah, I do." I looked down nervously before making myself look at Brett. The little girl in his arms was watching me and gave me a huge, toothless smile. "Hey, cute baby."

"My little sister, Kitty." I couldn't help smiling. Brett looked so proud when he said that. I couldn't imagine Trent ever looking that way while telling anyone I was his little sister.

"You were in my seminary class last term. Brother Anderson's class, right?"

I nodded and felt my face flaming red. "He was a good teacher."

"Yeah, I liked him, too. That was a pretty fun class."

I thought so, too, but mostly because Kelly was in it. He was nice to look at, and he'd had good comments to make in class.

Brett turned Kitty around so her back was against his chest. Now that she could see everyone, she wouldn't stop kicking her legs and making loud babbling sounds.

Brett laughed and kissed the top of Kitty's head. "She has to get her two cents in, I guess."

I smiled and watched Kitty smile and babble back at me. "I'll bet she's a lot of fun."

Brett beamed his wide grin at me. "Oh, yeah—she's the best!"

Kelly laughed and shook his head at me. "Watch out. You stick around, and you'll get play-by-play details of everything she's been doing lately!"

I pretended to act horrified. "Oh—well, I'm sure that'd be great, but I have to buy some—milk! Yeah, that's right—some milk!"

Kelly burst out laughing again. "Good excuse, Jamie—escape while you can!"

Brett grinned widely at me. "Yeah, well—we've got to get out of here, too. My mom would freak if she knew we had Kitty with us."

I laughed and waved with a "See ya—" before I hurried by them. I turned around one more time and almost tripped when I caught Kelly still grinning at me. I nearly tripped over my feet again when Brett slowly winked at me. I whipped my head back around and stepped into the doorway of the drugstore but stopped short when I heard a low whistle from Brett.

"I know those legs from somewhere."

And then Kelly's voice. "Girls' basketball team. Not bad, huh?"

"Not bad at all!"

Something about the way Brett Colton said that last comment, slow and with a smile in his voice, made my face burn. I whirled around without seeing where I was going and almost fell over the magazine rack near the doorway. I tripped my way past it and practically ran to hide in the back of the store where the milk was, my heart pounding the whole time.

I stared at my face in the reflection of the glass door in front of the rows and rows of milk and watched my mouth slowly grin. *I guess I'm really not that bad. Not bad at all.*

"Too bad Kyle wasn't here to see!" I was shocked to realize I'd not only thought that but said it out loud, too. And that I'd meant it, and not just so I could've used it to thumb my nose at him. I was still thinking it all over when I walked back into Grandpa's house.

"James, you'll never guess what Anna just told me!" Grandpa looked so excited, waving me over to the kitchen table where he and Anna were seated, that I was afraid he was going to explode.

Anna looked both pleased and embarrassed. "Oh, really, it's nothing, Harold. It's nothing, James. Really!"

"What? What's nothing?"

Grandpa pulled a chair out for me and made me sit down first. "Well, Anna and I have been planning our wedding, and I couldn't wait anymore to tell her that I want to take her to Hawaii for our honeymoon, and guess what? She's just told me she can get us a good discount on the tickets since her husband used to work for the airlines. Isn't that great?"

Anna tried to shush Grandpa. "Oh, it's not a big deal—"

I had to stop her, though. "Not a big deal, Anna? Sure, it's a big deal! That's great. Does that mean the doctor said you can go after all?"

Grandpa shook his head. "No, we still can't go for a few months or so. But now I can take Anna to more than just Hawaii, since I'll have airplane money to spare!" Grandpa didn't stop there. "And guess what else? We've ordered one of those big, three-layer cakes for our wedding at that nice bakery down the street. Anna's having them put real flowers on it and everything!"

"That sounds really nice." And I meant it, too. I actually got a kick out of listening to them excitedly rattle off all the plans they'd made for their big day that would be here in a few short weeks, until Grandpa stopped and looked at me thoughtfully.

"James, I have something else for you that I meant to give you on your birthday, but you seemed out of sorts later on, so I didn't. But I think maybe now might be a good time."

Grandpa hurried into his bedroom. He came out a minute later and placed a small, square gold box in my hand. The box was old and familiar, and as I slowly opened the lid, my heart pounded when I saw the beautiful ring resting on a bed of white tissue paper inside. A gold ring, with two tiny, perfectly carved gold tulips on their sides with a small diamond between the two flowers. I hadn't seen it since the day I arrived at Grandpa's for the summer.

"It's—it's Grandma's engagement ring. The first one you gave her!"

Grandpa smiled. "You remembered!"

"Of course, but are you sure, Grandpa? I mean, maybe Aunt Gracie, or Sarah—"

Grandpa shook his head and squeezed my hand. "I thought it would mean more to you, now that you've been hearing all of these stories about how we got together and everything."

I stared at the sparkling ring again before reaching out to hug Grandpa. "I'll treasure this forever, Grandpa. I can't believe you're giving it to me!"

Grandpa patted my back as he hugged me. "I know you'll take good care of it, James. Just like you're taking good care of my old memories, recording my life history for me and everything."

I hugged Grandpa tighter. "I love your stories, Grandpa!"

Anna smiled as I showed her Grandma's ring. "It's absolutely lovely, James." Anna turned to Grandpa and patted his arm. "How about you tell us some more, Harold?"

I nodded and nudged Grandpa. "Yes, I want to know what happened after you rescued all the sheep!"

Grandpa winked. "Go get the tape recorder, James, and I'll pick up where I left off!"

FORTY-THREE

The Supe decided to send a bunch of us, including me, Bud, and Landon, back to the Veyo Camp instead of the spike camp early Friday morning. On the way to Veyo from Modena, the wind blew and it snowed, so I had a heck of a time getting back to camp. I didn't ride to the Veyo Camp in the Cat with Landon and Bud but was asked to drive one of the CCC trucks back instead. The truck didn't have a snow plow on the front of it, but it did have chains on the wheels. I'd rigged up an old Coleman lantern in the truck to keep warm and replaced the glass around the wick with a cylinder piece of metal stove pipe. The hood of the truck had a vent that could be opened and closed, so by keeping it opened just a crack, the smoke and fumes would go outside. That kept me plenty warm on the way back to camp.

The road cut over to Enterprise, so I decided to make a quick stop there to see if Lilly wanted to go to the dance that night with me. She was excited to see me, which was pretty exciting for me. Vivian for once seemed happy to see me, too, especially when I told her that Landon was already at the Veyo Camp and that I'd make sure he came back that night for the dance, too. I told Lilly I'd come pick her up, and before I could head back to the truck, she grabbed the front of my coat with both hands and gave me a fast kiss on the lips.

"Don't be late!"

I whistled and sang all the way back to camp.

The guys were worn out when I arrived and were snoozing in their bunks.

"Well, are we going to the dance tonight or what?" I yelled as loud as I could.

That got all the guys awake and hurrying to get cleaned up. The dance had already started, so we had to move fast. I hadn't seen Lilly in weeks, and now that Christmas was almost here, I wanted to get her something nice. I'd wandered through the one store in Modena trying to make up my mind between either a little bottle of perfume or a lace handkerchief, and since I never could decide which Lilly would like more, I'd gone ahead and bought both.

It'd been cold, stressful work digging people out of the mountains, so even though I'd promised Lilly to give up my smoking and drinking, I'd picked up the weed habit again. There were always cigarettes in all of the trucks, but after the first few weeks on the mountain, I started to feel guilty about my promise to her and made myself stop smoking. It wasn't doing me any good, and I wasn't about to let smoking cause me to miss out on being with Lilly.

"My good shirts are all dirty. Any of you got a shirt I can borrow tonight?"

"Here, Addison, how about this one?"

Bud tossed me one of his nice shirts, but since Faye hadn't gotten after him to quit the weed, he'd never stopped. When I put the shirt on, I could smell tobacco all over it.

"Holy Moses—your shirt stinks!" I moaned.

Bud laughed. "It's just good old tobacco. It's the best choice you've got tonight, so it's either this shirt or one of your dirty shirts. So what's it going to be, tobacco or sweat?"

Having to pick between two evils, I figured the tobacco smell was the better of the two stinks. None of us wore our heavy work clothes to go to the dances, even though it was freezing cold outside. We'd wear our oxfords and light pants and borrow each other's shirts. Then we'd put the big CCC army overcoat around us. As long as the trucks ran and we could get some heat in the trucks, we were fine and stayed warm.

I was dressed up in my nicest pants and shoes, wearing Bud's nice, although smoke-smelling shirt, and had my gift for Lilly all wrapped up and ready to go. Once we arrived at Lilly's home, Vivian ran outside to meet Landon at the truck while I walked up to the door and knocked. Lilly opened the door, looking more beautiful than I remembered. She smiled that wonderful slow smile of hers and took a hold of my hand.

"Come in!"

I took off my coat and with my present in hand went over and sat down on the couch beside her.

"I wanted to get you something for Christmas—" I couldn't say anything else, because I could tell Lilly wasn't listening to me. Her eyes weren't shining anymore but looked suspicious instead. And she was sniffing—sniffing hard.

"What in the world is that smell?!"

Before I could explain, she grabbed my sleeve and took a big whiff of the shirt. With that, she lit into me like crazy about my promise not to smoke anymore, and here I was, supposedly caught red-handed. Boy, I got chewed out good and proper. She wouldn't let me get even one word in edgewise. She was too far gone into her tirade.

"When I think of how I told you I wasn't about to go with a man who smoked, and how I believed that you'd given up such a rotten, stinking habit—"

"Will you let me talk for just five seconds—please?!" I'd never gotten that loud and firm with Lilly before, so after her jaw dropped, it snapped back shut.

"I'm listening."

So then I finally was able to explain to her it was Bud's shirt with the tobacco smell. "I told you I was staying away from cigarettes, and I have. All my shirts are dirty, so borrowing this shirt from Bud was the best I could do, since I barely got into Veyo tonight. But thanks for thinking the worst of me right off. Oh—and by the way. Merry Christmas." I dropped my present into her lap and got up and stormed over to the front door. "So are we going to go to the dance or what? Bud and Landon and everyone are waiting."

I felt bad when I saw the look on her face. This wasn't at all the way I'd thought it would be to see her again. I certainly hadn't imagined fighting with her about anything. She mumbled something about needing to get her coat. I watched her set my unopened present on the table by the couch before she left the room.

Ol' Kurt Harris was at the dance and spotted Lilly and me right off. We'd barely stepped onto the dance floor after saying less than five words to each other driving over to the dance at the church house when Kurt Harris came barreling over to us.

"Hey, Lilly—good to see you again! Mind if I cut in?"

Kurt wasn't even looking at me, but I felt cold all over as it hit me that Lilly had still been going to the Friday night dances and Kurt had, too. I let go of Lilly and stepped back. For all I knew, by now, she probably liked dancing with Kurt better anyway.

"Thank you, Mr. Harris, but I'd really like to dance with Harold. I'm sorry. You'll forgive me, won't you?"

I didn't know who was more surprised—Kurt or me. Kurt mumbled something I couldn't hear and stomped off the dance floor. Lilly smiled and put her left hand back on my shoulder. She slipped her right hand into mine, and we picked the waltz back up. I was still annoyed thinking about Kurt, though, wondering how much dancing the two of them had been doing, so of course, I had to go and ruin everything.

"You sure you wouldn't rather dance with Kurt? Since you two have become so close and everything?"

Lilly's smile was gone in an instant. "I said no to him, didn't I?"

"Yep. You picked me over Kurt. I'm honored."

I decided to ignore whatever Lilly was muttering and looked around the dance floor and at all the people standing and sitting around the edges of the floor by the walls instead.

"So where's your dad? I don't see him here tonight."

"He's taking care of our cattle. He'll be bringing them into town from our ranch up in the North Hills soon. I'm surprised you noticed he's not here."

I snorted. "It's hard not to notice someone who stares at me like he wishes I was dead."

That pretty much ended any conversation between us. Neither of us tried talking anymore after that.

Kurt watched us dance, with a big ugly scowl on his face, before storming out of the church. Which was fine with me, although I felt like storming out myself. But I didn't, and although Lilly and I hardly talked, we kept on dancing together for the rest of the song. And then she danced with someone else, so I did, too, and after that happened too many times in a row, I went back over to her and asked her to dance before anyone else could. I didn't even sneak outside for the typical CCC refreshments that I knew were hiding in one of the trucks.

Towards the end of the night, Lilly and I were dancing together, and we danced our way over to where one of the windows had been cracked open. Lilly made a horrible face and put her hand over her mouth for a second.

"What in the world is that smell?!"

"If you're going to keep giving me grief over this shirt—"

"It's not your shirt. Your shirt smells wonderful in comparison. It's something else—something nearby—"

I didn't even have to try and smell anything. The stink hit me in the face the second we danced near the opened window and the next breeze filtered in. It smelt like dead skunk. I could just imagine who was responsible for putting something so foul near the only open window. The smell was so bad it didn't take long before everyone smashed into the farthest corner of the church house away from the window to dance, but the wind was blowing the air in just enough to move the smell everywhere fast. That pretty much served as the swan song of the evening, so I took Lilly home and left without kissing her even once.

FORTY-FOUR

By the time Landon and Bud had finished saying good-bye to
Faye and Vivian and we headed back to camp, it was really late.
We'd all come in the same CCC pickup truck together, and the
wind had blown enough snow all over the dirt road we'd opened up
from Veyo into Enterprise that we had to plow through dirty snow and
mud and muck to get back. None of us had drunk anything that night,
which was both good and bad. We were all completely sober, but we
were freezing cold, because there wasn't any alcohol in our stomachs to
keep some kind of an inner fire going and also because we didn't have
our heavy CCC winter clothes on. Even though we had our big CCC
army overcoats on, our legs and feet were freezing in our oxfords and
light pants, but as long as the truck kept running, we were all right.

At about five o'clock in the morning, we were a third of the way back
to the Veyo Camp when the worst possible thing happened. The truck
let out a strange, dying noise and then jerked to a halt.

"Hey, what just happened?"

"I don't know—it just quit!" I stepped on the brake and shoved it in
gear before trying to start the truck back up again. No matter what I did,
though, the truck was dead. Completely dead. It wouldn't make any
noise except for a "click" while I tried to turn the engine over.

"Move over and let me try!"

First Landon tried, and then Bud tried, but none of us could get the truck going. Finally I jumped out of the cab and stomped through the snow in my oxfords, soaking them all the way through in two steps, and threw both sides of the hood open. I only had the light of the moon to help me see under the hood, but from what I could tell, everything looked okay inside.

Bud leaned out the passenger window. "What's the matter?"

"Nothing, so far as I can tell!"

Both Landon and Bud jumped out in their oxfords and sloshed over to me to take a look under the hood. Neither of them could find anything wrong with the engine, either.

We were all so dumbfounded we didn't know what to do. Instead of finding some wood and building us a fire where we could keep warm, like we should have, we all sloshed back through the mud and snow in our freezing, sopping wet oxfords and sat in the truck without saying anything, only staring straight ahead of us at nothing. Every so often I'd try starting the engine up again, but it was as dead as could be.

After a few minutes, Landon wouldn't stop squirming. "My feet—I can't move my feet!"

I couldn't move my feet, either. "Yeah, my feet feel numb, too—"

"I don't mean numb—I mean I can't move them off the floor!"

I tried to move my shoes and within seconds, we all realized the same thing. Our shoes had frozen to the floor! We had no choice but to pull our feet out of our shoes and sit on them to keep our feet warm. We cried like babies, we were so cold. We sat huddled in that truck crying on and off from five in the morning until the sun finally came up.

Bud was the first to make us move. "We've got to get out and build a fire. Come on!"

Somehow we got our frozen selves out of the truck and stiffly moved around to get our blood flowing again. We found some wood and built a fire to warm ourselves up and dry out our shoes. While Bud and Landon examined the engine, I took a good look at the fuel line and then crawled underneath the truck to follow the line under the cab of the truck and over to where the gas tank was behind the cab of the truck on the driver's side.

It only took one look at the portion of the line near the gas tank before I let a few good obscenities fly.

"Some rat cut off the gas line!"

"Are you kidding me?!"

A second later, Bud and Landon joined me underneath the truck to take a look.

Landon scratched his head. "It must've happened while we were at the dance."

"Think so?" I grumbled.

Landon ignored me. "Probably used a pair of pliers. You'd just have to squeeze the gas line real tight with pliers, and it'd snap the line easy."

I could just picture Kurt Harris after he stormed out of the dance reaching in under the hood with a pair of pliers and squeezing the gas line until it broke. And laughing the whole time he did it.

Bud climbed out from under the truck first. "Think we can jerry rig this and get back to camp okay?"

I crawled out from under the truck with Landon and shook my head. "The Enterprise Camp, maybe, but not the Veyo one."

The fuel pump was located on the side of the engine by the driver's door, so once we'd found a pair of pliers in the truck's tool box, we broke the fuel line off close to the fuel pump itself. Landon found a canteen cup in the truck, so we siphoned gas out of the gas tank, filled the canteen cup with gas, and bent the broken and now short fuel line into the canteen cup. We kept the half of the hood by the driver's side folded down flat against the side of the truck, and Landon—he had to sit on the fender of the front wheel with his feet on the runningboard of the truck, holding that canteen cup against the fuel line while I jumped back in the truck and turned the engine over. That ol' fuel pump sucked the gasoline out of the canteen cup and into the fuel pump, then into the carburetor system, and finally we got that truck moving again.

It was slow going. Landon had to sit on the fender, holding the canteen cup, and every so often we had to stop and siphon more gas out of the gas tank and into that canteen cup. It was well past noon by the time we finally made it back into Enterprise. Landon was half sick and starting to ramble funny and sweat like mad. Bud and I thought for sure he had pneumonia. I drove the truck right up to Lilly's house, and Bud and I carried him between us up to the front door while poor Landon moaned and cried. I kicked the door with my foot and yelled for someone—anyone—to open up. Lilly herself opened the front door.

"Oh, my lands—get inside, quick!"

From the noise we made carrying poor Landon in, Lilly's three sisters came running downstairs to see what was going on, while Lilly's mom came hurrying in from the kitchen, gripping a towel in her hands. Vivian screamed and burst into tears when she saw Landon, and Lilly stared all bug-eyed for a second before grabbing Vivian's arm. Lilly's mom took control pretty fast.

"Get out of the way, girls. We need to get him by the stove in the kitchen!"

It was too bad Landon was so sick. Otherwise, he really would've enjoyed all the fuss those five women made over him. We carried him to the rocking chair by the big wood-burning stove in the kitchen while Vivian wrapped a blanket tight around him. Lilly took his shoes off, and Rachel and Beth got busy helping their mom get some sort of soup into a bowl for him. Boy, they took good care of him and babied him up good. Vivian grabbed the bowl of soup out of Rachel's hands and fed him a few bowls of the stuff while Bud and I took the truck over to a mechanic in town and got it fixed.

I wished like crazy I could talk to Lilly for even just two minutes, but we were hours late back to camp. As soon as the truck was ready to go, Bud and I loaded Landon back into the front seat with us—he was now back to his joking, grinning self and flirting with Vivian something fierce. He got a kiss out of her before we left. I wasn't sure Lilly would want one from me, so all I did was tell her good-bye, and she did the same back.

FORTY-FIVE

I stayed away from Kyle for the next few days, and the fact made me sad. We'd been best friends for so long, and now it seemed like every time I turned around, something stupid had to happen to make me feel uncomfortable to be around him. But even if I'd wanted to see him and Grandma June, I wouldn't have been able to. August was here, and between helping Grandpa and Anna with their wedding plans, plus the family reunion in southern Utah coming up, I didn't have a lot of time left for anything else. I'd planned on going with my parents and Trent and Sarah, since I thought for sure Grandpa and Anna wouldn't be going, but I was wrong.

"You really still want to go to the family reunion, Grandpa?"

Grandpa stared at me in surprise before laughing. "Of course I do, James. You're going to come along with Anna and me, aren't you?"

Now I was the one staring in surprise. "You're *both* going?"

Grandpa tweaked my nose. "Of course—I'm excited to go. It'll be fun!"

From the last showdown with my great-aunts, I had a bad feeling about the family reunion. But Grandpa looked so happy, and Anna was so willing to go just to make Grandpa happy that I couldn't say anything negative. "Sure. I'd rather go with you two anyway!"

I tried to act all happy, but Grandpa folded his arms and looked at me almost sternly. "I know that look, James. What's going on in that head of yours?"

I shrugged nervously. "It's just that, well, Great-Aunt Vivian and everyone—they weren't that nice the last time they were here, and I think Great-Aunt Vivian said to rethink coming to the family reunion or something like that—"

Grandpa brushed that aside and laughed. "Oh, don't worry about them. Everyone will feel a lot better about things once Anna and I are good and married. You'll see!"

I smiled and nodded, but I couldn't make myself believe it.

FORTY-SIX

I t was a long drive down to southern Utah. I knew we'd have to leave a few days in advance in order to get to Enterprise on the date the family reunion was set to start, but Grandpa had other ideas.

"It won't take a whole week to get to Enterprise, Grandpa!"

Grandpa smiled and ruffled my hair. "I know that. I thought it might be fun to take a few detours along the way, if that's okay with you, James."

I shrugged and looked at Grandpa's grinning face curiously. "I don't have anywhere else to be. Where are we stopping?"

"That's a surprise. You'll see!"

I threw in a couple more shirts and pairs of shorts into my traveling bag, and soon the three of us were loaded up in Grandpa's truck and heading out on the highway for southern Utah.

"Head 'em up, move 'em out, hot dig, let's go!" Grandpa whistled and hummed to himself as we cruised down the highway, going faster than most people his age would drive.

Anna squeezed Grandpa's hand before turning to me, seated on her right in the cab of the truck. "You remembered the tape recorder, didn't you, James?"

"I did. I've got it here under the seat."

"Well, we're going to be like this for quite a few hours on the highway. Harold, how about recording some more of your history?"

I leaned forward to see Grandpa. "Yeah—I want to know what

262

happened after Kurt Harris cut the gas line to your truck and poor Uncle Landon nearly froze to death. I mean, if you're in the mood, Grandpa. Are you?"

Grandpa winked at Anna before grinning at me. "I'm always in the mood!"

FORTY-SEVEN

Everyone back at camp had been wondering where we'd been all day when we finally made it back late that afternoon after we got the gas line repaired, but that's what happens to guys when they're chasing girls and don't take care of themselves and somebody like Kurt Harris doesn't like someone like me.

Bud and Landon and I moved back over into the Enterprise Spike Camp a day later because the Supe needed Landon and Bud to be part of the shifts to drive the two Cats and me to drive one of the Walters to help clear more snow around Enterprise. All of us CCC guys worked twelve-hour shifts clearing snow for days on end. I wanted to see Lilly on Christmas, but two days before, a terrible snowstorm blew in, leaving four to five feet of snow on the level.

The day after the storm, I woke up early with a feeling that wouldn't go away that we needed to go over to Lilly's home and check on everyone. Even though the Supe had told the three of us that we didn't have to clear snow that day, I couldn't shake the thought that kept coming into my head that we needed to get over to Lilly's home. And as soon as possible.

"I'm sure Lilly's fine. Go back to sleep!" Bud had no desire to go anywhere, but since going to Lilly's meant Landon could see Vivian, Landon was on board to go to Lilly's house.

"Come on, Bud. It's better than hanging around here doing nothing all day!"

We cleared a path with the Walter over to Lilly's home to make sure everything was okay at their house, but it only took one look at Lilly's tear-streaked face along with the noise of four other sobbing women to know everything wasn't okay. Once I scraped the snow off my boots and stepped inside the house, Lilly ran right up to me and threw her arms tight around my neck.

"I've been praying you'd come!"

"Praying?" I took a hold of both of her hands and made her sit on the couch while Landon tried to comfort Vivian, who was crying so hard she was practically hysterical.

Lilly wiped her eyes with the back of her hand and took a deep breath. "My father's with the cattle up on our winter ranch in the North Hills."

"The North Hills? Where's that?"

Lilly's mom spoke up. "Just north of Old Hebron. You take this road in front of our house and keep heading north about five miles or so and you'll reach the hills."

I frowned. "What's your dad doing up there?"

Lilly wiped more tears from her eyes. "We always keep our cattle in the North Hills during the winter to graze. We have a cabin up there, and there's a lot more winter feed there, too, so it's easier to keep better track of the cattle during the winter."

Lilly's mother spoke up again. "The cattle have been up there for some time, doing just fine, but my husband was afraid a bad storm might come soon. He took a horse up to the North Hills to bring the cattle back into town the day before the storm hit."

Lilly gripped my arm. "He hasn't come back yet." Tears started falling down her cheeks again. "I've been praying all morning that you would come—that maybe you and Landon—"

I hurried and pulled her close. "We'll go get your dad. Don't worry anymore."

I was ready to go charging out the door, but Bud yelled for me to wait and reminded me of something I'd nearly forgotten about that was really going to put a huge snag in our rescue.

Neither of the Cats was in camp.

When the snowstorm hit, one of the two Cats had been left up on the mountain by a ranch near Enterprise, and the other Cat was up on the road to the Enterprise reservoir, just as stuck in the snow as the one on the mountain.

"Well, then the three of us are going to have to go rescue the Cats first!"

In order to get over to the reservoir to where the first Cat was, we'd have to take horses, so the girls hurried us over to one of their neighbor's homes. The father at that home let us borrow two horses along with a real work horse and a flat platform they called a "lizard" that looked something like a long sleigh.

We rode the horses towards the reservoir up along the canal bank where the snow was bowed off a little. The road was plowed in so deep over the horses' bellies that they couldn't make it, so we had to stop and pick a trail for them. I rode the big work horse with the lizard attached to the back of it. The lizard was big enough to haul a fifty-gallon drum of diesel fuel, so we loaded one on it so we'd have some fuel to start the Cats once we reached them. Along with the drum of fuel, we loaded a good-sized tub, a tool box, some oil, and some other things we needed. I dragged the whole load on that lizard-sleigh with the work horse behind Bud and Landon on their horses, who broke the trail for me.

We got a fire going the second we found the Cat. Then we drained the Prestone out of it and into the tub over the fire and got it good and hot. After it started boiling, we poured it back into the Cat. Then, we drained the oil out into the tub, got it boiling hot, and poured it back in the Cat, too. We took all the plugs out after that and cleaned them and heated them up before putting them back. We'd found out by experience that we could start the Cats pretty easy in the snow and cold if we heated the plugs up, too. The whole process took us a long time, but we finally got the Cat to start up.

Landon took the wheel of the Cat, and with Bud and me on the horses again, we trudged up the mountain to the ranch where the other Cat was and went through the whole process again until we got the other one started, too. Bud took the wheel of the second Cat, and I followed both of them down the mountain, riding the work horse with their two horses tied behind the lizard.

We got back on the road towards Hebron and the North Hills, and with the Cats in front of me to break the trail, it only took us an hour or so to finally get up on the North Hills where Lilly's dad was, stuck in the snow with all of his cattle.

Lilly's dad had done his best to keep the cows from lying down in the snow. Cows would die if they didn't keep moving. Icicles were frozen a foot long on the nose of every cow, and when we drove up to Lilly's dad, I could see the snow had frozen to such a hard crust that the ice was cutting the chest of his horse, making it bleed. I thought he was going to cry when we plowed our way over to him, but instead, for the first time, I saw him smile.

"I've been trying to get my cattle into town, but the snow's too deep. We went as far as we could, but when we got here, we were just too bogged down by the snow to go any further. I've just been doing my best to keep the cows on their feet instead."

"Landon and Bud are on the Cats. We'd better get you and your cattle back into town before you freeze any further!"

I pulled Lilly's dad off his horse and put him in the Cat with Landon to get warmed up, since his chaps and clothes were frozen solid. It was amazing how he'd kept himself going in the cold. He didn't have anything on his head except for his cowboy hat, and since his ears were open to the weather, they were redder than cherries.

Once we had him all settled into the Cat with Landon, Landon and

Bud got the Cats pointed down the hill and bulldozed a road in the snow down off the North Hills and over towards Enterprise. I followed behind with all of the horses and the lizard still hooked behind me. The cattle all followed along without any prodding, right behind our little convoy.

We'd left to go rescue the Cats and the cows early that morning, but by the time we finally got back into Enterprise, it was dark, and it'd turned bitter cold. The Cats ate a lot of gas, and we were about out of fuel, so we left them right at the border line into Enterprise. Bud, Landon, and Lilly's dad got back on their horses, and Lilly's dad took over the cattle from me.

I was so cold and frozen that when we rode up to Lilly's house, I just fell off the horse into the snow. I didn't know whether I was going to pull through, and at that point, I didn't care. Lilly and her mother and all her sisters came running out of the house, and with Landon and Bud's help, they took me in and undressed me and stuck me in a tub of cold water. Boy, that brought me back among the living again.

Lilly had my clothes hanging in the kitchen by the wood-burning stove to dry, and once I was settled in the kitchen wrapped in a blanket, I watched while she hustled around getting me something to eat. Vivian did the same for Landon, and Beth and Rachel took care of Bud. Lilly hovered over me, asking, "Do you want more soup? More bread? More hot chocolate?" the whole time I was trying to eat, but it was nice. Really nice.

Lilly waited until everyone had left the kitchen to sit down beside me at the kitchen table and sneak me a piece of apple pie.

"It's the last piece. I made it myself from apples I picked during the fall."

I grinned and cut into the pie. "Does this mean you're not mad at me anymore?"

Lilly looked shocked. "Me mad at you? I thought it was you who was angry with me!"

"I'm not mad anymore."

Lilly's eyes sparkled when she smiled at me. "Well, neither am I. In fact, I have something else I need to thank you for."

"Oh?"

"Yes—for the Christmas present. I love the handkerchief—it's going to be my Sunday one. And the perfume smells wonderful. I have some on now. Do you like it?"

Lilly tilted her head to one side to let me smell where she'd put some on her neck, but I kissed her neck instead. Lilly squealed and jumped, but she didn't move away. I couldn't resist the opportunity to give her a real kiss, and lucky for me, she didn't pull away. In fact, she let me kiss her again, longer this time.

Lilly pulled back enough to brush a lock of hair out of my eyes. "So now that you're back safe and sound, tell me all about your adventure rescuing my father today."

After I'd gone through the whole story, Lilly's eyes watered, and she gripped one of my hands in hers. "I prayed so hard—I knew Heavenly Father would hear and answer my prayer. I knew he'd send you here—I just knew everything would turn out all right, and it did—it did!"

I wasn't surprised God had answered Lilly's prayer. She was nearly an angel herself, she was so good all of the time. What surprised me was the idea of Him using me to answer her prayer. But at the same time, I knew that was exactly what He had done.

"I guess I must not be all bad if God Himself thought I could help out."

"You don't give yourself enough credit, Harold. You risked your life to save my father's. Not everyone does heroic things like that!"

I couldn't help chuckling at that. I was a lot of things, but one thing I wasn't was a hero.

Lilly disagreed, though. And she wasn't the only one. Once my clothes were dry enough to put on, even though by then it was in the early hours of the morning, Bud and Landon and I knew we needed to get back to camp. Bud ran outside to get the Walter started up, and Landon and I were about to follow him, but Lilly's dad stopped us.

"I have something I need to say to you boys." I wasn't surprised to hear his nice speech thanking us for rescuing him and his cattle, but his last words about knocked me flat on my back. "I've always wanted to see my girls marry good LDS boys who can take them to the temple, but after what you two did for me—saving my life and saving my cattle—I can't discourage you two from courting my daughters. And I won't. You're both fine young men."

Vivian and Lilly's mouths were hanging open as wide as mine and Landon's were, but after Lilly's dad shook Landon's hand and then my hand, the girls ran to their dad, squealing and hugging him before Vivian jumped into Landon's arms and Lilly threw her arms around me.

"You see—Heavenly Father answers all prayers—every one!"

The next morning, Bud and Landon and I went back up with more fuel in the drum on the sleigh and gassed up the Cats and plowed a few more paths around Hebron. A bunch of the cattle ranchers in town had their cattle down and around Hebron in the cedar trees where the snow wasn't quite as deep, but because of the recent storm, their cattle were stuck, too. Once we'd made a few more paths for them, they were able to use the road we'd plowed with the Cats all the way from Hebron into Enterprise as well. The ranchers put their cattle in the fields down in town where we'd put Lilly's father's cattle, so I moved some haystacks with the Walter into the fields in town so they could keep their cattle fed, too.

Landon and I spent Christmas that year with Lilly and Vivian and their whole family. Whenever we came by, we were always invited in, so we spent the rest of the winter—when we weren't pushing snow—going to the dances with Lilly and Vivian and getting to know their family inside their home.

Before the winter was over, people in town said they wished their daughters were going with CCC guys, too, because the trails we plowed led from the barracks up to Winsor's store, up to Lilly's home, down over to the church house and Faye's home, up to the schoolhouse, and back. We only plowed the roads that Lilly, Vivian, and Faye needed, so those were the only places in town that had paths for walking. Everyone had to climb over the snow everywhere else. The snow was so high it went right over the top of the fences around the houses. Nobody even tried to shovel it. Everyone just packed it down and walked on top of it.

That winter was a hard one, but we got through it okay. Us CCC boys opened lots of the roads, and we rescued most of the cows and sheep out of the snow in the mountains and into town where they could be fed, which helped out the people in town. But best of all, I could see Lilly whenever I wanted to, and that meant more to me than anything else.

FORTY-EIGHT

Grandpa had a big tent he'd thrown into the back of the truck along with some other gear, so we stopped at a KOA that night before heading back on the road and into northern Utah. Once we turned away from Salt Lake City and into Parley's Canyon, I knew we were heading towards Ashley National Forest and the Uinta Mountains, even without seeing any signs.

"Grandpa, are we going camping for a few days? That's your surprise, isn't it? Since we couldn't go for my birthday this year!"

Grandpa smiled and kept looking straight ahead as he drove. "Yes and no. You remember camping here, do you?"

"Sure—lots of times!"

"We haven't been back up here since you were about seven or eight, though."

I laughed. "You don't forget scenery like this, Grandpa!"

Grandpa smiled and nodded slowly. "No, you don't, James. You're right about that."

The trees on the mountains were just starting to change their colors from deep greens to golds and reds. I stared silently out the window as we drove along, winding through small towns and weaving our way up and down hills before we finally entered Ashley National Forest.

Grandpa stopped at the first campground we came to within minutes of entering the forest. The Yellowstone campground, which consisted of a small group of campsites almost in a circle with an outhouse nearby, was surrounded by tons of tall, skinny, white-barked quaking aspen trees that were shaking their small, dark green oval leaves in the breeze. The Yellowstone River was running fast, hardly more than a hop, skip, and a jump away. The sky was incredibly blue, the sun was shining, and the air smelled wonderfully mountain fresh and clean. Nothing could compare to being up high in the mountains. Nothing.

I jumped out of the truck once Grandpa ground it to a halt and looked carefully at the campsites around me. "Hey—this is where we camped the last time we came up here as a family, right, Grandpa?"

Grandpa nodded before beckoning for me to follow. "Very good. Come on, James, and bring your camera. I want to show you something."

Anna moved more slowly out of the truck and stretched her arms above her head. "I'm going to stay here and rest and set up some lunch. Is that okay?"

Grandpa smiled and gave Anna a quick kiss. "We won't be gone long. I promise!"

I followed Grandpa up the graveled, one-lane road until he turned right, moving fast into the middle of a thick bunch of quaking aspen trees. I fought my way, tripping over rocks and long wild grass, trying to keep up with him.

"Grandpa—what—where are you going?"

"Just come see!"

I stumbled as fast as I could until I saw him standing excitedly on a large slab of cement with weeds and wild grass growing in some of the larger cracks.

Grandpa was shaking his head in amazement with his hands on his hips, just staring at the slab before him. "Can't believe even this much is still here!"

I hurried forward to stand on the slab beside him and stared at the cement. "What is it?"

Grandpa turned to smile at me. "What do you think it might be, James?"

I frowned and studied the large rectangular slab more closely. "Well, it looks like maybe a building was here once."

Grandpa laughed and clapped his hands. "Exactly!"

My mind raced as a memory fought its way into my brain, and I remembered playing on big slabs of cement like this as a little kid on camping trips and finding "chalk" rocks with charcoal in them so I could draw pictures on the cement. Trent and I had played tic-tac-toe that way, and Sarah had carefully drawn hopscotch boards.

My heart beat fast as I turned to look at Grandpa. "Is—is this one of the—" I watched Grandpa's face beam at me before realization hit me good and hard. "We're standing in your old Moon Lake winter CCC campsite, aren't we?"

Grandpa laughed and hugged me. "Yes, this is where one of the old buildings was. One of the barracks for us enrollees to sleep in. And look over here, James—" Grandpa gave me a minute to take a few pictures before he hurried me across the gravel road to show me an even better foundation with part of the cement wall around it still intact. "Another building."

"Like in your old pictures!"

I snapped a few more photos before Grandpa hurried me farther up the hill until we came to two huge slabs that had gigantic stone fireplaces attached at one end of each of the two slabs. One of the fireplaces was more brick than stone, but both were impressive.

"The mess hall and rec center. Oh, we had some fun times here. Lots of dances. Us CCC boys built all of these buildings and the fireplaces and roads—everything—ourselves."

I moved forward to touch the smooth rocks placed tightly together to form the fireplace before me. "Wow! These fireplaces are huge!"

Grandpa nodded and craned his neck to look up at the top of the fireplace, easily at least twenty feet high in the air. "Yep, they are. You can see the top of the chimney sticking out of the mess hall that used to be here, in some of my Uinta Camp pictures—remember?"

I nodded and had Grandpa take my picture in front of the fireplace before snapping a couple of him standing in front of it as well.

Grandpa raced around in the trees like a kid on an Easter egg hunt, pointing out more of the cement slabs to me. "Here's where the officers lived, and over here was the bath house and the headquarters for the officers. And over here's where the doctor had his office."

I snapped pictures like crazy, chasing Grandpa through the trees as he excitedly pointed everything out to me.

"And see all these rocks lined up like so, on either side here? Those were set up to line both sides of the foot paths from building to building in camp."

Grandpa raced even deeper into the trees until he stopped, laughing at the remains of a wooden building that had crashed into a big hole in the ground.

I stood beside him, gasping to catch my breath, and stared at the building before snapping a picture or two. "I can't believe the building is still here. How come it is?"

Grandpa laughed again. "No one would've wanted the wood from this building. Can you guess why?"

I stared at the mess of wood everywhere and the big hole beneath it before I laughed, too. "This one—and that crashed-in building over there—these were the latrines, right?"

Grandpa grinned. "Right. No one wanted to try and salvage this wood!"

"Is that why there isn't anything but the cement slabs from the rest of the buildings?"

Grandpa nodded. "Yep. After this camp closed down for good, whatever remained of the buildings would've been scavenged by people in need. Things were hard back then, with the Depression still going on and the threat of war on the horizon. But we also took apart what we could to use for the next camp we were being moved to, if we'd finished the jobs where we were and no one was going to be coming in to replace us."

Grandpa walked back over to the gravel road and followed it until he stopped in front of a grassy area lined on both sides with quaking aspen trees. The area was wide enough for a truck to drive through and stretched out before us for yards and yards.

"What's this?"

Grandpa shook his head in amazement. "That used to be one of the main roads into the camp back in the '30s. Can't believe I can still see it!"

"It's pretty amazing." I snapped a picture of the road that was now grass while Grandpa turned to walk back up the "new" gravel road before turning off the road again to walk up a small grassy hill. I ran to catch up with him and found him staring at a funny-looking hole in the ground surrounded by cement.

Grandpa smiled at me, pointing at the hole. "What do you think this was for, James?"

I frowned as I studied it and then looked around at the cement foundations I could see from the hilltop, trying to picture the area as it would've looked in the 1930s with all of the CCC buildings and how it looked in Grandpa's CCC photo album.

"Oh—it's the flagpole base, isn't it?"

Grandpa laughed and squeezed my shoulders. "Good job, James!"

I crouched down to study the small circle of cement around the hole more closely and snapped a picture. "And look—there's a bunch of letters and numbers carved in the cement—"

Grandpa crouched down beside me and smiled. "What's carved there, James?"

I frowned and studied the numbers more closely. "Let's see—oh, 1934—the year. And F37—that's the Uinta Camp number, isn't it?"

Grandpa's eyes sparkled. "And here I thought maybe you weren't really listening to me ramble on and on this summer!"

"And this—1345—that's the company number, right?"

Grandpa laughed. "Definite A+ for you, James. I'll have to call your history teacher!"

I watched Grandpa stand up and turn in a slow circle to look out over the landscape without any more words before he finally motioned me to follow him back down the little hill.

"Let's get in the truck and drive over to Moon Lake so you can see a few things there."

Anna was too comfortable dozing in a reclining lawn chair, so Grandpa and I drove over by ourselves and parked at the lodge at Moon Lake, barely a stone's throw from the lake. Grandpa jumped out of the truck and hustled me over to see the little red log cabins lining the lake near the lodge.

"Hey—I remember fishing along here and seeing the cabins when I was little!"

Grandpa smiled proudly, running his hand along the wood logs of one of the cabins. "I helped build these original cabins. And look here—"

I jogged behind Grandpa's fast, excited pace as he followed the line of cabins to a hiking trail fork in the road with a sign pointing to Lake Fork straight ahead or the Brown Duck Trail that led to the left and up the mountain.

"See that Brown Duck Trail?"

"Yeah."

"During the late spring or early summer of '36, while I was still at Moon Lake Camp, besides building the campgrounds and cabins and roads, we also built a head house for the spring heads."

I frowned and squinted up at Grandpa, shading the sun from my eyes. "Head house? For spring heads?"

Grandpa nodded. "Way up on the mountainside where the springs came out and ran down the mountain, we built a little cement building around the spring heads so the animals couldn't get in and tromp the springs out or contaminate them. We needed those springs to hook pipes into in order to get water into the campgrounds for campers to use. We had a trail we used to get to the springs—this one here." Grandpa pointed at the trail leading to the Brown Duck Trail. "They used to load up all us CCC boys with a sack of gravel, a sack of sand, and a sack of cement in a pack on our backs. We'd start off carrying fifty pounds up the trail, but before the hike to the top was over, we were only carrying about ten pounds apiece, 'cause the load on our backs got heavier the farther up the mountain we went. It was definitely a good, hard hike. At least a mile. Probably more, I'd guess. But I was big and strong then, so I carried my fifty pounds to the top of the trail to where we were building the head house every time. Did it over and over." Grandpa chuckled and shook his head. "We worked hard. Had to mix the cement up there on the mountain and drag all the supplies we needed up there on our backs. So now you know where the water comes from that gets to these campgrounds."

I nodded and looked at the trail. "Yeah, I guess I do."

"And the dam—there's a dam up here at Moon Lake. The Cs built the dam up here, too." Grandpa sighed and looked wistfully up the trail and even walked up it a bit before slowly walking back down to where I was standing by the sign. "I'd sure like to see if that old head house has held up all these years, or if they've done something else to keep the water safe and flowing into the campgrounds."

"We've got time if you want to hike up there, Grandpa."

Grandpa smiled sadly. "I wish I could, James, but I don't think my heart could take it this time."

"Maybe next summer, huh?"

Grandpa nodded slowly. "Maybe. If I can't go, you'll have to go and see it for me. Would you do that for me, James?"

I was taken aback by the pleading look on Grandpa's face and stepped towards him to take his hand. "Sure, Grandpa, but you'll be there with me. You'll make it!"

Grandpa smiled at me and patted my hand in his. "I will, James. Don't worry. I'll be there, one way or another."

Grandpa stared at the trail for a few seconds longer before motioning me back to the truck. He was silent for the few minutes' drive back to the Yellowstone campground and Anna, and he was pretty quiet through lunch, too, although his eyes never stopped moving, looking around at the mountains and trees and grassy land all around us.

After lunch, we walked again through the remains of the camp and showed Anna all the cement foundations and the flagpole and fireplaces before Grandpa loaded us back into the truck and followed a road that led us up higher into the mountains. The trees were thick, and as I watched them zoom by from the window on my right, I was jerked forward when Grandpa suddenly jammed on the brakes, stopped the truck, and climbed out of the driver's seat.

I jumped out of the truck myself and watched Grandpa slowly walk away from the truck before staring into the trees. Everything was so quiet I could only hear the wind rustling through the quaking aspen leaves. And Grandpa—his eyes had tears in them.

I was hesitant to ruin the moment, but I had to speak. "Grandpa?"

Grandpa didn't respond, but when he did, his voice was quiet and hoarse and almost hollow. "This is where the fire was—this is where Max died. Max!" Grandpa's voice had turned into an almost sad wail, and I felt tears close off my throat as Grandpa again sadly called out "Max!" I slipped my hand into his, and although I could only see young trees that had never known fire, I knew Grandpa had moved into another place and time.

We stood there together, my hand firmly holding his, before Grandpa squeezed my hand and fished for his handkerchief in his pants pocket with his other hand. After wiping his eyes and blowing his nose, Grandpa turned to me with that pleading look on his face again. "Next summer when you go camping, have your dad bring you and your brother and sister here. They haven't been here in a while, either. You'll show them the old CCC sites, okay?"

I squeezed Grandpa's hand with both of mine. "But you'll be there to show them, Grandpa. You'll be there, too!"

Grandpa smiled sadly and nodded. "Yes, honey. I'll be there. I promise."

FORTY-NINE

We stayed overnight at the Yellowstone campground in Grandpa's tent and then moved on south the next morning towards Cedar City.

"I've got a few more places I'd like to show you along the way, James. Do you mind?"

"'Course not, Grandpa. As long as you're up for it, so am I. And I've got plenty of film for my camera. Are you up for it, Anna?"

Anna grinned at me. "I am!"

I grinned back before leaning forward in the cab of the truck to look at Grandpa. "Well, since we're going to be driving for a while, I want to know what happened after you and Uncle Landon saved my great-grandpa!"

Grandpa turned his head from watching the stretch of highway he was driving to give me a quick wink. "Turn the recorder on, and I'll get my jaw working!"

FIFTY

The spring of 1937 came all too soon, as did the news that our camp was moving to Eureka for our next projects. Having to move out of Enterprise and away from Lilly was bad enough, but in the process of getting all the paper work done to move to Eureka, one of the clerks in the office got my paper work all mixed up. I was packing my gear up the day before we were supposed to leave when I got the bad news.

"I'm going where?"

"You're being sent up to Salt Lake to Fort Douglas, the main CCC camp in Utah."

"Who all is going with me?"

"No one else. Just you."

I couldn't help but wonder if the ol' Supe did it on purpose to get rid of me for good. Before I knew what was happening, I was on a train for Salt Lake City. The second I got to Fort Douglas, I put up a fight with the officers at the CCC camp to get out of Salt Lake City and over to Eureka where the boys were so I could be with them.

"Well, it's going to take at least a week to get this all sorted out, so you might as well make yourself useful while you're here. Based on your file, it looks like you've done a lot of truck driving."

"Yes, sir."

"Well, then, we'll set you up to drive the 'officer car.'"

Driving the "officer car" wasn't so bad a job. All I had to do was play chauffeur and take an army officer out to different camps for inspection. One of the officers I drove around was pretty good, but the other officer I had to drive for was a rat. He did everything he could to make my life even more miserable than it already was, being up there in Salt Lake away from all the guys and from Lilly, too.

The only good thing about being up north was that I got to monkey around Salt Lake a little bit. Every day I'd wander over to where the Salt Lake Tabernacle was and then I'd go look at the Salt Lake Temple. I knew how badly Lilly wanted to be married in one of those temples, and as I looked up at that great big, fancy Salt Lake one, it seemed impossible to think I'd ever be allowed inside the likes of a building like that. But then I'd remembered a conversation Lilly and I had about the temple not long before I was sent up to Salt Lake.

"I don't know that I'll ever be perfect enough to go inside a temple, let alone get married inside one."

"Oh, Harold—you don't have to be perfect to go inside a temple. If we had to be perfect, none of us would ever go inside, and then none of the Lord's work could ever get done. Don't you see? He wants everyone to be able to go inside and gain the blessings that can only be found in the temple."

"Then why all the red tape to get in?"

"It's the Lord's house. It's the most holy, sacred place on earth, so we have to be clean and worthy to go inside. And even though it may seem like there are a lot of things we have to do before we can go inside, Heavenly Father's actually being pretty lenient with us."

"Lenient? What do you mean?"

"He could've made it a lot harder to get in, but instead, He only asks us to follow and live the simplest and most basic principles of the gospel. And in return, we gain all kinds of blessings and knowledge that can only be found in His house."

Lilly seemed pretty sure that even someone like me could eventually be allowed inside a temple, and I hoped she was right. I'd been going to the LDS meetings at camp for a few months now, and I even went to church at the camp in Salt Lake while I was at Fort Douglas.

After a week went by and nothing was said to me about being moved to Eureka, I put up another squawk, but the Captain had something to say that really surprised me.

"No need to get so upset, Addison. You'll be heading out tomorrow for Eureka, thanks to one of the superintendents at the Eureka CCC Camp. He's been calling me every day and doing some pretty fancy footwork to get you back into his camp again. He told me I'd be better off letting you go before you caused bad luck for me, too."

I couldn't believe the ol' Supe would go through all of that for me. I had to believe Lilly was right—that God really did answer prayers, because I sure had been praying for this all week.

I finally got back out to the Eureka CCC Camp, out by the Jericho sand dunes. The barracks at the Eureka Camp were big, wide barracks, different from the ones we had up at Moon Lake, and they had iron army cots with mattresses on them.

"Addison!"

"I can't believe it!"

Bud and Landon were so excited to see me when I walked into the barracks that they both jumped on me and knocked my gear off my back. I was glad to see them, too, and in seconds, we were laughing and wrestling and horsing around. It didn't take long before we had that barracks tore to pieces. By the time we finished wrestling around, most of the ol' army cots were bent out of shape, but we were together again, and at that moment, nothing else mattered.

FIFTY-ONE

O nce the middle of April arrived, after I'd been at the Eureka Camp for two months, I realized just being with Bud and Landon again wasn't enough. I was thinking about Lilly and missing her too much, so I decided to get out of the Cs. Even though the Depression was still on, I thought I could go home and find a job and put some money away, and then I'd be able to see Lilly any time I wanted to and stay for as long as I wanted down in Enterprise.

I'd been in the Cs nearly three whole years, so the captain of the camp had no problem giving me an honorable discharge. When the ol' Supe found out I was leaving, he called me into the officers' quarters to meet with him about it.

The Supe sat me down in a chair across from the desk he was sitting at and just stared at me with his arms folded for a few seconds.

"Well, Addison, what are you going to do now?"

"Well, I think I'm going to put me up an office."

"What kind of office?"

"I don't care what kind of office, just long as it's got a chair and a desk in it, and I don't have to be in the Cs."

The Supe had a good laugh over that, but what he said next shocked me. "Well, believe it or not, Addison, I'm going to miss you. You kept things exciting. And you did a good job. I haven't seen a better truck driver the whole time I've been in the CCC. If you decide to work in the

real world driving truck, let me know. I'd be happy to give a good refer-
ence for you."

I was pretty shocked. The ol' Supe—he'd turned out to be an okay
guy after all. All I could manage to say was thanks and that I was still
planning on finding myself an office job.

The Supe just grinned in return, and we stood up and shook hands.
"All the same, Addison, the offer still stands."

FIFTY-TWO

When we pulled into Cedar City, Grandpa stopped so we could have lunch, but after we'd finished off our sandwiches and chips, Grandpa was quick to herd us back into the truck.

Anna frowned, watching Grandpa down a couple of his heart pills. "Really, Harold—we've driven all day with hardly a break for you. Do you want me to drive for a while?"

"No, no, I'm fine. I want to show James a few things before we lose the light."

Grandpa turned off the main street of town onto the road that led up towards Cedar Mountain, and again, the area was familiar to me.

He grinned. "It's the road to the Duck Creek Camp. We've gone camping up here a few times, too."

"You helped build the campgrounds when you were in the CCC, didn't you?"

Grandpa nodded. "I did. I've got lots of good memories here, too. Good memories of those times in the Cs, both in the Uintas and up here on Cedar Mountain."

I thought about that as I stared out the window, looking at all the tall, skinny pine trees and grassy meadows with little purple flowers we passed along the way until we finally made it to the Duck Creek Camp area. Within seconds of passing the visitors' center, Grandpa ground the truck to a stop and jumped out of the cab.

"Come here, James."

I followed Grandpa into a grassy meadow surrounded by tall pine trees across the street from the campgrounds and watched him tramp through waist-high grass until he stopped and turned to me, beckoning me closer.

I hurried over to Grandpa's side with my camera and followed him onto a few more cement foundations like I'd seen in the Uinta Mountains. Some of the foundations Grandpa showed me weren't cement at all but large squares of hard-packed dirt, sometimes with tufts of wild grass struggling their way through the earth.

"This is where your Cedar CCC Camp was, isn't it?"

Grandpa nodded and stretched his arm to point toward the mountains ahead of us. "Us enrollees slept in tents way farther back in the meadows there. The main buildings and officers' quarters were up here, where these foundations are. This big cement foundation here is where the mess hall was. And across this street is where the garage was where we kept the trucks and things."

I snapped all kinds of photos of the foundation marks while Grandpa wandered slowly through the meadow, studying the remains of the few building foundations left.

"See here, James—here's more of those rocks we put down for the walking trails in camp."

I nodded and took a few photos of the softball-sized rocks snaking through the grass in semistraight lines.

Grandpa squinted up at the sky that had been slowly filling with dark clouds over the past hour. "The weather changes fast up here in the mountains. It's going to rain before too long, and there's something else I want to show you, James. Something kind of interesting."

We piled back in the truck, and although within minutes the clouds burst and rain really poured down on us, Grandpa easily maneuvered the truck past Navajo Lake and over a washboard road into the Spruces Campground, where we stopped at a small picnic area near the lake with an outhouse nearby. I pulled the hood of my jacket up over my head and followed Grandpa when he jumped out of the truck. He practically ran in the rain, past the outhouse and up a small hill. I couldn't see what he was running towards, but once I ran around the outhouse, too, I could see on top of the little hill behind it another small, black and gray rock building with doors painted bright red and vented windows painted red as well.

"See this, James?"

I frowned as I looked over the building, hugging my camera inside my jacket from the rain. "It's just another outhouse."

Grandpa threw his hands up in the air. "Not just another outhouse! It's the original one! Us CCC boys built this one. And it's still here! It's the only actual building left standing that we built in the Cs up here on Cedar Mountain." Grandpa chuckled and shook his head. "An outhouse, of all things!"

I did my best to protect my camera with one hand from the rain and snap pictures with the other and then carefully snuggled my camera back inside my jacket while Grandpa stared at the old little building without even noticing the rain pouring down on him. "Funny how much things change, and yet some things remain the same, you know?"

I nodded. "Sure, Grandpa."

Grandpa laughed. "You'll see what I mean when you're older." Grandpa slowly ran his hand along the damp, rocky wall of the small building before finally turning to me with a sad smile.

"Well, we better get going so we can make it to Enterprise before it's really dark. And if you're not feeling too tired, we can break out the recorder and I'll tell you what happened when I finished my days with the Cs."

FIFTY-THREE

S o after talking with the Supe, I got out of the Cs. Bud and Landon gave me a ride into Eureka, and from there I boarded a train and rode into Salt Lake, where I caught the D&RG train and finally made it back home to Price. I couldn't find any work, though, and the main problem I'd been having was still there: I missed Lilly. I was thinking about her all the time, so I finally talked my brother into letting me borrow his Model A car to drive down to Enterprise to see Lilly and bring her back up to Price for the yearly band concert competition.

I drove down Friday afternoon and spent the night at the camp in Veyo. Then I headed over to Enterprise early Saturday morning. When I pulled up to Lilly's house and hurried up to the front door, for just a second, I was afraid of how she'd act when she saw me again. It'd been quite a while, but when she opened the door and saw me, she squealed in an amazingly high pitch.

"Harold!"

A second later, she'd thrown her arms around my neck and given me a good, long kiss, and I knew I had nothing to worry about anymore.

Even though it was barely seven o'clock in the morning, we had to get going to make it to Price in time for the band concert. Most of the roads were dirt with rocks, so we bounced around on the seat of my brother's car, just sailing along, going not even thirty miles an hour. That was about top speed for the ol' Model A. It was so nice to be with Lilly again that it felt like we were flying. I was feeling so happy I couldn't help getting a little crazy. I even dared teach Lilly one of the cleaner, funny drinking songs Bud and Landon would sing when they were plastered.

We'd been singing along at the top of our lungs when I spied three girls walking along the side of the road on the driver's side. There was a swamp along the road by where the girls were walking, so I just let the car coast up along beside them, and then I pounded my left fist real loud and fast against the inside of the car door. The girls screamed, and they all jumped right into the water! Lilly laughed and laughed. I thought she'd die laughing before we made it to Price.

We drove into Price early in the afternoon without having to make too many stops along the way. Besides stopping a few times to pour water on the radiator, we only got a flat tire once, and it didn't take me hardly any time at all to get it fixed.

The best place to watch the band concert was along Main Street. Bleachers had been set up here and there along both sides of the road, so I grabbed a blanket out of the car and found a good spot up high on one of the bleachers near the town park. Lilly just stood there in the road, staring at me, while I spread the blanket out nice.

"What's the matter?"

"I thought we were going to a band concert!"

"We are!"

"Here? Right in the middle of the street?"

"Yep—right here in the middle of the street!"

I jumped off the bleachers and took Lilly's hand and helped her up the bleachers to where I'd spread the blanket. She'd packed a nice picnic lunch for us, so we ate our sandwiches on the bleachers while we waited for the performance to start.

"Tell me some more about this band concert I'm about to see."

"Well, it's more than just your average band concert."

Lilly laughed. "Clearly. We're not exactly sitting in a concert hall!"

I laughed, too. "I guess I should've explained the whole thing better. It's actually more of a competition instead of a concert. Here in Price, we have a band contest every year. All the schools from all around the county, Salt Lake City—all around the state—even from Colorado—come to Price to march and perform to see who's the best."

Lilly smiled. "Sounds pretty neat!"

I grinned back. "I went to Carbon High School. Our school band took first place quite a few years in a row and even went back to Chicago to the World's Fair and marched and placed in the competition back there. We won some good prizes and recognition in Chicago. In fact, I marched in this competition myself when I was a kid."

"You did?"

Lilly looked so surprised I couldn't help laughing. "Yup. When I was in junior high, I played the snare drum in the high school band, so I got to march one year in this competition. It was quite an experience."

"Hidden talents all over the place—I had no idea you were musically inclined!"

I laughed loud again. "I'm not, but it was fun pounding on that drum and wearing one of those fancy band uniforms."

Lilly smiled again. "What did your uniforms look like?"

"Our school colors were black and orange, so we wore white pants and shirts with a black tie and then this orange-and-black cape tied around our necks with a black tam hat on our heads. I looked better than Zorro in that getup."

Lilly giggled. "I'm sure you did!"

"We'd march here down Main Street and then turn up towards the park around the corner. All the people in town would take in band kids from all the different schools to sleep in their homes. There'd be cots set up in all the old empty stores and the gyms and the basement of the church and the library. We'd put kids up all over town and feed them everywhere we could. Then after the contest was over, there'd be a big dance up at the Silver Moon Dance Hall to celebrate the winners."

"Is there going to be a dance tonight?"

I winked at her. "I wouldn't have brought you here if there wasn't going to be a dance!"

Lilly smiled and slipped her hand into mine, and we sat there holding hands, watching all the bands play and march by us in their nice uniforms while we cheered them on from the stands. Lilly enjoyed it more than I'd thought she would. She even stood up on the bleachers by me to stomp her feet and cheer loud when my high school's band came marching through.

Once the competition was over, we wandered around town and made our way over to the dance up at the Silver Moon Dance Hall. It was so crowded we could hardly dance with all the kids from out of town and all the town people from Price, but we had a lot of fun anyway.

"You've been awfully quiet—and smiling, too. What are you thinking about?"

Lilly was looking up at me, almost expectantly, her eyes sparkling all over. I hadn't realized I'd been so quiet, waltzing around the floor with her.

"I just realized this is the first time I've been to the Silver Moon that I didn't have to crawl in a window or promise the owner, ol' Johnny Manatee, that I'd work off my dancing the next day by cleaning up the hall. I actually had money to buy a ticket to get in!"

"That's the only reason you're smiling?"

She looked so disappointed I couldn't help laughing and squeezing her around the waist. "That and the fact that it's been really nice tonight, not having anyone like Kurt Harris cutting in on me out here on the dance floor while I'm dancing with you."

Lilly smiled her slow smile. "Much better answer!"

It was dancing there at the Silver Moon Dance Hall that I realized it wasn't going to be enough to dance with her that night. I wanted to dance with her every night, from now on until forever had passed away. It scared me to think about it, but it was a good kind of scary. My mouth felt all dry and my heart was pounding funny when I tried to tell her all that, but even so, I knew what I wanted, and it was right there in front of me.

Lilly was staring up at me all wide-eyed. "Harold—what are you saying? Are you saying what I think you're trying to say?"

"What would you say if I asked you to come with me and find someone in town who could marry us?"

Her eyes were still as wide open as they could go, and then she just sort of gasped. "Are you serious?"

"I wouldn't have said what I did if I wasn't!" She still hadn't given me an answer yet, so I prodded her again. "Don't you want to marry me?"

"Of course I do—yes, of course I do!"

That was all I needed to hear, so I kissed her—right there in the middle of the dance floor. I told her I loved her, and she whispered back that she loved me, too. I was so happy I thought I'd burst. I grabbed her hand, and we hurried out of the dance, and with my arms around her, we waltzed in the street towards where I knew the justice of the peace lived.

The closer we got to his house, though, the quieter Lilly got until I couldn't get her to say anything at all.

"Well, this is it. The next house is his."

Lilly stopped in the middle of the street and wouldn't move. "I don't see a light on."

"It's okay—"

"No, it's not—it's not right—"

"He won't mind being woken up to marry us. My family's known him for years."

"No—you don't understand. It's not that. It's just—"

Before I knew what was happening, Lilly burst into about a million tears.

"What—what's the matter? What did I do?"

Lilly could hardly even talk and that scared me. "I'm sorry, Harold, but I can't—I can't do this. Not here, not without my family, not without you asking for my father's permission—and not when we can't go to—to—"

"To the temple?"

Lilly nodded and kept crying. I sighed and handed her my handkerchief. "You know I'm not near ready to get married in the temple."

"I know you're not ready now, but—"

"I don't know that I'll ever be ready enough to go into any temple."

Lilly shook her head hard. "Don't say that."

I sighed and ran a hand through my hair. "You know, Lilly, I don't get you. You want to do what all good LDS girls do and get married in the temple, so why are you with me at all?"

Lilly wiped her nose and smiled. "That's easy. I love you. And I see something in you. Something very real and very special."

"Oh, yeah? What?"

Lilly kept smiling. "Potential."

I didn't know what to say to that. No one had ever said they'd seen that in me before.

"My father sees it in you, too, now. He wouldn't let me see you at all if he didn't see something wonderful in you, too."

I was sorely disappointed, but at the same time, I had this funny feeling that Lilly was right. Timing was everything, and our timing tonight wasn't right at all.

"I guess I better take you home then, huh?"

Lilly nodded. "I guess so."

FIFTY-FOUR

So we didn't end up getting married that night, but I kept making trips over to Enterprise to see Lilly. And I'd go to church with her and her family on Sundays when I was in town. I still couldn't find any work in Price, so I found myself going over to Enterprise more and more. Sometimes I'd go through Eureka, down to the CCC camp, and pick up Landon and Bud and take them down to Enterprise, too. We'd all spend some time with the girls there, and then I'd take Bud and Landon back to the Eureka Camp and head back over to Price.

I didn't realize how lonely Landon was for Vivian until he announced that he was getting out of the Cs, too. Once Landon left the Cs, we didn't see too much of Bud, because he chose to stay in the Cs for a while longer. Landon went back to Vernal, but he'd come down to Price, and we'd hitchhike to Enterprise and spend some time with the girls. We'd pitch hay for Lilly's dad to help take care of the cattle and pay for our room and board while we stayed at their home for a week or so at a time. Lilly's dad had a lot of land and kept us busy during the day pitching hay, working in the garden behind the house, and taking care of the horses, pigs, and chickens—just any type of work that he needed us to do. Lilly's dad had an old granary near the barn that Lilly's brother Marshall slept in when he was in Enterprise, so we'd sleep out in the granary with Marshall at night, since there wasn't any room in the house.

At that time, the house was small and had only a few rooms: the kitchen, the parlor, and Lilly's parents' bedroom downstairs; and a room upstairs for the four girls.

By the time the summer of '37 arrived, Landon and I were practically living in Enterprise, we were there so much of the time. Neither of us had been able to find any jobs in Vernal or in Price, with the Depression still going on full force.

Both Landon and I were talking marriage a lot with our girls then, even though neither of us had a job. Even though Landon was only seventeen, while I was twenty-two, he worked up the courage to ask Lilly's dad first for permission to marry Vivian, and once he got it, both he and Vivian were ecstatic. When Lilly heard, she didn't look happy about it at all. I was sure it was because Landon wasn't ready to take Vivian to the temple, either, so I figured it would be useless for me to ask for her father's permission, since I knew she'd say no to me anyway.

A few days went by with Lilly giving me a little of the cold shoulder. I couldn't help feeling baffled as to why I was being punished. I was out in the barn, wondering what I'd done wrong, raking out dirty straw and raking in clean straw for the horses, when I looked up and saw Lilly standing calmly with her arms folded, leaning against the door to one of the horses' stalls.

"You nearly scared me to death! How long have you been standing there?"

Lilly just looked at me without blinking before she blurted out, "Don't you want to marry me anymore?"

"What? Of course I want to marry you!"

"Then how come you haven't asked my father for his permission, too?"

I hadn't felt okay about asking yet, because I wasn't sure Lilly would be willing to marry me since I still wasn't ready to go to the temple.

Lilly sighed. "I know you're not ready to go to the temple yet, but you're on your way, and that means something to me. Tell me this: Do you *want* to go to the temple?"

I'd had that exact question running through my mind for weeks now, and as I stood there looking at Lilly, I realized that I *did* want to go to the temple someday. Someday soon, so I slowly nodded my head.

"I want to be with you forever."

Lilly's eyes teared up, and she ran to me and threw her arms around my neck. "Will you ask for my father's permission to marry me now?"

I smiled and hugged her tight. "Yes. Most definitely, yes!"

FIFTY-FIVE

So, you and Grandma didn't get married in the temple?"

"No, not at first. Things worked out okay for us in the end, but I wouldn't recommend taking the kind of chance your grandma did. She always told me I had potential, so she wouldn't give up on me. But I'd advise you not to take such a risk. More often than not, heartache's the result of choosing someone you can't go to the temple with. You're a good girl, James. You'll make it easier on yourself if you stick to dating good LDS boys and marry in the temple right off instead of having to wait like your grandma and me. Promise you'll try to do that?"

I smiled at the worry in Grandpa's voice. "I promise, Grandpa."

Anna pointed to the sign up ahead. "Looks like the next exit is for St. George!"

"I'd kind of like to take a look at Pine Valley if we have some time. Is that all right with you two girls?"

Anna smiled and squeezed Grandpa's hand. "Sounds wonderful to me. Do you mind, James?"

"Of course not—we've got lots of time!"

Pine Valley was absolutely beautiful, tucked behind the mountains near St. George. We had to drive over a few cattle crossings, and each time we did, Grandpa would laugh.

"Hear that, James? That's some good ol' mountain music!"

We drove past the old white Pine Valley Chapel and headed straight for the campgrounds but stopped in the visitors' parking lot and climbed out of the truck to stretch our legs while Anna decided to check out the rest rooms.

"Come on over here, James!"

I followed Grandpa across the small street leading to the parking lot and over to Pine Valley Reservoir. It was easily one of the prettiest man-made lakes I'd ever seen, surrounded by tall pine trees and mountains.

"Wow—this is so beautiful. And you helped build it, didn't you, Grandpa?"

Grandpa smiled proudly. "Yeah, I did—and all of the campgrounds further up, too. It all turned out really nice."

I took a few pictures before Grandpa and I slowly walked the dirt path the length of the reservoir and stood together, watching the water ripple and wave on the reservoir, before we turned and headed back to where Anna was waiting by the truck.

"Enterprise and the reunion next. Are you girls ready?"

Anna smiled and nodded, and although I had a sick feeling in my stomach, I smiled and nodded, too.

When we drove into Enterprise an hour later, Grandpa couldn't stop excitedly pointing out all kinds of buildings on Main Street.

"See, James—that's where Day's Garage used to be. And right here next to it used to be the Old Holt Store. And the Corner Café. And across the street here is Lund's Store. The old Winsor Store used to be here by the Corner Café. Winsor's was the best because it had ice cream and a soda fountain. They even *made* their own ice cream, and oh, it was *de*-licious!"

Anna and I couldn't help laughing.

"That good, huh, Grandpa?"

Grandpa smiled and nodded. "The best! And see—right here by where Winsor's used to be—see that house, James?"

I stared at the small white house with a cement path leading to it. "That's Grandma's house, isn't it, where she grew up?"

We all jumped out of the truck and stood outside the fence so I could take pictures of the house before Grandpa stepped through the gate. My jaw dropped a good two inches as I watched him walk fast across the front lawn toward the side of the house.

"Grandpa—stop!"

Grandpa only threw a "What for?" over his shoulder.

"You—we can't just go tromping onto someone else's property! We could get arrested!"

Grandpa stopped, threw back his head, and laughed. "We won't get arrested. Your Great-Aunt Rachel owns the home now, and besides—we're family! No one would tell Lilly's grand-daughter that she can't take a peek at her own great-grandpa's backyard!"

The idea still made me nervous, but with an encouraging wave from Grandpa, I followed him around the house and into the gigantic backyard.

"Here's where the granary was, James, over by the side of the house. And the barn and stables were way at the back by the property line. The chickens and pigs were kept here in front of the barn, and right here behind the house where we're standing is where the garden was planted every year. And another big garden was planted over to the right and another one down in back by the barn. And over on the left in front of the garden—that's where the fruit trees were, and the calf pasture, too."

"Amazing!"

I took more pictures before Grandpa motioned me to follow him back to the truck. "I've got something else to show you, James."

Grandpa turned off Main Street, and soon we were on 200 South.

"See here, James? This is the old high school. And over here is where the open-air dance hall was, right here by the high school."

It was amazing, standing on the cement floor where my grand-parents had danced together so many times. Grandpa had his faraway smile on as he walked slowly around the old floor, and I knew he was thinking about Grandma.

I stared out the window as we slowly drove up and down the wide streets of the town until Grandpa stopped near a field several blocks from the main streets of Enterprise.

"This is the last stop, James. Do you know where we are?"

I frowned, looking over the field, before realization happily dawned. "Is this where your Enterprise Spike Camp was?"

Grandpa smiled and nodded. Then he motioned me to follow him before pointing out all the cement foundation marks similar to those in the Uintas and on Cedar Mountain.

"Oh, Landon and Bud and I had some good times here!"

I snapped at least a dozen pictures before I moved through the field to stand by Grandpa, who still had his faraway look on his face.

"Grandpa, whatever happened to Bud? Did he and Faye get married, too?"

Grandpa was quiet for a few moments before he shook his head slowly. "No, he and Faye didn't get the chance."

I frowned. "Didn't get the chance? What do you mean?"

"World War II happened. It took Bud away. And it took Tucker, too." Grandpa turned to smile at me sadly. "They didn't come home."

"Oh—I didn't know—I'm so sorry, Grandpa—"

Grandpa shook his head as he reached for my hand and patted it with his other hand. "It was a long time ago, James."

Anna jumped out of the truck then and hurried over to where we were standing in the middle of the field. "Harold—James—it's almost two o'clock!"

Grandpa raised both eyebrows as he turned to me in surprise. "I didn't realize it was so late! Everyone's probably already over at the church for the reunion by now."

I shrugged and stuffed my camera back into my jacket pocket. "That's okay. Now we can make an entrance, right?"

Anna laughed. "Exactly. We're fashionably late. It's never good to be the first ones to arrive anyway."

Grandpa grinned at us both as we jumped back into the truck. "Well, we certainly won't have to worry about that!"

Grandpa was right. There were plenty of cars and trucks in the parking lot by the time we arrived at the church house. We hurried into the building, and after spying the rest rooms at the end of the hall, I tugged on Grandpa's sleeve to stop him from walking into the gym.

"I'm going to check out the bathroom. I'll catch up with you in a few minutes, okay?"

Grandpa smiled and patted my shoulder. "Okay, James. We'll see you inside!"

My hair was a little bit of a mess, after wandering the town with Grandpa and Anna in the light summer breeze, but I quickly smoothed it behind my ears and washed my hands and splashed some water on my face before heading back down the carpeted hall to the gym.

I'd barely arrived at the propped open, heavy oak double doors to the gym, but after taking one look inside, I couldn't make my feet take me past the doorway.

Grandpa was maybe fifteen yards in front of me holding Anna's hand. Gripping it, actually. Both Anna and Grandpa had their backs to me, but I could see the faces of my three great-aunts in front of them. None of them looked happy, but at least they were all trying to be civil. Coldly civil, but still civil. The conversation between the group had probably been limping uncomfortably along for the past few minutes while I'd been in the bathroom.

I was too far away to hear what was being said, with all the other relatives milling around, but I could tell the conversation was starting to heat up. I was sure whatever was being said now wasn't anything good, especially since other people in the room kept glancing over to where Grandpa and Anna were standing. Great-Aunt Vivian had obviously had enough and was now clearly chewing Grandpa out something fierce. And Great-Aunt Beth and Great-Aunt Rachel—they were throwing "and another thing" type of lines at him, too. Great-Uncle Landon and Great-Uncle Robert were standing with them, and to their credit, looked uncomfortable and actually embarrassed, but I knew neither of them would even try to stop any of my great-aunts.

My heart was pounding, and somehow I made my feet inch into the room. I moved a few yards closer and finally caught a little of the conversation-slash-argument going on between Grandpa and my great-aunts. I watched while Great-Aunt Vivian pulled on Grandpa's arm, moving him a few feet away from Anna.

"Harold, I thought we made it clear that if you were planning on coming to this reunion, then you weren't to bring her!"

Something about the way Great-Aunt Vivian said "her"—as if Anna was something awful and almost vulgar—made me want to jump right in the middle of their circle and add a few choice words of my own.

Grandpa tried to stay calm. "Now, Vivian—"

Unfortunately, Great-Aunt Vivian didn't feel like being calm. "It's embarrassing, Harold. Just completely embarrassing and shocking to have you bring this—this woman with you when Lilly hasn't even been gone six months! I can just imagine what everyone here is thinking."

I watched Grandpa grab Anna's hand again and pull her over to him and Great-Aunt Vivian. "Well, everyone's just going to have to get used to seeing Anna if they want to see me, because Anna and I are getting married!"

All three of my great-aunts were starting to spin into orbit over that revelation. I knew I wouldn't have to strain to hear any of their voices after Grandpa's announcement, and I was right.

Great-Aunt Beth had her hand at her throat as if she was choking. "Obviously, Harold, you have absolutely no respect for our sister. It was bad enough to find out you've been—*dating*—so soon after her death, but now to get married, too—"

And Great-Aunt Rachel looked like she was going to be sick. "I don't even want to think about how this would make Lilly feel—how hurt she'd be—"

I wasn't sure how I thought Grandpa would react, but hearing Grandpa snort and yell back shocked me.

"Don't tell me how Lilly would feel. You have no idea how she'd feel about anything!" Grandpa actually pointed a finger at Great-Aunt Vivian.

"You can't tell me what to do, Vivian. I'm not like Landon and Robert. I've never had a ring in my nose!"

The horrified looks on my great-aunts' faces and even on my two great-uncles' faces made me guiltily want to break out my camera and snap a few photos for posterity, but I refrained. I couldn't stop cheering a little inside. I'd never heard Grandpa all angry and defensive like that, and although it surprised me, I was strangely proud of him, too. Great-Aunt Vivian could be too much of a bully if she was allowed to be, and I was glad to see Grandpa trying to put her in her place.

But Grandpa wasn't finished yet. "Well, it looks like we're being cut out, Anna. And that's fine. When you told me that I could come to the reunion but I couldn't bring Anna, I was sure you didn't really mean it. I thought you were just upset. But I guess you meant it, so—to the devil with you!" My three great-aunts gasped, but Grandpa continued. "If Anna can't come and be part of things like this, then I won't come, either!"

Grandpa gripped Anna's hand and whirled around towards the open doors. I hustled back into the hall myself and tried to pretend I hadn't seen a thing and waited until Grandpa came stomping out of the gym with Anna. Eavesdropping wasn't exactly classy, and I didn't want them to know I'd heard any of the conversation, even though I was sure I wasn't the only person who'd heard all the words being fired back and forth.

"Change of plans, James. Looks like they're going to have to have their reunion without us. Is that going to break your heart?"

I shook my head quickly. "Nope. Not at all, Grandpa."

"Well, I don't feel like hanging around anymore. Do you mind if we start heading back for home? We won't stop and dawdle this time."

"Whatever you want to do is fine with me, Grandpa. Is that okay with you, Anna?"

Anna looked so relieved I thought she was going to sag into a heap on the ground. "I think going home sounds like a wonderful idea."

FIFTY-SIX

Grandpa grumbled about my great-aunts the whole first day's drive towards home, even though Anna quietly and patiently tried to calm him down.

"Just forget about it, Harold."

"Forget about it? After how they acted?"

"Please, Harold. You need to calm down. For your heart's sake, if nothing else!"

Grandpa had been wheezing a lot on the way home, but he refused to let Anna take a turn driving.

"I need to blow off some steam. I need something to do, and right now, driving's all I've got. I'll let you know if I need you to take over, Anna."

There weren't any fun stories or stops along the way, and that made me sad. But I kept quiet and let Grandpa vent and Anna soothe him with her quiet, calm voice until we stopped at a KOA for the night.

The next day, the drive started out better. Grandpa had calmed down and was humming and singing funny old campfire songs to make Anna and me laugh. The only problem was that he kept wincing and lightly beating his chest with his fist now and then, even after he'd taken his heart medication.

"Harold, please pull over and let me drive. You're tired, and I know your chest is hurting."

Grandpa shook his head and patted Anna's hand. "I'm fine. Really, I'm fine!"

But Grandpa wasn't fine, and all three of us knew it, even if Grandpa was too stubborn to admit it.

We were about an hour away from home when it happened. One second, Grandpa was coughing, and the next, he was gasping and wheezing, and a second later, he'd jerked the truck off the highway and screeched it to a stop on the shoulder of the road, sending dust flying everywhere while Anna grabbed the wheel, shrieking "Harold! Harold!"

I didn't think I'd ever catch my breath again. "Grandpa! Are you okay—"

Grandpa's voice was hardly more than a whisper. "I'm okay. Just get me home. My chest hurts—hurts something awful—"

My heart was pounding as I gripped the dashboard. I couldn't make myself move—

"James, get out—get out of the truck now! I'm going to need to drive."

My fingers were shaking so badly I could hardly get my seatbelt off, but the second I was out of the truck, so was Anna. I stood without moving and watched while she ran around the truck to open the driver's door and climbed inside.

"James, help me move your grandpa over. You keep him comfortable."

Anna pushed and I pulled, and together we helped Grandpa move into the middle of the seat and belted him in place. Anna got the truck back in gear and in seconds, we were back on the highway again, with Anna driving fast. Really fast. Grandpa slumped against my shoulder, and with shaking hands, I mopped his forehead with paper towels and tried to get him to drink some water.

"We'll be home soon, Grandpa. Hold on—just hold on!"

FIFTY-SEVEN

By the time we got home, Grandpa had taken another pill for his heart and was feeling a little better.

"I was just pushing myself too hard and letting myself get too steamed up. I'm fine now. Really. You two are getting all fired up over nothing!"

Anna folded her arms and frowned at Grandpa, watching him carefully and slowly stretch himself out on his bed. "Harold, really—we need to get you to the hospital!"

I could feel worry lines creasing my forehead. "Yeah, Grandpa. Listen to Anna. You need to see a doctor. Or maybe I should call Dad—"

Grandpa waved his arm at both of us. "It's my heart, and I know if I need a doctor or not. Or if I need anyone to call Ben. And I don't. So you two little mother hens can quit squawking and just let me get some rest, all right? I'll be just fine in the morning."

Anna sighed and rubbed her temples. "Maybe I better stay for a while—"

But Grandpa would have none of it. "No need, Anna. You're tired, too, and it's late. Why don't you go home and get some sleep, and I'll see you in the morning, okay?"

I didn't want Anna to leave, and I wanted Grandpa to let us take him to the hospital, but Grandpa was pretty insistent.

"I'm fine, James—just fine!"

I had a sinking, bad feeling that wouldn't go away for the next two days while Grandpa rested quietly in his room. I put the tape recorder by his bed, but Grandpa just seemed to want to rest by himself. I'd check on him constantly, and Anna did, too, but Grandpa continued to insist he was fine.

"I just need to take it easy. The road trip took the wind out of my sails. That's all. Just need some time to recuperate. I'll be fine."

After two days of carefully watching over Grandpa, I couldn't stop feeling stressed as I watched Anna pull her car out of the driveway to go home to sleep, and by 3:00 A.M., I knew why.

It was the crash that woke me up, but the dull thump had me scrambling out of bed and racing to Grandpa's room.

"Grandpa!"

The lamp by Grandpa's bed was now in pieces on the floor, and Grandpa was lying in a crumpled heap a few feet from the broken lamp. My heart pounded as I raced over and fell to my knees beside him.

"Grandpa—are you okay? Grandpa??"

Grandpa could only gasp and try to nod his head.

"I'll get your medicine—hold on!"

I jumped up and ran to the bathroom and grabbed Grandpa's heart pills out of the mirrored medicine cabinet. My hands were shaking so badly that I knocked every bottle out of the cabinet and onto the floor trying to find his heart pills, and when I did, I raced back into the bedroom only to find Grandpa lying still. Way too still.

"Grandpa!" My heart raced faster as I fell back on my knees beside him. *Help me, Heavenly Father—oh, please, help me!* I put my head to his chest, trying to hear a heartbeat. I felt his faint breath tickling my ear, and the fact sent a wave of relief rushing through my chest. A second later, Grandpa turned his head towards the sound of my voice and slowly opened his eyes to stare in wonder at me.

"Lilly?"

Tears formed in my eyes as I shook my head. "No, Grandpa—it's me—James. Jamie."

Grandpa wearily closed his eyes and nodded. "James—yes, Jamie."

"Grandpa—we need to get you back in bed—I'll call for help—"

I moved to put Grandpa's arm around my shoulder, but he stopped me. "Wait a minute, please—Jamie—I'm sorry—I'm so sorry—"

"Sorry? You don't have anything to be sorry about, Grandpa—"

Grandpa tried to shake his head. "I shouldn't have lost my temper—down in Enterprise—at the family reunion. That was the wrong way to handle things. They're good people, and they loved Lilly, too."

"It's okay, Grandpa—"

"No, it's not." Grandpa's voice was hardly more than a whisper as he struggled for breath between his words. "I should've told them—I wanted to tell them—" Grandpa gasped for breath and swallowed hard. "I agonized for so long over marrying Anna when everyone was against it, but one night—one night, I had a dream that I saw Lilly—your grandma—standing here in this room at the foot of the bed, just smiling at me, and I knew—I just knew she approved, and that she was happy I wouldn't have to be alone anymore. She—she didn't want me to be alone. I wanted to tell them—I wanted to—"

"It's okay, Grandpa—"

Grandpa coughed and sighed before looking at me with tears in his eyes, too, as I gripped his hand tight in both of mine. "You're so much like my Lilly—so much." Grandpa slowly patted my hands with his free hand. "You've been so good to me, Jamie—I'm so glad you stayed with me. I've enjoyed every minute we've had together this summer. You're my best friend—you know that, don't you?"

I nodded, fighting hard not to cry.

"My hero," Grandpa whispered slowly. "You're my hero, Jamie."

I could feel the tears coming now. "You'll always be mine, Grandpa," I whispered back.

Grandpa slowly drew my hand to his lips and kissed the back of it before smiling and closing his eyes again.

I could feel panic rising from my chest into my throat. "Grandpa, I'm going to get help, okay? Just hold on! Please, hold on!"

I dropped the bottle of pills and jumped up to race for the phone in the kitchen. Before I knew what I was doing, I'd called Grandma June's house. It took three rings, but someone finally answered.

"Hello?"

Kyle's sleepy voice took me aback. "Kyle?"

"James?" Kyle was clearly awake now.

"Kyle—I—I think Grandpa just had a heart attack—" I could feel the panic rising higher in my throat, strangling my voice.

"Have you called an ambulance?"

An ambulance? My panic level shot higher. "I—I can't remember the number for 911!"

"It *is* 911! Hang up and call the number right now. I'll be right over, okay?"

Kyle hung up before I could, and somehow I got my fingers to dial 9–1–1 on the rotary phone. A second later, a 911 operator was on the line with instructions after I somehow gave her Grandpa's address.

"Please don't hang up until the ambulance gets here!"

"I won't, honey. You just hold on, okay?"

I had to set the phone down for a second when Kyle pounded on the locked back door. I almost bawled when I saw his incredibly concerned face—concern for Grandpa, concern for me, too—but a second later, he'd raced by me to run into Grandpa's room to check his pulse and airway before trying to get him in a more comfortable position.

"Have you called Anna yet?"

My voice was trembling horribly as I fell to my knees beside Kyle. "No—just you and the ambulance—"

"I'll call her. She needs to know."

"My dad—I need to call my dad—"

Kyle turned and shocked me by reaching out to give me a tight, brief hug. "It's okay, James. I'll call him and tell him to call Gracie. Just calm down and breathe, okay?"

Everything became a gigantic blur after that. The ambulance—Kyle calling Anna, calling my dad—EMT technicians loading Grandpa up onto a stretcher—it was crazy, crazy, and seconds later, I climbed up into the back of the ambulance to sit by Grandpa while I held his hand tight in mine as the ambulance screeched and wailed, flying down the road to the hospital.

"Just hang on, Grandpa, please hang on!"

FIFTY-EIGHT

Hospital waiting rooms are easily one of the worst places in the entire world to have to be in. I didn't know how long I'd been sitting in the waiting room in the critical care unit waiting for Anna, my dad, Gracie, Kyle, the doctor with any news, but it seemed like forever. And even though I'd been sitting in nervous silence for an eternity, there was a moment when I could feel that everything had changed. Something was gone.

I'd barely looked up from staring at my hands gripped tight in my lap when the elevator door in front of me opened and my dad rushed into the room. He looked at me, and I could see fear and sadness and horror all rolled into one terrible ball in his eyes and on his face, but before he could say anything, the doctor appeared around the corner.

"I'm too late—he's already gone, isn't he?" Dad asked.

The doctor nodded and spoke softly. "I'm so sorry. He had a massive heart attack . . ."

I didn't want to hear anything more. And I didn't have to, because Aunt Gracie had been close behind Dad and had heard everything, and now she was crying. Loudly. Dad turned to put his arms around her, and the two were ushered by a nurse into Grandpa's hospital room.

"Do you want to go in with them, James?"

I shook my head at the doctor and gripped my hands together

tighter, and it was then that I saw someone I'd missed before, hidden from my view by Dad and Aunt Gracie when they'd arrived.

Anna. She was standing motionless by the elevator with Kyle, her eyes wide open in shock, with tears streaming down her cheeks.

"Anna!" I stood up to walk over to her, but she tried to smile and motioned me back into my chair. Slowly she walked over to sit down on the couch beside me. I reached out to put my arms around her and cried on her shoulder. She cried a little on mine before finally pulling away and smoothing my hair, trying to smile through her tears. When Anna did speak, her words truly stunned me.

"Your grandpa and I were supposed to be married next week."

"I know—I'm so sorry—"

Anna tried to smile again and shook her head. "Will you do something for me? For your grandpa?"

I nodded slowly. "Of course. Anything."

"Your grandpa loved you in that beautiful lavender dress you two picked out for your birthday. I hope you won't put it away now. You won't, will you?"

"I—I don't know. I won't have anywhere to wear it now—"

"Of course you will. You'll wear it to his funeral, won't you?"

I couldn't help feeling a little startled. "I—I don't know if I should—"

Anna reached out and gripped my hand. "Well, I do. Your grandpa would want you to. Promise me you will, all right?"

I didn't trust myself to try and talk, so I only nodded. I could feel tears slipping fast down my face while Anna gathered me close in another fierce hug.

FIFTY-NINE

The next few days were a blur. I'd wanted to stay at Grandpa's until the funeral, but neither of my parents was about to let me. Dad had me packing up my stuff and on the road back home with him within an hour of leaving the hospital. We didn't speak the entire drive home, and once we entered the house, I headed straight for my bedroom. I hardly talked to Mom or Dad, and Trent and Sarah thankfully left me alone. By the next morning, though, I made myself rejoin the family at the breakfast table, and as I did my best to be a part of the family, it was a definite welcome surprise to have Trent and Sarah play nice, too.

Even though I'd promised Anna I'd wear my new lavender dress, on the day of Grandpa's funeral I wasn't sure if I should wear the dress after all and spent a good fifteen minutes that morning sitting on my bed, staring at the dress spread out on my lap. I was so deep in my dilemma I hadn't heard Sarah softly knock and enter my room.

"It's beautiful."

I looked up at Sarah standing in the doorway, smiling tentatively at me. "Yeah, it is, isn't it?"

"Are you going to wear it?"

I shook my head slowly. "I'm not sure."

Sarah walked over and sat down beside me. "Well, in case you decide to wear it, how about I help you with your hair, okay?"

I nodded dully, not really caring what Sarah was going to do to me, and just sat like a rag doll on a stool in the bathroom while she silently rolled up my hair in hot rollers and even dared dust some makeup on my face.

Sarah didn't say anything until she was finished with my face and hair. "I think if you wore the dress it'd be a nice tribute to Grandpa. He was so excited about that dress on your birthday."

I still wasn't sure I should, but at the last minute, I decided to wear it. After slipping on the semi-high heels Sarah had bought me for my birthday, I took a deep breath before looking in the full-length mirror in Sarah's room to see what kind of damage she'd done to my face and hair—and forgot to release the air in my lungs.

Poor Sarah looked worried and even wrung her hands. "You don't like it, do you?"

I shook my head as I kept staring into the mirror. "It's not that. It's— I don't recognize myself!"

And I didn't. At all. Sarah had brushed the curls out until they were big, shiny waves that came to the middle of my back. And the makeup— I didn't look made up. Just different. A better kind of different. More sparkly and glowing. And paired up with the dress and shoes, I looked—

"Beautiful, Jamie. Just beautiful!" Mom had crept up and hugged me from behind, resting her chin on my shoulder as we both looked into the mirror.

"It's a pretty dress, isn't it?"

Mom nodded and smiled. "Yes, it is, but I wasn't referring to the dress."

My eyes widened as I looked at Mom's smile in the mirror. "You weren't?"

Mom shook her head. "You're beautiful, Jamie. And you've grown so much this summer, spending time with your grandfather, and being there for him. I'm so proud of you."

I stared at our reflection together until Mom squeezed my shoulders. "What's wrong, Jamie?"

"Nothing. I mean, not nothing. It's—it's Anna—"

Mom nodded and smoothed my hair. "She's become someone special to you, hasn't she? Like Grandma June."

I nodded. "I'm worried about her. Sad for her, too."

"I know, honey. I'm sad for her, too."

I didn't get a chance to say anything else, because Dad knocked on Sarah's door to hustle us into the car, and within half an hour, we were at Grandpa's ward house for the funeral.

I'd forgotten about the short viewing and family prayer that had to take place before the actual funeral. I definitely received a few strange looks over my choice of dress that made me blush and squirm, but Sarah gripped my hand and smiled at me and whispered, "Grandpa would love that you're wearing the dress." After that, I didn't care what anyone thought of me in my fancy dress anymore.

When Kyle and Grandma June came through the viewing line, I only had a second to see the stunned look on Kyle's face when he saw me before Grandma June grabbed me up into a hug.

"Oh, James, honey—I'm so sorry—so sorry about your grandpa. How are you holding up, sweetie?"

"I'm doing okay, Grandma June. Really."

"That's my James, always brave. Just like your grandma always was! And you—look how pretty you look! Your grandpa would be so thrilled to see how beautiful you are."

"Oh, Grandma June—" Grandma June pulled me into another hug, and as she did, I could see Great-Aunt Vivian making a beeline straight for my dad, who was standing by my mom near a dozen different arrangements of flowers several feet behind Grandma June. Great-Aunt Beth and Great-Aunt Rachel were close behind, all of them wearing shocked, stricken looks on their faces that made me dully wonder what kind of look had been on my face all day.

Great-Aunt Vivian made it to my dad first, and before he could've refused, she threw her arms around his neck, sobbing almost out of control.

"If I'd have known he didn't have more time—if I'd only known, I wouldn't have—I'm sorry—I'm so sorry!"

Dad was kind and hugged her back. I couldn't hear what he was saying, but I could tell it was something nice and that he was trying his best to calm her wailing. And then Great-Aunt Beth had tearful hugs for my dad and my mom as well, followed by Great-Aunt Rachel. Great-Uncle Landon and Great-Uncle Robert soon joined them with equally sorrowful, regretful, shocked looks on their faces, and Sarah and Trent moved to stand with the group while everyone took turns hugging each other. As for me—I could only stand frozen, watching.

Grandma June had pulled back to look at me worriedly with her hands gripping my upper arms. "James, honey, are you all right?"

I nodded dully while I watched my dad easily accepting the apologies and words of remorse and the pleas for forgiveness. Even Aunt Gracie hurried over to the group with Blake and Maxwell in tow and seemed happy to join in with this moment of forgiveness.

Easy for all of you—easy for you now–

"Hey, James, are you okay?"

Kyle. I'd forgotten how nice he looked in a suit and wished we were both dressed up for some other reason than a funeral. My grandpa's funeral. I only had a second to smile a brief "Hey, you" back before the family prayer announcement was made. As Grandpa's friends and ward members filed out of the quiet room, I could see Anna sitting alone on a chair near the casket, looking down at her hands clutching a lace hanky in her lap. My great-aunts were still in their huddle with the rest of my family across from where Anna was sitting, all of them trying to smile through their tears, looking at me expectantly. I didn't even have to think about it. One second I was looking across the room at them, then at Anna, and the next, I'd walked over to Anna's side, and as she stood, I gently reached for her hand and felt her grip it tightly as we stood together during the family prayer. I kept her hand tight in mine as we followed the casket into the chapel, and seated on the front row of the chapel with the rest of my family, I continued to hold her hand throughout the entire funeral.

Grandpa's church house had three sections of benches in the chapel. Kyle was also seated on the front row on the section to the right of Anna and me with Blake and Maxwell. All three were pallbearers, along with Dad and Trent and a young married man who'd been my grandpa's home teaching companion. I slightly turned my head after the opening prayer to see Kyle and was shocked to find him looking at me. Intently. I knew I was blushing, but Kyle smiled briefly before turning his head to look down at the funeral program in his hands.

Like at Grandma's funeral, Dad had asked Trent to give the eulogy. He did an incredibly nice job of it, but what surprised me the most was when after a long pause with his head down, he lifted his head and looked straight at me.

"Most of you have seen my sister Jamie, who's seated here on the front row. Our grandpa bought the dress she's wearing for her sixteenth birthday a couple of weeks ago, and she's wearing it today in honor of him."

My heart was pounding. I hadn't expected anything like that from Trent, and the fact that he'd done something so nice made tears start up in my eyes. Anna squeezed my hand, and Sarah, who was seated on the other side of me, reached over and squeezed my other hand.

Dad had asked Clay Anderson, who'd spoken at Grandma's funeral, to be the main speaker. It was strangely comforting to have the same person speak nice things about Grandpa. Someone who'd known both of my grandparents for a long time. And Kyle played the piano and sang like he'd done before, too, this time singing one of Grandpa's favorite hymns, making tears start in my eyes again.

When the funeral finally ended, Anna gripped my hand. "Will you ride with me to the grave dedication, James?"

I nodded. Once we'd arrived at the cemetery, Anna switched off the car and quietly broke the silence we'd shared during the drive.

"You look beautiful, James. Just beautiful. Thank you for wearing the dress your grandpa bought for your birthday."

I nodded before turning to look at Anna's sad face. "Anna—" I wasn't sure how to say what I wanted to say—what I'd wanted to say for some time now. Anna was looking at me questioningly, so I took a deep breath and tried not to cry. "Thank you for making the last months of my grandpa's life so happy."

Anna's lips trembled as her eyes filled up with tears before she reached out to pat my hand. "Oh, James—I could say the same to you. This summer with you has meant the world to your grandpa."

"It's meant everything to me—" And now I *was* starting to cry, so I closed my mouth and swiped at my eyes with the back of my hand.

Anna reached out and put her arm around me. "James," she whispered. "I know you have a special closeness with June—your Grandma June—but I want you to know, you'll always be welcome in my home."

I could feel the tears building up again, but I made myself smile. "I may just take you up on that, Anna."

Anna smiled back and squeezed my shoulders. "I hope you will, James!"

The wind was stiff and cold, as it always was at this cemetery, and the white folding chairs lined up in rows on either side of the casket were just as hard as they'd always been. Dad dedicated Grandpa's grave, and as I sat between Trent and Sarah with Blake and Maxwell seated across from me on either side of Aunt Gracie, I caught both cousins looking at me soberly. I gave both a brief smile and was surprised to see the smile returned from both of them.

After the prayer was over and everyone stood and quietly milled around, talking and offering condolences here and there, I was surprised when Anna's visiting teaching companion touched my arm and said, "I knew that was the dress Harold bought for you the minute I saw you in it!" but I was truly touched when several people from Grandpa's ward followed after her, commenting on the dress Grandpa had bought for me. I couldn't believe Grandpa had told so many people about his "date" with me.

I'd done my best to avoid my great-aunts, who to their credit had each been trying to catch me by myself, but I wasn't about to talk to any of them. Not today. I'd barely moved strategically behind a tree that would keep them from seeing me when I felt someone lightly touch my shoulder from behind.

I jumped and whirled and then smiled. It was Clay Anderson, Grandpa's friend.

"So that's the dress?"

I nodded my head.

"Harold told me all about your date and how you didn't want him to buy this dress because it was expensive, but he said he'd had such a wonderful time with you that he just had to buy it. He couldn't stop talking about how beautiful you looked in that dress. He was right. You're beautiful."

I was afraid I'd start crying again, so on an impulse, I put my arms around him and hugged him briefly instead before turning to run as best I could in my high heels to Dad's car where I could see my family waiting for me.

SIXTY

he Relief Society had set up a luncheon at Grandpa's church house after the funeral. As soon as we were inside and friends and relatives had crowded around my family and before anyone could stop me, I sneaked out one of the side doors by the classrooms and walked as fast as I could over to Grandpa's house. I had my key to Grandpa's house on a long string I'd tied around my neck, safely hidden from view inside the front of my dress. After looking around cautiously for a second, I carefully turned the key in the lock and stepped inside.

I stood in the kitchen without moving for probably a good solid minute. The room still looked the same, as if it expected Grandpa to come walking in the door any second. I wandered slowly through the house and tried to force away the ugly realization that this would probably be the last time I'd see it like this before it would be emptied and eventually sold.

When I quietly stepped into Grandpa's bedroom, I saw his old red CCC photo album on the dresser where he'd kept it since I'd found it hiding under his bed the day I'd arrived for the summer. I picked the book up and hugged it to my chest and felt tears slipping fast down my cheeks.

I turned then and let my eyes roam slowly around the room, staring first at each of the lavender walls until my eyes rested on the lamp table by Grandpa's bed. The black and white picture of Grandma, smiling and leaning against the old tree in Enterprise, was still there, and by that was Grandpa's tape recorder.

I moved around the bed to sit on the edge by the table and lifted an envelope that was sitting on top of the recorder. Inside were the last pictures Anna had taken, including the pictures of me in my new dress and bare feet, grinning and standing by Grandpa, who was smiling proudly at the camera with his arm around me while I leaned against him with my arm around his back. I slipped the photos of Grandpa and me into the CCC photo album and then turned to place the tape recorder in my lap.

I stared at the recorder for a moment before wiping my eyes. I gently pressed the eject button and removed the tape inside. Grandpa had written the date on the tape, and I was shocked to realize the date was the day after we'd brought him home from the hospital. The tape was filled on both sides, and although I knew hearing Grandpa's familiar voice was only going to make me start crying again, I took a deep breath, reinserted the tape in the recorder, and pushed the play button.

SIXTY-ONE

So after Lilly and I decided to get married, and Landon and Vivian were making their plans to get married, I tried to work up my courage to ask Lilly's dad for permission to marry her. It was a harder job than I thought it would be, so after a few days went by, Lilly started pushing at me. We were out in the back of the house one afternoon when Lilly wouldn't stop egging me on like crazy.

"Look—there's my father now. He's crossing the street to go over to his mother—my grandmother's house."

I looked over my shoulder, and sure enough, he was halfway across the street.

"This may be your only chance to catch him alone for a while!" Lilly gave me a good, hard shove. "Go ask him!"

I took a deep breath and jogged over to Lilly's dad. I caught him by the arm out in the middle of the street. He turned around and looked at me without smiling. My heart pounded hard and fast, and I although I tried to talk normal, I could only stutter and stammer like an idiot.

"Mm—Mister—Grant, ahh, wwould you let me marry your daughter?"

I waited for what felt like hours while he looked me over carefully and folded his arms across his chest. "Well, Mr. Addison, I'm relieved you've finally asked. My wife's been worried about having you and Landon living with us, not married to our daughters or anything."

"So Lilly and I, we've got your blessing and permission, then?"

Lilly's dad only frowned. "I didn't say that."

I couldn't believe what I was hearing. He'd told Landon yes, but me—

"Let's go back across the street and sit down in the house for a minute, Mr. Addison."

"If you're going to say no, you can just say it now, right here!"

"I'm not saying anything until we're away from prying eyes!"

He had a point there, so I shut my mouth and followed him nervously back across the street and into the house, where he motioned me to sit down on the couch while he sat in a chair across from me and stared stonily at me. Before he could start in on me, I decided to go ahead and say my piece and hope—maybe even pray—for the best.

"Mr. Grant, I know how much you want your daughter to be married in the temple. Would it help if I told you I want that, too?"

"It would."

I took a deep breath. "Well, I do. I've been going to church more now than I ever have in my whole life, but you know as well as I do that it takes more than that to go to the temple."

Lilly's dad frowned deeper. "How much more would it take for you?"

"I—I need more time. I'm still breaking myself from booze. And coffee, too. But I'm done with the cigarettes. You can rest easy on that!"

Lilly's dad raised one bushy eyebrow. "At least you're being honest. Landon was, too. I wouldn't want to see either of you go to the temple unworthily."

I nodded and realized I was shaking. "My thoughts exactly, sir."

"Any idea how much longer it would take you to be ready?"

"I can't give you a count of days, sir, but I can say that I think it would be a mistake for Lilly and me to put off getting married, even though it would be outside the temple for now."

Lilly's dad glared hard. "And why is that?"

"As much as I love being near Lilly and appreciate you letting me live here—both Landon and me, since we're still looking for jobs—"

"Yes?"

And now my voice was shaking funny. "Well, I love Lilly, and she loves me. I—I don't want to be without her anymore."

Lilly's dad sighed. "I know you love her. And heaven knows, she loves you, too. I'll give you permission to marry my daughter, if you'll make me a promise that you'll take her to the temple as soon as you can."

So I made that promise, and while we shook on it, I knew I would keep it. Not because it was important to him, or even to Lilly anymore, but because it was important to me.

And I did keep that promise. A little over two years after we were married, on the 19th of July, 1939, Lilly and I were married in the temple in Manti, Utah. It'd taken a lot of hard work, but one thing the Cs taught me was that I could handle hard work. And that I wasn't afraid of it. The satisfaction of accomplishing something I never thought I could do was a pretty big thing for me. I don't know if I could've done it without Lilly, though. She didn't push me. Just held my hand and walked with me.

We went to church every Sunday, and when I finally got a job that moved us far away from Enterprise, we met Clay Anderson and his wife, Milly. And June Jansen and her husband. They were good friends and walked with us, helping us prepare for the temple. But what made the experience of going to the temple even better was knowing that Vivian and Landon were sealed in the Salt Lake Temple the same month Lilly and I were sealed in the Manti Temple.

As Lilly's dad shook my hand, he nodded. "Since neither of you two boys has found any work, then I guess you'd just as well stay here and pitch hay to earn your board and pay for your wives."

So we decided we'd stay in Enterprise for a while. I had to hitchhike back to Price to get some money somehow to buy a ring for Lilly. One of my sisters had a job and was working then, so she was willing to let me borrow some money from her. I found a ring with just a small diamond in a nice setting with a tiny gold tulip on either side of the diamond. My sister thought it was pretty, so I figured Lilly would like it, too. Once I got back to Enterprise, Lilly and I made arrangements to hurry down to St. George and get our marriage license.

In the meantime, Landon and Vivian went ahead and got married without us. I couldn't feel too bad about it. Because they'd eloped, no one else got to be a part of the marriage ceremony, either. Rachel, Beth and Faye and a bunch more of their friends wanted to shivaree them, which sounded like a good idea to Lilly, since her nose was bent out of joint by Vivian going off and getting married without telling her.

There was a new bunch of guys from North Dakota who were in the Veyo CCC Camp and in the Enterprise Spike Camp, so I went over to the spike camp to see if they'd loan me one of the CCC trucks. If it wasn't for the fact that two of the guys we talked to thought Rachel and Beth were cute, they probably wouldn't have loaned us the truck, but they did. The two guys came along with us, riding in the front seat with Lilly, Rachel, Beth, and me while Faye and the rest of the girls rode in the back. We drove all over town, but we couldn't find Vivian and Landon anywhere. Someone had hidden the two of them real good.

On the next Friday night, June the 25th, 1937, a week after Landon and Vivian eloped, I picked up Lilly in my best suit to take her to the LDS bishop's home in Enterprise to get married. When I knocked on the front door, she opened it, wearing that pretty lavender dress she was wearing the first time I saw her, looking more beautiful than I'd ever seen her look before. Both of her parents were dressed up, too, and went to the bishop's house with us as witnesses. No one else in the family came with us, so the four of us walked over to Bishop Joseph A. Terry's place, and we were married. It wasn't the temple wedding Lilly had always dreamed of, but as I slipped that little diamond ring with the gold tulips onto her finger, I promised her we'd go there someday soon, and with the bishop's permission, kissed her, this time as her newly wedded husband.

Lilly hugged me tight and whispered softly, "I know. I know we'll get there. Line upon line, one step at a time."

SIXTY-TWO

I wanted to celebrate the happiest day of my entire life, so after we left the bishop's home, all four of us walked over to the high school where the open-air dance was being held out on the tennis court that was never used for anything but dancing, and we danced and danced and danced. We didn't tell anybody we'd just gotten married, and Lilly's parents didn't, either.

"Are you ready to go home now?"

We'd been slowly waltzing around the floor, but Lilly's question made me trip and nearly send her crashing to the floor. Two couples near us were trying hard not to laugh but not hard enough.

"Well, I definitely am now!" I grumbled.

Lilly laughed and grabbed my hand. "Come on!"

We dodged couples as we hurried off the dance floor and then had to dodge everyone else standing around the edges of the floor, when some old married couple in town—probably past eighty years old—stepped up and blocked our way out.

The old lady smiled at Lilly and said, "You two aren't leaving, are you?"

Lilly blushed real pretty and quickly said, "We decided to leave early tonight. We just want to go home is all."

Then the old man grinned and spoke up. "Home? Whatcha going home for?"

I knew if I didn't say something good fast, we'd get stuck

hem-hawing around with them all night, so I said back, loud and slow enough for them both to hear just fine, "Well, we're just going home so we can practice making babies."

I thought Lilly was going to faint from embarrassment, but it worked. The old lady's mouth fell open in shock, while the old man threw back his head and laughed. I hustled Lilly right out of there, and although she acted all shocked and outraged at first, pretty soon we were both laughing our heads off, waltzing down the street to Lilly's home.

Neither of us knew where Vivian and Landon had been since they got married, and with Marshall not home from the dance yet, we went to the granary to be alone.

Lilly pulled back when I tried to lead her by the hand into the granary. "My brother sleeps in here."

"He'll be at the dance most of the night with his girlfriend, and then he'll want to take her home and spend some time with her, so we'll probably have this place to ourselves tonight."

We had to find some place to spend our first night of marriage alone together, so we went ahead and took over the granary for the night. I was sure Marshall would be gone most all night visiting with his girlfriend in town, but we'd only been asleep maybe an hour when I was rudely awakened by a fist plowed into my face.

"What the deuce are you two doing in bed here together?!"

Lilly screamed, but before Marshall could cause any more damage to my face, I dodged his next punch while Lilly hid under the blanket.

"Stop it—just stop it! We're married, I tell you—we're married! Tell him, Lilly!"

"Sure you are! Next you're going to tell me you just barely got married tonight!"

"We did! I'm telling you the truth!"

This wasn't exactly the way we'd planned to let everyone in Lilly's family know we were married now, but before things got any uglier, Lilly kept the blanket tight under her chin and yelled, "We did—we did! Just go ask Mother and Father—they'll tell you! They were there!"

Marshall just stood there, dumbfounded, staring back and forth from me to Lilly until Lilly finally shrieked, "Now get out of here!" which I was happy to see him do, right after he fell all over himself trying to apologize and congratulate us at the same time.

SIXTY-THREE

So the day after we were married, we gave Marshall back his bed in the granary. In the summertime there in Enterprise, everyone slept outside, just like everyone did up in Price. All the kids in town would put their beds out under the trees at the side of the houses to sleep. Lilly and I got a hold of a big steel bed that we set up under one of the trees near the back of the house. Out in back of the house, Lilly's dad had an orchard with apple trees, so Landon and Vivian had hooked up an ol' swinging bed between two of the apple trees in the orchard. It was like a hammock. They'd slept in it about a week, but after they got a good look at that steel bed Lilly and I had put up back at the corner of the house, Landon and Vivian wanted to trade us. We didn't want that old swinging bed, though, because it was too much like a hammock to try to sleep in. But they wouldn't stop pestering us about it, and it was while they kept whining at us to trade them that an idea popped into my head.

"Okay, Landon—enough's enough. We'll trade you."

Poor Lilly nearly choked. "Harold!"

"Go ahead—take the bed. And enjoy it!"

I nearly had to drag Lilly away, who was about ready to scratch my eyes out.

"What in the world did you do that for? I don't want to sleep in the swinging bed!"

I hustled her over to where Landon and Vivian couldn't see us or hear us. "Did you see how Rachel and Beth were acting at breakfast this morning, all giggly-like, asking us how we were liking sleeping in that steel bed?"

Lilly rolled her eyes. "They were just being silly girls, that's all."

"I don't think so. There's something going on there with them."

"What do you mean?"

"Since they missed out on shivareeing Landon and Vivian, I think they're going to go after us instead!"

Lilly didn't know what to say to that, but we figured we better not take our chances. Besides, Vivian and Landon still needed their shivareeing.

I didn't want to sleep in the swinging bed, either, so while I rigged us up an old cot that night and put a mattress on it and fixed it up for a bed, strategically hidden near the steel bed, Lilly kept Rachel and Beth busy far away from where I was. Rachel and Beth and all their friends knew where we'd been sleeping, but they didn't know that we'd switched beds with Vivian and Landon during the day.

We all went to bed that night, and Vivian and Landon—they fell asleep in the steel bed right away, but Lilly and I purposely stayed awake, waiting to see what might happen that night. It didn't take long before our wait was rewarded.

"Lilly! Look—look over there!"

Lilly sat up beside me on the cot, and we peeked through the bushes in front of us. Rachel and Beth had a bunch of their girlfriends with them, and they came sneaking up to that old steel bed, hoping to shivaree Lilly and me.

"They've got something with them—it looks like—buckets! Buckets of something—"

A second later, we found out exactly what they had in those buckets. All of the girls came right up to that steel bed, and in one big throw, all at the same time, they dumped buckets of ice cold water on Landon and

Vivian. Poor Landon and Vivian—we could hear them easily from where we were hiding. In fact, the whole town probably heard them.

"Aah, aah, water—wwhoo wwhhoo threw—who threw—who threw—who put that water—oh, oohh,—I'm all wet! Cold! I'm freezing!!"

We laughed and laughed. I thought Lilly and I would split our sides laughing. We could hear Rachel and Beth and their gang where they'd run out in the street laughing, "Oh, we got Vivian and Landon—we didn't get Lilly and Harold!"

I knew they'd come looking for us next, so I hurried and scooted Lilly off the cot. "Come on! Grab a couple of quilts, and let's get out of here!"

We sneaked off down to the barn before anyone could see us and climbed up the ladder to the top level of the barn. We dragged the ladder up after us, and then we laid our quilts and pillows on top of the hay and spent the rest of the night there.

And that's the way we beat Landon and Vivian in getting shivareed. Vivian and Landon finally got caught up with for hiding out for their shivaree, and they got a good soaking out of it. They had to go back to the ol' swinging bed after that to get to sleep that night.

That's the way things happened down there in Enterprise when we got married. Being a part of the Cs and meeting and marrying Lilly marked the end of one chapter of my life and the beginning of a new one.

It was—and is—a good life.

SIXTY-FOUR

I thought I'd find you here."

I'd been sitting in Grandma's old swing, looking down at my feet pushing against the wooden boards, slowly swinging back and forth for I didn't know how long. I'd walked outside and sat down in the swing after the tape clicked off following Grandpa's final words and had been so deep in my own thoughts that I couldn't believe I hadn't heard Kyle walk across the lawn towards me.

"I just needed a minute by myself, I guess."

Kyle leaned against the swing, loosened his tie, and tried to smile. "More like an hour. Everyone's wondering where you are."

"Everyone? Who's everyone?"

"You know—your mom and dad, and all your family. And my grandma, too." Kyle's smile faded as he looked at me seriously. "Your great-aunts were looking for you, too. They want to talk to you."

I frowned and looked back down at my feet again. "I don't want to talk to them."

"You can't hide from everyone forever, you know."

"Maybe not, or maybe I can."

Kyle was quiet for a moment before giving me a nudge. "Hey, I have something I wanted to give you for your birthday."

"Oh, yeah?"

Kyle laughed. "Don't look all suspicious!"

"What is it?"

"You have to come inside for it."

Kyle held onto the swing with one hand to steady it while he reached for my hand with the other to help me out of the swing. The fact that he did both surprised me, and the way he smiled at me touched me inside and made my heart jump. I slowly smiled back at him, which made him smile even bigger. I wasn't sure what to think of that, but a second later, Kyle was opening the back door for me and hurrying me into Grandpa's house and into the living room.

"Sit down here." Kyle gently pushed me into a chair near the piano. Then he sat down on the piano bench and smiled nervously at me.

"So—here's your birthday present. I hope you like it."

I watched with my mouth opening slightly in surprise as Kyle turned to the piano and began to play softly and slowly, chord after chord, carefully connecting each chord with single notes, smoothly building in volume as he played with easy control. I listened intently with my heart pounding as the chords changed into an incredibly beautiful melody that danced from his fingers up and down the keyboard in intricate patterns that were absolutely amazing. It was the most beautiful song I'd ever heard, and in seconds, tears were forming in my eyes and blurring everything because I knew the song. I'd heard him play it before.

I was doing my best not to let the dam of tears come in a flood by the time his amazing, powerful, emotion-filled playing turned back into the quiet, controlled, beautiful chords that he'd started the song with before the notes quietly slipped into the silence that now filled the room.

"That was amazing, Kyle. I can't believe it—it was so beautiful—"

Kyle turned his head to smile at me hopefully. "You liked it?"

"Liked it? I loved it! That's the song I heard you playing that one day at Grandma June's—"

Kyle nodded. "Yeah, I'm sorry I got ugly with you. I'd been working on it for a while, and I wanted it to be a surprise."

I could feel my eyes widening. "You mean—you—you wrote this song for me?"

Kyle smiled and nodded.

"Wow. I can't believe it. You've got an amazing talent, Kyle."

Kyle stood up, opened the bench cover, and reached inside. "I meant to give this to you on your birthday, but things got—strange."

I could feel myself blushing now. "Yeah, they did."

Kyle turned and handed me several pages of music paper with penciled notes all over, but what made my hands tremble was the title, "Jamie," printed in big capitals at the top.

"You named it after me?"

Kyle looked at me steadily. "I named it *for* you."

I didn't want Kyle to see me cry, but no one had ever done anything so special for me before. No one but Kyle—and Grandpa.

"I have to tape you playing this, Kyle. If I go grab Grandpa's tape recorder, will you play it again?"

"Sure, Jamie—whatever you want—"

But I was running into Grandpa's room for the tape recorder then, and once I'd entered Grandpa's room and picked it up off the bed, it hit me hard and all at once—*I'm never going to be in this house—this room— like this, ever again.* And then, there was no stopping any of the tears I'd been holding back since the day at the hospital when Grandpa died, and I cried and cried and turned into a huge, blubbering mess.

One second I was looking around the room, clutching the tape recorder, crying hard, and the next, Kyle had entered the room.

"Jamie? Are you okay?"

I turned to look at Kyle, knowing I had tears staining my face all over, and even though Kyle looked concerned and sad and understanding all at once, I couldn't help getting a little hysterical. With my free hand, I snatched up Grandpa's CCC photo album.

"These are mine now! No one else can have them—no one!"

I dumped the recorder and the photo album onto the bed and reached under the bed to grab the small box of tapes that held the rest of Grandpa's stories he'd recorded for me all summer long.

"And no one can take these from me—no one!" I ran to the other side of the bed and grabbed Grandma's smiling black and white photo and added it to my pile. Then I whirled to the closet and shoved hanger after hanger aside until I found that beautiful lavender dress.

"And this is mine, too—no one can take anything else away—"

I sat down hard on the bed then and dropped the dress on my pile before picking up the CCC photo album again, hugging it hard to my chest while I cried and cried and couldn't seem to make myself stop, even if I'd wanted to stop.

One second, I was crying like crazy, and the next, Kyle had quietly moved to sit by me, gently taking the photo album out of my hands before he gathered me up tight in his arms and let me cry and cry and cry on his shoulder for I didn't know how long. I could feel his hand slowly stroking my hair and his voice saying softly, "It's going to be okay, Jamie. It's going to be okay," and somehow, that kept me from feeling like a complete idiot for losing it in front of him.

I slowly drew away from Kyle enough to see his face. "It's just—I need—I need to be able to remember him—see something that I can touch every day to remind me of him so I don't ever forget him—"

Kyle smiled and gently brushed my hair off my cheeks. "It's okay to want to keep things. There's something about being able to touch things that belonged to someone you love—things they had with them all the time. It's almost like you're still touching them in some way."

"Yes—that's it—"

Kyle smiled sadly. "I felt the same way when my grandpa died. I still have an old watch he used to carry. And I still keep it by my bed. When I hold it in my hand, he doesn't seem so far away."

I nodded and looked down before looking up at Kyle again, who was steadily watching me. "I want to go sit in the swing again, Kyle. It might be the last time I can—"

Kyle nodded, and after I picked up the CCC photo album in one hand, Kyle held my other hand as we walked back outside and climbed into the swing, this time with Kyle sitting on the same side as me.

I opened the photo album, and together we looked at all the pictures of Grandpa in the CCC as a young man with all of his old CCC buddies—Landon, Bud, Max, Tucker. There were even some pictures of the superintendent he'd told me about.

"Is that the one Grandpa Harold nearly drove insane?"

I laughed and was surprised that I could. "Yeah, that's him."

Kyle stopped me from turning the page when one of the Enterprise pictures caught his eye. "Wow—this is a cool picture. That's your grandparents in the middle, isn't it?"

I smiled and nodded at the picture of Bud, Grandpa, and Landon on their knees dressed up in suits for a dance, with Faye, Grandma, and Vivian standing behind them, each girl with her arms around her man's neck.

"On the way to the family reunion, Grandpa and Anna and I stopped and looked at all of Grandpa's old CCC campsites."

Kyle turned to look at me in surprise. "Wow—really?"

"I didn't know when I was little, but all these places Grandpa showed me—that's where my family always camped at every summer."

Kyle shook his head. "That's amazing! So you grew up spending your summers on the places your grandpa helped to build in Utah. That's pretty cool."

"I didn't know it then." I shook my head back. "Grandpa was so determined to see all of these places again. I think he knew it was his last chance."

Kyle took hold of my hand. "I'll bet it meant a lot to him that you were there with him. Especially since you've been listening to all of his stories and taping them all summer long."

I nodded and closed the photo album before looking at Kyle curiously.

"That night I called Grandma June—you were there. Why were you?"

Kyle shook his head slowly. "It was weird. I don't usually sleep over, but that day—I just had this feeling I shouldn't go home. I thought at the time maybe my grandma needed me."

"I'm glad you were there."

Kyle squeezed my hand and looked at me steadily again. "So am I."

We slowly pushed the swing in silence for a few moments before I softly tried to speak again. "I just—I just hate that I was really starting to get to know my grandpa and what he was like when he was young. I loved hearing his stories and things about my grandma when she was young. My grandma didn't keep a journal, so all I really had left of her was Grandpa's stories and memories, and now he's gone—"

Kyle squeezed my hand again. "At least you got a lot of stuff on tape. You have your grandpa's actual voice! You can hear him tell his stories any time you want. You don't realize what an amazing, special thing you've got here. I'd do anything to hear my grandpa's voice again."

I sighed and shook my head. "I know you're right. It's just—I'm sad it's all over. I hate that there won't be any more stories to hear ever again."

And now Kyle was shaking his head. "You've still got your dad. And your Aunt Gracie. I'll bet they know a lot of stories."

I couldn't help lifting an eyebrow. "My Aunt Gracie?"

"Well, she did name one of her sons 'Maxwell.' I'll give you one guess who he's named after."

The thought stunned me. *Of course.* I couldn't believe I hadn't realized it before.

"I'm sure my grandma could tell you stories about your grandparents when they were young and first moved into this ward. And that man who spoke at both your grandparents' funerals." Kyle turned in the swing towards me and tucked a wayward strand of hair behind my ear before speaking softly. "Plus, you've still got your great-aunts and uncles who I bet could tell you a ton of stories, if you'd give them a chance."

I could see my great-aunts in my mind again, tearfully approaching my dad at the viewing right before the family prayer. I pushed the memory away.

"You don't know, Kyle—you weren't there."

Kyle frowned. "What do you mean?"

"My great-aunts. They don't know that I saw how they treated my grandpa. Not just at the family reunion, but before, too. Here at Grandpa's house. I saw how they talked to him. They think after being mean to his face, now he's gone, they can come crying, saying sorry, and begging for forgiveness, and that makes everything okay—"

Kyle shook his head. "I doubt they think that makes everything okay now. But they *are* sorry, I'm sure."

"I don't care—they shouldn't have been mean to him!"

Kyle sighed and squeezed my hand again. "They miss their sister. They love her, and they're sad she's not here anymore. People do crazy things when they're really sad. I know."

"But they're—old. I thought by now they wouldn't act like—well, like I do!"

Kyle laughed. "Just because they're older doesn't mean they're perfect. They're doing the best they can, like everyone else."

Kyle's words made me shiver, echoing something Grandpa had tried to tell me not too long ago.

"You cold?" Kyle put his arm around me and rubbed my arm. I couldn't help jumping a bit, but Kyle pretended not to notice. We sat together like that in silence with me not moving, and Kyle rubbing my arm while he gently pushed the floor boards with his feet, making the swing slowly rock back and forth.

I finally made myself dare to break the silence. "I always thought it was hard to forgive someone who hurts you, but I think maybe it's harder to forgive people when they hurt people you love."

Kyle nodded without saying anything back, but after a moment, he tugged a lock of my hair, making me turn to look at him. "Everyone deserves a second chance, don't you think?"

"Even when they've hurt you pretty bad?"

Kyle slowly nodded. "I think it's pretty important to be willing to give someone who's hurt you a second chance. I mean, if you really care about the person."

Something about the way Kyle said those words, along with the hopeful way he was looking at me, made me wonder if he was still talking about my great-aunts and uncles.

I looked down at my feet. "I was thinking during the funeral how people see funerals as an ending, you know? I mean, today's been an ending for everyone else, but for Grandpa, today's a new beginning." I could feel my lips widening into a slow smile as I turned to look at Kyle. "I think it's a new beginning for me, too."

Kyle grinned before his face turned serious. "I meant to tell you earlier—you look nice. Really nice."

I lifted an eyebrow. "'Really nice'?"

Kyle laughed. "More than just nice. Pretty. Beautiful, I mean."

I smiled back. "You think I look good in this dress?"

Kyle nodded slowly as he stared at me. "I do."

"Sarah thought so, too. She wants to take me clothes shopping for school and help me figure out hair and makeup and all that for school. I think she wants to tone down my tomboy look."

Kyle actually looked worried. "A while back, you said you weren't going to be on the girls basketball team next year. Were you serious?"

I laughed. "Of course not. I love the game too much. It'd be stupid to stop doing something I like and that I'm good at, right?"

"I think so."

Kyle's look of relief made me burst out laughing. "I'm becoming more and more versatile—that's all. I can wear makeup *and* play basketball!" Kyle laughed, and so did I before I bumped him in the side with my elbow. "You're forewarned, though. Just because I may have makeup on my face doesn't mean I can't kick your rear on the court!"

"Yeah, I know—you don't need to rub it in!" I helped Kyle push the swing with my feet, and we stayed that way, pushing the swing together, until he hesitantly spoke again. "Jamie?"

"Yeah?"

"I—I wanted you to know—I'm sorry about—about what happened outside. On your birthday."

"What are you sorry about?"

Kyle looked away, all embarrassed, and actually blushed. "You know—I'm sorry I kissed you."

"You are?"

Kyle turned back fast to look at me and grab my hand. "No! I mean—I'm sorry it—you know—upset you so much."

I shook my head. "The kiss didn't upset me, Kyle. It's why you kissed me that bothered me. I wish it'd been different."

"So do I."

"You do? How do you wish it would've been?"

"I wish it'd been something like this."

And then with his arm tightening around me, Kyle leaned in, and I did, too, and he kissed me. A much better kiss than before. And when he drew away, I kept looking right at him and felt my lips widening into a slow smile while he gave me his elf grin back.

"See—second chances *are* a good thing, Jamie!"

I couldn't help laughing, and Kyle laughed, too, until I stopped and looked at him soberly.

Now Kyle lifted an eyebrow at me. "What?"

"You called me Jamie again."

"That's your name."

"Everyone's always called me James. Even you."

Kyle shook his head and picked up a lock of my hair. "I should've stopped calling you that a long time ago."

I couldn't decide if my heart was pounding more over his words or the way he was looking at me now, but before I could make up my mind, Kyle kissed me again. I could feel a smile growing on my face again as Kyle drew his face away a bit.

Kyle smiled back and lightly touched my nose with his. "Hey, you hungry now?"

"You know, I think I could go for some funeral potatoes right about now."

Kyle laughed. "Do you want to take your grandpa's CCC book inside first?"

I turned to look at the book, and my heart started to pound as I brushed my hand over the cover. Grandpa wouldn't want this to be put away—he wouldn't.

"I thought maybe my family would like to see it. And maybe Uncle Landon. And Aunt Vivian. I don't know—maybe my cousins and Trent and Sarah would be interested in it, too."

I couldn't look at Kyle's face while I said that, but when I did, he looked happy. Surprised and happy. A second later, he had his arms tight around me in the kind of hug that made it hard for me not to cry.

"They're going to go crazy when they see it. Your dad and your aunt are going to be pretty excited to see it, too."

I nodded before leaning forward to grab my high heels where I'd kicked them onto the grass by the swing. Kyle was faster, though, and quickly picked up both shoes before bending down to hold first one and then the other for me to slip my feet into. *Just like that Cinderella story.*

"Thanks." I could feel my lips growing into a slow smile as Kyle brushed a few strands of grass off my shoes before reaching for the photo album. He grinned back and helped me off the swing, keeping my hand tight in his as we slowly walked across the lawn.

Right before we crossed the street towards the church, I stopped and took one last look at Grandpa's house over my shoulder. I caught my breath as a peaceful, comforting warmth grew inside me, wrapping around me like a thick, soft blanket as I watched the old white swing continue to rock slowly back and forth.

Kyle nudged me then and squeezed my hand. "You ready?"

That smile was still on my face as I looked at Kyle and nodded. "I am now. For anything and everything."